Also by **Diana Palmer**

DIANA PALMER

The Cowboy's Winter Bride

All the characters in this book have no existence outside the imagination
of the author, and have no relation whatsoever to anyone bearing the
same name or names. They are not even distantly inspired by any
individual known or unknown to the author, and all the incidents are
pure invention.

All Rights Reserved including the right of reproduction in whole or
in part in any form. This edition is published by arrangement with
Harlequin Enterprises II B.V./S.à.r.l. The text of this publication or any
part thereof may not be reproduced or transmitted in any form or by any
means, electronic or mechanical, including photocopying, recording,
storage in an information retrieval system, or otherwise, without the
written permission of the publisher.

This book is sold subject to the condition that it shall not, by way of trade
or otherwise, be lent, resold, hired out or otherwise circulated without the
prior consent of the publisher in any form of binding or cover other than
that in which it is published and without a similar condition including
this condition being imposed on the subsequent purchaser.

M&B™ and M&B™ with the Rose Device
are trademarks of the publisher.

First published in Great Britain in 2009
Harlequin Mills & Boon Limited, Eton House,
18-24 Paradise Road,
Richmond, Surrey TW9 1SR

THE COWBOY'S WINTER BRIDE © Harlequin Books S.A. 2009

Heart of Ice © Diana Palmer 1984
Carrera's Bride © Diana Palmer 2004

ISBN: 978 0 263 87716 8

024-1209

Harlequin Mills & Boon policy is to use papers that are
natural, renewable and recyclable products and made from
wood grown in sustainable forests. The logging and
manufacturing processes conform to the legal environmental
regulations of the country of origin.

Printed and bound in Spain
by Litografia Rosés S.A., Barcelona

The prolific author of over one hundred books, **Diana Palmer** got her start as a newspaper reporter. One of the top ten romance writers in America, she has a gift for telling the most sensual tales with charm and humour. Diana lives with her family in Georgia.

Heart of Ice

Dear Reader,

Of all the books I've ever done, *Heart of Ice* is one of my own personal five favourites. I loved seeing these characters come alive on paper. Having been to the northwest, specifically to Montana and Wyoming, I know the beauty and grandeur of the country and the warmth of the people who live there. This book will always remind me of some wonderful times I spent in the Rockies.

I hope that you enjoy this book, and that it gives you the same sense of wonder that I feel each time I go to New York City, or to the vast western states. I love the elegance of New York City and the grandeur of Wyoming equally. This book is about both. It is a story of contrasts and differences, but also of compromise and understanding.

Thank you for your kindness to me over the years, and a special hello to my adopted "family" all over the country and around the world.

Love,

Diana Palmer

Chapter One

"You didn't!" Katriane wailed at her best friend. "Not at Christmas!"

Ada looked pained and visibly shrank an inch. "Now, Kati..." she began placatingly, using the nickname she'd given the taller girl years ago. "It's a huge apartment. Absolutely huge. And you and I will be going to parties all over town, and there's the charity ball at the Thomsons'... It will be all right, you'll see. You won't even notice that he's here."

"I'll notice," Kati said shortly. Her reddish gold hair blazed in the ceiling light, and her brown eyes glared.

"It's our first Christmas without Mother," Ada tried again. "He's got nobody but me."

"You could go to the ranch for Christmas," Kati suggested, hating the idea even as she said it.

"And leave you here alone? What kind of friend would I be then?"

"The kind who isn't sticking me with her horrible brother during my one holiday a year!" came the hot reply. "I worked myself to the bone, researching that last book. I was taking a rest between contractual obligations…just Christmas. How can I rest with Egan here!"

"He'll be fun to have around," Ada suggested softly.

"We'll kill each other!" Kati groaned. "Ada, why do you hate me? You know Egan and I don't get along. We've never gotten along. For heaven's sake, I can't live under the same roof with your brother until Christmas! Have you forgotten what happened last time?"

Ada cleared her throat. "Look, you planned to set that next big historical in Wyoming, didn't you, on a ranch? Who knows more about ranching in Wyoming than Egan? You could look upon it as an educational experience—research."

Kati just glared.

"Deep down," Ada observed, "you both probably really like each other. It's just that you can't…admit it."

"Deep down," her friend replied, "I hate him. Hate. As in to dislike intensely. As in to obsessively dislike."

"That's splitting an infinitive," Ada pointed out.

"You are an actress, not an educator," came the sharp retort.

Ada sighed, looking small and dark and vulnerable. So unlike her elder brother. "I may wind up being an educator, at this rate," she said. "I am sort of between jobs."

"You'll get another one," Kati said easily. "I've never seen anyone with your talent. You got rave reviews in your last play."

"Well, maybe something will turn up. But, getting back to Egan…"

"Must we?" Kati groaned. She turned, worrying the thick waves of her long hair irritatedly. "Don't do this to me, Ada. Uninvite him."

"I can't. He's already on the way."

"Now?" Kati looked hunted. She threw up her hands. "First my royalty check gets lost in the mail when my car payment is due. Now I wind up with a sidewinder to spend Christmas with…."

"He's my brother," Ada said in a small voice. "He has no one. Not even a girl friend."

"Egan?" Two eyebrows went straight up. "Egan always has a girl friend. He's never between women."

"He is right now."

"Did he go broke?" Kati asked with a sweet smile.

"Now, Kati, he's not that bad to look at."

That was true enough. Egan had a body most men would envy. But his face was definitely not handsome. It was craggy and rough and uncompromising. Just like Egan. She could see those glittering silver eyes in her sleep sometimes, haunting her, accusing her—the way they had that last time. She hated Egan because he'd misjudged her so terribly. And because he'd never admitted it. Not then, or since.

She folded her arms over her breasts with a curt sigh. "Well, Mary Savage used to think he was Mr. America," she conceded.

Ada eyed her closely. "He's just a poor, lonely old cattleman. He can't help it if women fall all over him."

"Egan Winthrop, poor? Lonely?" Kati pursed her lips. "The old part sounds about right, though."

"He's thirty-four," Ada reminded her. "Hardly in his dotage."

"Sounds ancient to me," Kati murmured, staring out over the jeweled night skyline of Manhattan.

"We're both twenty-five." Ada laughed. "Nine years isn't so much."

"Fudge." She leaned her head against the cold windowpane. "He hates me, Ada," she said after a minute, and felt the chill all up and down her body. "He'll start a fight as sure as there's a sun in the sky. He always starts something."

"Yes, I know," Ada confessed. She joined the taller woman at the window. "I don't understand why you set him off. He's usually the soul of chivalry with women."

"I've seen him in action," Kati said quietly. "You don't have to tell me about that silky charm. But it's all surface, Ada. Egan lets nobody close enough to wound."

"For someone who's been around him only a few times in recent years, and under the greatest pressure from me, you seem to know him awfully well," Ada mumbled.

"I know his type," she said shortly. "He's a taker, not a giver."

"Neither one of you ever gives an inch," Ada remarked. She studied her friend closely. "But I had to invite him. He's the only family I have."

Kati sighed, feeling oddly guilty. She hugged the shorter girl impulsively. "I'm sorry. I'm being ratty and I don't mean to. You're my friend. Of course you can invite your awful brother for Christmas. I'll grit my teeth and go dancing with Jack and pretend I love having him here. Okay?"

"That I'll have to see to believe."

Kati crossed her heart. "Honest."

"Well, since that's settled, how about if we go and get a Christmas tree?" Ada suggested brightly.

Kati laughed. "Super," she said and grabbed up her coat to follow Ada out the door. "And if we get one big enough," she mumbled under her breath, "maybe we can hang Egan from one of the limbs."

They trudged through four tree lots before they found just the right tree. It was a six-foot Scotch pine, full and bushy and perfect for their apartment. They stuffed it into the back of Kati's Thunderbird and carried it home, along with boxes of ornaments and new tinsel to add to their three-year supply in the closet.

Ada went out to get a pizza while Kati tied ribbon through the bright balls and hung them lovingly on the tree. She turned on some Christmas music and tried not to think about Egan. It seemed so long ago that they'd had that horrible blowup....

It had been five years since Kati first set eyes on Egan Winthrop. She and Ada had met at school, where both were majoring in education. Ada had later switched to drama, and Kati had decided to study English while she broke into the fiction market in a small way. Three years ago, after graduation, they'd taken this apartment together.

Egan and Kati had been at odds almost from the first. Kati got her first glimpse of the tall rancher at school, when she and Ada were named to the college honors society in their junior year. Egan and Mrs. Winthrop had both come. Kati had no relatives, and Ada had quickly included her in family plans for an evening out afterward. Egan hadn't liked that. From the first meeting of eyes, it had been war. He disapproved vehemently of Kati's chosen profession, although he was careful not to let Ada or his mother see just how much he disliked Kati. They'd hardly spoken two words until that fateful summer when Kati had flown out to the ranch with Ada for the Fourth of July.

It had been the first year she'd roomed with Ada, almost three years ago. Ada's mother had been diagnosed with cancer, and the family knew that despite the treatments, it would only be a matter of a year or two before she wouldn't be with them. Everyone had gone to the Wyoming ranch for the July Fourth holidays—including Kati, because Ada refused to leave her alone in New York. Kati's parents were middle-aged when she was born, and had died only a little apart just before she finished high school. She had cousins and uncles and aunts, but none of them would miss her during the July vacation. So, dreading Egan's company, she'd put on a happy face and gone.

She couldn't forget Egan's face when he'd seen her getting off the plane with his sister. He hadn't even bothered to disguise his distaste. Egan had a mistaken

view of romance writers' morals and assumed that Kati
lived the wild life of her heroines. It wasn't true, but it
seemed to suit him to believe that it was. He gave her
a chilly reception, his silvery eyes telling her that he
wished she'd stayed in New York.

But his cousin Richard's enthusiastic greeting more
than made up for Egan's rudeness. She was hugged and
hugged and enthused over, and she ate it up. Richard
was just her age, a dark-haired, dark-eyed architect
with a bright future and a way with women. If he hadn't
been such a delightful flirt, the whole incident might
have been avoided. But he had been, and it wasn't.

Richard had taken Kati to the Grand Teton National
Park for the day, while Mrs. Winthrop soaked up the
attention she was getting from her son and daughter.
She was a lot like Ada, a happy, well-adjusted person
with a loving disposition. And none of Egan's
cynicism. Kati had liked her very much. But she and
Richard had felt that Mrs. Winthrop needed some time
alone with her children. So they'd driven to the park
and hiked and enjoyed the beauty of the mountains
rising starkly from the valley, and afterward they'd
stopped in Jackson for steaks and a salad.

On the way home, Richard's car had had a flat tire.
Richard, being the lovable feather-brain he was, had no
spare. In that part of the country on a holiday night,
there wasn't a lot of traffic. So they walked back to the
ranch—which took until four in the morning.

Egan had been waiting up. He said nothing to Richard,
who was so tired that he was hardly able to stand. Richard
went inside, leaving all the explanations to Kati.

"You live down to your reputation, don't you?" he asked with a smile that chilled even in memory. "My God, you might have had a little consideration for my mother. She worried."

Kati remembered trying to speak, but he cut her off with a rough curse.

"Don't make it worse by lying," he growled. "We both know what you are…you with your loose morals and your disgusting books. What you do with my cousin is your business, but I don't want my holidays ruined by someone like you. You're not welcome here any longer. Make some excuse to leave tomorrow."

And he walked away, leaving Kati sick and near tears. She hadn't let them show, she was too proud. And she'd managed to get to bed without waking Ada, who shared a room with her. But the next morning, cold-eyed and hating Egan more than ever, she packed her suitcase, gave some excuse about an unexpected deadline and asked Richard to take her to the airport.

They were on the porch when Egan came out the front door, looking irritated and angry and strangely haggard.

"I'd like to speak to you," he told Kati.

She remembered looking at him as if he were some form of bacteria, her back stiff, her eyes full of hatred.

"Go ahead," she told him.

He glared at Richard, who cleared his throat and mumbled something about getting the car.

"Why didn't you tell me what happened?" he asked.

"Why bother, when you already knew?" she asked in glacial tones.

"I didn't know," he ground out.

"How amazing," she replied calmly. "I thought you knew everything. You seem to have made a hobby out of my life—the fictionalized version, of course."

He looked uncomfortable, but he didn't apologize. "Richard had been drinking. It was four in the morning—"

"We had a very long walk," she told him curtly. "About fifteen or twenty miles. Richard wasn't drunk; he was tired." Her dark eyes glittered up at him. "I didn't like you much before, Mr. Winthrop, but I like you even less now. I'll make a point of keeping out of your vicinity. I wouldn't want to contaminate you."

"Miss James…" he began quietly.

"Good-bye." She brushed past him, suitcase in hand, and got into Richard's car. Ada and Mrs. Winthrop had tried to talk her into staying, but she was adamant about having an unexpected deadline and work pressure. And to this day, only she and that animal in Wyoming really knew why she'd left. Even Richard hadn't been privy to the truth.

That episode had brought the antagonism between Egan and Kati out into the open, and their relationship seemed to go from bad to worse. It was impossible for Kati to stay in the same room with Egan these days. He'd find an excuse, any excuse, to nick her temper. And she'd always retaliate. Like last year…

Egan had been in town for some kind of conference and had stopped by the apartment to see Ada. Kati had been on her way to a department store in downtown Manhattan to autograph copies of her latest book,

Renegade Lover, a historical set in eighteenth-century South Carolina. Egan had walked in to find her in her autographing clothes—a burgundy velvet dress cut low in front, and a matching burgundy hat crowned by white feathers. She'd looked like the heroine on the front of her book, and he immediately pounced.

"My God, Madame Pompadour," he observed, studying her from his superior height.

She bristled, glaring up at him. "Wrong country," she replied. "But I wouldn't expect you to know that."

His eyebrow jerked. "Why not? Just because I'm in oil and cattle doesn't make me an ignoramus."

"I never said a word, Mr. Winthrop, honey," she replied, batting her long eyelashes at him.

The term of endearment, on reflection, must have been what set him off. His lips curled in an unpleasant smile. "You do look the part, all right," he replied. "You could stand on the street corner and make a nice little nest egg…"

She actually slapped him—and didn't even realize she had until she felt her fingers stinging and saw the red mark along his cheek.

"Damn you!" she breathed, shaking with fury.

His nostrils flared; his eyes narrowed and became frankly dangerous. "Lift your hand to me again, ever," he said in that low, cold tone, "and you'll wish you'd never set eyes on me."

"I already do, Egan Almighty Winthrop! I already do."

"Dress like a tramp and people are going to label you one," he rejoined. His eyes cut away from her with distaste. "I wouldn't be seen in public with you."

"Thank God!" she threw after him, almost jumping up and down with indignation. "I wouldn't want people to think I cared so little about who I was seen with!"

At that moment, luckily, Ada had rushed in from her bedroom to play peacemaker. Without another word, Kati had grabbed up her coat and purse and had run from the apartment, tears rolling down her cheeks. It was a miracle that she managed to get herself back together by the time she reached the department store.

That was the last time she'd seen Egan Winthrop. And she never wanted to see him again. Oh, why had Ada agreed to let him come, knowing the state of hostility that existed between Egan and her? Why!

She put the last ball on the tree, and was reaching for the little golden angel that would sit atop it when she heard the door open.

It must be Ada with the pizza, of course, and she was starved. She reached up, slender in jeans and a pullover yellow velour sweater, laughing as she put the angel in place. As she moved, she knocked into one of the balls, but caught it just in time to keep it from dropping to the carpet.

"Back already?" she called. "I'm starved to death! Do you want to have it in here by the tree?"

There was a pregnant pause, and she felt eyes watching her. Nervous, she turned—to find herself staring at Egan Winthrop. Her hand clenched at the sight of him—so powerful and dark in his gray vested suit—and the fragile ball shattered under the pressure.

"You little idiot," he muttered, moving forward to force open her hand.

She let him, numb, her eyes falling to the sight of his dark hands under her pale one where blood beaded from a small cut.

"I…wasn't expecting…you," she said nervously.

"Obviously. Do you have some antiseptic?"

"In the bathroom."

He marched her into it and fumbled in the medicine cabinet for antiseptic and a bandage.

"Where's Ada?" he asked as he cleaned the small cut, examined it for shards, and applied the stinging antiseptic.

"Out getting pizza," she muttered.

He glanced up. He'd never been so close to her, and those silver eyes at point-blank range were frightening. So was the warmth of his lean, powerful body and the smell of his musky cologne.

His eyes searched hers quietly, and he didn't smile. That wasn't unusual. She'd only seen him smile at Ada or his mother. He was reserved to the point of inhibition most of the time. A hard man. Cold…

Something wild and frightening dilated her eyes as she met that long, lingering look, and her heart jumped. Her lips parted as she tore her gaze down to the small hand that was visibly trembling in his big ones.

"Nervous, Katriane?" he asked.

"Yes, I'm nervous," she bit off, deciding that a lie would only amuse him. If granite could be amused.

"How long did it take Ada to talk you into this visit?" he asked.

She drew in a heavy breath. "All of a half hour," she said gruffly. "And I still think it's a horrible mistake."

She looked up at him defiantly. "I don't want to spoil Christmas for her by fighting with you."

His chin lifted as he studied her. "Then you'll just have to be nice to me, won't you?" he baited. "No snide remarks, no deliberate taunts…"

"Look who's talking about snide remarks!" she returned. "You're the one who does all the attacking!"

"You give as good as you get, don't you?" he asked.

Her lower lip jutted. "It's Christmas."

"Yes, I know." He studied her. "I like presents."

"Is anyone going to give you one?" she asked incredulously.

"Ada," he reminded her.

"Poor demented soul, she loves you," she said, eyeing him.

"Women do, from time to time," he returned.

"Ah, the advantages of wealth," she muttered.

"Do you think I have to pay for it?" he asked with a cold smile. "I suppose a woman who sells it expects everyone to…"

Her hand lifted again, but he caught it this time, holding it so that she had to either stand on her tiptoes or have her shoulder dislocated.

"Let go!" she panted. "You're hurting!"

"Then stop trying to hit me. Peace on earth, remember?" he reminded her, oddly calm.

"I'd like to leave you in pieces," she mumbled, glaring up at him.

His eyes wandered from her wild, waving red-gold hair down past her full breasts to her small waist, flaring hips and long legs. "You've gained a little weight, haven't you?" he asked. "As voluptuous as ever. I suppose that appeals to some men."

"Ooooh!" she burst out, infuriated, struggling.

He let her go all at once and pulled a cigarette from his pocket, watching her with amusement as he lit it. "What's the matter? Disappointed because you don't appeal to me?"

"God forbid!"

He shook his head. "You'll have to do better than this if you want to keep a truce with me for the next few days. I can't tolerate hysterical women."

She closed her eyes, willing him to disappear. It didn't work. When she opened them, he was still there. She put away the antiseptic and bandages and went back into the living room, walking stiffly, to clean the debris of the shattered ball from the beige carpet.

"Don't cut yourself," he cautioned, dropping lazily into an armchair with the ashtray he'd found.

"On what, the ball or you?" she asked coldly.

He only laughed, softly, menacingly; and she fumbled with pieces of the ball while he watched her in that catlike, unblinking way of his.

"I thought Ada told me you'd stopped smoking," she remarked when she was finished.

"I did. I only do it now when I'm nervous." He took another long draw, his eyes mocking. "You give me the jitters, honey, didn't you know?"

"Me and the cobalt bomb, maybe," she scoffed. She threw away the debris and ran an irritated hand through her hair. "Do you want me to show you to your room, like a good hostess?" she asked.

"You'd show me to the elevator and press the Down button," he said. "I'll wait for my sister and a warmer welcome."

It was Christmas, and he'd lost his mother, and she hated the surge of sympathy she felt. But knowing he'd toss it right back in her face kept her quiet. She went to the window and stared down at the busy street. "Ada, hurry," she wanted to scream.

"I saw your book advertised on television the other day," he remarked.

She turned around, arms folded defensively over her breasts. "Did you? Imagine, you watching television."

He didn't take her up on that. He crushed out his half-finished cigarette. "It sold out at the local bookstore."

"I'm sure you bought all the copies—to keep your good neighbors from being exposed to it," she chided.

His eyebrows arched. "In fact, I did buy one copy. To read."

She went red from head to toe. The thought of Egan Winthrop reading *Harvest of Passion* made her want to pull a blanket over her head. It was a spicy book with sensuous love scenes, and the way he was looking her over made it obvious what he thought of the book and its author.

"I like historical fiction," he remarked. "Despite having to wade through the obligatory sex to get to it."

She flushed even more and turned away, too tongue-tied to answer him.

"How do you manage to stay on your feet with all that exhaustive research you obviously do?"

She whirled, her eyes blazing. "What do you mean by that?" she burst out.

He laughed softly, predatorily. "You know damned good and well what I mean. How many men does it take?"

The door opened just in time to spare his ears. Ada walked in and her face glowed with joy as she saw her brother. She tossed the pizza onto a chair and ran to him, to be swung up in his powerful arms and warmly kissed.

"You get prettier all the time," he said, laughing, and the radiance in his face made Kati feel like mourning. She'd never bring that look to Egan's face.

"And you get handsomer. I'm so glad you could come," Ada said genuinely.

"I'm glad someone is," he murmured, glancing at Kati's flushed, furious face.

Ada looked past him, and her own expression sobered. "Ooops," she murmured.

Kati swallowed her hostility. She wouldn't ruin Christmas for Ada—she wouldn't. She pinned a smile to her lips. "It's all right. He patched me up when I cut my hand. We're friends now. Aren't we?" she asked, grinding her teeth together as she looked at Egan.

"Of course," he agreed. "Bosom pals." He stared at her breasts.

Ada grabbed him by the hand and half dragged him from the room. "Let me show you where to put your suitcase, Egan!" she said hastily.

Kati went to take the pizza into the kitchen and make coffee. And counted to ten, five times.

Chapter Two

"How have you been?" Ada asked her brother as the three of them sat around the dining room table munching pizza and drinking coffee.

"All right," he said, staring at the thick brown mug that held his coffee. "You?"

Ada smiled. "Busy. It's helped me not to dwell on Mama."

"She's better off," Egan reminded her quietly.

"I know," Ada said, her eyes misting. She shook her head and grabbed another slice of pizza. "Anybody else for seconds? There are three slices left."

"No more for me," Kati said with a speaking glance at Egan. "I wouldn't want to get more voluptuous than I already am."

"Nonsense," blissfully ignorant Ada said. "You're just right. Come on, have another slice."

"Go ahead," Egan taunted.

"Why don't you?" she dared him.

"And be accused of making a pig of myself?" he asked innocently.

"Who would be so unkind as to call you a pig?" Kati asked sweetly.

"Excuse me," Ada interrupted, "but it's Christmas. Remember? Holly and mistletoe…?"

"Mistletoe?" Egan glanced at Kati. "I'd rather drink poison."

Kati glared back. "Ditto!"

"Let's watch television!" Ada suggested frantically. She dragged Kati into the living room and quickly turned on the set. "I'll clear the table, you keep Egan company."

"You're just afraid of getting caught in the line of fire," Egan accused as his sister rushed out of the room.

But Ada only grinned.

Egan eased down into the armchair he'd vacated earlier and stared at Kati. He'd taken off his coat and vest. Both sleeves of his white silk shirt were rolled up and the neck was opened. He didn't wear an undershirt, and through the thin fabric, bronzed muscles and a thick pelt of hair were visible. That bothered Kati, so she carefully avoided looking at him while the evening news blared into the room.

"How's the writing going?" Egan asked conversationally.

"Just fine, thanks," she replied tersely.

"What are you working on now?"

She swallowed. Ada had finked on her, she just knew it. "Actually, I'm doing another historical."

"On...?"

She cleared her throat. "Wyoming," she mumbled.

"Pardon?" he said.

Her lips made a thin line. "Wyoming," she said louder.

"A historical novel about Wyoming. Well, well. Have you done a lot of research?"

She glanced at him warily. "What do you mean?"

"Historical research," he clarified, watching her. "You'll have to mention cattle-ranching, I imagine?"

"Yes," she said grudgingly.

"Know a lot about it, city lady?" he mocked.

She glared at him. "I have been on a ranch before."

"Sure. Mine." He stared down his nose at her. "I don't imagine they have many big cattle ranches in Charleston?"

"We have good people," she returned. "With excellent breeding."

His eyebrows arched. "Yes, I know. My grandmother came from Charleston."

She glared at him. "Did she, really?" she asked coldly.

He smiled softly. "She used to say it was where the Cooper and Ashley Rivers meet to form the Atlantic Ocean."

She'd heard that, too, in her childhood in the South Carolina coastal city, and she had to bite her lip to keep from smiling with him.

"She was a redhead too," he continued, waiting for a reaction.

"My hair isn't red," she said, predictably.

"Honey and fox fur," he argued, studying it.

She flushed. That sounded oddly poetic, and she didn't like the tingle that ran through her.

She glanced at her watch. "Excuse me. I'd better put on a dress."

Egan glared. "Going somewhere?"

"Yes." She left him sitting there and went to find Ada. "Jack's coming for me at seven," she reminded her friend. "I've got to get dressed."

"I'll go keep Egan company. Lucky you, to have a boyfriend in town." She sighed. "Mine's out at sea again."

"Marshal will be back before you know it," she murmured. "Sorry to run out on you."

"You'll have fun." Ada grinned. "And so will I. I like Egan. He's great company, even if he is my brother."

Well, there was no accounting for taste. She couldn't imagine Egan being great company; but then, she wasn't related to him.

She put on a black cocktail dress and wore red accessories with it. Her eyes gave her a critical appraisal. She'd twirled her hair into a French twist and added a rhinestone clip to it, and she liked that elegant touch. She grinned. Jack would love it.

Jack Asher was a reporter for *The New York Times,* a political specialist who was intelligent and fun to be with. She'd known him for several months and enjoyed the occasional date. But things were still platonic between them because she didn't want any serious involvement. She was too independent.

The doorbell rang while she was putting a gloss of

lipstick on her mouth, and she knew Ada would get it. Then she remembered that Egan was here, and rushed to finish her makeup and get back into the living room.

Jack was standing in the hall, talking to Ada while Egan glared at him.

He cleared his throat when Kati joined him, looking painfully relieved to see her.

"Hi, lady," he said with a forced smile. He was blond and blue-eyed and not nearly as tall or muscular as Egan. Sadly enough, in comparison he looked rather pale and dull.

But Kati grinned at him and Ada as if nothing were wrong. "Had to find my purse, but I'm ready when you are. Night, Ada. Egan," she added, glancing his way.

Egan didn't answer her. He was still glaring at Jack with those dangerous narrowed eyes glittering like new silver while he smoked a cigarette. Ada made a frantic gesture, but he ignored her too.

"Night, Ada," Jack said uncomfortably and led Kati out the door.

"Whew!" Jack exclaimed when they reached the elevator. "I felt like an insect on a mounting board for a second there! Is he always like that? So…uncommunicative?"

"Egan?" Kati's eyes flared up. "He's usually much too communicative, if you want to know. We're stuck with him for Christmas. Ada invited him because their mother died earlier this year. She felt sorry for him, being all alone."

"I should think so," Jack said gently. "Well, maybe he talks to her." He frowned. "You don't like him, do you?"

"Not one bit. Not one ounce. Not a fraction." She glared at the elevator.

Jack laughed. "Poor guy!"

"Not Egan. Feel sorry for me. I'm stuck in the same apartment with him for the next week," she moaned.

"You could always move in with me," he offered.

She laughed, knowing the offer was a joke, just as it always had been. They didn't have that kind of relationship. "Sure I could. I can just see your mother's face."

"Mother likes you." He chuckled. "She'd probably be thrilled."

"Only because she could pump me for my latest plots." She grinned. "You know she's one of my biggest fans. Sweet lady."

"She's sweet, all right. Well, where do you want to go? The Rainbow Grill?"

"Let's save it for a special time. How about the Crawdaddy Room at the Roosevelt?"

He chuckled. "You just like to go there because of their pudding," he accused.

"Well, it is terribly good," she reminded him.

"I know, I know. Actually, I like it myself."

She followed him into the elevator and put the confrontation with Egan right out of her mind.

A prime rib, a salad, several hard rolls and a dish of delicious whiskey pudding later, Kati sat drinking her coffee and looking around at the elegant surroundings. She saw a nice little old German waiter she knew from other visits there and smiled at him.

"Friend of yours?" Jack asked her.

"Everybody's my friend." She laughed. "I used to think New York was a cold place until I moved here. New Yorkers just take a little getting to know. And then they're family. I love New York," she sang softly, and laughed again.

"So do I. Of course, I was born here," he added. He looked out the window at the traffic. "I've got tickets for a modern ballet, if you'd like to use them."

"Could we?"

"Sure. Come on."

He led her down a side street where a group of people were just entering what looked like an old warehouse. But inside, it was a theater, complete with live orchestra and lighted stage and some of the most beautiful modern ballet she'd ever watched. The people onstage looked like living art: the women delicate and pink in their tulle and satin, the men vigorous and athletic and vibrant. Kati had been going to the ballet for years, but this was something special.

Afterward, they went to a lounge and drank piña coladas and danced to the hazy music of a combo until the wee hours.

"That was fun," she told Jack when he brought her home. "We'll have to do it again."

"Indeed we will. I'm sorry I didn't think of the ballet weeks ago. I get free tickets."

"Let's do it again even if we have to pay for them," she said, laughing.

"Suits me. I'll call you in a few days. Looks like I may have to fly down to Washington on that latest scandal."

"Call me when you get back, okay?"

"Okay. Night, doll." He winked and was gone. He never tried to kiss her or make advances. With them, it was friendship instead of involvement, and she enjoyed his company very much. Jack had been married and his wife had died. He wanted involvement even less than she did and was glad to be going out with someone who wouldn't try to tie him up in wedding paper.

Dreamily, she unlocked the apartment door and stepped inside. She closed the door and leaned back against it, humming a few bars of the classical piece that had accompanied one of the pieces at the ballet.

"Do you usually stay out this late?" Egan asked from the living room. He was standing by the window with a glass of amber liquid that looked like whiskey in his hand.

She stared at him. "I'm twenty-five," she reminded him. "I stay out as late as I like."

He moved toward her slowly, gracefully, his eyes holding hers. "Do you sleep with him?" he asked.

She caught her breath. "Egan, what I do with anyone is my business."

He threw back the rest of his drink and set the glass on a small table in the hall, moving toward her until she felt like backing away.

"How is he?" he asked lazily. Then he caught her by the shoulders and held her in front of him, looking down quietly, holding her eyes.

Her lips parted as she met that intimidating stare. "Egan..."

His nostrils flared. The lean fingers that were

holding her tightened. "Is he white all over?" he continued in a faintly mocking tone. "City boy."

"Well, there aren't many cattle to herd up here," she said tautly.

"No, but there are too damn many people. You can't walk two steps without running into someone," he complained. "I couldn't survive here. Answer me. Do you sleep with him?"

"That's non—" she began.

"Tell me anyway. Does he do all those things to you that you write about in your books?" he asked, studying her. "Does he 'strip you slowly,' so that you can 'feel every brush of his fingers…'"

"Egan!" She reached up to press her fingers against his lips, stopping the words as she flushed deeply.

He hadn't expected the touch of her fingers. He caught them and held them as if he wasn't sure what to do with them. His eyes held hers.

"Is that the kind of man you like, Katriane Desiree?" he asked, using the full name that she didn't know he'd ever heard.

She watched him helplessly. "I like…writers," she managed.

"Do you?" He brought her hand to his mouth and kissed its warm palm softly, slowly. His teeth nipped at her slender forefinger.

"Egan," she breathed nervously.

He took the tip of her finger into his mouth and she felt his tongue touching it. "Afraid?" he murmured. "Don't they say that a woman is instinctively afraid of a man she thinks can conquer her?"

She wrenched away from him like an animal at bay. "You'd be lucky!" she whispered. Was that her voice, shaking like that?

He stared at her, sliding his hands into his pockets, and the action stretched the fabric of his trousers tight over the powerful muscles of his legs. "So would you," he returned. "But one of these days I might give you a thrill, honey. God knows, my taste never ran to virgins. And an experienced woman is…exciting."

She felt the blood rush into her face, and she whirled on her heel. If she stayed there one second longer, she'd hit him! Boy, wouldn't the joke be on him if he ever tried to take her to bed! Egan, in bed….

She went straight into the bathroom, oblivious that she might wake Ada, and ran herself a calming cool shower.

Chapter Three

Kati didn't sleep. Every time she closed her eyes, she could feel the hard grip of Egan's fingers on her shoulders, the touch of his mouth against her hand. She hated him, she thought miserably; that was why she couldn't sleep.

She dragged into the kitchen just after daylight, with her long gold and beige striped caftan flowing lovingly over the soft curves of her body. Her tousled hair fell in glorious disarray around her shoulders, and her dark eyes were even darker with drowsiness.

With a long yawn, she filled the coffee pot and started it, then she reached for the skillet and bacon and turned on the stove. She was leaning back against the refrigerator with a carton of eggs in one hand and butter in the other when the kitchen door opened and Egan came in, dressed in nothing but a pair of tan slacks.

He stopped at the sight of her and stared. She did some staring of her own. He was just as she'd imagined him without that shirt—sexy as all get-out. Bronzed muscles rippled as he closed the kitchen door; a mat of hair on his chest curled down obviously below his belt buckle. His arms looked much more powerful without a concealing shirt, as did his shoulders. She could hardly drag her eyes away.

"I thought I'd fix myself a cup of coffee," he said quietly.

"I just put some on," she said.

He cocked an eyebrow. "Does that mean I have to wait until you drink your potful before I can make mine?" he asked.

She glared at him. So much for truces. "There's a nice little coffee shop down on the corner," she suggested with a venomous smile.

"I'll tell Ada you're being unkind to me," he threatened. "Remember Ada? My sister? The one whose Christmas you said you didn't want to spoil?"

She drew in a calming breath. "Do excuse me, Mr. Winthrop," she said formally. "Wouldn't you like to sit down; I'll pour you a cup of coffee."

"Not until you tell me where you plan to pour it," he returned.

"Don't tempt me." She reached up into the cabinet for a second cup and saucer while he pulled out a chair and straddled it.

When she turned back with the filled cups, she found him watching her. It unnerved her when he did that, and she spilled coffee into one of the saucers before she could set them on the table.

"Couldn't you sleep?" he asked pleasantly.

"No," she said. "I'm not used to sleeping late. I'm at my best early in the morning."

A slow, wicked smile touched his hard mouth. "Most of us are," he commented.

It didn't necessarily mean what she thought it did, but she couldn't help the blush. And that increased her embarrassment, because he laughed.

"Will you stop!" she burst out, glaring at him. "Oh, why don't you take your coffee and go back to bed?"

"I'm hungry. Don't I smell bacon?"

"Bacon!" She jumped up and turned it just in time. It was a nice golden brown.

"Going to scramble some eggs, too?" he asked.

"No, I thought I'd let you drink yours raw," she said.

He only laughed, sipping his coffee. "I like raw oysters, but I draw the line at raw eggs. Want me to make the toast?"

"You can cook?"

"Don't get insulting." He stood up and found the bread and butter. "Get me a pan and some cinnamon and sugar."

She stared at him.

"Cinnamon," he said patiently. "It's a spice—"

"I know what it is," she grumbled, finding it. "Here. And I've lined the pan with aluminum foil. It's all yours."

"Ungrateful woman," he muttered as he mixed the cinnamon and sugar in the shaker she'd handed him. He buttered the bread and spread the mixture on top.

"Don't get conceited just because you can make cinnamon toast," she mumbled. "After all, it isn't exactly duckling *a l'orange*."

"I'd like to see you cook that," he remarked.

She cleared her throat. "Well, I could if I had a recipe."

"So could I." He turned on the oven and slid the toast in under the broiler. "Get me a pot holder."

"Who was your personal slave yesterday?" she asked, tossing him a quilted pot holder.

"I liked the old days," he murmured, glancing at her. "When men hunted and women cooked and had kids."

"Drudgery," she scoffed. "Women were little more than free labor...."

"Cosseted and protected and worried over and loved to death," he continued, staring down at her. "Now they're overbearing, pushy, impossible to get along with and wilder than bucks."

"Look who's talking about being wild!" she burst out.

He stared down his nose at her. "I'm a man."

She drew in a breath and let it out, and her eyes involuntarily ran over him.

"No argument?" he asked.

She turned away. "Your toast's burning."

He took it out—nicely browned and smelling sweet and delicate—and put it on a plate while she scrambled eggs.

"I like mine fried, honey," he commented.

"Okay. There's a frying pan; grease is in the cabinet. If you're too good to eat my scrambled eggs, you can mutilate your own any way you like."

He chuckled softly, an odd sound that she'd never heard, and she turned to look up at him.

"Firecracker," he murmured, his eyes narrow and searching. "Are you like that in bed?"

She jerked her eyes away and concentrated on the eggs. "Wouldn't you like to get dressed before we eat?"

It was a mistake. A horrible mistake. Because then he knew what she hadn't admitted since he walked into the room. That, stripped to the waist, he bothered her.

The arrogant beast knew it, all right. He moved lazily until he was standing just behind her...so close that she felt him and smelled him and wanted nothing more out of life than to turn around and slide her hands all over that broad chest.

His hands caught her waist, making her jump, and eased her back against him so that she could feel the warm, hard muscles of his chest and stomach against her back. The caftan was paper-thin, and it was like standing naked in his arms.

She felt his fingers move to her hips, caressingly, and her hand trembled as it stirred the eggs to keep them from burning.

"Egan, don't," she whispered shakily.

His breath was warm and rough in her hair, because the top of her head only came to his chin. The fingers holding her hips contracted, and she felt the tips of them on her flat stomach like a brand.

"Put down that damned spoon and turn around," he said in a tone she didn't recognize.

She was shaking like a leaf, and God only knew what would have happened. But noisy footsteps sounded outside the kitchen door, and an equally noisy yawn followed it. Egan let go of her and moved away just as Ada walked in.

"There you are!" she said brightly, watching her best friend stir eggs. "I'm starved!"

"It'll be on the table in two shakes," Kati promised, hoping her voice didn't sound as shaky as it felt. Damn Egan!

"I'd better get dressed," Egan commented, winking at Ada as he went past her. "I think I bother somebody like this."

Kati made an unforgivable comment under her breath as he left the room.

"At it again, I see," Ada sighed wearily.

"He started it," Kati said through her teeth. "I didn't ask him to walk in here naked."

"What?" Ada blinked.

Kati looked at her friend with a pained expression. "Oh God, isn't he beautiful?" she whispered with genuine feeling.

Ada chuckled gleefully. "Well, I always thought so, even if he is my brother. But isn't that something of a strange admission for you to make?"

"It slipped out. Just forget it." She dished up the eggs. "I think I'd better put something on too."

"Don't be long," Ada cautioned. "The eggs will congeal."

"I'll hurry."

She ran for her bedroom and closed the door just as Egan opened his. A minute's grace! She got into her jeans, blue T-shirt and shoes, and barely stopped to run a brush through her hair. She hoped it would be a short week. She hadn't expected Egan to have this kind of effect on her. In all the years she'd known him, he'd never even tried to make a pass at her. Now, in less than two days, he'd made more impact on her guarded emotions than any other man had in all her twenty-five years. She was going to have to get a hold on herself. She didn't know what kind of game Egan had in mind, but she wasn't playing.

He was wearing a brown velour pullover when she came back, one that emphasized his dark hair and complexion and the hard muscles she'd already seen.

"We left a little for you," Egan commented as she sat down. He pushed aside his empty plate and poured himself another cup of coffee from the hotplate on the table.

"How kind of you," she said pleasantly. She held up her cup and Egan filled it, studying her far too closely.

"What does your boyfriend do for a living?" he asked unexpectedly.

"Jack isn't my boyfriend," she said. "He's a man I date. And he's a political reporter for *The New York Times*."

He leaned back in his chair while Ada bit her lower lip and looked apprehensive.

"Is he really?" Egan asked. "He doesn't look like he gets much exercise. A little overweight, wouldn't you say?"

She glared at him. "He works very hard."

He only laughed, and sipped his coffee. "If I took him home with me, I could break him in one day."

"You could break the devil in one day," Kati said, exasperated. "What business is it of yours who I date?"

"Now, that's a good question," he replied. His eyes narrowed, and there was a smile she didn't understand on his chiseled lips. "Maybe I feel sorry for the poor man. He does know what you do for a living, doesn't he? Must be hell on him, having everything he does to you turn up in a book...."

"Egan." Ada groaned, hiding her face in her hands.

"You overbearing, unspeakable, mean tempered..." Kati began in a low tone. She threw her napkin down onto the table and stood up.

"You sure got up on the wrong side of the bed," Egan commented. "Here I am a guest in your apartment—"

"I'd sooner invite a cobra to breakfast!" she burst out.

"You should have," he murmured, glancing at the plate he'd just emptied. "He might have enjoyed burned eggs and half-raw bacon."

She tried to speak, couldn't, and just stormed out of the room.

She left the apartment before Ada could get out of the kitchen, and wandered around the streets shivering in her thin jacket for an hour before she gave up and went back. It was too cold for pride, anyway. All she'd accomplished was to let Egan see how unreasonably she reacted to his prodding. She'd just have to grit her teeth, for Ada's sake.

Egan was nowhere in sight when she got back, and Ada looked apologetic and worn.

"I don't understand him, I just don't," Ada groaned. "Oh Kati, I'm sorry. If I'd realized how bad things were between you, I'd never have invited him."

Kati was generous enough not to remind her friend that she'd tried to warn her. She sat down on the sofa with a hard sigh.

"I'll manage. Where is he?" she added darkly.

"Gone to spend the day with some girl friend of his," Ada said absently. "He said he might not be back until late."

Why that simple statement should make her feel murderous, Kati didn't know. But something gnawed inside her at the thought of Egan with another woman.

"I wonder how much he had to bribe her?" she asked nastily.

"Shame on you," Ada said.

But Kati didn't apologize. And she didn't dwell on her confused emotions, either. She wanted no complications in her life, especially with someone like Egan Winthrop.

She and Ada went shopping later in the day and ate out at a little Italian restaurant just down the street from their apartment. They watched television and eventually went to bed. And Egan didn't come back. Not that night. Not until the next morning.

Kati was sitting on the living room floor with pages littering the area around her. They were galleys of her latest book, which had come that morning by special messenger, and she was going over them. Ada was at auditions for a new play, hoping to be home by lunch if she didn't get held up at the theater during tryouts. That was a laugh. Most of the time, it took hours. Despite the appointments the hopefuls were given, something always went wrong. Ada had never gotten back when she thought she would, and Kati was dreading Egan's arrival. She felt wild when she thought of his not coming in at all, and angry because she didn't understand why. She didn't even *like* the man, for God's sake!

There was a loud knock at the door an hour later, and when she opened it, Egan was standing there looking faintly amused and as immaculate as when he'd left. Still in the same clothes, of course....

She glared at him. "Lose your key?" she asked.

"I thought I'd better not use it, in case you were... entertaining," he said.

She let him in, slammed the door and went back to her comfortable sprawl on the floor.

"Coffee's hot if you want some," she said icily. "I'm busy reading."

"Don't let me interrupt you. I thought I'd have a quick shower and change clothes. I've got a lunch date."

Why oh why did she feel like smashing plates? She frowned and concentrated on what she was doing. Minutes later, he was back, dressed in a navy blue pin-stripe suit with a white silk shirt and a blue and burgundy tie. He looked regal. Sexy. Unbelievably handsome for such an ugly man. If he was dressing like that in the middle of the day, he must be on his way to the Waldorf, she thought. And God only knew with whom.

"Ada didn't worry, did she?" he asked, checking his watch.

"Oh, no. She's used to people staying out all night," she lied deliberately, lifting her eyes. It shocked her, the flash of reaction in his face before it was quickly erased.

His eyes ran over her: the gray slacks and burgundy silk blouse she was wearing, her feet hose-clad and without shoes. Her hair was loose, and flowed in waves of reddish gold silk down her shoulders; her face was rosy and full of life.

His scrutiny made her nervous, and she dropped her eyes back to the page she was reading.

He moved closer and suddenly bent to pick up a page. His eyebrows rose as he read, and a slow smile touched his mouth.

"You do put your heart into it, don't you?" he murmured.

She reached up and took the page out of his hands, glancing at it. She blushed and tucked it under what she was reading. Why did he have to pick up *that* page? she groaned inwardly.

"Is that what you like with a man?" he continued maddeningly, his hands in his pockets, his eyes intent. "I've never done it in a bathtub, but I suppose—"

"Will you please go away?" she groaned, letting her hair fall over her eyes. "I don't care where you've done it, or with whom, just please go eat your lunch and leave me to my sordid occupation."

"I suppose I'd better. Stockbrokers sure as hell don't have time to waste."

She looked up as he turned to leave. "Stockbroker?" she murmured incredulously.

He glanced down at her from his formidable height with an expression she couldn't decipher. "I'm a busi-

nessman," he reminded her. "I do have the odd invest-
ment to look after."

"Yes, I know," she said quickly. "I just thought—"

"That because I was out all night, it was with a
woman—and that I was meeting her for a leisurely
lunch?" he suggested in a menacing tone.

She turned back to her work, trying to ignore him.
It wasn't easy when he loomed over her that way.

"The reasons I stayed away might shock you, city
girl," he said after a minute.

"I don't doubt it for a minute," she muttered.

"And that wasn't what I meant. It might have something to do with you."

The careless remark brought her eyes up, and he
held them relentlessly for so long that she felt currents
singing through her body.

"I didn't expect you to start trembling the minute I
put my hands on you," he said in a harsh undertone.
"Not after all these years. We've been enemies."

"We still are," she said in what she hoped was a con-
vincing tone, while humiliation stuck like bile in her
throat.

"Dead right," he said coldly. "And it's going to stay
that way. I don't want complications during this holiday."

"Ditto," she said curtly. "And don't go around flattering your ego too much, Egan," she added. "I was half
asleep at the time!"

His darkened eyes searched hers in the stillness that
followed, and she was aware of him in a way she'd
never been aware of a man before. Of his height and
strength, of the devastating effect he had on her senses.

"Saving your pride, Kati?" he asked quietly.

She studied her long fingernails. "I like my life as it is," she said. "I'm on the go too much for relationships of any kind. And what you'd have in mind...!" she began.

"Now who's flattering their ego?" he asked shortly, glaring down at her. "My God, I don't mind experience in my women, but I draw the line at promiscuity!"

She scrambled to her feet and was ready to swing when the dark look on his face worked some kind of witchcraft and left her standing helplessly with her fists clenched.

"You slapped me once and got away with it," he said quietly. "If you do it again now, we'll wind up in bed together."

She felt her body tremble at the words. "No," she bit off.

"Yes." His chest rose and fell heavily, and his eyes cut into hers. "Don't you realize that the way we react to each other is like flint and steel? All it would take is a kiss. Just that. And we'd burn each other alive. I've known that from the very beginning."

She hadn't, and the thought of Egan as a lover made her face burn. She had to smother a gasp as she turned away with her arms folded protectively around her slender body.

"Don't worry. You're safe, city girl," he said in a mocking tone. "I'm not that desperate. Just don't push me too far."

She couldn't even face what he was insinuating. Egan was the enemy. He was going to stay that way too, if she had to bite her tongue in two. She stared blankly out the window.

"And it's Ada that's auditioning for acting jobs," he commented sarcastically. "Playing innocent?"

She didn't have to play, but he'd never believe it. He'd just shocked her to her nylon-clad feet, and she was lost for words. It was a little frightening to be threatened with a man's bed, just for provoking him. She hadn't been aware that she *was* provoking him until now. Which automatically led to her asking why she did it, and that was frightening as well.

"Kati," he called softly.

She stiffened. "Will your stockbroker wait?" she asked quietly.

He frowned at her stiff back. "What the hell's the matter with you?"

"You threaten me with sex and then ask me what's wrong?" she burst out, staring at him nervously over one shoulder.

He blinked, as if she'd shocked him. "It wasn't a threat."

She flushed and walked away.

"Will you stop doing your Lady Innocent act and look at me?" he growled.

She walked into her bedroom and slammed the door. On an afterthought, she locked it, too. There was a string of unprintable curses from the vicinity of the living room before the front door slammed violently and the room became quiet.

It wasn't going to be possible to stay in the same apartment with Egan after this, she thought miserably.

She'd just have to check into a hotel until he left. Having to put up with his incessant verbal aggression was bad enough; but when he started threatening to make it physical, that was the end. The very end.

The conceited beast—to accuse her of being so vulnerable that she'd jump into his bed at the first opportunity. She groaned as she recalled the touch of his hands on her hips, the wild tremors that had run through her untried body. She gritted her teeth. She'd have to get away from him. Because what if he did that again? The real problem was telling Ada she was leaving without spoiling the poor girl's Christmas.

Chapter Four

Kati had half her clothes in her suitcase by the time Ada came home from her tryout. She still hadn't decided what she was going to do, beyond checking into a hotel down the street. She knew for certain that she couldn't take one more night of Egan.

"What are you doing?" Ada asked hesitantly, pausing in the doorway of Kati's room.

"Cleaning out my drawers," came the terse reply.

Ada cleared her throat. "Where are you taking what was in them?"

"To a hotel."

Ada leaned back against the doorjamb wearily. "Egan came home."

"How did you ever guess?" Kati asked pleasantly. She closed the lid of the suitcase.

"You're adults," Ada argued. "Surely you should be able to get along just during Christmas holidays? Peace on earth?"

"There is no peace where your brother is," Kati said vehemently. She tossed back a strand of hair and glared across the room. "I find it no less than miraculous that he can get people to work for him at all!"

The other woman sighed. "Amazingly enough, most of the hands have been with him for years. He has hardly any turnover." She glanced at Kati. "And he gets along wonderfully with women, as a rule. Polite, courteous, attentive—"

"We are talking about the same man?" Kati had to ask. "The big ugly one who's been staying here for two days and one night?"

Ada shook her head, laughing. "Oh, Kati. Kati." She moved out into the hall. "You win. I'll pack, too. We'll let Egan have the apartment and we'll both go to a hotel."

"Now hold on," Kati protested. "It's Christmas, and he's your brother, and the whole point of asking him here—"

"Was not to ruin your Christmas, believe it or not," Ada said gently. "You're like a sister to me. How can I let you leave alone?"

Kati bit her lower lip and stared helplessly at the suitcase. She didn't know what to do anymore.

"Maybe if you pretend he's not here?" Ada suggested softly.

Kati looked up. "He won't let me. He keeps making horrible remarks; he says..." Her face flushed, and she couldn't meet the curious look in her friend's eyes. "He has this strange idea about where I get material for my books."

"Suppose I talk to him?"

"That would make it worse." She moved the suitcase aside and sat down heavily. "I'll stay. I can't come between the two of you, not at Christmas."

"You're a doll." Ada grinned.

"I wish I were. Maybe then he'd let me alone," came the muttered reply.

"Just treat him like someone you've never met before," Ada suggested.

"That's an idea."

"Anything's worth trying once."

"Yes. Where do you keep the arsenic?"

"Shame on you! It's Christmas!"

"All right, I'm easy," Kati agreed. "Where's the holly stake?"

Ada threw up her hands and left the room.

It was late that evening when Egan came in, looking disheveled and out of sorts. He glared at Kati as if every ill in the world could be laid at her feet.

"We, uh, saved you some supper, Egan," Ada said.

"I'm not hungry," he returned gruffly, but his eyes still didn't leave Kati.

"I'll bring you some coffee," Kati said pleasantly and with a polite smile.

Egan stared after her blankly. "Concussion?" he asked Ada.

Ada laughed, going to help her friend in the kitchen.

"It's working," she whispered as they filled a tray. "He thinks you're sick."

"When hasn't he?" Kati muttered. She sliced some pound cake, added some dessert plates, forks and napkins to their coffee service, and carried the loaded tray into the living room.

Egan was sprawled in the big armchair that he'd appropriated since his arrival. He glared up from its depths as Kati put the tray down on the coffee table.

"I said I wasn't hungry," he repeated.

"Oh, the cake isn't for you," Kati said sweetly. "It's for Ada and me."

That seemed to make him worse. He sat up and took the cup of black coffee Kati poured him, sipping it. He seemed to brighten all at once. "Too weak," he said, staring at her.

She ignored the challenge. "Is it?" She tasted hers. "Yes," she lied, "it certainly is. I'll make some more."

"Don't bother," he returned curtly, leaning back with the cup and saucer held on the palm of one large, lean hand. "It'll do."

She nibbled at her cake and idly watched television. The program they had chosen was a romantic comedy about detectives.

"Isn't he dashing?" Ada sighed as the leading man came into view.

"Oh, rather," Kati said theatrically. "So handsome." She glanced at Egan with a lifted eyebrow.

Egan glanced back at her with hard eyes. But he didn't say a word.

"Did you settle that business with our stockbroker?" Ada asked when the commercial came on.

"Yes," Egan replied curtly. He finished his coffee

and stood up. "I think I'll get some sleep. It's been a trying day. Good night." He walked out without a word to Kati.

"It's barely nine," Ada murmured, scowling after him. "Egan never goes to bed this early."

"Maybe it's his conscience bothering him," Kati suggested. "About the abominable way he's been treating me?"

"Dream on, my best friend," came the sighing reply.

The phone rang and Ada dragged herself over to answer it, brightening when she heard the caller. "It's Marshal!" she whispered to Kati.

Kati grinned. Ada's boyfriend had been away for several weeks, and the joy of homecoming was in her eyes. She moved the phone into the hall while Kati finished watching television.

"He wants us to double up tomorrow night at the Rainbow Grill. Want to ask Jack?" Ada asked.

"I'd love to, but Jack's still out of town. How about Friday night?"

"Fine! I'll make sure it's okay with Marshal."

"You'll make sure what's okay?" Egan asked, stopping in the doorway with his tie in his hand and his shirt unbuttoned over his broad chest.

"A date, Friday night," Ada volunteered. "Want to come along? I've got a super girl friend—"

"I can get my own women," he said with a tilt of his mouth. "Friday? I'll ask Jennie. What time?"

Kati's heart sank, and it showed in her eyes. Egan happened to look her way; he smiled with pure malice.

"What's the matter, honey, will I cramp your style if I come along?" he asked her.

Kati remembered almost too late the role she'd chosen to play. Polite hostess. No personalities. No hostilities. Christmas. Good cheer.

She gritted her teeth. "You're welcome, of course," she said with a frozen smile.

Egan's heavy eyebrows lifted. "My God, get a doctor," he told Ada.

Kati smiled even brighter. "Now, I think I'll say good night, too. I have this headache…"

"But it's only nine," Ada wailed. "Don't both of you go to bed and leave me alone."

"Don't you want peace and quiet?" Egan asked his sister.

Ada glanced from one to the other of them and sighed. "Well, I think I'll come, too. I need my beauty sleep, I guess."

"Some of us might benefit from it," Kati muttered, glaring up at Egan.

He chuckled softly. "Think I'm ugly?"

She flushed. Her eyes involuntarily ran over the craggy contours, the broken nose, the hard, cruel mouth. For some odd reason, she couldn't quite look away. His eyes caught and held hers, and they stood staring at each other in a silence that blazed with new tensions.

"Excuse me," Ada murmured, trying to hide a grin as she edged past Kati's frozen form and into her own bedroom. "Good night!"

Egan's chest was rising and falling roughly as he

stared down at Kati. "Do you?" he asked in an odd tone.

She swallowed. Her throat felt as if it were full of cactus. Her lips parted, and Egan watched them hungrily. She realized all at once that he hadn't just been making threats earlier in the day. He wanted her!

"I...I'm tired," she managed, starting to move.

One long, hard arm came out, barring her path. "I wasn't threatening you this afternoon," he said tautly. "I was telling you how it would be. You can't be blind enough not to see how we are with each other, Kati," he added half under his breath.

She moved gingerly away from that long arm. "I...have a boyfriend...whom I like very much," she said shakily.

He eased forward, just enough to let her feel the warm strength of his body, the heat of his breath against her reddish gold hair. "Liking isn't enough."

Her eyes came up to meet his. "Isn't it?"

His fingertips touched her throat like a breath, feeling its silky texture, stroking it sensuously. "You smell of roses," he said in a husky whisper.

Her fingers caught his, trembling coldly against their warm strength as she tried to lift them away from her throat.

He caught her hand and moved it to his chest—easing it under the fabric and against thick hair and warm muscle—and her breath jerked in her throat. He felt as solid as a wall, and the wiry pelt of hair tickled her fingers as he flattened them against him. His expensive cologne filled her nostrils, drowning her in its masculine scent.

"Forgotten what to do, Kati?" he murmured roughly.
"Shall I refresh your memory?"

She lifted her eyes dazedly to his, and they were
wide and curious as they met his glittering gaze.

His head bent so that his hard face filled the world.
"'She tore his shirt out of the way,'" he quoted huskily,
"'and ran her fingers, trembling, over his hard,
male…'!"

"No!" Recognizing the passage, she flushed hotly.
Immediately, she dragged her hand away and shrank
from him as if he'd burned her.

He laughed, but there was an odd sound to it, and
his eyes blazed as she reached behind her for the
doorknob to her room.

"Doesn't your reporter friend like having you do
that to him?" he asked huskily. "Or does he prefer what
comes later?"

She whirled on a sob, pushing open the door. She
started to slam it, but he caught it with a powerful hand
and she couldn't budge it.

"I hate you," she breathed shakily, frantic that Ada
might hear them.

"So you keep telling me," he replied. "You're the
one with no scruples, honey, so stop flying at me when
I throw them back at you."

"I'm not what you think I am," she cried.

"No kidding?" he murmured insolently, letting his
eyes punctuate the insult.

"You go to hell, you ugly cowboy!" she said furiously.

He studied her flushed face and black eyes
amusedly. "Ada used to talk about her sweet-tempered,

easygoing friend. Before I ever met you, I imagined a retiring little violet. You were a shock, honey."

"What do you think you were?" she returned.

He laughed softly. "No woman's ever pulled the wool over my eyes. It didn't take reading your books to tell me what kind of woman you were. All I had to do was watch you in action."

"The car broke down," she reminded him. "Richard and I had to walk for miles…!"

"Aren't you tired of lying about it? I told you," he added, letting his eyes narrow sensuously, "experienced women turn me on."

"Then why don't you go out and find the friend you spent the night with?" she retorted hotly.

His eyebrows went up and he grinned. "Did that bother you?"

She brought her heel down hard on his instep, without warning; and while he was off balance, she slammed the door and locked it.

"Kati!" he growled furiously.

"Go ahead, break it down!" she dared him. "I'll be screaming out the window until the police come!"

There was a muffled curse; a door opening; Ada's voice, almost hysterical; and Egan's, angry but conciliatory. Minutes later, two doors slammed almost simultaneously. With an angry sigh, Kati started stripping off her clothes and heading toward the shower. She was furious enough not to mind that the water was ice-cold.

Chapter Five

Egan was gone, blessedly, when Kati woke up late the next morning. Jack called to say he was back in town and asked Kati out for dinner. Grateful for the respite, she was waiting for him on pins and needles at six that afternoon.

Ada had been sympathetic about her brother's strange behavior, adding that he had a sore foot and it served him right. It was the first time Kati ever heard Ada say anything against Egan.

"Do you think I'm scandalous?" Kati asked unexpectedly when she and Jack were relaxing over coffee after a satisfying steak.

He stared at her. "You?"

"Because I write what I write," she added. "It's important."

"No, I don't think you're scandalous," he said

honestly and smiled. "I think you're extremely talented, and your books are a joy to read."

"You don't think I lead a wild life?"

He only laughed. "No, I don't. What's wrong? Are you getting unpleasant letters again?"

"Oh, no. It's…" She sighed and propped her chin on her hand. "It's Egan."

"Please, don't spoil a perfect evening," he said with a restless movement. "He has a glare that could stop a clock."

"Tell me about it," she muttered. "He's giving me fits about what I write."

"Doesn't he realize the difference between fiction and fact?"

"Not if he doesn't want to," she said with a short laugh. "Egan makes up his rules as he goes along. He's a law unto himself out West."

"I got that idea, all right." He studied her sad face and reached out impulsively to pat her hand. "He'll leave after Christmas," he said bracingly.

"Roll on, New Year," she murmured, and sighed as she sipped her coffee.

They went dancing after dinner, and for a while Kati forgot all her troubles. She drew interested glances in the black dress she was wearing. It had a peasant bodice with a full, swirling skirt, and left her creamy shoulders bare. With her hair in a high coiffure, and a minimum of makeup, she wore the designer gown with a flair.

She felt on top of the world, until she went into the apartment and found Egan waiting in the hall.

"Where's lover boy?" he asked, glaring past her at the closed door. "Doesn't he come in for a nightcap?"

He was wearing a dress shirt rolled up to the elbows and half unbuttoned in front, with his black slacks. Obviously, he hadn't spent the evening at home, either, and his proprietary air irritated Kati even more. She was still fuming from last night.

"He doesn't wear a nightcap," she said with sweet venom, "and I don't lend mine."

His chin lifted at an arrogant angle and he looked at her long and hard, his dark eyes narrowing on her bare shoulders.

Self-conscious with him, she hunched her shoulders so that the elastic top came back into place, demurely covering everything south of her collarbone.

"Shy of me?" he asked quietly, moving forward.

She felt like running. Where was Ada, for heaven's sake? She couldn't get past him to her room to save her life, and she knew it.

"Where's Ada?" she asked quickly.

"In her room, talking to Marshal," he said. "Why? You're a big girl, now; you don't need protecting, do you?"

Oh yes, she did, but obviously she couldn't count on her best friend tonight.

She felt the impact of his rough, warm hands—with a sense of fatalism. Her body jerked under the sensation as he deliberately began to slide the fabric away from her shoulders and down.

"Isn't this how you had it?" he breathed, bending. His chest rose and fell roughly, and she drowned in the warmth of his body.

"Egan…" she began.

"Don't talk. Stand still." His mouth smoothed over her shoulder, leaving a fiery wake. His fingers held her upper arms, digging in as his teeth nipped slowly, tenderly at the silken flesh.

"Don't," she moaned, eyes closed, throat arching as if it invited him—begged him—to do what he pleased.

"You want it," he whispered huskily. "So do I. Desperately…!" She felt his tongue and the edge of his teeth as he moved over the warm expanse of her shoulders and her collarbone in a silence blazing with promise.

His breath sounded oddly jerky as he drew her body against him. "You taste like the sweetest kind of candy," he said under his breath, and his fingers were hurting, but she was too shaken to care. "Baby," he whispered, his mouth growing urgent now as it found her throat, the underside of her chin. His hands moved up to catch in her hair, careless of its neat bun, as he bent her head back and lifted it toward his hard, parted lips. "Baby, you make me ache…!"

His mouth was poised just above hers, and at that moment she'd have given him that and anything else he wanted. But before he could lower his head, the sound of a door being opened shattered the hot silence.

"Oh, damn," Egan ground out. His fingers bruised her, and his eyes were blazing as he pushed her away and turned as if he were blinded by his own passion— a frustrated passion like that which was making her tremble.

"Marshal's sick of the sea, but they won't let him come home," Ada sighed, oblivious to the wild undercurrents around her. "Why couldn't I find myself a man instead of a sailor? Hi, Kati. Have a good time?"

"Sure," Kati said, smiling through a haze of unsatisfied longing. She glanced toward Egan and saw his eyes, and she flushed wildly. Her eyes went to his mouth and back up; and he muttered something terrible under his breath and slammed into his room without even the pretense of courtesy.

"What's the matter with him?" Ada asked softly.

"Beats me," her friend replied blandly. "Gosh, I'm tired. We went dancing and my feet are killing me!"

"Well, I hope you don't wear them out before Friday night," Ada laughed. "Sleep well."

"I'll do my best," came the muttered reply, and she went into her room and almost collapsed. He hadn't even kissed her, and she was trembling like a leaf. Heaven only knew what would happen if he ever really made a heavy pass. She couldn't bear to think about it! She went to bed and lay awake half the night brooding, only to wake with a splitting headache the next morning.

Egan brooded all day. He moved restlessly around the apartment, like a man aching for the outdoors. Even Kati felt vaguely sorry for him.

"You'll wear ruts in the carpet," she murmured after lunch, while Ada was taking her turn at the dishes.

He turned with his hands rammed deep in his pockets and stared at her. "If I do, I'll buy you a new one."

"That wasn't what I meant," she said, trying hard to hold on to her temper. She searched his hard face, but she couldn't quite meet his eyes. "You hate being indoors, don't you?"

"With a passion," he agreed shortly. "I couldn't live like this."

"New York is full of things to see," she suggested. "There's Central Park, and the Statue of Liberty, the Empire State Building—"

"I've already seen them once," he said. "And I've walked the streets. What I want, I'm not going to find out there."

She lifted her eyes and had them trapped.

He moved closer so quickly that she hardly saw him coming before he was towering over her. "I want you," he said, his voice like warm velvet in the sudden silence of the room. "I'm through pretending."

"Well, I don't...I don't want you," she said in a breathless little voice. "I have a boyfriend—"

"No competition whatsoever," he returned. "What are you afraid of? I'm not brutal in bed. I wouldn't hurt you."

She flushed deeply, and just stopped herself from slapping him. "I liked it better when you hated me," she said angrily, glaring up at him.

His eyes searched hers. "Was it ever that?"

Her lips parted, but before she could find an answer, Ada was through with the dishes and Kati stuck to her like glue until it was time to leave for dinner that evening.

Jack grinned as he saw Kati in her burgundy velvet dress. "What a dish," he murmured. "And I like your hair down like that."

"Thank you. You aren't bad yourself. Jack, you know Marshal," she said, indicating the tall, dark young man beside Ada.

"Sure." Jack extended his hand. "Good to see you again."

"Same here," Marshal replied. He hugged Ada close. "I still love the sea, but sometimes I get a little hungry for the shore."

"I can imagine. Uh, wasn't your brother supposed to join us?" Jack asked Ada with evident reluctance.

"He's meeting us at the Rainbow Grill," Ada said. "And I made reservations in advance."

"Good girl," Jack said. He took Kati's arm. "Well, let's get it over with," he murmured under his breath.

"It will be all right," she promised as Ada and Marshal fell back. "We can have the waiter pour wine over his head if he starts anything."

"You don't think he would?" Jack asked, horrified.

She patted his arm. He wasn't the type for public scenes, although Kati wouldn't have minded dousing Egan any old where at all. "No, I don't," she promised. "Don't worry. Everything will be fine."

She was to remember those words vividly a little later, when Egan joined them at their table overlooking the colorful lights of the city sixty-five floors down. He had on his arm a windblown little blonde who looked and dressed like a woman who loved money, and her first glance at the other women was like a declaration of war.

"So this is Ada," the blonde gushed, heading straight for Kati.

"Wrong woman," Kati said shortly. "That's Ada."

The blonde shrugged, gave a careless smile and turned to greet a highly amused Ada. "So you're Ada. How nice to meet you at last. I've just heard so much about you from Egan. We've known each other for a long time, you know. He calls me every time he gets to New York. I'm a model."

As if that didn't stick out a mile, Kati thought as the blonde sat down near her and almost choked her with expensive perfume.

"Isn't this the most gorgeous place?" the blonde enthused. "I love the atmosphere. And isn't the combo great?"

Kati couldn't say. She hadn't been able to hear them play, or hear their sultry-voiced vocalist sing, for the newcomer. And just as she was wondering how she'd eat because of the perfume, Egan slid into the seat beside her and ruined her appetite completely.

"Jennie Winn, this is Katriane James and her date," Egan volunteered.

Kati glared at him. "Jack Asher," she supplied.

"Nice to meet you, I'm sure," Jennie murmured. "What do you do, Mr. Asher?" she asked Jack and batted her impossibly long eyelashes at him.

He perked up immediately, the turncoat. "I'm a political columnist, for the *Times,*" he said.

Jennie beamed. "Are you, really? Oh, I just adore intelligent men."

Kati had to muffle a giggle with her napkin. Really, she was behaving impossibly, but that blonde couldn't be for real!

"Something amuses you, Miss James?" Egan asked with ice in his tone.

She got herself under control. "I got strangled, Mr. Winthrop," she managed.

"On what? The air?"

"Now, Egan, honey," Jennie crooned, glaring past him at Kati. "You just relax, and later I'll take you back to my place and soothe you."

Kati bit almost through her lip to keep from howling. She didn't dare look at Egan—it would have been the very end.

"Jennie, look at the menu," Egan said curtly.

"Whatever you say, sugar."

"I want the beef Wellington," Ada said. "How about you, Kati?"

"Do they serve goose here?" Egan asked under his breath.

"If they do," Kati replied with a venomous smile, "yours is probably sizzling on the grill right now, sugar."

He glared at her and she glared back at him. Sensing disaster, Jack quickly intervened.

"Kati, didn't you want to try that duckling in orange sauce?"

She tore her eyes away from Egan's and smiled across the table. "Yes, I did."

By then the waiter was back, elegant in his white jacket, to take their order. By and large, Kati loved New York waiters. They had a certain flair and grace of manner that set them apart, and they were unfailingly polite and kind.

"I want prime rib," Jennie said nonchalantly. "Rare, honey."

"A woman after my own heart," Egan murmured. "I'll have the same."

Kati wanted to mutter something about barbarism, but she kept her mouth shut with an effort. And when the food came, she was far too involved in savoring every morsel to waste time on Egan Winthrop.

But the coffee and dessert came, eventually, and while Kati toyed with her superb English trifle, Egan leaned back and eyed Jack.

"I read your column on the Washington scandal," he told the younger man.

"Did you?" Jack asked with a polite smile.

"Interesting, about the deficit in the agency's budget," he continued. "Apparently your man was allocating funds on paper that never reached the recipients. The audacity of politicians constantly amazes me, and so does the apathy of the public."

Jack perked up. "Yes. What I can't understand is how he expected to get away with it," he said, forgetting his dessert as he went into the subject.

Egan matched him, thought for thought, and the ensuing conversation fascinated Kati. She listened raptly, along with everyone else at the table except Jennie—who looked frankly bored to death.

"You know a hell of a lot about politics for a rancher, Mr. Winthrop," Jack said finally, on a laugh.

"I took my degree in political science," came the cool reply. "Ranching pretty much chose me, rather than the other way around. When my father died, there was Ada and my mother to look after, and no one else to assume control of the property. There was a lot of it." He shrugged. "The challenge is still there," he added with a smile. "Cattle are a lot like politics, Mr. Asher. Unpredictable, hard to manage and sometimes just plain damned frustrating."

Jack laughed. "I imagine so."

"Oh, can't we stop talking about such boring things?" Jennie asked in a long-suffering tone. "I want to go to the theater, and we've got tickets to that hit musical on Broadway. We'll be late if you talk all night."

Egan gave her a look that would have stopped traffic.

Jennie flushed and cleared her throat. "I mean, whenever you're ready, sugar," she said placatingly.

Kati lifted her chin with faint animosity. She'd have told him where to go, instead of pleading with him like that. He knew it, too. Because he glanced at her and caught the belligerent gleam in her eye, and something wild and heady flashed between them when he smiled at her.

Her lips trembled, and she grabbed her coffee cup like a shield.

"See you later," Egan told them, picking up the tabs. "My treat. I enjoyed the discussion," he told Jack.

Before anyone could thank him, he and Jennie were gone and Jack was shaking his head.

"And I thought he hated me. My God, what a mind. He's wasted out West."

Ada beamed. "He was offered an ambassadorship, did you know?" she asked. "He knows everybody in

Washington, right to the top. But he turned it down because of mother and me. Since then, he's given everything to the ranch."

"Not quite everything," Marshal murmured. "His girl was a knockout."

"I'd have liked to knock her out," Kati muttered, flushing at Ada's shocked look. "Well, she must have bathed in perfume; I could hardly breathe," she said defensively.

But Ada only grinned, and Kati hated that knowing look. So she was jealous! She caught her breath. She was jealous? Of Egan? She picked up the untouched wineglass and helped herself.

Egan wasn't home when they finally got back to the apartment, and Kati could just picture him with that sizzling blonde. It made her ache in the oddest way. She took a shower and got ready for bed and then paced and paced around her room.

"Is something bothering you?" Ada asked minutes later, coming in to check on her. It wasn't like Kati to pace. "You're getting to be as bad as Egan about wearing ruts in the carpets."

Kati lifted her shoulders helplessly, grabbing at the ribbon strap that kept sliding off. The green gown was far too big, but she liked its roominess. "I'm just restless."

Ada studied her friend quietly. "He's a man," she said softly.

Kati blushed all the way down her throat and turned away.

"I'm sorry, I shouldn't have said that," Ada said hesitantly. "But, you see, I can't help noticing the way you look at him. And the way he looks back. Normal people don't fight like the two of you do. Anything that explosive has to…well, there has to be something pretty powerful to cause it, don't you see?"

"I hate him," Kati said through her teeth. "That's powerful, all right."

"But you want him."

Kati's eyes closed. "Tomorrow is Christmas," she said. "The day after, he'll go back to Wyoming and I'll go back to my sordid books, and we'll both be better off. There's no future with your brother for any woman, Ada, and you know it." She turned around, her face stiff with control. "He's not the happily-ever-after kind."

Ada looked worried. "He says that, but no man really wants to get married, does he? It kind of takes the right woman."

Kati laughed huskily. "A woman like Jennie. She suits him just fine, doesn't she?" she asked venomously.

Ada shook her head. "She numbs the hurt, that's all. He's a lonely man."

"He got hurt once and never wants to be again, is that how it goes?" Kati asked.

"I don't think Egan can be hurt, Kati," came the soft reply. "He doesn't let anyone close enough. I know less than nothing about his private life. But I think he's more involved with you right now than he's ever been before."

"He's never touched me," she bit off.

"Yes, I know. I didn't mean physically," Ada said.

"I mean emotionally. Don't you realize that's why he hits at you so hard?"

"He hits at me because he wants me," she told the other woman bluntly. "He said so. He thinks I'm easy."

Ada looked horrified. "Well, did you tell him the truth?"

"Of course not! I don't owe your horrible brother any explanations— Let him just keep his disgusting image of me!"

Ada frowned slightly. "Kati, he isn't a man to let go of something he sets his mind on. I think you'd better tell him."

"Why bother? He'll be gone day after tomorrow," she repeated.

"Kati—"

"Go to bed and stop worrying about me," Kati said gently, and hugged her concerned friend. "Egan and I will go on being enemies, because I won't give in and he'll give up. He makes a nice enemy."

"You wouldn't think so if he'd ever really been yours," Ada replied.

"Anyway, we both need our sleep. It will all work out, somehow. Sleep well."

Ada gave up. She smiled as she went out. "You, too."

But Kati didn't. Not until the wee hours of the morning. And Egan still hadn't come home. He was with that blonde, kissing her with that wide, cruel mouth that had tormented hers so sweetly....

Something woke her. She didn't know what. But she felt the light on her eyelids and the coolness of air on her skin, and her dark, drowsy eyes opened slowly.

He was standing beside the bed, wearing nothing but a pair of slacks, with his broad chest sensuously bare and a cup of black coffee in one hand. And he was looking at her in a way that brought her instantly alert and wary; his glittering silver eyes were on fire.

She frowned slightly as she realized that he wasn't looking at her face. Her eyes shifted, and she noticed to her embarrassment that the loose gown had shifted in the night, leaving one perfect breast pink and bare.

Her hand went to jerk the bodice back up.

"No, Kati," he said in a husky undertone, and his eyes went back up to hers. "No. Let it happen."

He moved close, setting the coffee on the table. He dropped smoothly down beside her, and she hated the sudden weakness and hunger of her body as she stared up at him. Her hair was spread out on the pillow like a ragged halo of red and gold, her cheeks rosy with sleep, her eyes sultry. And he looked just as disheveled, just as attractive to her, with his hair tousled, his muscular arms and chest bare and tanned.

His hands went under her head, both of them, and he eased down so that his chest rested on her partially bare one.

She gasped at the unfamiliar sensation of skin on skin, and her eyes dilated under the piercing scrutiny of his.

"I'm going to kiss you until you can't stand up," he said roughly, bending. "My God, I want your mouth…!"

He took it, with a hard, hungry pressure that frightened her. Her slender hands lifted quickly to his shoulders and started to push—until they discovered the rough silkiness of his skin, the power in his bunched muscles. She ran her hands slowly down his arms, feeling the tension of the hard muscles, and back up again, to the hard bone of his shoulders.

Meanwhile, his mouth was slowing, gentling. He lifted it so that it was poised just over hers, and he looked at her for a long moment.

"You don't like it hard, do you?" he asked in a gruff undertone. "I do. Hard and hot and deep. But I'll make the effort, at least."

He bent again, coaxing her lips. It was an education in sensual blackmail. She lay tense under the crush of his torso, feeling each brief, soft contact like a brand. Her lips parted because she couldn't stop them, her breath was coming in short gasps and her heartbeat was shaking her. She hadn't known that women felt like this, despite the novels that bore her name. All her research had come from books, from films and television and bits and pieces of gossip. But what Egan was teaching her bore no resemblance to any of that. He was making her catch fire, and she was moving and reacting in ways that embarrassed her.

"That's more like it, baby," he breathed. "Much, much more like it. Now," he whispered, letting his hands slide down the long, bare line of her back, "now, if you want my mouth, come up and get it."

Blind, aching, she arched up and caught his hard mouth with hers, kissing him with enough enthusiasm to make up for her lack of experience at this kind of impassioned caress.

She felt his tongue go into her mouth, and she moaned sharply at the intimacy.

He lifted his dark head as if the sound had shocked him, and looked down at her rigid, anguished features. His free hand tugged slowly at the other strap of her gown and his eyes followed its movement.

"Do you want me, Kati?" he asked quietly. "Shall I get up and lock the door?"

Her mind cleared instantly with the words as she stared up into his blazing eyes. He was asking her a straightforward question, and the answer would have been an unqualified *yes*. But he was offering a quick, temporary merging of bodies that would shame her when her sanity returned. And what in heaven's name would Ada think?

As if he sensed the indecision, his hand stilled on her arm. "Second thoughts?" he asked softly.

"I...can't," she whispered, searching his narrow eyes.

"I understand," he murmured, glancing toward the door with a wry smile. "We're not likely to be alone much longer."

He thought it was because of Ada, and it didn't really matter, did it? Whatever the reason, the result was going to be the same.

He looked back down at her and shifted so that the thick hair on his chest rubbed against her soft bareness; he smiled at her reaction.

"Like it?" he murmured arrogantly, and his hand came up to tease the softness under her arm, making her gasp.

"You have to stop that," she told him in a halting tone.

"Do I?" He bent and brushed his mouth lightly over hers while his fingers toyed with the silken skin and edged slowly, relentlessly, toward the hardening nub that would tell him graphically how he was affecting her.

"Egan?" she whispered in a voice that sounded nothing like her own. Her fingers lifted, catching in his hair, and her body was no longer part of her. It was his, all his, and every inch of it was telling him so.

His nose rubbed against hers as his mouth brushed and lifted; and his fingers made nonsense of principles and morals and self-respect.

"Kati?" he whispered, sensuously. He nipped at her lower lip. "Kati, take my hand and put it where you want it."

It was the most wildly erotic thing she'd ever heard or dreamed or thought. Helplessly, she reached out for his hand and carried it to the aching peak, and pressed it there.

"Oh God," she ground out, trembling, her face pressing into his hot throat, her body shuddering with the force of her own hunger.

"Silk," he whispered, his own voice rough and unsteady. "You're silk. So soft, so whisper-soft." His mouth found hers and he kissed her so tenderly that tears welled in her eyes, while his hand cupped and his thumb caressed, and it was the sweetest ache in the world that he caused her.

And then, all at once, the bodice was back in place, the sheet was over her and she was lying, shaking, in the bed as he propped up pillows and set her against them like a big doll.

"Ada," he ground out, handing her the cup with hands that trembled.

Her own trembled, and between them they just got it steady as Ada opened the door without knocking and came in yawning.

"Morning," she murmured, grinning at them. "I've got breakfast. Bring your coffee with you. Thanks for taking it to her, Egan."

"My pleasure," he murmured, and went out without a backward glance.

"Bad mood again?" Ada grimaced. "I thought it might mellow him up if I sent him in with your coffee. I guess I goofed again. Well, hurry up and dress, I've got something special!" Ada added and went out the door laughing.

Kati sat there with tears suddenly rolling down her cheeks, so shaken and frustrated that she wanted to scream the roof down. She should have listened to Ada, she told herself. Ada had known what she didn't—that Egan was relentless when he wanted something. And what he wanted now was Kati.

Chapter Six

Ada had made fresh croissants—so light and flaky they could almost fly—and she had real butter to go on them. But Kati didn't taste anything she ate. She felt as if she were in the throes of some terrible fever, and every time she glanced at Egan, it got worse.

He was wearing a shirt and his boots now, with his dark slacks, and he was still beautiful. Kati could hardly drag her eyes away.

"You must have been late last night," Ada remarked to her brother. "I didn't hear you come in."

"I let myself be talked into going to a party after the show," he muttered. "Damned bunch of freaks. It was like a drugstore in there."

"You left," Ada said with certainty.

"I left. And took Jennie with me. And she screamed

bloody murder all the way back to her apartment." He laughed shortly. "Which got her nowhere at all. She knew how I felt about that from the beginning, I never made any secret of it."

"Things are different in the city, Egan," Ada said sadly. "Very different."

His head lifted. "Geography doesn't change what's right and what isn't," he said shortly.

"I know that," Ada agreed. "I don't like it any more than you do, but I don't feel I have the right to dictate to the rest of the world. Kati and I just keep to ourselves."

He glanced at Kati then, his eyes sweeping over her pale jersey blouse and slacks possessively. "Are you an old-fashioned girl in that respect, at least?" he asked, but he didn't sound so sarcastic as usual. "Do you drink and pop pills and smoke pot?"

"I drink cola," she replied. "And I do take aspirin when my head hurts." She watched him with wide eyes. "But I don't think I've ever tried to smoke a pot. What kind of pot did you have in mind?"

He burst out laughing. It changed his entire face, erased some of the hard, leathery lines. He looked faintly attractive, despite that cragginess. "My, my, aren't we sharp this morning?"

She lowered her eyes before he could read the embarrassment in them. "Eating improves my mind."

"I know something better," he remarked just as she lifted the coffee cup to her mouth.

"Don't move!" Ada gasped as hot coffee went all over the table and into Kati's lap. "I'll get a towel!"

She disappeared, and Egan mopped at her legs with a napkin.

"That was damned poor timing on my part," he muttered. "I didn't mean to make you hurt yourself."

She looked up into his silver eyes, astonished. "That's a first," she breathed.

He looked back, his gaze intent. The napkin rested on her thigh. "Did I tell you how lovely you are?" he asked under his breath. "Or what it did to me to touch you like that?"

She felt her lips part helplessly. "Egan, about... what happened—"

"I want it again," he breathed, bending so that his mouth threatened hers. "I want you against me so close that I can feel your heart beating."

"You don't understand," she whispered weakly.

"You want me," he returned huskily. "That's all I need to understand."

It was true, but it wasn't that uncomplicated. And before she could tell him how complicated it really was, Ada was back and the moment was lost. And she was trembling again.

She walked around like a zombie, going through the motions of helping Ada in the kitchen. They invited Marshal and Jack over for dinner the next day, since neither of them was going to try to go home for Christmas. And getting everything ready was a job.

Egan watched television and paced. Finally he got his jacket and hat and went out, and Kati almost collapsed with relief. She ached every time she looked at him, until it was torment to be within seeing distance.

He came in just as the annual Christmas Eve specials were beginning on the public broadcasting station, and he tossed his hat onto the hall table and shed his jacket.

"Culture," he murmured, watching the opera company perform.

"Go ahead, Mr. Winthrop, make some snide remark," Kati dared, feeling young and full of life because her heart leaped up just at the sight of him.

He smiled at her, with no malice at all on his dark face. "I like opera."

"You?"

"Well, there was a report awhile back on music and milk production," he told her, dropping easily into his armchair, "and it seems that cows produce more milk when they're listening to classical music."

Kati smiled. "It must cost a lot."

"What?"

"Having the orchestra come all the way out to the ranch."

"You little torment," he accused and reached out to tug a lock of her long hair playfully.

Ada, watching all this, just stared at them.

"Something wrong?" Egan asked her.

Ada shrugged. "Not a thing in this world, big brother."

He grinned at her. "Where's your boyfriend?"

"Begging for liberty on his knees," she told Egan. She laughed. "If he gets it he'll be here any minute."

"I'd bet on him." He glanced at Kati. "How about yours?" he asked tautly.

"Jack's making calls to his family," she said. "He won't be over until tomorrow."

He didn't say anything, but he settled down in the chair to watch the programs with an oddly satisfied smile.

Marshal came a few minutes later, and Egan even joined in when they sang Christmas carols during the next program. They drank eggnog and ate cake, and Kati thought she'd never been so happy in her life.

Ada led Marshal under the mistletoe on his way out at midnight and kissed him lovingly, winking at Kati as the two of them moved out into the hallway.

"I'm going to walk Marshal to the elevator," she called back. "Don't wait up."

"Don't fall down the elevator shaft!" Kati called after her.

The door closed on a giggle. Which left Kati alone with Egan and trembling with new and frightening emotions.

He stood up, holding out his hand. She put hers into it unhesitatingly and let him lead her to the mistletoe. His lean, strong hands caught her waist and brought her gently against the length of his hard body.

"I've waited all day for this," he whispered, bending.

She stiffened, but his hands smoothed down over her hips and back and he nudged his face against hers gently.

"I know how you like it, baby," he breathed. "I won't hurt you this time, all right?"

She was beyond answering him. Her body throbbed. Throbbed! It was the most incredible physical reaction she'd ever had in her life, and she couldn't control it.

His mouth opened and hers opened to meet it, inviting the new intimacy, and she drowned in the magic of the long, sweet kiss. She breathed him, the tangy fragrance of cologne and, closer, the minty hotness of his mouth.

"I want you," he whispered, his voice shaking.

She drew back a little, trying to catch her breath and regain her sanity. It was impossible, but she couldn't even speak. They were simply torturing each other with this kind of thing. But how could she explain it to him?

He rested his forehead on hers and his eyes closed on ragged breaths. Against her hips, his body was making an embarrassing statement about his feelings, and she withdrew just enough to satisfy her modesty.

"Still playing games, Kati? You don't have to put on any acts for me. That virginal withdrawal—"

"Egan, you have to listen to me," she managed, looking up.

"I've got an apartment two streets over," he said on a harsh breath. "One even Ada doesn't know about. We could be there in fifteen minutes, and she'd never have to know."

Her breath caught in her throat. His eyes were blazing with it, and she knew her own legs were trembling. For one wild second she looked up at him and knew how it would be between them. She could almost feel the length of him without clothes: the silken slide of skin on skin, the aching pleasure of being touched by those lean, expert hands...

"Come with me, Kati," he said unsteadily. "We're just torturing each other. I've got to have you."

"I can't," she ground out. She lowered her chin so that her tormented eyes were on a level with his chest, and her trembling fingers pressed against his warm shirt.

His fingers tautened on her waist, moved to her hips and jerked them into his. "I ache," he whispered. "You know what I'm feeling."

Her eyes closed. She wasn't stupid; she could imagine that it was ten times worse for him than it was for her. But she couldn't undo all the years of conditioning. Flings weren't for her. She had too much conscience.

"I'm sorry," she whispered. "I'm so sorry, Egan, but I can't."

He drew in an angry breath, and she stiffened because she knew he was going to go right through the ceiling. She couldn't even blame him; she should never have let him touch her.

But oddly enough, he didn't say a word. He loosened his grip on her hips, allowing her to move away, and drew her gently into his arms. He held her, his head bending over her, his heartbeat shaking both of them, until his breathing was normal again.

Her hands felt the warm strength of his back even through his shirt, and she loved the protected feeling she got from being close like this. Her eyes closed and, just for a moment, she allowed herself the luxury of giving in completely, of pretending that he loved her.

"I could make you," he whispered at her ear. "I could take the choice away."

"Yes, I know," she agreed softly. Her cheek nuzzled against his chest.

"This kind of passion is a gift," he said quietly. "I could give you pleasure in ways you've never had it with another man. Not because I'm any damned prize in bed, but because we react to each other like dynamite going up."

"I can't," she replied softly. "I want to, but I can't."

His hand smoothed her long hair gently. "Because of him?"

She drew in a steadying breath. She was going to have to tell him, and it wasn't going to be easy.

The door opened, thank God, and Ada walked in, stopping dead when she saw the two of them wrapped in each other's arms.

"Wrestling match?" she guessed. "Who's winning?"

"Mistletoe," Egan murmured, nodding upward. "Damned potent stuff. She's got me on my knees."

"That'll be the day," Ada grinned.

Kati pulled away, and he let her go with obvious reluctance. "And I didn't poison you, either," she murmured, trying to keep it light.

"Didn't you?" he returned, but there was a difference in him now, a strangeness.

"No fighting," Ada said. "It's Christmas day."

"So it is," Egan said. "Where's my present?"

"Not until morning," Ada returned.

"Damn." He looked down at Kati. "I like presents. What did you get me?"

"Not until morning," she echoed Ada.

He lifted an eyebrow. "I hate waiting," he murmured, and only Kati knew what he meant.

"All good things come to him who waits, though,"

Ada interrupted; and then wondered why Kati blushed
and Egan laughed.

The girls went in to bed, but Kati didn't sleep. She
wanted Egan. And there was more to it than that. She
was beginning to feel something she'd never expected.
She thought ahead to the next day, when he'd leave for
Wyoming, and the world went black. She couldn't
imagine a day going by without the sight of him. Just
the sight of him.

She sat straight up in bed and stared at the wall. She
hadn't known that it could happen so quickly. Of course,
it could be just physical attraction. She did want him very
much, and it was the first time she'd wanted any man.
She knew nothing about him really, except bits and
pieces. So how, she asked herself, could she be in love
with him?

"Love," she whispered out loud. She licked her dry
lips and put it into words. "I…love…Egan." The sound
of it made tingles all the way to her toes, and when she
closed her eyes she could feel his mouth on hers; she
could taste the minty warmth of his lips. Shivers went
all over her like silvery caresses, and she caught her
breath.

You have to forget all that, she told herself. Because
what Egan wanted was the limited use of her body, to
sate his own hunger. And once he'd had it, he'd be off
to new conquests. Like Jennie. Her eyes clouded with
bridled fury. Jennie! She'd like to rip the girl's hair out.

She lay back down and closed her eyes. Well, that
was his kind of woman, anyway. All she had to do was
grit her teeth and bear it until he left. Then she could

pull her stupid self together and forget him. Her eyes opened. It was over an hour before she could close them in sleep.

Chapter Seven

The thought of the condominium bothered Kati. She couldn't help remembering that Egan had said Ada didn't know about it, which meant he kept it for only one reason. If he was willing to take Kati there, he must have taken other women too. In the cold light of morning, she was glad she'd had the sense to resist him. Egan only wanted her. Someday, with a little luck, there would be a man who'd love her.

But if she was inclined to be cool and collected, Egan wasn't. He watched her covetously when she joined them for breakfast. His silver eyes roamed over the pretty red vest and skirt she was wearing with a long-sleeved white blouse, and he smiled appreciatively.

"Very Christmasy," he murmured.

She smiled as coolly as possible. "Thank you."

She allowed him to seat her, expecting Ada to plop down beside her as usual. But instead, Egan slid into Ada's usual place, so close that his thigh touched hers when he moved.

"I can help," Kati volunteered quickly.

"No," Ada said as she dished up everything and carried it to the table. "Just sit. We'll both have enough to do later."

So she sat, nervously, hating the close contact because she could feel Egan as well as smell the warm, manly fragrance of his body. He was dressed up, too, in a navy pinstripe suit that made him look suave and sophisticated. And all the time she picked at her bacon and eggs, he watched her. It was as if he were launching a campaign, with her as the objective. And it was getting off to a rousing start.

Ada noticed the tension and smiled. Kati flushed at that smile, because she knew her friend's mind so well.

It didn't help that Ada finished early and announced that she just had to have a shower before she dressed.

"Afraid to be alone with me?" Egan teased gently when the door closed behind his sister.

"Oh yes," she admitted, looking up with fascinated eyes.

His own eyes seemed unusually kind and soft, and he smiled. "Why?" he asked. "Because of last night?"

She lowered her eyes to his smooth chin, his chiseled mouth. She remembered the feel of it with startling clarity.

"Don't hide." He tilted her face back up to his and

studied it quietly. "I can wait. At least, until you've had time to break it off with Asher."

So that was what he thought! That was why he'd been so patient last night. He assumed that she was sleeping with Jack and had to end the affair before…

She caught her breath. "But I can't—"

"Yes, you can," he said. "Just tell him how it is. He doesn't seem to be so unreasonable to me. In fact—" he laughed shortly "—he hardly touches you in public. A man who's committed to a woman usually shows a little more warmth."

"I don't like that kind of thing, around people," she murmured.

"Neither do I, for God's sake," he bit off. "But when people get involved, it happens sometimes. A look, a way of touching, a hand that can't let go of another hand—there are signs. You and Asher don't show them."

"He's…very reserved," she returned.

"So are you. Even alone with me." He leaned closer and brushed his mouth over hers like a breath. "Ada won't be gone that long. And then we'll be surrounded by people. And I won't be able to do this to you…."

His hand contracted behind her head, catching her hair, tangling in its fiery depths to press her mouth to his. As if passion were riding him hard, he bit at her closed lips and shocked them into parting. And then she was his. Totally his, as he explored the soft warmth of her mouth expertly, possessively.

When he stopped, her hands were clenched in his thick hair, and she moaned when he lifted his mouth.

"No more, baby," he whispered huskily. "We don't have the luxury of privacy, and I had a hard enough time sleeping last night as it was. A man can only stand so much."

Her eyes opened slowly and she looked up at him drowning in the silver of his eyes. "I didn't mean to tease," she whispered. "It wasn't like that."

"I know that," he replied quietly. "You were with me every step of the way, from the first second I touched you. Circumstances have been the problem. I need to be alone with you. Completely alone." He drew in a slow breath. "Come back to Wyoming with me, Kati."

Her eyes dilated. "What?"

"You said you had to research that damned book. All right. I'll help you. Fly out with me in the morning, and I'll show you everything you need to know about ranch management."

She studied his hard face. She knew exactly what he was saying: "during the day." His eyes were telling her that he had different plans for the night, and she already knew exactly what *they* were.

"Still afraid?" he asked thoughtfully, watching the expressions change on her young face. "Let's get it out in the open. Why? Do I strike you as a brutal man? Do you think I'd be kinky in bed or something?"

Her face burned and she looked down. "I've never thought about it."

"Liar. You've thought about it every second since yesterday morning, just like I have." He bent his head and kissed her quickly, roughly. "It was just the way I told you it would be. We touched each other and exploded. I wanted you, and it made me rough at first. But it won't be that way anymore. I promise you, Kati. I'll be as tender a lover as you could want."

"You...you never seemed gentle," she said involuntarily. "And you've been so harsh with me...."

He brushed a lock of hair back from her cheek and frowned as he looked down at her. "It's the way you write, damn it," he said. "So...openly."

"Egan, I don't make love with strange men in bathtubs," she said. It was one of the ironies of her life that she could write torrid romances at all. But the writing never embarrassed her. It was as if the characters did what they wanted to, taking over as the words went onto paper. The situations arose from the characterizations, not out of her own personal experience.

He shrugged. "That may be. But no man likes to think he's being used for research."

Her eyes opened wide. Her eyebrows went straight up. "You don't imagine that I...that I'd even consider—" She felt herself puffing up with indignation. "Oh, you monster!"

She jerked up from the table, glaring down at him as she fought tears of pure fury. "What do you think I am, damn you, an exhibitionist? What I write comes out of nowhere! The characters create themselves on paper, and their own motivations produce the love scenes! I do not write from personal experiences with a multitude of lovers!"

"Now, Kati," he began, rising slowly.

"But you just go on thinking whatever you please,

Egan," she continued. "You just go right ahead. I don't care. I don't need you at all!"

And she turned, tears in her eyes, and ran from the room, colliding with Ada.

"Hey, what's the matter?" Ada asked gently.

"Ask Dracula!" came the broken reply, and she threw a last accusing glare at Egan before she went into her room and slammed the door.

It was a bad start for the day. And it didn't help that when she got herself together and came back out, Egan had vanished. She'd overreacted, and she was ashamed. But his opinion of her had hurt in unexpected ways and brought home how he considered her widely experienced.

Wouldn't he be shocked, she thought miserably, to know how innocent she was?

In fact, the love scenes in her books were mild compared to those in other genres. They were sensuous, but hardly explicit. That was why she was able to write them. She didn't have to go into a lot of explanations that she'd have to dig out of anatomy books anyway—because she didn't know the first thing about fulfillment, except what she'd learned second-hand.

"Will he be back?" Kati asked miserably when Ada told her that Egan had walked out.

Ada lifted her shoulders helplessly. "I don't know. Things were going so well this morning. What happened?"

"He accused me of doing my own research for the love scenes," she muttered. "In bathtubs with strange men." She hid her face in her hands. "You can't imagine how it hurt to have him think so little of me!"

"Then why not tell him the truth, my dumb friend?" Ada asked. "He doesn't read minds, you know."

"Because..." She clenched her fists and hit the air impotently. "Because," her voice lowered, "the only thing about me that attracts him at all is my 'experience.'"

Ada gaped at her. "You're in love with him," she said half under her breath.

Kati smiled sadly. "Doesn't it show? Hasn't it always shown? Ada, I'd walk over a gas fire just to look at him."

"And I thought you hated him."

"I did. Because he hated me, and I knew it would never be more than that." She smoothed her hair. "And now it's worse, because he's like a bulldozer and I'm terrified of him."

"I warned you," Ada reminded her. "He's utterly relentless."

"He wants me to go home with him," she said.

Ada's face brightened. "He does?"

"Don't be silly, I can't go! If I do, he's bound to find out what an absolute idiot I am, and then where will I be? He'll throw me out on my ear!"

"And then again, he might not."

"I'm no gambler, Ada. Losing matters too much. I'd rather stay here and pull the pieces together. Maybe it's just a physical infatuation and I'll outgrow it," she added hopefully.

"If you'd walk through fire just to look at him,

darling," Ada said gently, "it's got to be more than physical. And you know it."

"But what can I do?" Kati wailed. "Ada, I'm not the kind to have affairs. I'm too inhibited."

"Not when you write, you aren't!"

"That's different. When I write, I'm a storyteller, telling a story. In real life, I get too emotionally involved, and then I can't let go. And Egan hates even the idea of involvement."

"He looked pretty involved to me this morning. He could hardly take his eyes off you long enough to eat," Ada remarked.

"You know why, too."

"Men are attracted first; then their emotions get involved. Look at Marshal and me! He liked my legs, so he called me. And now here we are almost engaged!"

"And here it is Christmas and I've ruined it again," Kati moaned.

"No, you haven't. Egan will be back when he cools down. He's mad at himself, I'll bet, not at you." She smiled. "He didn't mean to hurt you."

Tears welled up in her eyes and she turned away. "I never meant to hurt him, either."

"Then cheer up. It will all work out, honest it will."

"So you keep saying. I'll try to listen this time."

They had everything ready just as Marshal and Jack arrived, and the four of them stood around and talked until noon.

"Should we wait for Egan?" Marshal asked.

"Well," Ada said, biting her lower lip. "I don't know when he'll be back."

Even as she said the words, the front door opened and Egan walked in. He tossed his Stetson onto the hall table.

"Waiting for me? I got held up at Jennie's," he added, glancing toward Kati with pure malice in his eyes.

So much for Ada's helpful optimism, Kati thought as she took off her apron. She didn't even look at him again, and her entire attitude was so cool and controlled that she felt she deserved an Oscar for her performance all the way through the holiday meal. The turkey was perfectly browned, the ham beautifully glazed. Egan, at the head of the table, carved, and Ada passed the plates down. He said grace, and everyone was far too busy to talk for the first few minutes.

Kati was just bursting with fury about Jennie. She could imagine what Egan had been doing and why he'd been held up. She was rigid with the effort not to get up and fling the turkey carcass the length of the table at him.

"The cherry pie is delicious," Jack offered as he finished his last mouthful and followed it with the rich black coffee Ada had made.

"Thank you," Kati said with a smile.

"Kati does all the desserts," Ada told Marshal. "I'm no hand at pastry."

Egan hadn't touched any of the pies or fruitcake. He barely seemed to eat anything, like Kati. Her eyes found his across the room, and it was like lightning striking. She felt the longing she'd been fighting down all day coming to life again. It was incredible that she could look at him and go to pieces like this.

"Well, I hate to eat and run," Jack said, "but I promised my cousin I'd stop by and see him and his family this afternoon. There are so few of us left these days."

"Yes, I know what you mean," Ada said quietly, and her face showed the loneliness Kati knew she must feel this first Christmas without her mother.

"I'm sure you do. I'm sorry, I didn't mean to bring up such a sad subject," Jack apologized.

Ada smiled. "Don't be silly. Happy Christmas, Jack. I'm glad you could come."

"Me, too," Kati said, avoiding Egan's eyes as she got up to walk Jack to the door.

"I enjoyed it," Jack said. "Merry Christmas!"

Kati saw him out into the corridor. "I'll see you later, then."

Jack stared down at her quietly. "Do you realize how that big cattleman feels about you?" he asked unexpectedly.

Her face paled. "What?"

"He watched you as if he'd bleed to death looking. And the one time I smiled at you, I thought he was going to come over that table to get me." He laughed self-consciously. "If you get a minute, how about telling him that we haven't got anything serious going? I'd like to keep my insurance premiums where they are."

She laughed too, because they were friends who could ask such things of each other. "I'll do my best. Want to spend New Year's with us?"

"As far as I know, I don't have a thing planned.

But," he added with a wink, "you might. So let's leave it alone for now, and I'll call you. All right?"

"All right. Merry Christmas," she added.

"You, too." He bent and kissed her lightly on the cheek. He was just lifting his head when Egan appeared in the doorway with eyes that glittered dangerously.

"You're taking a long time just to say good-bye," he muttered.

"Discussing the weather," Jack said quickly. "Damned cold outside! In here, too. Bye, Kati!" And he took off for the elevator with a grin.

Egan caught Kati's hand in his, holding it warmly, closely, and pulled her just inside the door. They were out of view of the living room, and when he closed the outside door, they might have been alone in the world.

"I can't stand it," he ground out, gripping her arms as if he were afraid she'd fly out of his reach. "You're driving me out of my mind, damn it!"

"You started it," she bit off, keeping her voice down.

"I didn't mean it, though," he returned in a harsh undertone. His hands loosened their grip, became caressing, burning her even through the blouse's long sleeves. "Kati, I'm so used to hitting at you…but this morning I didn't mean to."

Her lower lip trembled as she looked up at him. "You went to her," she said shakily.

Every trace of expression left his face, and only his eyes showed any emotion at all. They glittered at her like silver in sunlight. "I didn't touch her," he said huskily. "How could I? All I want in the world is you!"

Her lips parted, and before she could speak, he bent

and caressed them slowly, sensuously, with his own. His breath was suddenly ragged, uneven, and the hands that were on her arms moved up to cup her face and hold it where he wanted it.

"Are you going to fight me every inch of the way?" he asked in a strained tone.

"I'm not," she protested dazedly.

"Then kiss me," he murmured.

She didn't understand what he meant until the pressure of his mouth forced hers open and she felt his tongue in a slow, even penetration that made her blood surge.

She gasped, and he deepened the kiss even more. She felt his body tremble, and he groaned softly— deep in his throat—like a man trying to control the impossible. He whispered her name under his breath and his arms went around her like chains. He crushed her into the taut muscles of his body until she hurt, and she didn't care. She wanted to be closer than this, even closer, with nothing in the way…!

"Kati?" Ada called from the living room.

In a fever of hunger, Kati watched Egan lift his head and take a slow, steadying breath.

"We're talking, all right?" he asked in what sounded like an almost normal tone.

"Oh, excuse me!" Ada called back. "Never mind!"

Egan's eyes burned down into Kati's. "Are you all right?" he whispered, watching the tears shimmer in her eyes.

"Yes. I…just…just feel kind of shaky," she stammered.

He took her hands to his hard chest and held them over the vest. "So do I," he said. "From the neck down. My God, you stir me up!"

Her eyes searched his slowly, curiously. "You're a passionate man," she whispered. "I imagine most women make you feel that way."

He shook his head very slowly. "I'm not promiscuous, Kati. I'm selective. It takes a very special woman."

She felt unreasonably flattered, but then, she wasn't thinking straight. How could she, this close to him, wanting him with a fever that was burning her alive?

"I'm scandalous, remember?" she said. "I seduce men to help me with my research—"

He stopped the words with a touch to her lips. "I'm not a virgin. How can I sit in judgment on you?"

"If you'd listen to me," she said softly, "I'd tell you."

"I don't want to hear it," he said curtly. "The past is over. We'll go from here. Are you coming home with me?"

And there was the question she'd wanted and dreaded, staring her in the face. She looked at him and knew she wasn't going to be strong and sensible. She could feel herself falling apart already.

"You won't...expect too much?" she asked hesitantly.

"Listen," he said, brushing his fingers over her warm cheek, "as far as I'm concerned, you're coming to learn about ranching for a book. You don't have to pay for your keep, Kati. In any way," he emphasized. "I'll let you come to me. I won't ask more than you want to give."

She lowered her eyes to his vest and wondered again, for the hundredth time, what it would be like with him—and knew that it was suicide to think about it.

"Come home with me," he said, tilting her face up to his. "The snow's sitting like a blanket on the Tetons, and the river's running through it like a silver thread. I'll show you where the buffalo used to graze and the mountain men camped."

He made it sound wildly romantic, and his eyes promised much more than a guided tour. It was crazy! She was crazy!

"I'll go home with you, Egan," she whispered.

His breath caught and he studied her eyes for a long moment before he bent to kiss her softly, slowly on her swollen lips. "There's a bear rug in front of the fireplace in my den," he breathed at her lips. "I've wondered…for years…how it would feel on bare skin, Kati."

A tiny, wild sound escaped from her throat, and he lifted her in his arms to kiss her roughly, possessively, until the whole world compressed into Egan's mouth and arms.

"Er-ahmmmm!" came a loud noise from the doorway.

Egan drew away with shaky reluctance and let Kati slide back to her feet just as Ada peeked around the corner.

"Marshal and I wondered if you'd like to go walking and look at the city," Ada asked, trying not to look as pleased as she felt.

"I'd like that," Egan said, smiling down into Kati's rapt face. "Would you?"

"Yes," she said dreamily.

"I hope you don't mind living alone for a couple of weeks, Ada," Egan added as he grabbed his hat and topcoat. "Because I'm taking Kati to Wyoming."

"You are?" Ada burst out, her face delighted.

"To help her with the book," he added, glaring at his sister. "Research, period."

"Oh, of course," Ada said, getting a firm grip on herself. "What else?"

Kati didn't dare look up. It would have blown her cool cover to pieces. Then Egan caught her small hand in his big one as they went to the elevator, and every thought in her head exploded in pleasure. Her fingers clung, locking into his. She walked beside him feeling as if she owned the world, oblivious to the beauty of New York City in holiday dress. Her present was right beside her.

It was almost dark when they came back to the apartment, after looking in store windows and eyeing the decorations around Madison and Fifth Avenues. Then they exchanged presents, and Kati was overwhelmed when she opened Egan's gift. It was a silver bracelet—pure silver with inlaid turquoise, and surely not a trinket. She looked up, pleasure beaming from her dark eyes, to thank him.

"Do you like it?" he said on a smile. "I like mine too."

She'd given him a new spinning reel, something Ada said he'd appreciate. Although, at the time, pleasing Egan hadn't been on Kati's list of priorities, now she was glad she'd bought it. She saw the real appreciation in his eyes.

All too soon it was bedtime, and Ada was seeing Marshal out in a protracted good night.

"You'll have to get up early," Egan told Kati as they said their own good night at the door of her room. "I want to be out of here by eight."

She smiled. "I'll pack tonight. I have to bring my computer."

"One of those portable ones with a built-in telephone modem?" he asked knowledgeably.

She nodded. "It's my lifeline. I can't manage without it. It even has a printer built in."

"I carry one with me when I travel," he said. "We inventory our herds on computers these days, and use them to print out the production records for sales. I even sell off cattle by videotape. Ranching has moved into the twentieth century."

"I'll feel right at home," she said, laughing.

"I hope so," he said, his face softening as he looked down at her. "No strings, baby. I won't back you into any corners."

She nodded. "Sleep well."

"Without you?" he murmured wistfully. "No chance."

He bent and kissed her lightly. "Night."

And he was gone.

She walked into her room and closed the door, feeling impossibly happy and terrified all at the same time. What was going to happen when, inevitably,

Egan discovered that her reason for going wasn't his reason for inviting her? Because things were bound to come to a head. And either way, he'd discover for himself that she wasn't the worldly woman he thought her. What would he do? She shuddered. He'd probably be furious enough to put her on the first plane to New York.

She reached for the doorknob. She almost went to tell him that she'd changed her mind. But the prospect of even a few days alone with him—to glory in his company—was like the prospect of heaven. And she was too besotted to give it up. Just a day, she promised herself. Just one day, and she'd confess everything and let him do his worst. But she had to have that precious time with him. It would last her all her life. It would be all she'd ever have of him.

Chapter Eight

Her first sight of the Tetons as she and Egan flew over Jackson Hole made Kati catch her breath.

Seated beside Egan in the ranch's small jet, she stared down at the velvety white tops of the jagged peaks with wonder.

"Oh, it's beautiful," she whispered. "The most beautiful thing I've ever seen!"

"You've never been here in the winter, have you?" he asked, smiling. "I'd forgotten. Honey, if you think this is something, wait until I get you on the Snake."

"Snake?" Her ears perked up and she looked at him apprehensively.

"River," he added. "From the ranch house, we overlook the Snake, and the Tetons look like they're sitting over us."

"I knew it was spectacular in the spring and summer," she sighed, staring back out the window. "But this is magic."

He watched her with quiet, smiling eyes. "I was born here, but it still sets me on my heels when I come home. A lot of battles have been fought over this land. By Shoshone and Arapaho and the white man, by ranchers and sheepmen and rustlers."

She glanced at him. "Are there still rustlers out West?"

"Of course, but now they work with trucks. We have a pretty good security system, though, so we don't lose many. Feeding the cattle during the winters is our biggest problem," he said. "We're pretty fanatical about haying out here, to get enough winter feed. A cow won't paw her way through the snow to get food, Kati. She'll stand there and starve first."

"I didn't know that," she said, fascinated.

"You've got a lot to learn, city lady," he said with a soft laugh. "But I'll teach you."

That, she thought, was what she feared. But she only smiled and watched the familiar lines of the big two-story white frame house come into view as they headed for the landing strip beyond it.

"How old is the house, Egan?" Kati asked after Egan had told the pilot to take the jet to the Jackson airport where it was based.

"Oh, I guess around eighty or ninety years," he said. He led her to a waiting pickup truck. "My grandfather built it."

"And called it White Lodge?" she asked, remembering that the ranch also was called by that name.

"No. That was my grandmother's idea. She was Shoshone," he added with a smile.

She studied him quietly. "And your grandfather? Was he dark?"

He nodded. "The sun burns us brown. Despite all the damned paperwork, I still spend a lot of time on horseback."

"Hi, Boss!" Ramey yelled out the window of the pickup truck.

"Hi, Ramey!" Egan called back. He opened the door and put Kati inside, jerking a thumb at Ramey to get him out from behind the wheel.

"I ain't such a bad driver," Ramey grumbled.

"I don't care what kind of driver you are," Egan reminded him as he got in next to Kati and shut the door. "Nobody drives me except me."

"On account of Larry ran him into a tree," Ramey explained as he shut his own door just before Egan started down the snowy ranch road. The young boy grinned at Egan's thunderous look. "Broke Larry's nose."

"Hitting the tree?" Kati asked innocently.

"Hitting the boss's fist afterward," Ramey chuckled.

Kati glanced at Egan. "And I thought you were the sweetest-tempered man I'd ever met," she said dryly.

Ramey's eyebrows arched. He started to speak, but Egan looked at him and that was all it took.

"Don't reckon you got a Chinook tucked in your bag somewheres?" Ramey asked instead, his blue eyes twinkling.

"A what?" Kati asked blankly.

"Chinook," Egan said. "It's a warm wind we get here in the winter. Melts the snow and gives us some relief." He looked over her head at Ramey. "How's the feed holding out?"

"Just fine. We'll make it, Gig says. Gig is our foreman," Ramey reminded her. "Kind of came with the ranch, if you know what I mean. Nobody knows how old he is, and nobody's keen to ask him."

"The answer might scare us," Egan chuckled. "Damn, this stuff is deep!"

He was running in the ruts Ramey had made coming to the landing strip, but it was still slow, hard going, and powdery snow was beginning to blow again.

"It'd be faster if we walked," Ramey suggested.

"Or rode." He shot a quick glance at Kati, letting his eyes run over her beige dress and high heels and short man-made fur coat. "God, wouldn't you look right at home on horseback in that? I almost made you change before we left Ada's."

She started to object to the wording and then let it go. Why start trouble?

"No comeback?" Egan chided. "No remarks about my tyrannical personality?"

"Why, Mr. Winthrop, I'm the very soul of tact," she said haughtily.

"Especially when you're telling me to go to hell," was the lightning comeback.

She flushed, noticing Ramey's puzzled look.

"We, uh, sometimes have our, uh, little differences," she tried to explain.

"Yes, ma'am, I recall," Ramey murmured, and she

remembered that he'd been nearby when she had walked furiously off the ranch that summer.

She cleared her throat. "Well, you do have the Tetons at your back door, don't you?" she asked Egan, who seemed to be enjoying her discomfort.

He followed her gaze to the high peaks rising behind the house. "Indeed we do. And the river within sight of the front door," he added, indicating the winding silver ribbon of the Snake that cut through the valley far below the house.

"Elk and moose and antelope graze out there during the winter," he told her. "And buffalo used to, in frontier days."

"I've never seen a moose," she said.

"Maybe this time," he told her.

She watched as Egan's elderly housekeeper waddled onto the front porch, shading her eyes against the blinding white of the snow. Egan left the truck idling for Ramey and lifted Kati off the seat and into his hard arms. The sheepskin coat he wore made him seem twice as broad across the chest and shoulders.

"You're hardly equipped for walking in the snow," he murmured, indicating her high heels. "I hope you packed some sensible things."

"Hiking boots, jeans and sweaters," she said smartly.

"Good girl. Hold on."

She clung as he strode easily through the high blanket of snow and up onto the steps, his boots echoing even through the snow against the hard wood. Dessie Teal was watching with a grin, her broad face all smiles under her brown eyes and salt-and-pepper hair.

"I never would have believed it," she muttered as Egan set Kati back on her feet. "And I don't see a bruise on either one of you."

"We don't fight all the time," Egan said coolly.

"Well, neither do them Arabs, Egan," Dessie returned, "but I was just remarking how nice it was that you and Miss James seemed to be in a state of temporary truce, that's all."

"She came to research a book about Wyoming in the old days," Egan told the old woman gruffly, his eyes daring her to make anything else of it.

Dessie shrugged. "Whatever you want to call it. A book about frontier days, huh?" she asked, leading Kati into the house. "Well, you just go talk to Gig, he'll tell you more than any book will. His daddy fought in the Johnson County range war."

Kati asked what that had been about and was treated to fifteen minutes of Wyoming history, including references to the range wars between cattlemen and sheepmen, and the ferocity of Wyoming winters.

"My brother froze to death working cattle one winter," Dessie added later, when Kati had changed into jeans, boots and a sweater and was drinking coffee with the housekeeper in the kitchen. "He fell and broke his leg and couldn't get up again. He was solid ice when one of the men found him." She shivered delicately. "This ain't the place for tenderfeet, I'll tell you." She paused in the act of putting a big roast into the oven. "How come you and Egan ain't fighting?"

"He's trying to get me into bed," Kati returned bluntly and grinned wickedly at the housekeeper's blush.

"I deserved that," Dessie muttered and burst into laughter. "I sure did. Ask a foolish question… Well, I might as well make it worse. Is he going to?"

Kati shook her head slowly. "Not my kind of life," she said. "I'm too old-fashioned."

"Good for you," Dessie said vehemently. "Honest to God, I don't know what's got into girls these days. Why, we used to go two or three dates before we'd hold hands with a boy. Nowadays, it's into bed on the first one. And they wonder why nobody's happy. You gorge yourself on candy and you don't want it no more. At least, that's how I see it."

"You and I should join a missionary society," Kati told her. "We don't belong in the modern world."

Dessie grinned at her. "Well, speaking for myself, I ain't in it. Can't get much more primitive than this, I reckon, despite all the modern gadgets Egan bought me for the kitchen."

"I understand what you mean." She leaned back in the chair and sipped her coffee. "Did Egan really not want to be a rancher?" she asked.

Dessie measured that question before she answered it. "I don't think he knew exactly what he did want. Politics used to fascinate him. But then, so did business. And that's mostly what ranching is these days; it's business. He has Gig to look after the practical side of it while he buys and sells cattle and concentrates on herd improvement and diversification." She grinned sheepishly. "What big words!"

"Is he happy?" Kati asked, because it mattered.

"No," Dessie said quietly. "He's got nobody except Miss Ada."

Kati studied her coffee cup, amazed at how deeply that hurt her. "He's…not handsome, but he has a way with him. And he attracts women," she added, remembering Jennie.

"Not the right kind of women," came the tart reply. "Not ever one he could bring to this ranch. Until now."

Kati blushed to the roots of her hair.

"Now what are you doing?" Egan growled from the doorway, taking in Kati's red face and Dessie's shocked expression at his sudden appearance. "Talking about me behind my back, I guess?"

"Well, who else is there to talk about?" Dessie threw up her hands. "I never see anybody except you. Well, there's Ramey, of course, but he don't do nothing interesting enough to gossip about, does he?"

Egan shook his head on a tired sigh. "I guess not. Damn. You and your logical arguments." He took off his hat and coat. "What's for dinner? I'm half-starved."

"You're always half-starved. There's some sliced turkey in the refrigerator, left over from my solitary Christmas dinner I had all by myself, alone, yesterday."

Egan glanced at the old woman. "Did you have a good time?" he asked.

"I told you I ate by myself!" Dessie growled.

"Well, I guess that means you didn't have any company," Egan said pleasantly.

"Wait," the housekeeper said, "until tonight. And see what I feed you for supper."

"Let me die of starvation, then," he said. "I'll call up Ada and tell her you won't feed me, and see what you do then!"

Dessie threw down her apron. "Hard case," she accused, her lower lips thrusting out. "Just hit me in my weakest spot, why don't you?"

Egan grinned, winking at Kati, who was seeing a side of him she hadn't dreamed existed. She liked this big, laughing man who seemed so at home in the wilderness.

He even looked different from the man in the pinstripe suit in Ada's apartment. He was wearing denim now, from head to foot, and a pair of disreputable brown boots that had seen better days—along with a hat that was surely obsolete. The only relatively new piece of apparel he had was the sheepskin coat he'd just taken off. But he seemed bigger and tougher and in every way more appealing than the sophisticated executive.

"You look different," Kati remarked absently, watching him.

He cocked an eyebrow as he carried turkey and mayonnaise to the table. "I do?"

"His looks ain't improved," Dessie argued.

"Just mind your own business, thank you," he drawled in her direction and watched her go back to her roast. "And don't burn that thing up like you did the last one!"

"I didn't burn nothing up," she shot back. "That stupid dog of yours got in here and reared up on my stove and changed the heat setting!"

"Durango doesn't get in the house," he told her. "And he isn't smart enough to work a stove, despite being the best cattle dog I own."

"Well, I wouldn't turn my back on him," she muttered. She put the roast in the oven and closed the door. "Excuse me. I got to go to the cellar and get apples. I thought you might like an apple pie. Not that you deserve one," she added, glaring back as she went out the door.

He only laughed. "Get the bread, honey, and I'll make you one too," he told Kati.

"Where is it?"

"In the breadbox."

She got up and went to the cabinet to get it, but before she could turn around, he was behind her, the length of his body threatening and warm.

"Fell right into the trap, didn't you?" he breathed, turning her so that her back was against the wall. With his hands on the wall beside her, he eased down so that his body pressed wholly on hers, in a contact that made the blood surge into her face.

"God, it's wild like this, isn't it?" he said unsteadily. "I can feel you burning like a brand under every inch of me."

She opened her lips to speak, and he bent and took them. His mouth was cold from the outdoors, but hers warmed it, so that seconds later it was blazing with heat. A moan growled out of his throat into her hungry, wanting mouth.

She felt his tongue, and her eyes opened suddenly, finding his closed, his brows drawn, as he savored the pleasure. But as if he felt her looking at him, the thick lashes moved up and his darkening silver eyes looked straight into hers.

On a caught breath he lifted his lips just fractionally over hers. "Now, that's exciting," he whispered. "I've never watched a woman while I kissed her."

But obviously he was going to, because his eyes stayed open when he bent again, and so did hers. The hunger and need in his kiss inflamed her, and her hands found their way to the top button on his shirt.

She'd never wanted to touch a man's bare skin. She couldn't remember a time in her life when the thought had appealed. But it did now. She could feel the crush of his hips and thighs over hers, and explosive sensations were curling her toes.

Her fingers toyed with his top button while she tried to decide how risky it would be. He was hungry enough without being tempted further, and she wasn't sure she could handle him.

He lifted his head and watched her fingers. "Are you always this unsure of yourself with a man?" he asked under his breath. "Or is it just me? Touch me if you want to, Kati. I won't lose my head and bend you back over the kitchen table."

The wording made it sound cheap, made her sound cheap. The color went out of her face and she eased away from him.

He swore quietly, watching her get the bread and some saucers and start making sandwiches in a strained silence.

"What do you want from me?" he ground out.

She drew in a steadying breath. "I'd settle for a little respect. Not much. Just what you'd give any stranger who came into your house." Tears welled in her eyes as she spread mayonnaise. "I'm not a tramp, Egan Winthrop."

He watched a solitary tear land with a splatter on the clean tabletop, and his hands caught her waist convulsively, jerking her back against him.

"Don't...cry," he bit off, his fingers hurting.

"Don't touch me!" she threw back, twisting away from him.

He held onto the edge of the table, glaring as she wiped the tears away and finished making the sandwiches. She pushed his at him and went to put the knife in the sink.

He poured coffee into her cup and his, put the pot away and sat down. She followed suit, but she ate in silence, not even looking at him. Fool, she told herself. You stupid fool, you had to come with him!

Dessie came back to a grinding silence. She stared at them, apples in her apron, and grimaced. "I leave you alone five minutes and you start a war."

Egan finished his coffee and got up, not rising to the bait. "I've got work to do."

He grabbed his coat and hat and stamped out the door. Kati brushed away more tears. Dessie just shook her head and started peeling apples. After a minute, she got another bowl and knife and pushed them at Kati.

"Might as well peel," she told her. "It'll give your hands something to do while your mind works."

"Mine doesn't work," Kati replied coldly. "If it did, I'd still be in New York."

"Not many people get under his skin like that," Dessie commented with a slow grin. "Good to know he's still human."

"Well, I'd need proof," Kati glowered.

"I think you'll get it," came the laughing reply. "Now, peel, if you want an apple pie."

Kati gave in. And it *was* rather soothing, peeling apples. She had a feeling she was going to make a lot of pies before she got her research done.

Chapter Nine

After that little episode, Egan became remote. He was the perfect host, polite and courteous, but about as warm as one of the rocks on his land.

Kati decided that if he could play it cool, so could she. So she was equally polite. And distant. Oddly enough, there were no more violent arguments like the ones they had in the past. Once in a while, she'd notice Egan watching her over the supper table before he disappeared into his study to work, or during a rare minute in the morning before he went to his office down the road. But he kept to himself, and the affectionate, hungry man who'd brought her to the ranch seemed to have vanished into his former, cold counterpart.

But she did accomplish one of her goals. She learned enough about ranching to do a nonfiction work on it.

The logistics of supplies fascinated her. Egan's cows and second-year heifers were bred to drop calves in February and March. So during January, the ranch manager and his men were very much involved in pre-calving planning. That meant buying ear tags, identifying first-calf heifers, checking breeding dates to estimate calving dates and arranging for adequate facilities.

Because of the increased herd, move calving pens had to be added, but those were erected during the fall. The cowboys were closely watching the cows now to make sure there were no problems. One of the older hands told her that he always hated being a cowboy during this time of the year and at roundup in the spring, when the cattle had to be branded, vetted, and moved about fifty miles away to summer pasture.

Listening to the men tell about their adventures took up the better part of her days. She was careful not to interfere with their work, having been cautioned by the boss about that. But she was around during breaks and sometimes after dinner, with her pad and pen in hand, asking questions.

It would have been all right if Ramey hadn't asked her to go to a dance with him. Egan happened to overhear the question, and before Kati could even get her mouth open to say "No, thanks," Egan was on top of them.

"If you're through irritating the men," he told her cuttingly, "they need their rest."

She rose, embarrassed to tears but too proud to show it. "Excuse me, I didn't realize—"

"But, boss," Ramey groaned, "she wasn't bothering us!"

There was a loud tumult as the other cowboys in the bunkhouse agreed with pathetic eagerness.

"All the same, good night," Egan said in his coldest tone. He held the door open; Kati, seeing defeat, shrugged, calling a smiling good night to the men and walked knee-deep in the melting snow back to the truck she'd commandeered for the drive down.

"This way," Egan said curtly, taking her arm. He led her to his pickup truck and put her inside.

"I was just asking questions," she muttered. "You told me not to interfere with their work."

"I didn't say you could sleep with them," he growled.

"You pig!" she burst out. Her eyes blazed; her lips trembled with fury. "How dare you accuse me of such a thing!"

"Ramey asked you out—did you think I didn't hear him?" he asked. He fumbled for a cigarette, surprising her, because she'd seen him smoke only once or twice in the past few days.

"I was going to refuse," she replied. "He's a nice boy, but—"

"But not experienced enough for a woman like you, right?" he asked, smiling insolently.

Her breath stopped. "What exactly do you mean, 'a woman like me'?" she asked deliberately.

"What do you think I mean?"

She clutched the pen and pad in her hand and stared straight ahead.

"No comeback?"

"I won't need one. I'm going home."

"Like hell you are."

"What do you plan to do, Mr. Winthrop, tie me up in a line cabin?"

"Who taught you about line cabins?"

"Gig," she said uncomfortably, remembering the long, amusing talk she'd had with the sly old foreman.

"Gig never talks to anybody, not even me."

"Well, he talks to me," she shot back. "But I guess you'll accuse me of trying to get him into bed too!"

"You'd hate it," he said, lifting the cigarette to his mouth. "He only bathes once a month."

She tried to keep her temper blazing, but she lost and hid the muffled laugh in her hands.

He glanced at her, his eyes sparkling. "If I stop making objectionable remarks to you," he said after a minute, "do you suppose we might try to get along for the duration?"

"I don't think that's possible," she said, glancing at him. "You won't even give me the benefit of a doubt."

"I've read your books," he reminded her.

"How in God's name do you think Edgar Rice Burroughs wrote *Tarzan of the Apes?*" she exploded. "Do you believe that he swung from trees in darkest Africa? When he wrote the first book, he'd never even seen Africa!"

He pulled up at the front door and cut off the engine. "Are you trying to tell me that a woman could write a sexy book without having had sex?" He laughed. "No dice, baby. I'm not stupid."

"That depends on your definitions," she returned hotly. "About me, yes, sir, you are stupid."

"Only when you kiss me in that slow, hot way," he murmured, smiling wickedly, "and try to take off my shirt."

She slammed the pen against the pad impotently and glared at him.

"All right," he said after a minute and crushed out the cigarette. "I'll apologize for the crude remark I made in the kitchen. Will that pacify you?"

"I want to make something crystal-clear," she returned, gripping the pad tightly. "As far as I'm concerned, I'm here to research a book."

His eyes darkened and he studied her closely. "Put it in words, not innuendos."

"I don't want to be mauled around," she replied.

"Tell Ramey. He was the one who wanted to take you off into the woods," he said on a laugh.

"So did you!" she accused.

He shook his head. "No. I wanted to take you into my bed. There's a difference."

"Geographical," she countered.

He sighed and reached out to smooth a long, unruly strand of her hair. "I want you. I haven't made any secret of it. You want me, too. It's just going to take more time than I thought."

"I won't sleep with you," she told him.

"You will," he replied softly, searching her eyes. "Eventually."

"Is that a threat?" she asked, finding her fighting feet.

"No, ma'am," he said, grinning.

She glared at him uncertainly. "I don't understand you."

"You've got a whole lot of company," he told her. He dropped her hair. "Better get some rest. And don't go back to the bunkhouse at night. Keeps the boys awake."

"I have to find out some things about calving," she protested.

"Do you? What do you want to know?" he asked with a wicked smile.

"Oh, stuff your hat…!" she began.

"Now, now, you mustn't shock me," he told her as he got out of the truck. "I'm just an unsophisticated country boy, you know."

"Like hell," she muttered under her breath.

He opened her door and lifted her into his arms. She started to struggle, but he held her implacably and shook his head.

"Don't fight," he said. "We've spent days avoiding each other. I just want to hold you."

She felt a rush of feeling that should have made her run screaming the other way. But instead, she put her arms—pad and pen and all—around his neck and let him carry her. By the time he got to the steps, her face was buried in his warm throat and her heartbeat was shaking her.

"We haven't made love since we were in New York," he whispered as he carried her into his study and deliberately locked the door behind him.

She felt her lips go dry as she looked up at him. He was taking off his hat and coat, and the way he was staring at her made her feel threatened.

"No more games, Katriane," he said softly. He took away the pad and pen, and, bending, took off her warm coat and dropped it beside his on the chair. He lifted her off the floor. "I won't hurt you. But I've gone hungry too long."

There would never be a better time to tell him the truth. But just as she started to, he bent and pressed his open mouth against the peak of her breast. She cried out, shocked speechless at the intimacy of it even through two layers of cloth.

He didn't say a word. She felt him lower her, felt the soft pile of a rug under her back. And then his body was spreading over hers like a heavy blanket, making fires that blazed up and burned in exquisite torment.

His mouth moved up to hers, taking it with a power and masculine possessiveness that she'd never felt before. She wasn't even aware of what his hands were doing until he lifted her and she felt the slight chill of the room and the heat of the blazing fire in the hearth on her bare flesh.

"Egan," she protested shakily as he laid her back down.

"God, you're something!" he breathed, looking down with wild, glittering eyes on what he'd uncovered. His hands went to the buttons on his shirt and unfastened them slowly, methodically. He pulled the shirt free of his jeans and stripped it off, revealing bronzed skin that shimmered smoothly in the light of the fire.

Her eyes fastened on him hungrily, loving every rugged line of him, wanting the feel of his hard muscles against her own trembling softness.

There was only the crackle of the fire as they looked at each other, only its reddish glow in the room. She knew what he was going to do, but she was powerless to stop him. She loved him. Oh God, she loved him!

He came down slowly, easing his chest over hers by levering himself over her on his arms. His eyes held hers every second as he brushed his chest against her taut breasts and watched the wild, sweet surge of her body upward to make the contact even closer.

"Don't hold anything back with me," he said under his breath. "And I'll please you until you scream with it."

His mouth eased down as his chest did, and she reached up to catch his head in her hands, tangle her fingers in his hair while he kissed the breath from her swollen mouth.

She experienced her own power when she felt the tremor in his long body; and without thinking about consequences, she tugged his head up and shifted to bring his lips down to the bareness of her body.

"Kati!" he burst out as if she'd surprised him, and he dug his hands in under her back. His mouth opened, and she felt his tongue, his teeth at flesh that had never even known a man's eyes.

Her body rippled in his arms, on waves of sweetness, and she moaned as his mouth learned every smooth inch of her above the waist. He rolled suddenly onto his back, bringing her with him, and she felt his hands going under the waistband of her jeans onto the softness of her lower spine.

"Look at me," he said in a husky tone.

She lifted her head just as his clean, strong hands

contracted, and he smiled at the hunger he could read in her eyes.

He nipped her earlobe with his teeth and whispered things that excited and shocked, all at once, embarrassing things that she'd only read until that moment.

"Egan," she protested weakly.

"Just relax," he whispered, bringing her hips back against his in a slow, sweet rotation. "Let me show you how much I want you."

He ground her hips into the powerful, taut muscles of his own. She cried out as he freed one hand to bring her shaking mouth down onto his, thrusting his tongue up into it in a rhythm that said more than words.

"My room," he whispered. "Right now."

He rolled her over and handed her the blouse and sweater he had taken off her minutes before. "You'd better put those on," he said in a taut undertone. "In case Dessie's still up."

She clutched the cool things to her, staring at him like someone coming out of a trance.

"Well?" he ground out. "My God, you felt what you've done to me. I need you, damn it!"

She swallowed, trying to find the right words. "I need you too, Egan," she said shakily. "But there's something you'd... you'd better know first."

"What? That you aren't on the pill?" he demanded. "It's all right, I'll take care of it. I won't let you get pregnant."

She blushed and lowered her eyes to the jerky rise and fall of his chest. Her fingers tightened on the shirt and sweater. "I'm a virgin."

"My God, that's a good one." He laughed coldly. "Try again."

"I don't have to," she said, trying to hold on to her pride and her self-respect, both of which were slipping. "I've told you the truth."

"Sure, I'm a virgin, too," he told her. "Now can we go to bed?"

"Go right ahead," she said with venom in her tone. "But without me! Didn't you hear what I said, damn you, I'm a virgin!"

"At twenty-five?" he asked in a biting tone. "Writing the kind of books you write?"

"I've told you until I'm blue in the face that I don't research those love scenes—most of which are foreplay with a hint of fulfillment!" She flushed, avoiding his eyes. "And some of that is obligatory; I can't get historical fiction published without it. And as for men…" she added, lifting her face to glare at him, "most of them have felt as you do, that a woman's place in the modern world is to be available for sex and then disappear before anyone gets emotional. I can't live like that, so I don't indulge."

"Never?" he burst out.

"Never!" she returned. "Egan, didn't Ada ever tell you about my parents?"

His breathing was steadier now, but he still looked frustrated and full of venom. "That they were old?"

She took another steadying breath of her own. "My father was a Presbyterian minister," she whispered. "And my mother had been a missionary. Now do you understand?"

He looked as if he'd been slapped. His eyes went over her, right down to the fingers that trembled on her discarded top. "Why didn't you tell me?" he ground out. "My God, the things I said to you…!"

He got to his feet and grabbed up his shirt, shouldering angrily into it. "Get out of here," he said coldly.

She managed to get to her feet gracefully, pausing as she tried to decide between running for it and dressing first.

"Put on your blouse, for heaven's sake!" he snapped, and turned away again to light a cigarette with jerky motions.

She put on the blouse and pulled the sweater on over it without ever fastening a button. She couldn't even look at him as she walked toward the door. Her fingers fumbled with the lock, and when she pulled the door open, he still hadn't turned or said a word. She closed it quietly behind her with trembling fingers and went upstairs as quickly as she could. When she was safely in her room, with her own door locked, she burst into tears.

Chapter Ten

It was the most agonizing night Kati remembered spending. Egan had bruised her emotions in ways she hadn't dreamed possible. Rejecting her was enough of a blow. But couldn't he have done it gently? She cringed, thinking of the way he'd been, the things he'd said until she confessed. Ada had warned her. Why hadn't she listened?

Worst of all was the fact that she'd been more than ready to give in to anything he wanted of her. She'd wanted him to know the truth because he was so hungry that she was afraid of being hurt the first time. But her revelation had backfired. Instead of comforting her, he ordered her out of the room and turned his back.

Well, at least she knew how he really felt now, she

told herself miserably. She knew that he'd only wanted her, and there was no feeling on his part except desire. She couldn't remember ever hurting so much. She loved him. What she'd felt in his hard, expert embrace was something she'd never get over. But he'd turned away as if such devastating interludes were just run-of-the-mill. To him, they probably were. With good-time girls like Jennie.

She got up well before daylight. She packed quickly and dressed in her boots and jeans and a burgundy sweater. She decided to go downstairs and have break-fast, and make sure Egan had left the house before she called a cab. It was eight o'clock, and he was usually long gone by then. She didn't know how she could face him if he was still there, not after last night. It made her color, just remembering the things they'd done together.

Her footsteps slowed as she reached the kitchen. She pushed the door open part way and found Dessie put-tering around the stove. With a sigh of relief, she pushed it open the rest of the way and came face to face with Egan, who was just behind it picking up his hat from the counter.

She actually jumped aside. He looked down at her with an expression she couldn't read. His eyes were dark silver, cold, angry.

"I want to talk to you for a minute," he said curtly.

He didn't give her a chance to protest. He pro-pelled her through the door and down the hall to the living room. He shut the door behind them and stared hard at her.

"Before you start," she said in a painfully subdued tone, "I realize it was all my fault, and I'm sorry."

He pulled a cigarette from his pocket and lit it, his fingers steady. "We won't talk about last night," he said. "Stay the week out, finish your research. If you run off this morning, you'll just upset Dessie and Ada."

"What do you mean, if I run off?" she countered defensively.

"Aren't your bags packed already?" he asked, lifting his head at an arrogant angle.

Damn his perception, she thought furiously, turning her eyes to the curtained windows. "Yes," she snapped.

"Then unpack them. You came here, obviously, for a different reason than I brought you," he said with the old, familiar mockery. "Since your work is obviously so important, by all means indulge yourself. Just stay out of the bunkhouse after dark. We've got a couple of new men that I don't know well."

"The only people I really need to talk to are Gig and Ramey," she told him with what dignity she could muster. "Would you mind if I asked them up to the house?"

"Don't be ridiculous," he shot back through a cloud of smoke. "I don't play the master around here; the men are always welcome."

"I didn't mean it that way," she said. She wrapped her arms around her. "Please don't hate me, Egan."

He stood, breathing slowly, deliberately, while his eyes accused. "You knew why I invited you here, Kati," he said after a minute, and his manner was colder than the snow outside. "I didn't make any secret of wanting you. I assumed you felt the same way."

Her eyes lowered to his shirtfront. "I thought I could go through with it," she confessed. "But, last night—" She swallowed. "I was afraid that if I didn't tell you the truth, you'd hurt me."

He made an odd noise deep in his throat and turned away, smoking his cigarette quietly while the clock on the mantel ticked with unnatural loudness.

"I told you once that I like my women experienced. I meant it. I have no taste whatsoever for virgins." He took another harsh draw from the cigarette and moved restlessly around the room, oblivious to her slight flinch. "You're safe for the duration, Miss James," he said finally, glaring at her. "I wouldn't touch you now to save this ranch."

She would have died before she'd let him see how much that hurt. Her face lifted with what pride she had left. "I won't get in your way," she promised quietly.

"Well, that's comforting," he said sarcastically, and with a smile she didn't like.

Her arms tightened where she had them folded over her breasts. "If that's all, I'd like to have some coffee."

"Help yourself."

She left him, her heart around her ankles. It had been better when she hated him, when she didn't have the memory of his hungry ardor to haunt her. But he'd closed all the doors just now, and there wouldn't be any openings again. He'd as much as said so. Virgins didn't interest him.

She laughed miserably to herself. At least he hadn't guessed that she was in love with him. He hadn't understood that she couldn't have given herself without loving, and that was a blessing. She'd finish her research and get out of there. And once she did, she never wanted to see Egan again. It would be too painful.

For the rest of the day, she went through the motions of living without really feeling much of anything. Dessie noticed, but was kind enough not to say anything.

Finally, faced with imminent insanity or work, Kati chose work. She got out the portable computer and began to write, putting all her frustrations and irritations down on paper in a letter to Egan telling him just what she thought of him. She read it over and then erased every word from the screen without ever having fed it to her printer. She felt much better. Then she began work on the book.

Somehow, writing took all the venom out of her. She created without knowing how she did it, watching the characters unfold on paper, feeling the life-force in them even as she put the words down. When she looked at the clock, she realized that she'd been working for hours. She put the information on tape and then ran it off on the printer for hard copy. After a shower, she went downstairs to see if she could help Dessie with supper.

"No need," Dessie told her with a grin. "We've having beef stew and homemade rolls and a salad. Suit you?"

"Oh, yes! I love beef stew!" she enthused.

"You'll like this—it's our own beef. Want to sit down while I dish it up?"

Kati eased into a chair, noticing that only two places were set. "Just us two?" she asked as casually as she could.

"Boss is helping at the calving sheds. Had a handful of first-time heifers calving tonight, and they've already had to pull one. Gets expensive if you lose too many calves," she explained.

"Is the snow still melting?"

"No, worse luck," Dessie grumbled as she put the food on the table. "Weatherman says it's going to come again tonight. I've seen it so that the snow was over the door."

Kati's heart lodged in her throat. "That high?"

"This is Wyoming," came the laughing reply. "Everything's bigger out West, didn't you know? Now, don't you worry. The boys would dig us out if we got snowed in. And we could get another Chinook."

"I remember a painting by Russell," Kati murmured. "A drawing of a cow freezing in the snow, surrounded by wolves, with the legend 'waiting for a Chinook.' I didn't understand it until now."

"See? You're learning." She nibbled at her stew, watching the younger woman curiously. "Uh, you wouldn't care to tell me a little about this new book? I've read all your others."

Kati's face brightened. "You have?"

"Sure. Well, I know you, sort of." She shifted in the chair. "Gave the girls at the bookstore a charge when I told them that." She glanced up. "I like the books, though, or I wouldn't spend good money on them."

"Just for that," Kati said, "I'll tell you the whole plot."

And Dessie sat, rapt, sighing and smiling, while the entire book was outlined.

"What does the hero look like this time?" Dessie asked finally. "Is he blond like your others?"

"No, this one is dark and has silver eyes."

"Like Egan?"

Kati's face flamed red. "His eyes are…gray," she protested.

"Not when he's mad, they ain't. They're silver, and they gleam." She reached over and patted the young woman's hand. "Listen, I don't tell Egan nothing. I won't spill the beans, so don't start clamming up. These eyes of mine may be old, but they don't miss a lot. Besides," she added, sipping coffee, "this morning he ate sausage."

"What does that mean?"

"Egan eats bacon or ham. He hates sausage. I cook it for me." She grinned. "He wouldn't have noticed if I'd fed him raw eggs. In a nasty temper, he was."

And Kati knew why, but she wasn't rising to the bait. "Maybe his tastes have changed."

"Oh, I know that," Dessie said casually. "Yes, I do. Have some more stew."

The snow came all night, but Egan didn't appear. It was late the next morning before Kati got a glimpse of him. He came in cursing, stripping off his jacket as he strode toward his study.

"Damned bull," he muttered. "I should have had his horns cut off… Dessie!" he yelled.

She came running, her apron flapping, while Kati stood frozen on the staircase.

"What?" Dessie asked.

"That big Hereford bull of mine got Al," he grumbled. "Get some bandages and disinfectant and I'll drive you down to the bunkhouse to bandage him until I can get the doctor here. I've sent Ramey to fetch him." He jerked up the phone. "Kati!" he called.

She walked in as he was punching buttons. "What can I do?" she asked hesitantly.

"You can stay with Al's wife and keep her quiet," he told her. He held up his hand and spoke into the phone. "Brad, have the boys tracked that wolf yet? Well, call Harry Two Toes and get him to meet me at the house in twenty minutes. Tell him I'll pay him a thousand dollars for that damned wolf. Right." He hung up the receiver. "Al's wife, Barbara, is pregnant with their first child," he continued, his eyes dark and steady on hers. "I won't let her see him. She gets hysterical at the sight of blood, and she's miscarried twice already. Will you stay with her?"

"Of course," she said without hesitation. "How old is she?"

"Twenty. Just a baby herself. Al was trying to check a sore on that damned bull, and he turned wrong. It's my fault, I should have had him dehorned," he said shortly as he rose from the desk. "Got Al in the stomach. That's a bad place to get gored."

"If he works for you, he must be tough," she said quietly. "He'll be all right, Egan."

His eyes searched hers for a long moment. He turned away. "Get a coat, honey."

She thrilled to the endearment, although she knew

that he was worried and probably hadn't realized he was saying it. She ran up the stairs to get her overcoat and knitted hat, and hurried back. Dessie was already wearing a thick corduroy coat of her own, a floppy old hat and hightop boots.

"Let's go," Egan murmured, herding them out into the snow where the truck was parked.

It was slow going. The road was half obscured by the thick, heavy flakes that fell relentlessly. It seemed to take forever to get to the bunkhouse. Egan had Kati wait in the car while he got Dessie inside and checked to see how Al was. He was back minutes later.

"He's stopped bleeding, at least on the outside," he said heavily as he pulled the truck back onto the ruts. "But he's lost color and he's hurting pretty bad. He'll need to go to the hospital, I'm damned sure of that. I told the boys to get him into one of the pickups and put a camper over it and take him into town. I had Ken call Ramey on the radio and have him go on to the hospital instead of to the doctor's and alert the emergency room."

"It's starting out to be a rough day, isn't it?" she asked, thinking of the poor man's wife as well, who still had to be told about the accident.

"Worse." He lit another cigarette. "We had two cows brought down by a wolf and savaged."

"One wolf?" she asked.

"He's old and wily," he told her shortly. "I've lost cows and calves to him for several months now, and I'm at the end of my patience. I'm going to get an Arapaho tracker I know to help me find him."

"You must be losing a lot of money if the wolf is bringing down that many cattle."

"That's not why. I hate killing even a mangy wolf, with the environment in the mess it's in. But you've never seen a cow or a horse that's been attacked by a wolf." His jaws set. "They don't quite kill the animals, you see."

She did, graphically, and her face paled. "Oh."

"We'll trap him and free him in the high country." He turned the truck into the driveway of a small house not far below the bunkhouse.

"Will wolves attack people?" she asked uneasily.

"Not you," he said, half amused. "You won't be walking this ranch alone."

"That's not what I meant." She glanced at him silently.

"Worried about me?" he asked mockingly.

She turned away. "Maybe I was worrying about the wolf," she grumbled.

He got out and helped her over the high bank of snow. She noticed that he didn't offer to carry her this time, and she was glad. It was torture to be close to him, with all the memories between them.

"Try to make her rest as much as you can," Egan said before he knocked on the door. "I'll have Ramey call here just as soon as the doctor's examined Al."

"All right. I'll take care of her."

The door opened, and a pretty young girl with dark hair and eyes opened it. "Egan!" she said enthusiastically. "What brings you here?"

His eyes went from her swollen belly back to her face

and he grimaced. He pulled off his hat. "Barbara, my new Hereford bull gored Al," he said softly. "He's all right, but I've had the boys drive him in to see the doctor."

The girl's face went pale, and Kati stepped forward quickly, as Egan did, to help her back inside and onto a chair.

"I'm Kati," she told the girl as she led her to the chair and eased her bulky figure down into it. "I'm going to stay with you. He'll be all right, Barbara. Egan said so."

Egan looked down at her with a faint smile in his eyes. "I'll be out on the ranch with my tracker," he told Kati. "But if Al isn't home by dark, you'll stay in the house with us, Barbara."

"Yes, Egan," Barbara nodded numbly.

Kati left her long enough to walk out onto the front porch with Egan.

"Keep her as quiet as you can," he said. "If you need help, get Dessie."

"I will," she promised. She looked up at him, quietly searching the craggy lines of his face, loving him so deeply that she'd have followed him barefoot through the snow.

He glanced down at her, and the darkness grew in his eyes as they held hers.

"The wolf," she said uneasily. "You won't take chances?"

He moved close, framing her worried face in his hands, and stared down into her eyes for a long moment. "I never take chances, as a rule," he said. "Of course, I blotted my book with you."

"I don't understand."

"What would you call trying to seduce a virgin on a bearskin rug?" he asked dryly.

She flushed and he laughed.

"I lost my head that night," he told her. "I could have broken your young neck when you told me the truth."

"Yes, I know, and your temper hasn't improved since," she said miserably. "I shouldn't have said anything, I guess."

"I'd have blown my brains out afterward if you hadn't," he said. "Kati, I wasn't in any condition for initiation, ceremonies. You had me so worked up, I didn't know my name. That's why it took me so long to get over it."

"Oh," she murmured, studying him. He didn't look so formidable now. He looked...odd.

"I can't get too close to you, baby, don't you know? I don't want you any less right now than I did the first time I kissed you," he breathed, bending to her mouth. "But I could seduce you now without even trying. And that wouldn't be a good thing."

"It wouldn't?" she whispered, watching his mouth brush and probe gently at hers in the cold air.

"Don't they say," he whispered back, "that good girls almost always get pregnant that first time?"

"Egan...!" she moaned as his mouth found hers.

He lifted her against him and kissed her roughly, his mouth cool and hard and sure as it moved over hers. His gloved hand caught at her nape and brought her face closer; and she heard a deep, rumbling sound echoing out of his chest.

"We've got to stop this," he ground out as his mouth slid across her cheek, and he wrapped her up tightly in his arms. "It's just a matter of time before I go off the deep end if we don't. I could eat you!"

"Yes, I know," she whispered achingly. "I feel the same way."

He rocked her slowly in his arms while the wind whistled around the house and snow blew past them. "I have to go, Kati."

Her arms tightened. "Be careful. Please be careful."

He was breathing heavily, and his eyes when he lifted his head were silvery and wild. "I used to be," he said enigmatically. He let her go and tugged at a lock of her hair with rough affection. "See you, city girl."

She nodded with a weak smile. "So long, cowboy."

She turned and went back into the house before he could see the worried tears in her eyes.

"Would you like some coffee?" she asked Barbara with perfect poise. "If you'll show me where you keep everything, I'll even make it."

Barbara dabbed at her eyes and smiled. "Of course. Thank you for staying with me."

"I'm glad to do what I can for you," Kati replied. "Come on. Your man will be all right. You have to believe that."

"I'm trying to," the young girl replied. She glanced at Kati as they went into the kitchen. "Is Egan your man?"

Kati flushed. "No," she managed. "No, he's my best friend's brother. He's helping me with some research on a book I'm writing."

"You write books?"

"Yes. Those big historical things," Kati offered.

"It must be lots of fun." She got down cups. "I wanted to be a singer, but I married Al instead. We've been together two years now." She stared out the window at the thickening snow. "I love him so much. And we've been so excited about this baby."

"What do you want?" Kati asked, seeing an opening. "A boy or a girl?"

"Oh, a boy," Barbara said. "I've been knitting blue booties and hats. He'll be all right, won't he?"

"Egan said he would, didn't he?" Kati hedged.

Barbara smiled wanly. "I guess so. Egan's never lied."

Kati nodded, but her own mind was on that killer wolf and Egan out hunting it. An animal that would savage cattle three or four times its size would think nothing of attacking a man. She closed her eyes to the possibility. She couldn't bear thinking about it.

Two hours went by before the phone rang, and Kati answered it herself.

"Barbara?" came Ramey's voice.

"No, Ramey, it's Kati. How is Al?" she asked quickly.

"Madder than a skinned snake," Ramey chuckled. "He wants Egan to give him that bull for steaks."

"He's all right!" Kati told Barbara, laughing; and Barbara sat down heavily with a tired sigh.

"The boss might do it, too," Ramey laughed, "despite how much he paid for him. They're going to keep Al overnight, but he wants Barbara with him. Pack her a bag, will you? They're going to put a bed in the room for her."

"I sure will. Are you coming after her?"

"Guess I'll have to. Boss is still out with Charlie."

That was a worrying thought. "Will it take them long to find the wolf, do you think?" she asked hesitantly.

"Anybody's guess, Miss James. See you."

"Bye."

She hung up the phone with numb fingers. "Al wants you to spend the night with him at the hospital. They've even fixed you a bed," she said cheerfully. "He's going to be fine, but Ramey said they want to keep him overnight."

"Oh, thank God, thank God!" Barbara whispered. She took a minute to pull herself together before she became practical. "I'll pack my bag right now. Oh, my poor Al!"

Kati helped her get ready, knowing how she might feel in the same circumstances. And Egan was out tracking that wolf right now. What if something happened to him? How would she manage?

Ramey came and dropped Kati by the house on the way to depositing Barbara at the hospital. Kati waved them off and rushed to find Dessie.

"Is Egan back?" she asked the housekeeper.

Dessie shook her head. "It may take all night. Or longer," she told the obviously worried younger woman. "Kati, he's a rancher. This isn't the first time he's had to go tracking a predator; I doubt if it will be the last. It's something you get used to. Back in the old days," she added with a faint smile, "it was rustlers they chased. And they shot back."

"In other words, the wolf is the lesser of a lot of evils." Kati sighed. "Well..." She stuck her hands in the pockets of her jeans. "I guess I'll go work on my book."

"You do that. I'll straighten up the kitchen. Will you be all right by yourself? You won't get scared if I go on to bed?"

"Of course not." She was used to Dessie's early hours by now. "I'll just curl up in a chair and watch TV while I jot down a few notes. Today has been an education."

"I don't doubt it. Sleep well. Barbara doing okay, was she?"

"Yes. Just worried, and that's natural. But she handled it well."

"She's a cowboy's wife," Dessie replied. "Of course she did."

Kati nodded. She was beginning to understand what that meant. She wandered into the living room and watched television until bedtime. Still, Egan hadn't come back.

She paced and watched the clock and listened for the sound of a vehicle. But it didn't come. She thought about going up to bed, but knew she wouldn't sleep. So she curled up on the sofa to watch a late-night talk show. Somewhere in the middle of a starlet's enthusiasm for designer clothes, she fell asleep.

The dreams were delicious. Someone was holding her, very close; she could feel his breath at her ear, whispering words she couldn't quite hear. She smiled and snuggled close, clinging to a hard neck.

"Did you hear me?"

The sound of Egan's voice brought her awake. Her eyes opened heavily, and she blinked as she saw him above her.

"What time is it?" she asked sleepily.

"Six o'clock in the morning," he said, studying her. He was standing and she was locked close in his arms. She looked around and realized that they were in her bedroom. He'd carried her all the way from the living room and she hadn't known....

"I meant to go to bed," she protested.

"Yes, I imagine you did."

Her eyes searched his drawn face: the growth of beard on his cheeks and chin; the weariness that lay on him like a net. "Did you get the wolf?" she asked softly.

"Yes, honey, we got him." He bent to lay her on the bed and looked straight into her eyes. "Were you waiting up for me, Katriane?"

"No, I was watching television," she protested quickly.

He sat down beside her on the bed, still in his sheepskin coat and the wide-brimmed old hat he wore. He put his fingers over her mouth; they were cold from the outdoors, and he smelled of the wind and fir trees.

"I said," he repeated softly, "were you waiting up for me?"

"Well, you said the stupid creature would attack people, didn't you?"

"I didn't think you'd mind too much if he took a plug out of me," he murmured, studying her sleepy face.

"Isn't that the other way around?" she muttered. "You're the one with all the grudges, not me."

"I wanted you, damn it!" he burst out, glaring at her, and all the controlled anger was spilling out of him. "Wanted you, you naive little idiot! You write about it with a gift, but do you understand what it's like? Men hurt like hell when they get as hot as you got me that night!"

She dropped her eyes to his chest. "I wasn't going to say no," she managed curtly.

"But you knew I would," he returned. "You knew I'd never take you to bed once I had learned the truth. It's not my way."

"I wasn't thinking," she muttered.

"Neither was I. I brought you home thinking I could have you. You knew it. Then, just when I'm involved to the back teeth and aching like a boy of fourteen, you turn it off. Just like that."

She couldn't bear the accusation in his deep voice, the anger. Her eyes closed and her fingers clenched by her side.

"And the worst part," he continued, with barely leashed fury in his tone, "is that I think you did it deliberately, despite that lame excuse you gave about not wanting me to hurt you. I think you set me up, Kati, to get even."

That hurt more than all the other accusations put together. It made tears burn her eyes. "What an opinion you have of me," she whispered shakily, trying to force a smile to her lips. "First you think I'm a tramp, and then you try to seduce me, and now you think I'm a cheat besides."

"Don't try to throw it back on my head!" he growled.

"Why not?" She sat up, glaring. "Why not? You were the one who kept putting on the pressure, weren't you? And every time I tried to explain, you shut me up!"

"You knew why I invited you," he shot back. "For God's sake, what did you come out here expecting, a proposal of marriage!"

That was so close to the truth that it took all her control not to let him see it. "Of course not," she replied instead, as coolly as she could. "I expected to be allowed to research my book. And you told me," she added levelly, "that there were no strings attached. Didn't you?"

He sighed angrily but he didn't deny it. His eyes searched over her flushed, angry face, her narrowed eyes. "I guess I did."

Her breasts rose and fell softly, and she looked down at her hands. "As soon as the snow melts a little, I'll leave. I'll need some more data on Wyoming history and a few other related subjects, but I can get that in Cheyenne."

"Writing is all that matters to you, isn't it?" he asked coldly.

She met his eyes. "Egan, what else do I have?"

His heavy brows drew together. "You're young."

"I'll see my twenty-sixth summer this year," she replied. "And all I have to show for my life is a few volumes of historical fiction in the 'J' section of the library. No family. No children. No nothing."

"I'm almost thirty-five and in the same predicament, and I don't give a damn," he told her.

She studied his hard face. "I'm not even surprised. You don't need anyone."

"I do need the occasional woman," he replied.

"I'm sorry, but I don't do occasionals," she told him. "I'm the forever-after type, and if you'd really read any of my books, you'd have known it before you ruined everything."

"I ruined everything?" He glared at her thunderously. "You couldn't get your clothes off fast enough!"

"Oh!" Shamed to the bones, she felt the tears come, and she hated her own weakness. She tried to get up, but he caught her, his hands steely on her upper arms.

"I didn't mean to say that," he ground out. "Damn you, Kati, you bring out everything mean and ornery in my soul!"

"Then it's a good thing I'm leaving before you just rot away, isn't it?" she said, weeping.

He drew in a deep, slow breath. "Oh baby," he breathed, drawing her close against him under the unbuttoned sheepskin coat. "Baby, I don't want to hurt you."

His voice was oddly tender, although she barely heard the words through her sobs. She'd hardly cried in her life until Egan came along.

His arms enclosed her warmly and she felt his cold, rough cheek against hers as he held her. "You've had a hard time of it, haven't you? I wouldn't have asked you to stay with Barbara, but I needed Dessie more to get Al patched."

"I didn't mind, truly I didn't. She was so brave."

"She's had to be. Living out here isn't easy on a

woman. It's still hard country, and winters can be terrifying. Spring comes and there's flooding. Summer may bring a drought. A man can lose everything overnight out here." He stroked her hair absently. "It was even harder on Barbara. She was a California girl."

"She loves him, Egan."

He laughed shortly, the sound echoing heavily in the dark room. "And love is enough?"

"You make it sound sordid," she murmured at his ear, stirring slightly.

"Well, women set great store by it, I suppose," he said quietly. "I never did. What passed for love in my life was bought and paid for."

She flinched at the cynicism and drew back to look at him. This close, she could see every line in that craggy face. It held her eyes like a magnet, from the kindling silver eyes to the square chin that badly needed a razor.

"Haven't you ever loved anyone?" she asked gently.

"My mother. Ada."

"A lover," she persisted, searching his eyes.

"No, Katriane," he told her somberly. "The few times I tried, I found out pretty quick that it was the money they wanted, not me. What was it you called me that last time we got into it—a big, ugly cowboy?"

"I meant it, too," she said, not backing down. "But what I was talking about had nothing to do with looks. No, Egan, you aren't at all handsome. But you're all man, so what difference does it make?"

He stared at her, and she flushed, averting her eyes. She hadn't meant to let that slip out.

His fingers toyed with her hair and worked their way under her chin to lift it. He was closer than she'd expected—so close that all she could see was his nose and mouth.

"It's been...a long time since anyone waited up for me. Or worried over me," he said huskily. His breath came heavily. "Kati, you'd better not let me have your mouth."

But she wanted it. Ached for it. And her eyes told him so. He caught his breath at the blatant hunger in them.

"I'll hurt you," he ground out.

"I don't even care...!" She reached up, opening her arms and her heart, and dragged his open, burning mouth down onto hers.

He was rough. Not only in the crushing hold he had on her slender body, but the bristly pressure of his face and the ardent hunger of his mouth. His fingers tangled in her long hair and twirled it around and around, arching her neck.

His lips lifted, poised over hers, and he was breathing as raggedly as she was. "Open your mouth a little more," he said shakily. "Let me show you how I like to be kissed."

Her eyes opened so that she could look into his, and his hands clasped the back of her head as he ground his mouth into hers again, feeling it open and tremble and want his.

"Kati," he breathed as he half lifted her against him, while the kiss became something out of her experience. "God, Kati, it's so sweet...!"

She clung to him, giving back the ardent pressure until he groaned and his rough cheek slid against hers and he held her, breathing in shudders at her ear.

"Stop letting me do that," he ground out, tightening his arms. "It only makes things worse!"

"Yes," she whispered shakily. Her face nuzzled against his, her eyes closed, her body aching for something it had never had.

She began to realize what was happening to him, and it was her fault. She sat perfectly still in his arms and let him hold her until his breathing was steady, until the slight tremor went out of his arms.

"I'm sorry," she whispered.

"Yes, I know, but it doesn't help," he murmured.

"Well, don't put all the blame on me!" she sobbed, trying to push him away.

"I'm not trying to. Stop fighting me."

"Stop making horrible remarks."

He laughed. Laughed! He rubbed his face against hers affectionately; it felt like a pincushion. He lifted his head, and his eyes were blazing with laughter and something much harder to identify. He looked down at her, searching her eyes, her face, and looking so utterly smug that she wanted to hit him.

"You are something else," he said, and she remembered the words from the night he'd made love to her by the fire. She blushed scarlet, and he lifted an eyebrow. "Remembering, are you?" His eyes went down to her blouse and stayed there. "I'll never forget."

Her eyes closed because she couldn't bear the heat of his gaze. "Neither will I. I never meant—"

"Don't," he whispered, bringing her close again. "We made magic that night. I had this opinion of you, you see. For a long time. Kati, I wasn't telling the truth when I said I'd read your books, I'd only read a passage or two. Just enough to support my negative assessment of your character." He lifted his head and looked down at her. "Night before last, I read one. Really read it. There are some pretty noticeable gaps in those love scenes." He searched her eyes. "But some pretty powerful emotions in them, all the same. They were beautiful."

Her eyes burned with tears. "Thank you."

He touched her cheek softly. "I'd like very much to make love with you that way, Kati," he whispered. "I'd like to lie with you on a deserted beach in the moonlight and watch your body move, the way that pirate did in your last book…."

"Don't," she pleaded, burying her face in his shirt. She didn't feel at all like the very cool author who spoke to writers' clubs with such poise. She felt… young.

"So shy with me," he whispered, lifting her across his lap. "And I was the first, wasn't I? The first man to look at you, to touch you, to be intimate with you. My God, I ache just thinking about it, when it never mattered a damn before how many men I'd followed with a woman." His hands smoothed over her back gently while his face nuzzled hers. "I'm like a boy with you, Kati. When we share those deep, hot kisses, I shake all over."

Her fingers made patterns on his shirt, and she loved

the bigness and warmth of his body so close to hers. But he was admitting to nothing except desire. And she wanted much, much more.

"We'd better go and eat, I suppose," he murmured. "And I need a shave and a bath." He lifted his head and studied her pink cheek where his had scraped it, and he smiled slowly. "If we made love and I hadn't shaved, you'd look like that all over," he commented.

It brought to mind pictures that made her ache, and she couldn't get away from him quickly enough.

"There's just one thing," he added, watching her with a lazy smile. "If I ever turn up in one of those damned books, you're in trouble."

"I don't write about real people," she defended, and prayed that he'd never see the first few chapters of her new book before she had time to turn the hero back into a blond.

"You'd better not," he said; and although his voice was pleasant, there was a hard glint in his eyes. "What we do together when we make love is private. For the two of us alone."

She frowned. "You can't believe I'd do that!"

He searched her eyes slowly. "I'm not a writer. Explain it to me."

"It would take hours," she told him.

"I'm not leaving for the rest of the day," he told her. "Let me get my bath and shave. I'll meet you downstairs. You can ask me anything else you need to know about the ranch while we're at it."

The prospect of spending a day alone with him was heady and sweet. "All right," she said.

He winked and went out the door, already a different man. For the rest of the day, they talked as never before. He told her about the early days of the ranch and how his grandfather came by it. He told her about his own plans for it; his dreams; the career he once thought he wanted in politics. In return, she explained to him how she felt her characters come alive on paper and take over the actual writing of the book, right down to the love scenes. She explained how she researched the historical facts and how she'd learned to grit her teeth and smile when people asked where she had learned so much about intimacy when she was unmarried and apparently living alone.

"You see, it's just that you can't write fiction without a little romance." She sighed. "And these days, the more sensuous the better. I won't go the whole hog and write explicit scenes, but the sexiest books are the biggest sellers. I must be pretty accurate, though, because my reader mail is mostly kind."

He shook his head, sitting quietly by the crackling fireplace, watching her. "A virgin. Writing what you write. My God."

"Well, most fiction about scientists isn't written by scientists. Most fiction about lawyers isn't written by lawyers. It's just a matter of research, like anything else," she added.

"You do it very—"

The telephone interrupted him. Expecting news about Al, he sprang to his feet to answer.

"Hello?" His face changed. "Yes, how are you, Jennie?"

Kati felt her body go rigid. That woman! So they did have something going, even after he'd left New York.

"Yes, I know." He toyed with a pen-set on the desk. "Umm-hmm. Yes, we did, didn't we?" He smiled. "Here? No, I don't think that's a good idea, honey. We're snowed in. That's right, about five feet of it. No, we've closed the landing strip. You'd have to fly in to Jackson. Maybe. Tell you what, let's put it off until spring. Yes, I know you don't, but that's how it is, Jennie. No strings, remember? I told you at the very beginning how it was going to be. That's right. Sure. Next time I'm in town. So long." He hung up and turned, watching the expressions cross Kati's face.

"She wanted to stop over for a week or two on her way to California for a screen test," he volunteered. "I said no. Anything else you'd like to know?"

"She…was very pretty," Kati muttered.

"Surely she was. And experienced," he added deliberately. "But she wanted ties and I didn't."

"Freedom is your big problem, isn't it?" she asked on a laugh. "Well, don't look at me as if I had a rope in one hand—I don't want strings any more than you do," she lied, and looked away just in time to miss the expression that froze his face.

"I thought all you women wanted marriage," he said in an odd voice.

"Not now I don't," she returned as casually as she could. "I'm too involved in work."

"Going to remain a virgin for life, I gather?" he asked cuttingly. "Give up a home and children so you can keep writing those damned books?"

She looked up with a deliberate smile, in spite of the glittering anger in his eyes. "I like writing those damned books."

He turned away. "So I noticed. Don't let me hold you up, you probably have a lot of work to get through if you're leaving by the end of the week."

And he walked out of the room, leaving her speechless. Well, what had he expected her to say, she wondered achingly—that she loved him? That she'd lie on the floor and let him walk on her if she could stay with him?

Fat chance! If he could brush Jennie off so easily, when he'd obviously had an affair with her, what chance did she have? Probably he was just biding his time until he could get her into his bed. He knew she'd surrender, she thought miserably, he knew very well that she couldn't resist him. And once she'd given in, he'd be letting her down easily, just the way he'd done Jennie. And he'd be in pursuit of some new woman. With a tiny moan, she went upstairs and opened the case that held her computer. What a miserable end for a wonderful day!

Chapter Eleven

It wasn't hard to avoid Egan after that. He wasn't home. He worked from dawn until late at night and appeared only briefly to eat. He treated Kati with grudging courtesy, but he didn't come near her.

She packed Friday morning to go back to New York. The snow was melting again, and the skies were sunny and clear. Perhaps, she told herself, it was an omen.

"I sure am going to miss you," Dessie said gruffly as she had breakfast with Kati and Egan. "Been nice, having another woman around the place."

"I'll miss you, too," Kati said genuinely as she finished her eggs and drank her coffee. "I've learned a lot while I was here."

"I reckon Gig's talked more in the past week than he has since I've known him," Egan said mockingly.

He leaned back precariously in his cane-bottom chair to study her as he smoked a cigarette. He seemed to smoke all the time these days. "Have you satisfied your curiosity about ranch life, Miss Author?" he added.

"Yes," she said, refusing to let him irritate her. "And about the cattle business. Thank you for letting me come."

"My pleasure. Any time." He swallowed the rest of his coffee and got to his feet. "Ramey's going to drive you to the airport."

"Ramey?" Dessie burst out. "But Egan, you never let Ramey—"

"Just never mind, if you please," he told the old woman, a bite in his voice. He glanced at Kati hard, and his eyes accused.

"I'll clear this stuff away," Dessie murmured quickly and retreated into the kitchen with two empty platters.

"Have a safe trip home," he told Kati quietly. "And give Ada my love."

"I'll do that," she said stiffly.

He started to pass by her, paused, and suddenly jerked her out of the chair by her arms, hurting her as he dragged her against his chest.

"Damn you," he breathed furiously, with silver eyes that glittered dangerously. "Do you think your career is going to keep you warm at night? Will it give you what I did on that bearskin rug by the fireplace?" he demanded.

Her body melted against his and she wished she had the strength to hit him, but she was drowning in his eyes and the feel of his taut, powerful body.

"What are you offering me?" she asked. "A night in your bed?"

His hands tightened on her arms and he looked hunted. "I don't want you to leave," he said gruffly. "We'll work it out somehow."

"How?" she persisted. "Egan, I'm not like Jennie. I can't take an open affair."

"What do you want, then?" he asked under his breath, watching her. "Marriage?"

She searched his angry eyes defeatedly. "You'd hate me for that," she said with quiet perception.

"I don't know," he replied. "We might get used to each other; make a go of it."

She reached up, touching his face softly with her fingertips. "You'd better stick to girls like Jennie," she said softly. "I couldn't settle for what you'd be able to give me. I couldn't live on crumbs."

"I'm a rich man," he said curtly. "You could have anything you wanted, within reason. And in bed, I'd be everything you'd ever need."

"I know that," she agreed. Her fingers traced his hard mouth, feeling its automatic response with wonder. "But it's still not enough."

"Why not, for God's sake?" he growled, catching her wandering fingers roughly in his own.

"Because I'm in love with you, Egan," she said proudly, watching the reaction flare in his eyes, harden his face. "You can't match that with money or sex. I'd wither away and die of neglect and pity. No, I'd rather be totally alone than on my knees at your heart."

His lips parted and he couldn't seem to find the

right words. He touched her hair hesitantly. "You love me?" he whispered huskily, frowning as if he found the words incomprehensible.

"Occupational hazard," she whispered, trying not to cry. "I'll get over it. Good-bye, Egan."

His fingers tightened in her hair. "No, not yet," he said uncertainly. "Not just yet. You don't have to go right now—"

"Yes, I do," she said, on the verge of tears. "I'm running out of pride—" Her voice broke, and she tried to get away, but his arms tightened like a vice and he held her despite her struggles.

"Don't," he whispered, shaken. "Don't fight me. My God, Kati, don't run."

"Egan," she moaned.

"Egan!" Dessie called sharply from the kitchen. "It's the hospital on the phone! Something about Al— Can you come?"

He cursed under his breath, looking down at the tears on Kati's cheeks with eyes that frightened her. "Don't move," he said shortly. "Not one step. You hear me?"

She nodded, but the minute he was out of sight, she grabbed up her bag and made a run for the front door. She couldn't face him again, not after the fool she'd made of herself. If she couldn't have his love, she didn't want his pity. She couldn't bear it!

As luck would have it, Ramey was just getting out of the pickup truck. She dived in on the passenger side.

"Ramey, can you get me to the airport in Jackson in a hurry?" she asked quickly. "There's an emergency— I have to leave!"

"Emergency?" Ramey jumped back in and started the truck. "Why sure, Miss James. Don't you worry, I'll get you there!"

He turned the truck, and Kati reached down and very unobtrusively cut off the two-way radio.

"That noise is just awful," she murmured, "and I have such a headache. Can't we leave it off just until we get to town?" she asked with a pitiful smile.

He hesitated, then he grinned. "Sure. I don't reckon we'll need it."

"Good!" And then she began to talk furiously to keep his mind occupied. It didn't hurt her, either, to stop thinking about Egan and the look on his face when she'd confessed. She didn't know if she'd be able to hear his name again without going mad.

It seemed to take forever, and despite the four-wheel drive and snow tires, they almost bogged down a few times. But Ramey got her to the airport. It wasn't until she was getting out that she realized she'd left her computer at the ranch.

"I'll tell the Boss," Ramey assured her. "He'll get it to you."

That wasn't a comforting thought; the Boss would be out for blood. But she smiled anyway. "Thanks." She'd just do those chapters over on her stationary computer at the apartment, she assured herself; she could remember most of them.

"Have a good trip!" Ramey called and was off with a wave of his hand.

There was a seat on an outgoing plane to Cheyenne. She'd hole up there for a few days, letting only Ada know where she was. She wasn't strong enough to resist Egan, so she wasn't going to try.

She kept watching the door, although she couldn't help wondering why. Egan wouldn't come after her. Besides, she thought, he'd never make it through the snow anyway.

She checked her bag, went aboard with only her purse, and sat down heavily in her seat. It was over. She was leaving. Now all she had to do was get her mind off Egan and find some way of not thinking about him for the rest of her life. Facing Ada was going to be hard. Living with her would be sheer torture. She knew she'd die every time Ada mentioned her brother.

The plane was running now, and she knew it wouldn't be long until takeoff. She was just starting to fasten her seat belt when she heard a commotion in the back of the plane.

A sheepskin coat came suddenly into view, with a hard, furious face above it.

While she was getting over the shock, Egan reached down, unfastened her seat belt and scooped her up in his hard arms, purse and all.

"You can't do this!" she burst out, oblivious to the amused eyes of the other passengers.

"Like hell I can't," he replied curtly and carried her off the plane.

"Oh Egan, let me go!" she wailed as he walked back toward the terminal, burying her embarrassed face in his warm collar.

"I can't," he whispered huskily, and his arms tightened around her.

Tears rolled down her cheeks. He wanted her, that was all, but she didn't have the strength to walk away again, even if he'd let her. So she lay in his arms, crying softly, and let him carry her all the way to his pickup truck.

He put her in and got in beside her, picking up the radio mike as he started the truck. He gave his call letters and told somebody he was on his way back with Kati and signed off.

"My bag," she began.

"I hope it has a nice trip," he said curtly, glaring at her as he pulled out into the road. "I told you to stay put."

"I couldn't," she muttered miserably, staring into her lap. "I was too embarrassed."

"Best-selling author," he scoffed, glaring toward her. "The sensual mistress of the ages. And you can't tell a man you love him without blushing all over?"

"I've never done it before!" she burst out, glaring back at him.

His silver eyes gleamed. "You're doing a lot of firsts with me, aren't you, city girl? And the biggest and best is still to come."

"I won't sleep with you, Egan," she said angrily.

"Won't you?" He lit a cigarette and smoked it with a smile so arrogant she wanted to hit him.

"I want to go home!"

"You are home, honey," he replied. "Because that's what White Lodge is going to be from now on."

"Do be reasonable," she pleaded, turning toward him. "You're asking me to give up everything I believe in!"

"That's where you're wrong, Kati. I'm not asking."

"I'll scream," she threatened.

He gave her a wicked smile. "Yes, you probably will," he murmured softly.

"Oh, damn," she wailed.

"Now just calm down, honey," he told her. "When we get back to the ranch, I'll explain it all to you. Right now, you'd better let me keep my mind on the road. I don't want to spend the rest of the day sitting in a ditch."

She sighed. "How's Al?" she asked dully, remembering the phone call.

"On his way home. He called to get one of the boys to drive him. Now hush."

She folded her arms across her chest, feeling miserable and cold and helpless. He was taking the choice away from her, and she didn't know what to do. Didn't he realize what he was forcing on her? She wouldn't be able to go on living afterward, because the memory of him would burn into her like a brand and she'd never be free again. How could he be so cruel?

It seemed to take much less time getting back to White Lodge than it had leaving it. Egan pulled up at the steps and cut off the engine.

"I won't go in," she muttered.

"I figured you were going to be unpleasant about it," he said on a sigh. He got out, lifted her from the cab of the truck and carried her into the house.

"Dessie, take the phone off the hook," he told the amused housekeeper. "I've got a lot of explaining to do, and I don't want to be interrupted."

"Just keep in mind I'll be out here with my frying pan," Dessie told him, winking at Kati. "And keeping the coffee hot."

He laughed under his breath, carrying Kati into his study. He slammed the door behind him and put her down so that he could lock it.

She retreated to the fireplace, where a fire was crackling merrily, and glanced down at the bearskin rug. She quickly moved away, and Egan watched her as he took off his hat and coat, his eyes sparkling with amusement.

"It wasn't that bad, was it?" he asked, nodding toward the rug. "I thought you enjoyed what I did to you on that."

"Don't you have work to do?" she asked, moving behind his desk.

"Afraid of me, Kati?" he asked softly, moving toward her.

He looked devastating. All lean grace and muscle. His dark hair was mussed, and his eyes were sensual.

"Egan, let me go to New York," she said unsteadily, backing up until the wall stopped her.

He moved toward her relentlessly, until she was trapped between the hard wall and his taut body. He put his hands deliberately beside her head, the way he had in the kitchen that morning, and she trembled with the hunger to feel that hard body crushing down on hers.

"Now we talk," he said softly, watching the emotions play on her face. "You told me you loved me. How? Is it just a physical thing, or is it more?"

Her lips parted on a rush of breath and her body

ached for him. He poised there, taunting her; and, involuntarily, she moved against the wall.

"Tell me," he whispered, "and I'll do what you want me to do."

She swallowed, so weak with love that she couldn't even protest that arrogance. "I love you in every way there is," she told him. "Every single way."

"I've got a nasty temper," he reminded her quietly. "I like my own way. And I've lived alone for a long time. It won't be easy. There are going to be times when you'll wish I hadn't carried you off that plane."

Her body felt like jelly as she looked up at him. "I love you," she whispered. "I love you!"

He eased down over her, letting her feel the full, devastating effect the words had on him, and he smiled at the mingled hunger and embarrassment in her face.

"I'll want a son," he murmured, watching the effect of that soft statement. "Maybe three or four of them."

She smiled slowly, wonderingly. "I'd like that, too," she said, trembling as she realized what he was saying.

"No big wedding, though," he added under his breath as his body began to move slowly, sensuously, against hers. "Just the minister and some of the boys and Ada."

"Yes," she whispered, lifting her mouth, pleading for his.

"And if a word of what I'm about to do to you gets into print," he threatened with his mouth poised just above hers, "I'll chase you to Jackson with the truck."

"Yes, darling," she whispered back, standing on tiptoe to reach his open mouth with hers. "Egan, what are you going to do to me?"

"Come here and I'll tell you," he murmured on a soft laugh.

She felt his fingers taking away the sweater and opening the blouse, but she was too busy unbuttoning his shirt to care. Seconds later, hard, hair-roughened muscle pressed against soft, bare breasts; and she moaned, lifting her arms around his neck as she moved hungrily under him.

"Not here," he groaned. He lifted her and carried her to the rug, easing her down onto it.

"You can't imagine," she managed shakily as he lifted himself over her trembling body, "how many books I've read this scene in."

"You can't imagine," he countered, "how different this is going to be from reading." His hands slid under her, lifting her to the hard pressure of his hips, and he watched her with glittering silver eyes as she cried out. "You see?" he whispered unsteadily. "Kati, I'm drowning in you. Drowning in the feel of you, the taste of you."

He bent, and she gave him her mouth totally, moving instinctively under the weight of his taut body, loving the heaviness and hunger that was crushing her in pleasure.

"Like this," he whispered, guiding, and she felt him in a new and shocking way, and her eyes flew open incredulously.

His face, above hers, was hard with desire, his eyes glittering with triumph as he saw her pleasure in her eyes. "Now," he breathed, and his hands went under her thighs. "Now, just do what I tell you."

She felt his mouth on hers through a fog of incredible hunger, and somewhere in the middle of it, she began to cry. It was the sweetest maelstrom in the world. She felt the rough silk of his skin under her hands, and she touched him in ways she'd never dreamed of touching a man. Her legs tangled with his while he taught her sensations that shocked and burned and stung with pleasure.

"Please, Egan," she whispered into his ear, gasping as he lifted her hips closer. "Please, please!"

"I want you just as much," he whispered back. "But we're not going all the way."

"Egan!" she groaned.

"Trust me, Kati," he whispered. "Give me your mouth, and lie still."

She did, and somewhere in the back of her mind she felt as if she were dying as his body stilled on hers and his mouth began to lose its obsession with hers. He stroked her and whispered to her, and she cried helplessly as the urgency began to recede, to calm into a pleasant exhaustion.

"You and I," he whispered, "are going to burn up when we make love for the first time. I've never felt in my life what I feel when you put your hands on me."

She smoothed his dark hair with fingers that still trembled, and nuzzled against the hair over his hard chest. "Will it be enough?"

His lips brushed over her closed eyelids. "Look at me, little virgin," he whispered. "I want to watch your eyes when I say it."

Her heavy eyelids lifted and she saw his eyes burn like sunlight.

"I love you, Kati," he whispered softly. "I loved you the night you came walking home with my cousin, and I was so eaten up with jealousy that I ate you alive. I've loved you every day since and fought it with everything in me."

Her lips parted but she couldn't speak. Oh God, it was like having every dream of love she'd ever dreamed come true all at once!

"I thought you were having a fling," he said tightly. "Until the night we lay here together and you told me the truth. And I wanted to go through the floor, because I'd misread the whole situation, and I'd said things to you that still make me uneasy." He brushed the hair away from her cheeks and let his gaze drift down to her soft bareness. His jaw clenched and he dragged his eyes back up to hers, while his fingers stroked over skin no man had touched before. "Then you said you didn't want ties, and I realized that I did. I wanted my ring on your finger, for all time. But you were leaving. And I couldn't find the right words." He sighed heavily. "I was trying to, when you told me you loved me."

"I thought I'd embarrassed you," she said softly.

"You'd given me the moon, Kati," he replied, watching her. "The moon, the sun, the stars—I was speechless, just savoring the feel of it, the sound. And then Al called, and you got away. I'd have gone down on my knees to you…!"

"Egan," she breathed, drawing him close with possessive arms, clinging passionately to him. "Egan, it tore me apart to go! But I was afraid you'd pity me."

"I pitied myself for being so damned stupid—for ever letting you out of my sight. It will be the last time, too. As soon as I get a license, we're getting married. Tomorrow, if possible."

"But, I don't have a dress!"

"Get married in blue jeans, for all I care," he told her. "I just want to give you my name. My heart. My life."

Her eyes closed on a wave of pleasure. Tears welled up in them, at the magnificence of loving and being loved in return. She shuddered.

"Cold?" he whispered, concerned. "I'd forgotten how little we have on."

She did blush then, as he handed her her blouse and bra and watched her struggle to rearrange her jeans.

"Don't stare," she pleaded.

"I can't help it. You're so lovely," he said with a grin. He propped himself on an elbow, devastating without his shirt. "I guess we'll have to have at least one daughter to look like you." He caught her hand when she finished buttoning buttons and clasped it warmly to his hard, furry chest. "Can you live here with me and not miss the excitement of the city?"

"My darling," she said softly, "I carry my excitement around in my imagination, and I can work on the roof if I have to. There's a post office in Jackson. I have you to keep me warm and love me. What else do I need?"

He smiled slowly. "A good supply of sexy nightgowns," he murmured.

"Now, in that last book I wrote," she whispered, easing down beside him, "the heroine had this very modest white gown…"

"Which the hero ripped off on page fifty-six," he chuckled softly. "Yes, I know, but I like that scene in the bathtub. So, suppose tomorrow night you and I try it out?"

"I thought you were afraid of my research turning up in books," she laughed.

"Not since I've been reading them," he replied. "Anyway, they're giving me some good ideas."

She lifted her arms around his neck and pulled him down. "Suppose we just work on this bearskin-rug scene a little more?" she whispered at his lips. "I don't think I've got it the way I want it just yet."

"After we're married," he whispered back, his voice husky with emotion as he stared into her eyes, "we'll lie here together and go all the way. I'll let you feel this rug under you while I lie over you and—"

"Egan," she groaned, trembling, hiding her face.

He laughed softly as he pressed her back into it. "I can see that having a virgin for a wife is going to be educational," he mused.

"It's sort of the other way around right now, though," she reminded him. "You're the one doing the teaching."

"So I am." He rubbed his nose against hers. "And I'll tell you a secret, city girl. It's a hell of a lot more fun than fighting."

She smiled. Indeed it was, she thought as his lips nuzzled against hers. She caressed his back lovingly, and she wondered if Ada was going to be surprised

when they called her. Somehow, she didn't think so.
She reached up and pulled Egan's head down to hers.
Outside, the snow began to fall softly, again.

* * * * *

Carrera's Bride

Dear Reader,

Those of you who have read my books for a long time will already be familiar with the mysterious, elusive Marcus Carrera. His reputation was hinted at in *Paper Rose*, and he's made a substantial appearance in *Renegade*. He's also been mentioned from time to time in other books. Now he has a story of his own.

Marcus rescues a young woman in the hotel-casino he owns in the Bahamas. Her date, unknown to her, is a notorious money launderer, in league with a group of ruthless gangsters. Marcus rescues her from the man. She turns out to be a small-town girl from Jacobsville, Texas. They hit it off at first conversation. But Marcus has a reputation that frightens Delia when she finds out who he really is. Worse, her older sister dislikes him intensely and wants Delia to have nothing to do with him. Marcus, like Delia's sister, is keeping a dangerous secret. When Delia ends up on the firing line, she is the only one who can save Marcus's life. But at a terrible price.

This is one of the nicest stories I've had to tell so far. I really like Marcus, who isn't the black sheep he appears to be. And I like Delia, too.

I hope you enjoy the book!

Love,

Diana Palmer

Chapter One

It was a hectic evening at the Bow Tie casino on Paradise Island. Marcus Carrera was standing on the balcony smoking a cigar. He had a lot on his mind. A few years ago, he'd been a shady businessman with some unsavory contacts and a reputation that could send even tough guys running. He was still tough, of course. But his reputation as a gangster was something he'd hoped to leave behind him.

He owned hotels and casinos both in the States and in the Bahamas, although he was a silent partner in most of them. The Bow Tie was a combination hotel and casino, and his favorite of all his holdings. Here, he catered to an exclusive clientele, which included movie stars, rock stars, millionaires and even a couple of scalawags. He was a millionaire several times over.

But even though his operations had all become legitimate, he had to hold on to his vicious reputation for just
a while longer. The worst of it was that he couldn't tell
anyone.

Well, that wasn't entirely true. He could tell Smith.
The bodyguard was a really tough customer, an ex-ev-
erything military, who kept a six-foot iguana named
Tiny for a pet. The two of them were becoming a
landmark on Paradise Island. Marcus sometimes
thought his guests were showing up as much to see the
mysterious Mr. Smith as to gamble and lounge on the
sugar-sand beach behind the hotel.

He stretched hugely. He was tired. His life, never
calm even at the best of times, was more stressful lately
than it had ever been. He felt like a split personality.
But when he remembered the reason for the stress, he
couldn't regret his decision. His only brother was lying
in a lonely, ornate grave back in Chicago, the victim
of a merciless drug lord who was using a dummy corporation in the Bahamas to launder his illegal fortune.
Carlo was only twenty-eight. He had a wife and two
little kids. Marcus was providing for them, but that
didn't bring back their husband and father. It was a
damned shame to die over money, he thought furiously. Worst of all, the money-laundering banker who
had set Carlo up for the hit was still running around
loose and trying to help a renegade Miami gangster buy
up casinos on Paradise Island. They wouldn't be run
cleanly, as Marcus's were.

He took a draw from the cigar. It was a Havana cigar,
one of the very best available. Smith had friends in the

CIA who traveled to Cuba on assignment. They could buy the cigars legally and give them as gifts to whomever they pleased. Smith passed them on to his boss. Smith didn't smoke or drink, and he rarely swore. Marcus shook his head, chuckling to himself. What a conundrum the man was. Sort of like himself, he had to admit.

He lifted his leonine head to the breeze that blew eternally off the ocean. It ruffled his thick, wavy black hair. There were threads of silver in it now. He was in his late thirties, and he looked it. But he was an elegant man, despite his enormous height and build. He was well over six feet tall, as graceful as a panther, and just as quick when he needed to be. He had huge hands, devoid of jewelry except for a Rolex on his left wrist and a ruby ring on his left pinky finger. His skin was olive tan. It was set off stunningly by the spotless crisp white shirt he wore with his black dinner jacket and bow tie. The crease in his black slacks was knife-straight. His wing-tipped black leather shoes were so shiny that they reflected the palm trees on the balcony where he was standing, and the pale moon overhead. His fingernails were flat, immaculately clean. He was close-shaven and polished, never with a hair out of place. He was obsessive about grooming.

Perhaps, he thought, it was because he was so damned poor as a child. One of two sons of immigrant parents, he and Carlo had gone to work at an early age helping their father in the small automotive repair shop he owned with two other partners. The work ethic had been drilled into them, so that they knew that work was the only way out of poverty.

Their father had run afoul of a small-time local hood. He was beaten almost to death in his garage after he'd refused to let the hood use it for a chop shop, to process parts from stolen cars.

Marcus had been twelve at the time, not even old enough to hold a legitimate job. His mother worked as a cleaning lady for a local business in their neighborhood. Carlo was still in grammar school, four years behind Marcus. With their father unable to work, only what their mother brought home kept food on the table. But soon they couldn't pay rent anymore. They ended up in the street. Both of the elder Carrera's partners claimed that they had no obligation to him, since their agreement was only verbal. There was no money to hire attorneys.

It had been a bleak existence. Forced to ask for welfare, Marcus had seen his mother humbled and broken, while his father lay mindless in a bed from the massive concussion, unable to recognize his family, even to speak. A blood clot finished him a few months after the beating, leaving Marcus and Carlo and their mother alone.

When her health began to fail, Marcus was faced with seeing his brother and himself end up in foster care, wards of the court. He couldn't allow them to be separated. There was no family in the States to appeal to, not even any friends who had the means to help them.

With dogged determination, Marcus got a name from one of his tough friends and he went to see the local crime boss. His grit convinced the man that he was worth taking a chance on. Marcus became a courier for the mob, making huge amounts of money almost overnight. He had enough to get a good apartment for his mother and brother, and even managed health insurance for them.

His mother knew what he was doing and tried to discourage him, but he was mature for his age, and he convinced her that what he was doing wasn't really illegal. Besides, he asked her, did she want to see the family broken up and her kids made wards of the court?

The prospect horrified her. But she started going to mass every morning, to pray for her wayward son.

By the time Marcus was in his early twenties, he was firmly on the wrong side of the law and getting richer by the day. Along the way, he caught up with the drug boss who'd had his father beaten, and he settled the score. Later, he bought the garage out from under his father's two former partners and kicked them out into the street. Revenge, he found, was sweet.

His mother never approved of what he was doing. She died before he made his first million, still praying for him every day. He had a twinge of regret for disappointing her, but time took care of that. He put Carlo in a private school and made sure that he had the education Marcus lacked. He never looked back.

Women came and went in his life infrequently. His lifestyle precluded a family. He was happy for Carlo when the young man graduated from college with a law degree and married his childhood sweetheart, Cecelia. Marcus was delighted to have a nephew and then a niece to spoil.

Once, he let himself fall in love. She was a beautiful socialite from a powerful Eastern family with money to burn. She liked his reputation, the aura of danger that swirled around his tall head. She liked showing him off to her bored friends.

But she didn't like Carlo or the friends Marcus kept around, mostly people from his old Chicago neighborhood, who had as many rough edges as he did. He didn't like opera, he couldn't discuss literature, and he didn't gossip. When he mentioned having a family, Erin only laughed. She didn't want children for years and years, she wanted to party and travel and see the world. But when she did want them, it wasn't going to be with a man who couldn't even pretend to be civilized, she'd added haughtily. And that was when he realized that his only worth to her was as a novelty. It had crushed him.

By that time, Marcus had already seen most of the world, and he wasn't enchanted by it. The end came unexpectedly when he threw a birthday party for Erin at one of his biggest hotels in Miami. He missed Erin and went looking for her. He spotted her, disheveled and drunk, sneaking out of a hotel room with not one, but two rock stars he'd invited. It was the end of the dream. Erin only laughed and said she liked variety. Marcus said she was welcome to it. He walked away and never looked back.

These days, he'd lost much of his interest in women. It had been replaced by an interest in textiles and needlework. Nobody laughed at him since he'd started winning international competitions. He met a lot of women who were good with their hands, and he enjoyed their company. But most of them were married or elderly. The single ones looked at him oddly when they heard his name and the gossip. Nobody wanted to get mixed up with a hood. That was what had led to the decision he'd made recently. It was a life-changing event. But one he couldn't talk about.

He was sick of being a bad guy. He was more than ready to change his image. He sighed. Well, that wasn't going to be possible for a few months. He had to play the game to the end. His most immediate problem was finding a conduit to a necessary contact who was staying at a hotel in Nassau. He couldn't be seen talking to the man and, despite Smith's tight security, it was risky to use the telephone or even a cell phone. It was a knotty problem. There was another one. The man he was supposed to help in some illegal activities was due to talk to him tonight. So far, he hadn't shown up.

He put out the cigar reluctantly, but there was no smoking in the hotel or the casino. He couldn't really complain. He'd set the rules himself, after his young nephew and niece had come for a week with their mother, Cecelia. Smoking in the dining room had caused his nephew Julio to go into spasms of coughing. The boy was taken to a doctor and diagnosed with asthma. Since he had to protect Julio, and little Cosima, he decided to ban smoking in the resort. It hadn't been a popular decision. But, hell, who cared about popularity? He only smoked the rare cigar, though, he consoled himself. He didn't even really like the things anymore. They were a habit.

He stalked back into his luxurious carpeted office. Smith was scowling, peering at a bank of closed-circuit television screens.

"Boss, you'd better look at this," he said, standing straight. He was a mountain of a man, middle-aged but imposing and dangerous-looking, with a head shaved bald and green eyes that could be suddenly sparkling with amusement at the most unexpected times.

Marcus joined him, peering down. He didn't have to ask which monitor he should look at. A slight blond woman was being manhandled by a man twice her size. She was fighting, but to no effect. The man moved and Marcus saw who he was. His blood boiled.

"Want me to handle it?" Smith asked.

Marcus squared his shoulders. "I need the exercise more than you do." He moved gracefully into the private elevator and pushed the down button.

Delia Mason was fighting with all her strength, but she couldn't make her drunk companion let go of her. It was demeaning to have to admit that, because she'd studied karate for a year. But even that didn't help her much. She couldn't get away. Her green eyes were blazing, and she tried biting, but the stupid man didn't seem to feel the teeth making patterns in his hand. She hadn't wanted to come on this date in the first place. She was in the Bahamas with her sister and brother-in-law, getting over the lingering death of her mother. She was supposed to be enjoying herself. So far, the trip was a dead bust. Especially, right now.

"I do like…a girl with spirit," he panted, fumbling with the short skirt of her black dress.

"I hate a man who…won't take no for an answer!" she raged, trying to bring her knee up.

The man only laughed and forced her back against the wall of the building.

She started to scream just as his wet, horrible mouth crushed down onto hers. He was making obscene movements against her and groaning. She'd never been more powerless, more afraid, in her life. She hadn't even wanted to go out with this repulsive banker, but her rich brother-in-law had insisted that she needed a companion to accompany her out on the town. Her sister Barb hadn't liked the look of the man, either, but Barney had been so insistent that Fred Warner was a true knight. Fred was a banker. He had business at the casino anyway, he told Delia, so why not combine business and pleasure by taking Delia along? Fred had agreed a little reluctantly. He was already nervous and then he'd had one drink after another in the bar downstairs waiting for Delia, trying to bolster his courage. He mumbled something about getting into bed with a rattlesnake to keep his business going. It made no sense to Delia, who almost backed out of the date at the last minute. But Barney had been so insistent…

Delia sank her teeth into the fat lower lip of the man and enjoyed his sharp yelp of pain for a few seconds. But the pain made him angry and his hand suddenly ripped down the neckline of her dress and he slapped her.

The shock of the attack froze her. But just as she was

trying to cope with the certainty of what was about to happen, a shadow moved and Fred was spun around like a top and knocked down with a satisfying thud.

A huge man, immaculately dressed and menacing, moved forward with pantherlike grace.

"You son of a…!" the drunken man shouted, scrambling to his feet. "I'll kill you!"

"Go for it," a deep, darkly amused voice invited.

Delia moved forward before her rescuer could, and swung her purse at Fred, landing a solid blow on his jaw.

"Ouch!" Fred groaned in protest, grabbing his cheek.

"I wish it was a baseball bat, you second cousin to a skunk!" Delia spat, red-faced and furious.

"I'll loan you one," Marcus promised, admiring her ferocity.

Fred gaped at the man and his eyes flashed. "Who the hell do you think you are…!" Fred demanded drunkenly, moving forward.

Marcus planted a huge fist in his gut and sent him groaning to his knees.

"What a kind thing to do," Delia exclaimed in her broad Texas accent. She smiled at the stranger. "Thanks!"

Marcus was noticing her torn dress. His face hardened. "What are you doing here with this bargain basement Casanova?" he asked.

"My brother-in-law offered him to me as a companion," she said disgustedly. "When I tell Barb what he tried to do to me, she'll knock her husband out a window for suggesting this date!"

"Barb?"

"My big sister, Barbara Cortero. She's married to Barney Cortero. He owns hotels," she confided.

Marcus's eyebrows lifted suddenly, and he smiled. His luck had just changed.

She looked up at the big man with fascination. "I really appreciate what you did. I know a little self-defense, but I couldn't stop him. I bit a hole in his lip, but it didn't slow him down, it just made him mad, and he hit me." She rubbed her cheek and winced.

"He hit you?" Marcus asked angrily. "I didn't see that!"

"He's a real charmer," she muttered, glancing down at the drunk, who was still holding his stomach and groaning.

Marcus pulled out his cell phone and pressed in a single number. "Smith?" he said. "Come down here and take this guy back to his hotel. In one piece," he added. "We don't need any more trouble."

There was a reply. Marcus chuckled and flipped the phone shut. He looked at Delia curiously. "You're going to need to stitch that dress up," he remarked. He slid out of his dinner jacket and slid it over her shoulders. It was warm from the heat of his big body and it smelled of expensive cologne and cigar smoke.

She looked up at him with utter fascination. He was a handsome man, even with those two jagged white scars on his cheek, cutting through his olive complexion like roadmaps. He had big, deep-set brown eyes under thick eyebrows. He was built like a wrestler and he looked dangerous. Very dangerous.

"Stitches," she murmured, spellbound.

He was watching her, too, with amused curiosity. She was small, but she had the heart of a lioness. He was impressed.

The elevator opened and Smith walked out of it, powerful muscles rippling under his dark suit as he approached the small group.

"Where shall I deliver him?" he asked in his gravelly voice.

Marcus looked at Delia and lifted an eyebrow.

"We're all staying at the Colonial Bay hotel in Nassau," she stammered.

He nodded toward Smith, who put out one huge hand and brought Fred abruptly to his feet.

"Let go of me or I'll sue!" Fred threatened.

"Attempted sexual assault is a felony," Marcus said coldly.

"You can't prove that!" Fred replied haughtily.

"I've got cameras everywhere. You're on tape. The whole thing," Marcus added.

Fred blinked. He scowled and peered at the older man. Through the fog of alcohol, recognition stiffened his face. "Carrera!" he choked.

Marcus smiled. It wasn't a nice smile. "So you remember me. Imagine that. Small world, isn't it?"

Fred swallowed hard. "Yeah. Small." He straightened. "I actually came here to talk to you," he began, swaying unsteadily.

"Yeah? Well, come back when you're sober," Marcus said firmly, giving the man a look that he hoped Fred would manage to understand.

Fred seemed to sober up at once. "Uh, yeah, sure. I'll do that. Listen, this thing with the girl, it's all a…a misunderstanding," he added quickly. "I had a little too much to drink. And she just kept asking for it…"

"You liar!" she exclaimed.

"We've got tape," Marcus said again.

Fred gave up. He gave Marcus an uneasy look. "Don't hold this against me, okay? I mean, we're like family, right?"

Marcus had to bite his tongue to keep from spilling everything. "One more stunt like this, and you'll need a family—for the wake. Got me?"

Fred lost a shade of color. "Yeah. Sure. Right." He pulled away from Smith and tried to sober up. "I was just having a little fun. I was drunk or I'd never have touched her! Sorry. I'm really sorry!"

"Get him out of here," Marcus told Smith, and he turned away while the drunken man was still trying to proffer apologies and excuses. He gave Fred a long look.

"I'll…call you," Fred choked.

Marcus nodded without Delia seeing him.

He took Delia by the arm. "Come on, we'll get a needle and thread and fix your dress. You can't go home looking like that."

She was still trying to figure out what was going on. Fred seemed to know this man, even to be afraid of him. And strange messages were passing between them without words. Who was this big, dark man?

"I don't know you," she said hesitantly.

He lifted an eyebrow. "Repairs first, introductions later. You're perfectly safe."

"That's what my sister said I'd be with Fred," she pointed out, tugging his jacket closer. "Safe."

"Yeah, but I don't need to attack women in dark alleys," he stated. "It's sort of the other way around."

He was smiling. She liked his smile. She shrugged and her perfect lips tugged up. "Okay." She managed a smile of her own. "Thanks."

"Oh, I was just there to back you up," he said lazily, letting her go into the elevator in front of him. "You'd have done okay if you'd had a shotgun."

"I'm not so sure," she said. "He was inhumanly strong."

"Men on drugs or alcohol usually are."

"Really?" she asked in a faint stammer.

He gave her a worldly appraisal as the elevator carried them up to his office. "First experience with a drunk?" he asked bluntly.

"Well, not exactly," she confessed on a long sigh. "I've never had an experience like that, at least. I seem to draw drunks the way honey draws flies. I went to a party with Barb and Barney last month. A drunk man insisted on dancing with me, and then he passed out on the floor in front of God and everybody. At Barb's birthday party, a man who had too much to drink followed me around all night trying to buy me a pack of cigarettes." She looked up at him with a rueful smile. "I don't smoke."

He chuckled deeply. "It's your face. You have a sympathetic look. Men can't resist sympathy."

Her green eyes twinkled. "Is that a fact? You don't look like a man who ever needs any."

He shrugged. "I don't, usually. Here we are."

He stood aside to let her exit the elevator.

She stopped just inside the office and looked around, fascinated. The carpet was shag, champagne colored. The furniture was mahogany. The drapes matched the carpet and the furniture. There were banks of screens showing every room in the casino. There was a bar with padded stools curled around it. There were computers and phones and fax machines. It looked like a spy setup to Delia, who never missed a James Bond film.

"Wow," she said softly. "Are you a spy?"

He chuckled and shook his head. "I'd never make the grade. I don't like martinis."

"Me, either," she murmured, smiling at him.

He motioned her toward the huge bathroom. "There's a robe behind the door. Take off the dress and put on the robe. I'll get some thread and a needle."

She hesitated, her eyes wide and uncertain.

He pointed to the corner of the room. "There are cameras all over the place. I'd never get away with anything. The boss has eyes in the back of his head."

"The boss?" she queried. "Oh. You mean the man who owns the casino, right?"

He nodded, trying not to smile.

"You're a..." She almost said 'bouncer,' but this man was far too elegant to be a thug. "You're a security person?" she amended.

"Something like that," he agreed. "Go on. You've had all the hard knocks you're going to get for one night. I'm the last person who'd hurt you."

That made her feel guilty. Usually she was a trusting soul—too trusting. But it had been a hard night. "Thanks," she said.

She closed the door and slid out of the dress, leaving her in a black slip and hose with her strappy high heels. She put on the robe quickly and wondered at her complete trust in this total stranger. If he was a security guy, he must be the head guy, since he'd told the other guy, Smith, what to do. She felt oddly safe with him, for all his size and rough edges. To work in a casino, a man must have to be tough, though, she reminded herself.

She went out of the bathroom curled up in the robe that had to be five sizes too big for her. It dragged behind her like the train of a wedding gown.

Her rescuer was seated on the desk, wearing a pair of gold-rimmed reading glasses. Beside him was a sewing kit, and a spool of black thread. He was already threading a needle.

She wondered if he'd been in the military. She knew men back home who were, and most of them were handy around the house, with cooking and mending as well. She moved forward and smiled, reaching for the needle at the same time he reached for the dress.

"You sew?" she asked.

He nodded. "My brother and I both had to learn. We lost our parents early in life."

"I'm sorry." She was. Her father had died before she was born. She'd just lost her mother to stomach cancer. She knew how it felt.

"Yeah."

"I could do that," she said. "I don't mind."

"Let me. It relaxes me."

She gave in with good grace and sat down in a chair while he bent his dark head to the task. His fingers, despite being so big, were amazingly expert with the needle. And his stitches were short, even, and almost invisible. She was impressed.

She looked around the huge office curiously, and on an impulse, she got to her feet when she spotted a wall hanging.

She moved toward it curiously. It wasn't a wall hanging after all, she noted when she reached it. The pattern was familiar. The fabric was some of the newest available, and she had some of it in her cloth stash back home. Her eyes were admiring the huge beautiful quilt against one wall, hung on a rod. It was a symphony of black and white blocks. How incredible to find such a thing in the security office of a casino!

"Bow tie," she murmured softly.

His head jerked up. "What's that?" he asked.

She glanced at him with a sheepish smile. "It's a bow tie pattern, this quilt," she replied. "A very unique one. I could swear I've seen it somewhere before," she added thoughtfully. "I love the variations, and the stark contrast of the black and white blocks. The stitches are what make it so unique. There are stem stitches and chain stitches…"

"You quilt." It was a statement and not a question.

"Well, yes. I teach quilting classes, back home in Jacobsville, Texas, at the county recreation center during the summer."

He hadn't moved. "What pattern do you like best?"

"The Dresden Plate," she said, curious at his interest in what was primarily a feminine pursuit.

He put her dress down, opened a drawer in the big desk, pulled out a photo album and handed it to her, indicating that she should open it.

The photographs weren't of people. They were of quilts, scores of quilts, in everything from a four-patch to the famous Dresden Plate, with variations that were pure genius.

She sank back down in the chair with the book in her lap. "These are glorious," she exclaimed.

He chuckled. "Thanks."

Her eyes almost came out of their sockets as she gaped at him. "You made these yourself? You quilt?"

"I don't just quilt. I win competitions. National and even international competitions." He indicated the bow tie pattern on the wall. "That one won first prize last year in a national competition in this country." He named a famous quilting show on one of the home and garden channels. "I was her guest in February, and that quilt was the one I demonstrated."

She laughed, letting out a heavy breath. "This is incredible. I couldn't go to the competition, but I did see the winning quilts on the Internet. That's where I remember it from! And no wonder you looked so familiar, too. I watch that quilting show all the time. I saw you on that show!"

He cocked a thick eyebrow. "Small world," he commented.

"Isn't it just? I'm sorry, I don't remember your

name. But I do remember your face. I watched you put together a block from the bow tie quilt on that television show. Well, I'm impressed. Not that many men participate, even today."

He laughed. "We're gaining on you women," he said with a twinkle in his dark eyes. "There's a Texas Ranger and a police officer who enter competitions with me these days. We travel together sometimes to the events."

"You're good," she said, her eyes going back to the book of photos.

"I'd like to see some of your work," he remarked.

She laughed. "I'm not quite in your league," she said. "I teach, but I've never won prizes."

"What do you do when you're not teaching?"

"I run an alterations shop and work with a local dry cleaner," she said. "I do original fashions for a little boutique as well. I don't make a lot of money at it, but I love my work."

"That's more important than the amount of money you make," he said.

"That's what I always thought. One of my girlfriends married and had a child, and then discovered that she could make a lot of money with a law degree in a big city. She took the child and went to New York City, where she got rich. But she was miserable away from her husband, a rancher back home, and she had no time at all for the child. Then they filed for divorce." She shook her head. "Sometimes we're lucky, and we don't get what we think will make us happy. Anyway, I learned from watching her that I didn't want that sort of pressure, no matter how much money I could make."

"You're mature for your age. You can't be more than twenty…?" he probed.

Her eyebrows arched and she grinned. "Can't I?"

Chapter Two

"I'll bite, then," he murmured, going back to pick up her dress and finish his neat stitches. "How old are you?"

"Gentlemen are not supposed to ask ladies questions like that," she pointed out.

He chuckled, deep in his throat, his eyes on his fingers. "I've never been called a gentleman in my life. So you might as well tell me. I'm persistent."

She sighed. "I'm twenty-three."

He glanced at her with an indulgent smile. "You're still a baby."

"Really?" she asked, slightly irritated.

"I'll be thirty-eight my next birthday," he said. "And I'm older than that in a lot of ways."

She felt an odd pang of regret. He was handsome

and very attractive. Her whole young body throbbed just being near him. It was a new and unexpected reaction. Delia had never felt those wild stirrings her friends talked about. She'd been a remarkably late bloomer.

"No comment?" he queried, lifting his eyes.

"You never told me your name," she countered.

"Carrera," he said, watching her face. "Marcus Carrera." He noted her lack of recognition. "You haven't heard of me, have you?"

She hadn't, which he seemed to find amusing.

"Are you famous?" she ventured.

"Infamous," he replied. He finished the neat stitches, nipped the thread with strong white teeth and handed the dress back to her.

She took it from him, feeling suddenly cold. The minute she put the dress back on, their unexpected tête-à-tête was over. She'd probably never see him again.

"There's something about ships that pass in the night…" she murmured absently.

His jaw tautened as he looked at her, his reading glasses tossed lightly onto the top of the desk. He summed her up with his dark eyes, seeing innocence and attraction mingled with fear and nerves.

His eyes narrowed. He'd rarely been drawn to a woman so quickly, especially one like this, who was clearly from another world. Her connections were going to make her very valuable to him, but he didn't want to feel any sparks. He couldn't afford them right now.

"What's your name?" he asked quietly.

"Delia Mason," she replied.

"You're Southern," he guessed.

She smiled. "I'm from Texas, a little town called Jacobsville, between San Antonio and Victoria."

"Lived there all your life?" he probed.

She gave him a wicked grin. "Not yet."

He chuckled.

"Where are you from, originally?" she asked, clutching her dress to the front of his robe. "Not the Bahamas?"

He shook his head. "Chicago," he replied.

She sighed. "I've never been there. Actually, this is the first time I've ever been out of Texas."

He found that fascinating. "I've been everywhere."

She smiled. "It's a big world."

"Very." He studied her oval face with its big green eyes and soft, creamy complexion. Her mouth was full and sweet-looking. His eyes narrowed on it and he felt a sudden, unexpected surge of hunger.

She moved uncomfortably. "I guess I'd better get dressed." She hesitated. "Do the cabs run this late?" she added.

"They run all night, but you won't need one," he said as he closed up his sewing kit and put it away. He thought of driving her back himself. But it was unwise to start things he couldn't finish. This little violet would never fit into his thorny life. She couldn't cope, even if she'd been older and more sophisticated. The thought irritated him and his voice was harsher than he meant it to be when he added, "I'll have Smith run you back to your hotel."

The thought of a journey in company with the mysterious and dangerous Mr. Smith made her uncomfortable, but she wasn't going to argue. She was grateful to have a ride. It was a long walk over the bridge to Nassau.

"Thanks," she mumbled with suppressed disappointment, and went into the bathroom to put her dress back on.

She hung the robe up neatly and then checked her face in the mirror. Her breath sucked in as she saw the terrible bruise coming out on her cheek. She put a lot of face powder over it, but it didn't do a lot to disguise the fact that she'd been slapped.

She did the best she could and went back out into the security office. He was standing out on the balcony with his hand in his pockets, looking out to sea. He was a sophisticated man. He had a powerful figure, and she wasn't surprised that he was in security work. He was big enough to intimidate most troublemakers, even without those threatening dark eyes that could threaten more than words.

The wind caught strands of his wavy black hair and blew it around his ears. He looked alone. She felt sorry for him, although it was probably unnecessary and would be unwelcome if she confessed it. He wasn't a man to need pity, she could see that right away.

She thought of not seeing him again, and an emptiness opened up inside her. She'd just lost her mother. It was probably a bad time to get involved with a man. But there was something about this one that drew her, that made her hungry for new experiences, new feelings. She sighed heavily. She must be out of her mind. A man she'd only just met shouldn't have such an effect on her.

But, then, her recent past had been traumatic. The loss of her mother, invalid though she'd been, had been painful. It was worse because Delia's mother had never loved her. At least, not as she loved Barb; dear Barb who was beautiful and talented, and who had made an excellent marriage. Delia was only a seamstress, unattractive to men and without the live-wire personality of her much-older sister. It had been hard to live in the shadow of Barb. Delia felt like a bad copy, rather than a whole person. Her mother had been full of suggestions to improve her dull daughter. None of them had been accepted. Delia was satisfied with herself, loneliness and all. If only her mother had loved her, praised her even just once in a while. But there had been only criticism. A lifetime of it. She often wondered what she'd done to make her mother dislike her so. It really felt as if she were being punished for something. Nobody knew, least of all Barb, how difficult it had been for Delia at home. She'd done what was expected of her, always.

But when she looked at this man, this stranger, she wanted to do crazy things. She wanted to break all the rules, run away, fall off the edge of the world. She didn't understand why he should make her so reckless, when she'd always been such a conventional person. Apparently there was something to that old saying, that different people brought out different qualities in you, when you let them into your life. He must be a bad influence, because she'd never wanted to break rules before.

As if he sensed her presence—because he couldn't have heard her quiet steps above the wind as she joined him on the balcony—he turned suddenly and looked right at her.

She didn't say a word. She moved beside him and stared out over the ocean, enjoying the sound of the wind, and farther away, the subdued roar of the surf.

"You're very quiet," he remarked.

She laughed nervously. "That's me. I've spent my life fading into the background of the world."

He gave her an assessing gaze. "Maybe it's time that changed."

Her heart skipped a beat as she looked up at him in the dim light from the office. His dark eyes met hers and held them while the wind blew around them in a strange, warm embrace.

He made her think of ruins, of mysterious places in shadow and darkness, of storms and torrents of rain.

"You're staring," he pointed out huskily.

"I've never met anyone like you," she said unsteadily. "I'm just a small-town country girl. I've never been anywhere, done anything really reckless or exciting. I've never even been in a casino before in my life. But...but..." She couldn't find the right words to express what she was feeling.

His chin lifted and he moved a step closer, so that she could feel the strength and heat of his body close to her. "But you feel as if you've known me all your life," he said huskily.

Her eyelids flickered. "Well…yes…"

He reached out with one big, powerful hand and lightly brushed her cheek with his fingertips. She trembled at that whisper of sensation and shock waves ran down her slender body into her sensible stacked high heels.

"Oh, boy," he ground out.

"What's wrong?" she asked in confusion.

"And I'm old enough to know better, too," he said, obviously thinking out loud. He looked confounded, even irritated, so she wasn't really prepared when he suddenly reached for her.

His big arms lifted her up against him as his head bent. His dark eyes riveted on her soft, parted lips. "What the hell. It's midnight and you're about to lose a slipper…"

While she was trying to puzzle out the odd remark, his head bent, and his hard, warm mouth moved into total possession of her lips.

Instinctively she started to struggle, but his mouth opened and she gasped at the unexpected flood of sensation that left her trembling. But not with fear. She melted into the powerful muscles of his chest and stomach, and drowned in the clean, spicy scent of his skin. She felt the sigh of his breath against her cheek while the kiss went deeper and slower and hungrier…

In a daze of longing, she felt his arms crushing her against him while his face slid into her warm throat and he stood there in the wind, just holding her. His arms were warm against the chill of the wind coming off the ocean. She should have protested. She shouldn't be behaving this way with a total stranger, she shouldn't even be here with a man she didn't know.

But all the arguments meant nothing. She felt as if she'd just come home after a long and sad journey. She closed her eyes and let him rock her in his big arms. It was an intimacy she'd never felt in her life. Her mother had never been affectionate with her, even if Barb had. But that was in the past. Now, just the act of being held was a new experience.

Marcus was dumbfounded by what he'd done; by what she'd let him do. He knew by her response to him that she knew next to nothing about men. She didn't even know how to kiss. But she trusted him. She didn't protest, didn't fight, didn't resist. She was like a warm, cuddly kitten in his arms, and he felt sensations that he'd never experienced before.

"This was stupid," he said after a minute, the strain audible in his deep, raspy voice.

"You don't look like a stupid man to me," she said dreamily, smiling against his shoulder.

He drew in a long breath and slowly put her away. His eyes were as turbulent as hers.

"Listen," he began, his big hands resting involuntarily on her shoulders, "we come from different worlds. I don't start things I can't finish."

"Well, don't blame me," she said with dancing eyes. "I almost never seduce men on dark balconies."

He scowled. She had a quick mind and a quirky sense of humor. It didn't make things easier. She appealed to him powerfully. But he was at a point in his life when he couldn't afford attachments of any sort, especially her sort. She was more vulnerable than she might think. What he had to do might put her in the path of danger, if he kept her around. And he was in a bad place to start looking for romance.

"Ordinarily I wouldn't mind being seduced," he said. "But I'm not available."

She felt embarrassed. She stepped back, flushing. "Sorry," she stammered. "I didn't think…!"

"Don't look like that," he said harshly. He turned away from the embarrassment. "Come on. I'll have Smith drive you back."

"I could get a cab," she said, wrapping the tatters of her pride around her like an invisible cloak.

"Don't be absurd," he said, his voice curt.

Delia couldn't hide her discomfort at the thought of enduring the drive back to Nassau in the company of Mr. Smith.

"Surely you aren't afraid of him?" Marcus drawled softly. "You aren't afraid of me, and I'm worse than Smith in a lot of ways."

Her eyebrows arched. "Are you, really?" she asked in all honesty.

He chuckled in spite of himself. "You don't know anything about me," he murmured as he studied her with indulgent amusement. "That's kind of nice," he added thoughtfully. "It's been a long time since anybody was as comfortable with me as you seem to be."

"Now you're making me nervous," she told him.

He smiled. It was a rare, genuine smile. "Not very, apparently."

She moved a little closer, tingling all over as she approached him. He made her hungry. She gazed up at him. "I think I've got it figured out, anyway."

"Have you now?"

"You're Mr. Smith's boss," she said.

He pursed his lips and started to speak.

"You're a bouncer," she concluded before he could get the words out.

He was actually dumbfounded. He just stared at her with growing amazement.

"It's nothing to be ashamed of," she said firmly. "Somebody has to keep the peace in a place like this. Actually, my father was a deputy sheriff. I wasn't even born until after he died, so I don't remember him. But we still have his gun and gunbelt, and the deputy sheriff's badge he wore."

"How did he die?" he asked abstractly.

"He made a routine traffic stop," she said quietly. "The man was an escaped murderer."

"Tough."

She nodded. "Mom was left with me and Barb, although Barb was sixteen at the time, almost seventeen." She sighed. "Barb is beautiful and brainy. She married Barney, who's worth millions, and she's been deliriously happy ever since."

"So it's just you and your mother at home," he guessed.

She grimaced. "My mother died last month of stomach cancer," she said. "It's why I'm here. Barb thought I needed a break, so she and Barney squared it with my boss at the dry cleaner—I do alterations for them—and then they dragged me on a plane. I hope I still have a job when I go home. Nobody seems to understand how hard it is to get work in a small town. I have monthly bills to pay and hardly any savings, so my job is very important." She smiled ruefully. "Barb doesn't understand jobs. She married Barney just out of high school, when I was two years old, so she's never worked."

"Lucky Barb." He watched the expressions play on her delicate features. "I guess Barb helped when your mother was so sick?"

She nodded. "She paid all Mama's medical and drug bills, and even for a nurse to stay with her in the daytime while I worked. We'd never have made it without her."

"Did she do any of the nursing?"

"She came and stayed with us for the last few months of mother's life," she said quietly. "She and Barney decided that it was going to be too much for me, so they even got nurses to do the night shift. But mostly it was Barb who nursed her, until she died. Mother didn't want me with her. Barb and Mom were very close—it wasn't like that with Mother and me. She didn't like me very much," she added bluntly.

He revised his opinion of the older sister. She'd done her part.

"Are you close, you and your sister?"

She laughed. "We're closer than mother and daughter, really. Barb is terrific. It's just that she thinks I can't walk unless she's telling me how to do it. She's sixteen years older than me."

"That's a hell of an age difference," he pointed out.

"Tell me about it. Barb's so much older that I must seem more like a child than an adult to her."

He scowled. "How old was your mother when you were born?"

"Forty-eight," she laughed. "She said I was a miracle baby."

"Mmmm," he said absently.

"How old was your mother when you were born?" she asked curiously.

He chuckled. "Sixteen. In the old days, and in the old country," he drawled, bending closer, "women married young. She and my father were betrothed by their families. They only saw each other in company of a *dueña,* and they were married in the church. The first time they kissed each other was on their wedding day, or so my father always said."

She looked puzzled at the Spanish word he'd used for chaperone. "I thought you were Italian," she blurted out.

He shook his head. "My parents were from the south of Spain. I'm a first-generation American."

"Do you speak Spanish?"

He nodded. "But I read it better than I speak it. My parents wanted me and my brother to speak English well, so that we'd fit in better than they did."

She smiled, understanding. She moved slowly back into the office and he followed, closing the sliding door onto the balcony.

"I'll ride with you to your hotel," he said after a minute. He picked up the phone and told someone to take over for him while he drove into Nassau and back.

She took one last look at the beautiful black and white quilt in its frame on the wall. "That really is majestic," she remarked.

"Thanks. I'd love to see some of your work."

She grimaced. "I don't even have photos of it, like you do," she said. "Sorry."

"I may get down to Texas one of these days," he said offhandedly.

She smiled. "That would be nice."

He glanced back at her. "It might not be, when you know more about me," he said, and he was suddenly very solemn.

"That isn't likely."

"You're an optimist. I'm not."

"Yes, I noticed," she teased.

He chuckled as he opened the door to let her out into the hall.

Mr. Smith was waiting beside a huge black super stretch limousine in front of the hotel and nightclub.

Delia actually gasped. "You can't mean to drive me back in that!" she exclaimed. "Your boss will fire you!"

"Unlikely," Marcus said, with a speaking glance at Smith, who was trying not to laugh out loud. "Get in."

She whistled softly as she slid onto the leather seat and moved to the center, to give him room to get in.

Smith closed the back door and went to the driver's seat.

Delia was stagestruck. She looked around wide-eyed, fascinated by the luxurious interior. "You could go bowling in here!"

"It's nice when you're ferrying around a crowd of tourists," he stated. "Want something to drink?"

He indicated the bar, where a bottle of champagne and several bottles of beer and soft drinks were chilling in ice.

She shook her head. "No, thanks. Is that television?!" she added, indicating a flat screen just in front of her near the ceiling.

"Satellite television, satellite radio, CD player, phone…"

"It's incredible," she said softly. "Just incredible!"

"Your sister's married to a millionaire," he pointed out. "Don't you get to ride in limos?"

She shook her head. "There wouldn't be any need for her to drive down to Jacobsville in one. They fly to San Antonio and rent a car. At home, they've got a Jaguar sports car."

"I thought you might visit her and ride in limos," he teased.

"In New York?" she asked. She shook her head. "We'd usually go down to Galveston together for vacation on the beach. I've never been to New York, and since Barney travels so much and Barb goes with him, they're rarely home. I don't even go up to San Antonio unless I have to, when I buy supplies. I'm very much at home in the little house I shared with Mama. We have a handful of chickens and a dog named Sam."

"Who's looking after them?"

"A neighbor," she said. "Although, Sam's being boarded. He's bad to get in the road. You have to watch him constantly."

"What breed is he?"

She smiled. "He's a German shepherd—black with brown markings. I've had him for eight years. He's a sweetie."

"Any cats?"

She shook her head. "Mama was allergic. We couldn't even have Sam in the house."

Smith was pulling out into the main road that led over the bridge to Nassau. Marcus leaned back against the soft leather of the seat. "I've never seen a chicken close up, except on television," he remarked.

She grinned. "Come to Texas and I'll let you pet one."

"You can pet a chicken?"

"Of course you can," she said, laughing.

He liked the sound of her laughter. It had been a long time since he'd done much of that. His life was lonely and dangerous, and he had a natural suspicion of people. He'd seen women who looked like virginal innocents roll a man and take everything he had.

"Why were you at the club in the first place?" he asked unexpectedly.

She sighed. "Because Fred said he wanted to talk some business with the manager of the casino and we might as well go there as anyplace else on the island. But he got cold feet and started drinking." She was oblivious to the look on Marcus's leonine face. "He's mixed up in something illegal, I think, and there are some people he's dealing with who want to hurt him." She bit her lip as she looked up at Marcus. "I probably shouldn't have mentioned that. The owner of the casino's your boss, right?"

"Sort of," he confessed.

"Well, Fred kept throwing back hard liquor until he could hardly stand up. I wanted to go back to my hotel by then, because he was getting really out of hand. I had to fend him off in the taxi, and when we got to the club, I was going to go inside and call a taxi to take me back. But Fred got angry when I said that, and reminded me that he'd bought me an expensive dinner. He said I owed him a little fun," she added coldly. She grasped her purse tight in her hands and glanced at Marcus. "I guess I've led a pretty sheltered life until now. Do men really expect a woman to have sex with them just because they buy her a meal? Because if that's the way of it, I'm buying my own dinners from now on!"

Her expression amused him. He laughed softly. "Well, I can only speak for myself, but I've never considered a steak currency for sex."

She smiled in spite of her irritation. "It shows that I don't date much, huh?" she said matter-of-factly. "Even after I was in high school, I had to fight Barb and mother to get to go out with a man. Mother would call Barb if anyone asked me on a date. They said men were devious and they'd say all sorts of things to get you into bed with them, and then they'd leave you pregnant and desert you." She shook her head. "God knows where they got those ideas. Barb married Barney just after high school graduation, and Mother didn't go out with anybody at all after Daddy died."

"She didn't?" he asked abruptly, surprised.

"She was sort of old-fashioned, I guess. She said she

and Daddy were so happy together that any other man she dated would fall short of that perfection. So she spent her time doing charity work and raising me."

"I didn't think there were any women like that left in the world," he said honestly.

"What was your mother like?"

He smiled slowly. "She was the kind of woman who kissed cuts and bruises and made homemade cookies for her kids. She worked herself half to death to give us the things we had to have for school," he added, his face taut.

"Was she pretty?"

"What a question. Why?"

"Well, you're very good-looking," she said, and then flushed as she realized she might be overstepping boundaries.

He chuckled. "Thanks. I think you look pretty good, too."

"Oh, I'm plain," she replied. "I don't have any illusions about being beautiful. But I can cook, and I'm a fair seamstress."

He reached out and touched a loose strand of her blond hair, contemplating the high coiffure she wore it in. "How long is your hair?" he asked suddenly.

"It's to my waist in back," she said self-consciously. "My boss at the dry cleaner where I do alterations says I look like Alice in Wonderland with it down, so I keep it in a bun or a ponytail most of the time."

"You don't cut it, then?"

She shook her head. "I look terrible with short hair," she said. "Like a boy."

Both thick eyebrows went up. "Excuse me?"

She shifted on the seat. "I'm rather bosom-chal-lenged."

He burst out laughing.

She was really blushing, now. "I can't think of a better way to put it," she confessed. "But it's the truth."

His dark eyes were kind and indulgent. "Men have individual tastes in women," he said. "I come from a background where women have ample curves. They say it's what we're not used to that attracts us, and that's how it is with me."

She stared at him, uncomprehending.

"I don't like women with ample...bosoms," he explained.

She just looked at him, her eyes wide and hopeful. "You...don't?"

He shook his head. "And I've never met a woman who kept chickens until now, much less one who knew a Bow Tie pattern from a Dresden Plate."

She smiled. "I've never met a bouncer who could quilt before," she replied.

He chuckled. Let her keep her illusions. He'd never said what he did for a living on that quilt show he was on, or even in the competitions. He just said he was a Chicago businessman. He was enjoying this ano-nymity. It was rare for anyone not to recognize at least his name, if not his face.

"Would you like to see Blackbeard's Tower?"

Her lips parted. "Blackbeard, the pirate?" she asked.

"The very one." He leaned toward her conspiratori-ally. "He's not there."

She laughed. "That's all right, I'd rather see it without his ghost," She twisted her purse in her hands. "When?" she asked, without looking at him.

He hesitated. He had a meeting that he didn't really want to attend. Of course, he'd have to go. "I've got a lunch appointment. How about somewhere between one and two o'clock tomorrow?"

Her wide eyes lifted to his, radiant and happy. "I'd like that," she said huskily.

"I'll call for you in the lobby."

She smiled. "Okay!"

He hesitated. "You may hear some things about me when Fred tells your sister what happened," he told her. "Try not to believe them. Or at least, wait and make up your own mind when you get to know me a little better. Okay?"

She was curious, but she smiled. "Okay."

"One more thing," he added, when Smith was pulling up into the circular driveway that led to the hotel entrance. "If Fred calls you a liar and says it didn't happen—and he might—you tell your sister and brother-in-law that I've got a tape of it and they're welcome to look at it any time they like. It would stand in any court of law."

"You think I should have Fred arrested?" she exclaimed.

He was torn between what was right and what he was bound to do. He couldn't afford to have Fred in jail right now. "No," he lied. "But you shouldn't go out alone with him again."

"I don't plan to," she assured him.

Smith was opening the door. Tourists standing inside the glass doors were gaping at the huge black limousine.

"They probably think we're rock stars," she said with twinkling light eyes.

"Let them think what they like. You're sure you're okay?" he added.

She nodded. Her eyes caressed his broad face. "Thanks. For everything."

He shrugged. "You're welcome. I'll see you tomorrow."

"Between one and two, in the lobby," she agreed.

Smith held out a hand and helped her out on the passenger side of the huge vehicle. He grinned at her.

She flushed, because she was still nervous of him, and it showed.

"Well, good night," she said to Marcus.

He smiled. "Good night, angel."

She walked on clouds all the way into the hotel, past staring tourists, and straight into the elevator.

Barb was beside herself when Delia used the key to let herself into the suite.

Her blond hair was mussed from her busy, beautifully manicured fingers. "Baby, where have you been?" she exclaimed, rushing forward to hug Delia half to death. "Oh, I've been so worried! Fred came back with this wild tale about your being kidnapped by some gangster…!"

"Fred tried to assault me outside the casino in a dark corner," Delia said angrily, and she pointed to her cheek. "When I wouldn't cooperate, he slapped me!"

Barb gasped.

Barney, her husband, came into the room in an evening jacket. His balding head shone in the overhead light and his dark eyes narrowed. "So you're finally back! Fred was worried sick…"

"Fred assaulted me," Delia began again.

"Now, baby, you know that's not true," Barney said, his voice softening. "Fred told me you got a little upset because he was just slightly tipsy…"

"Look at my cheek!" she raged. "I wouldn't let him have sex with me, so he slapped me, as hard as he could!"

Barney hesitated, and his dark eyes began to glitter. "Fred said the owner of the casino gave you that bruise," Barney said, but with less confidence and growing anger.

"There's a videotape of the entire incident," she said curtly. "And the head of security for the hotel says you're welcome to see it. Both of you. Anytime you like!"

Chapter Three

There was a stunned silence. Barb's breathing was audible as she looked from her husband to her sister.

"I think Fred's lying," Barb said finally.

Barney stared at her. "Fred said she didn't do a thing for him, and he's used to real lookers. I'm sorry, baby," he told Delia, "but that's the truth. It doesn't make sense that Fred would be that out of line with a woman who didn't appeal to him."

"A bowl of gelatin would have appealed to him at the time, Barney," Delia said in her own defense. "He was stewed to the gills."

"I'll talk to Marcus Carrera," Barney said curtly. "He'll tell the truth. He may be a pirate, but he's an honest pirate."

"You know the head of security at the casino?" Delia asked.

"Honey, I don't know what *you've* been drinking," Barney said dryly, "but Carrera is the owner of the Bow Tie. The closest he comes to security is when he turns Smith loose on somebody who's tried to cheat him. They say he used to do his own dirty work in the old days in Chicago. Maybe he still does."

"Mr....Carrera owns the casino," Delia parroted.

"He owns lots of stuff," Barney replied casually. "Hotels and casinos, mostly, in the Caribbean and one off the coast of New Jersey. The Bow Tie's his newest one. He's been down here for a while. Since the oil drum incident, anyway."

Delia sat down, hard. She was feeling sick. "What oil drum incident?"

Barney chuckled. "This really bad character did something nearly fatal to one of Carrera's friends. They found him floating down the Chicago River in an oil drum. Well, most of him," he amended. "There are still a few parts missing."

"Parts?" Delia exclaimed.

"Now, now, baby, nobody said Carrera did it by himself. He's always had people around him who would do what they wanted him to," he continued. "But he's got a reputation that scares even bad people. Nobody ever crosses him unless they've got a death wish."

"That isn't what that Dunagan man said," Barb reminded her husband.

He frowned at her. "Dunagan was just passing on gossip," he said with deliberate firmness.

"Well, there is some gossip about that Miami

gangster—what's his name, Deluca?—who's trying to set up his own operation down here on Paradise Island. They say he's got his hand into all sorts of illegal gambling in Florida and now he wants to take over a casino or two in the Bahamas."

"He got caught for running an illegal betting operation," Barney replied. "He opened a couple of shops so people could bet on greyhound and horse racing. But he reneged on the payoffs or lied about the bets that were placed. He did three years. Had a really good lawyer," he added with a grin.

Barb gave him a cold look. "He's a crook."

"Sure he is," Barney agreed. "But he's got a lot of muscle, and that beautiful daughter who travels around with him. They say he uses her to set up men. But she's got the personality of a spitting cobra."

"How exactly did you get home, baby?" Barb asked suddenly.

"The head of security drove me over in a big black stretch limousine," Delia said with a big smile. "It was incredible!"

"I forgot you'd never been in one," Barney said, sighing. "I wanted to bring you up to stay with us in New York and show you the town. But your…mother wouldn't hear of it," he added curtly. "She hated my guts. She said she didn't want you around me."

"But, why?" Delia asked, appalled. Nobody had ever told her that.

Barb gave Barney a warning glance. "Mother was jealous of Barney because he took me away from her," she said. "They never got along, you know that."

"Yes," Delia admitted, "but that doesn't explain why she didn't want me to go to New York."

Barney turned away, looking uncomfortable. "She thought you might like it there and want to stay."

"She didn't want to lose you, baby," Barb said, but she didn't sound very comfortable herself.

"But she never liked me," Delia exclaimed.

"What?" Barb asked sharply.

Delia had never admitted that to them. She hated doing it now, but perhaps it was time to get it out in the open.

"She didn't like me," she confided miserably. "Nothing I did was ever right. She didn't like my hair long, but she liked it less if I had it cut. She didn't like the clothes I wore, they were too dowdy. She ridiculed the ones I designed and made myself. She said I was lazy and shiftless and that I'd never amount to anything…"

"Baby, you can't be serious!" Barb exclaimed, horrified.

"I never understood why," Delia said heavily, sitting down. "It was almost as if she hated me, but when I asked her if she did, she got all flustered and said of course she didn't, that it wasn't my fault that I was the way I was."

Barb and Barney exchanged curious glances. They not only looked shocked, they looked guilty. Delia wondered why.

"Baby, why didn't you ever tell me this?" Barb asked gently, her green eyes soft and loving.

Delia grimaced. "It wouldn't have been right, for me to talk like that about my own mother. And what could you have done, anyway? You and Barney had your own lives."

"She never said why she made it so hard on you?" Barney asked.

Delia glanced at him and thought, not for the first time, how strange it was that his face and hers were remarkably similar, from the small ears to the rounded chin and the very shape of his eyes. She'd even asked Barb once if he was kin to them, because of the resemblance. But Barb had laughed and said of course not.

Not that she didn't look like Barb, too, with the same green eyes and blond hair. Their mother had dark hair and blue eyes. But, then, Delia knew that she and Barb were throwbacks to their paternal grandmother, because Delia's mother had said so.

"I'm sorry," Barb said, moving to hug her sister close. She'd always been affectionate like that, since Delia's earliest memories. Barb hugged her coming and going, praised her, teased her, sent her presents on every holiday and birthday and all the time in between. Delia had never wanted for anything, especially not love. In fact, until three years ago, Barney and Barb had lived in San Antonio. They were always around. But when they were, Delia's mother was on her best behavior. She loved Barb best, and it showed. She was sharp with Delia, though, and Barb had occasionally remarked on it. She didn't realize how harsh their mother could be, when she wasn't there.

"Maybe I could come to New York and visit one day," Delia mentioned.

Barb's face lit up. "That would be great! We could take you to all the touristy places and you and I could go shopping together!"

Delia smiled. "I'd like that."

"We still haven't finished talking about Fred," Barney interrupted.

"She's not going out with him again," Barb said firmly, with an arm around her sister.

"I wasn't going to suggest that," Barney said gently. "But I need to have a talk with him about his behavior tonight," he added, dark eyes flashing. "He had no right to manhandle her!"

"I agree wholeheartedly," Barb said. "At least you got home safely."

"Yeah, and Carrera didn't send Fred home in a shoebox, either, apparently," Barney murmured.

"You said Mr. Carrera doesn't kill people," Delia reminded him. She couldn't believe that he did. She didn't want to believe it.

"He's calmed down a bit," Barney replied. He poured himself a drink. "He hasn't bumped anybody off recently, at least. He's keeping a low profile. I expect that's why he's down here in the Bahamas. Laying low."

"You look sick, baby," Barb said worriedly. She sat down beside Delia and patted her knee. "You've had a bad night. Why don't you go to bed and get some sleep?"

"I think I'll do that," Delia said.

"Did you actually talk to Carrera?" Barney asked curiously.

Delia nodded, her throat was too tight for speech.

Barney chuckled. "That's one for the books. He never mingles with the customers. I guess he was afraid you might sue him, if Fred's lying. He wouldn't like the publicity."

"I thought you believed Fred," Barb said curtly.

He shrugged. "If Carrera got involved, it's no wonder Fred's trying to smooth things over. Nobody wants to cross him. Least of all Fred. He's been working out a business proposition he wants to involve Carrera in. I don't know what sort, but Fred does have a genius for making money." He sipped his drink, frowning. "I might try to get in on it myself," he added with a glance at Barb.

"You stay out of business with Carrera," Barb said flatly. "I like you alive, warts and all."

"Did Smith bring you back to the hotel?" Barney asked Delia.

"He and Mr. Carrera did."

There were shocked stares.

"Fred tore my dress and Mr. Carrera sewed it up for me," she faltered.

Barney finished the drink in one swallow.

"That's right, he quilts," Barb said, brightening. "Delia teaches quilting. You told him, right?"

Delia nodded.

"No wonder he was nice to you," Barney agreed. "He's a sucker for a fellow quilter. We heard he gave a guy a week's paid vacation in one of his hotels for two yards of old cloth."

"Antique fabric is very valuable," Delia said softly, "and extremely hard to get."

"They say he keeps an album of his quilts," Barney chuckled.

"He does. I saw it. He's won international competitions," Delia replied. "His needlework is marvelous." She showed the mend to Barb, who couldn't find the stitches.

"That's really something," Barb had to admit.

"If he ever shoots me, I'll ask him to sew me a quilted shroud," Barney quipped.

Barb stared at him. "Why would he want to shoot you?"

Barney looked uncomfortable. Then he shrugged. "No reason right now. I had thought about suggesting we all take in a show at the casino. We might get special treatment now, what with him sewing up Delia."

Barb glowered at her husband. "We're not putting her in his path again. I do not want my baby sister running around with a criminal!"

"He's not a criminal. Not exactly," Barney said. "He's a nice guy as long as you don't try to steal from him or threaten anybody close to him."

"I don't want to find out," Barb said firmly. She turned to Delia. "You stay away from that man. I don't care how nicely he sews, either."

Delia wanted to tell them that Marcus had asked her out the next day, but she didn't quite have the courage. It was hard to stand up to Barb, who was mature and brimming with authority. Delia had never refused to do anything Barb asked.

But she remembered the hungry kiss she'd shared with Marcus on the windswept balcony, the feel of his arms around her, the warm strength of him in the cool evening. She tingled all over with memory. She wanted to be with him.

The only thing that bothered her was his reputation. What if he really did kill people...?

Barb was studying her expression. "Dee, did you hear me?" she asked. "I said, I don't want you going around with a gangster."

"I heard, Barb," Delia replied.

"He's loaded, you know," Barney interrupted. "They say he's worth millions."

"It's how he got it that bothers me," Barb replied.

"There are worse crooks heading up corporations all over the world," Barney said carelessly. "He's certainly got the midas touch when it comes to business. At least he's honest, and he never makes idle threats. He loves senior citizens."

"So does the Japanese mafia, the Yakuza," Barb shot back.

Barney threw up his hands. "Everything's black and white with you."

"I'll go to bed and let you two finish your argument in private," Delia offered.

"You do that, baby," Barb said gently. "I'm glad you're okay. Imagine, riding around Nassau in the company of a killer!"

"They never proved that he killed anybody," Barney argued.

"They never proved he didn't!"

Delia slipped out of the sitting room and closed the door on the loud voices. She got ready for bed in a daze. She couldn't believe what Barney said about Marcus. Surely she'd have sensed evil if it was in him. He'd been kind, and comforting. He'd even been affectionate. He was attracted to her, as she was to him. Was it so wrong to spend time with him?

She worried about what Barb would say. And then she thought, I'm a grown woman. I have to make my own decisions about people.

She remembered suddenly what Marcus had said to her, about not believing what she might hear about him; about waiting until she knew him better to make that sort of judgment.

It was going to be too much temptation anyway, to turn away from him now. She was already hooked. She couldn't stop thinking about him. She was going to go to Blackbeard's Tower with him, even if she had to do it covertly.

She remembered that he'd said he'd meet her in the lobby, and she began to worry. It was a long shot, but what if Barb and Barney happened to be in the lobby at the same time?

The thought kept her awake late into the night.

She dreamed about the hot kiss they'd shared on his balcony as well. She'd always been a sensible, practical sort of person. But when Marcus Carrera touched her, she lost her head completely and became someone else. She'd never understood why women gave up their principles and slept with men before they were married. But it was becoming clear that sometimes physical attraction overran caution. Her body throbbing, she felt stirrings that she'd never experienced in her life. She could barely stand to have the sheet touch her body, she was so feverish with just the memories. Marcus's body close to hers, his big hands flat on her back, his mouth biting into hers hungrily. She actually moaned. It was dangerous for her to see him again, because she wanted him with a blind, mindless passion. She knew already that she couldn't resist him if he put on the heat. And he might be as helpless to stop it as she already was.

She was very curious about sex. Her mother had been reticent and reluctant to even talk about it, just like Barb. But Delia had friends who indulged, and they told her the most shocking things about men and women in bed together. She thought of Marcus that way and her body ached for him.

She knew that if he asked her out, she'd go with him as often as he liked. She'd lived in a cocoon all her life, without refusing to do whatever she was told. But she was twenty-three now, and already falling in love with that big, dark man from the casino. For once, she was going to do what pleased her, and she'd live with whatever consequences there were. She wasn't going to spend the rest of her life alone without even one sweet memory to cherish in her old age. And if she had to go against Barb to do that, she was willing. It was, after all, her life.

When Delia woke, she felt as if she hadn't slept at all. She couldn't believe that Marcus was a killer, no matter what anyone said. He had been tender with her, generous, kind. Surely a gangster wouldn't have been so accommodating to a perfect stranger.

But what did she know about gangsters? She was a small-town girl with no knowledge of people with mob connections, except by gossip. There had been some excitement in Jacobsville, Texas, over the past few years. A drug lord had decided to build a distribution center there, and a group of local mercenaries had stopped him. A local girl had been kidnapped in revenge and taken to the drug lord's home in Mexico, and her stepbrother had rescued her. There had even been a shooting when Christabel Gaines and her guardian Judd Dunn had run afoul of a murderer; Christabel had been shot by one of the notorious Clark brothers, who had killed a young woman up around Victoria. Clark was now serving a life sentence without hope of parole.

But other than those episodes, Jacobsville was mostly a quiet place to live. Delia lived in a cocoon of kind people and rustic charm. She was unsophisticated, not really pretty, and rather shy.

So, why, she wondered, would a rich, worldly man like Marcus Carrera even want to take her sightseeing. If he was as rich as Barney said he was, surely he could get any sort of women he liked—beautiful women, talented women, famous women. Why would he want to take Delia out? Maybe he was desperate for company? She laughed at that thought. But then she remembered the torrid kiss they'd shared, and her heart raced. Perhaps he felt the same way she did. It didn't have a lot to do with looks, social position or wealth. Nobody could explain physical attraction, after all.

That fiery passion was unsettling to a woman who'd never felt it in her life. She couldn't even consider an affair, she told herself. And he didn't seem to be a

marrying man. Surely if he'd wanted to marry, he'd
have done it, at his age.

There was another consideration—if she was going
to go against her own best instincts and go out with
him, she'd have to lie to Barb. She'd never done that
in her life. Barb had loved her, sacrificed for her, taken
care of her even more than her own mother had. In all
honesty, she loved Barb more than she'd loved her
poor mother. But the alternative was to forget Marcus
and stand him up. Her heart ached at just the thought
of not seeing him again. This sudden hunger to be
with him, to hold him, to kiss him was overpowering.
She couldn't bear to stand him up. Even after only a
brief meeting, her eyes ached for the sight of him.

She told herself that she was an idiot. But she was
going to meet him, no matter what the consequences.
She couldn't help herself.

In the end, her fears of Barb seeing her with him in
the lobby evaporated when Barney had an emergency
call about his business back home. His headquarters
was in New York, but he was opening a new hotel in
Miami, and there were major problems with the contractor who was building it. The man had walked off
the job, with his entire crew, after an argument with one
of Barney's vice presidents. Barney was going to have
to fly there and solve the problem. Barb, who was in
charge of the interior design for the building, would
necessarily have to go as well, since the contractor had
been authorized to supply the materials she required.

"I hate leaving you here alone, baby," Barb said

worriedly. "Would you like to fly down to Miami with us while we sort this out?"

Delia thought fast. "I think I'd rather stay here, if you don't mind," she said. "I really wanted to get in some sunbathing on the beach."

"Are you sure you'll be okay?" Barb persisted.

"She's a grown woman, for God's sake. You're only her sister, not her mama," Barney said furiously.

Barb flushed. "Well, I worry!" she defended. "What about Fred?" she added.

"Fred's gone to Miami, too, for the week," Barney muttered, searching for his wallet. "I didn't know he had business interests there," he said with an odd smile.

"There!" Delia said, relieved. "That solves the problem."

Barb was frowning. "You aren't going off with Carrera anywhere, are you?" she asked suspiciously.

Delia managed to look dumbfounded. "Chance would be a fine thing!" she exclaimed. "I mean, look at me," she added, spreading her arms wide. "Tell me why a man that rich would look twice at a plain, nobody of a seamstress from a little town in Texas?"

"You are not plain!" Barb argued. "The right clothes and makeup and you'd be a knockout. In fact, we just outfitted you, didn't we, and you have yet to wear a single thing I bought you!"

"I will. I promise," Delia said in a conciliatory tone.

Barb sighed. "No, you won't. You spend your life in sweats and old shirts. In fact, you didn't even have any shirts without pictures or writing on them until I brought you down here and took you shopping."

"I'll wear the new clothes," Delia promised, and she meant it. Marcus might like her in something pretty.

"We need to talk about this," Barb continued.

"But not right now," Barney said impatiently, looking at his Rolex. "We have to go right now or we'll miss our flight."

"All right," Barb said reluctantly. She hugged Delia. "You keep this door locked while we're gone," she began. Barney was opening the door and motioning to her. "Don't open it unless you know who's outside!"

"Yes, Barb," Delia said automatically.

"And do not go out at night alone…" Barb continued.

Barney had her by the arm and was dragging her toward the door. She laughed. "Don't take candy from strangers!" she called merrily. "Don't go too near the ocean, and don't pet stray dogs!"

"I won't, I promise," Delia chuckled.

"I love you!"

The door closed on the last word.

"I love you, too!" Delia called after her.

There was a skirl of laughter and then, silence.

Delia tried on three of the new outfits Barb had bought for her before she settled on a simple white peasant blouse with a lace-edged white cotton skirt and a wide magenta cotton wrap belt. She'd found the outfit in one of the local stores and the saleslady, an elegant tall woman, had showed her how to wrap the belt around her waist several times and tuck it in. The result was very chic, especially with Delia's small waist.

She was vibrating with nervous energy and indecision about her choice when the phone rang and made her jump. She ran to answer it.

"Yes?" she said at once.

There was a deep chuckle, as if he knew she'd been sitting on hot coals waiting for him and was pleased by it. "I'm in the lobby," he said.

"I'll be right down."

She hung up and darted to the door, only then realizing that she was barefoot and had forgotten both her purse and the room key. With a rueful laugh at her own forgetfulness, she ran back to get her shoes and purse and key.

Eight breathless minutes later, she arrived in the luxurious lobby, having spent five minutes waiting for the elevator.

She stepped out into the lobby and looked around worriedly for Marcus. And there he was, lounging against the wall opposite the bank of elevators, lazily elegant and smiling.

He was wearing a green knit shirt with brown slacks. He looked big and expensive and sexy.

He was looking, too, his dark eyes intent on her trim figure and especially her wealth of long, wavy blond hair that she'd left cascading down to her waist in back.

He smiled then, warmly, and she went straight to him, almost colliding with another hotel guest she didn't even see, causing amused glances from passersby.

"Hi," she said huskily.

"Hi," he returned, his voice deep and soft. "Ready to go?"

She thought about the risks she was taking, the danger she could be in, the anger and betrayal that Barb was going to feel. But nothing mattered except that look in his dark eyes. She threw caution and reason to the winds.

"I'm ready," she said.

Chapter Four

Marcus could hardly believe this was the same shy, conservative woman he'd met only the night before. She looked exciting in that lacy white thing, with her long hair down. He'd had second thoughts about involving her in his life when it was in flux, but in the end, he hadn't had a choice. It had been pure luck that Fred had chosen to bring her along to the meeting they didn't get to have. She was Barney's sister-in-law and that gave him a connection to a badly needed contact. He could pass a message along in a very innocent way, through a woman he could pretend to be interested in. The fly in the ointment was Barbara, Delia's sister, who was not going to approve of her baby sister dating a gangster.

It was amazing, that of all the women he'd known—

and there had been some beautiful ones—he honestly was interested in her. It wasn't like him to be attracted to a small-town girl like Delia. She wasn't his style at all. Then, too, there was the question of his past. She thought he was a security guard. She had no idea who, or what, he really was. It wasn't fair to her to let her believe a lie. But he didn't dare tell her the truth. She didn't seem the sort of woman to be comfortable spending time with a gangster, even if he was reformed. And he needed her to spend time with him. For a few weeks, at least.

He reached out slowly and caught her cold, nervous fingers in his, linking them together. It was like touching a live wire. Her hand jerked in his, as if she, too, felt the electricity. Her breath caught audibly. She winced when she realized that he knew exactly what she was feeling.

"Don't look like that," he said in a deep, velvet tone, moving closer. "I feel it, too."

"I haven't slept," she choked, lost in his eyes.

"Neither have I," he replied curtly. He studied her perfect complexion, the faint flush on her cheeks a dead giveaway of her turmoil. "Where's your sister?"

"On her way to Miami with Barney. Some sort of crisis. And Fred's gone there, too," she added breathlessly.

"To Miami?" He looked thoughtful.

"So Barney said. God knows why, Barney says he's got no business interests there."

"None that Barney knows about, maybe," Marcus mused. He seemed distant for a moment. Then he blinked and smiled down at Delia. "I've got a big day planned for us. Let's go."

"Okay," she said softly.

He didn't ask any questions and she didn't tell him about Barb's warning about him. She was going to pretend that there were no complications. She was going to pretend she didn't know who he was, too. This was one day she was simply going to enjoy. It might be the only one she had with him. She wasn't going to waste it in worry.

They walked out the front door holding hands, but Mr. Smith and the limo were nowhere in sight. A cab was waiting at the entrance instead.

"I didn't want to raise eyebrows, in case your sister had told you something about me," he murmured.

"What would she have told me about you?" she wondered, pretending innocence.

His expression was priceless. He looked relieved. "What did you tell her?"

"That Fred assaulted me and the head of security at the hotel brought me home," she said simply.

"Not my name?" he persisted.

She grimaced. "I didn't think of it until it was too late…"

"Don't think of it," he said tersely. "I'll explain later."

He put her into the back of the cab and climbed in beside her. "Take us back to the Bow Tie, John," he told the driver.

"Yes, sir," the man said with a big grin. "You going around in disguise, huh, Mr. Carrera?"

"Big disguise, and you get a bonus for forgetting it."

"I'm your man."

"You can take her home tonight, as well," he told Harry. "For another bonus."

"I don't know who you are, Mr. Carrera," he said blithely. "Never met you in my life."

Carrera chuckled. "That's the spirit."

"What sort of disguise does he mean?" Delia asked wryly.

"Never mind," he replied. "I thought we'd have lunch before we go out."

"Lovely!" she said.

He felt guilty for a minute about the game he was playing. He didn't want to hurt her, but she gave him a connection he needed very badly. Apart from that, she appealed to him physically in a forbidden way. She was a sweet kid and he was going to spoil her a little, so she wouldn't lose by the association with him. She didn't ever need to know who he really was, and he didn't plan to tell her. Not until he had to, anyway.

They passed over the bridge to Paradise Island, and in daylight she was able to see the incredible assortment of boats moored at the big marina. There were sailboats and motorboats and ferry boats, carrying people from Nassau to Paradise Island on the water instead of the road.

"Just look at all the boats!" she exclaimed, looking out the cab's window. "There's one with black sails!"

"He must be a pirate then, huh?" he teased, following her gaze.

She turned her head and looked straight into his eyes. She felt him, strong and warm at her back, and her whole body tensed with hunger.

He saw that, enjoyed it, savored it. She couldn't hide anything from him. That was pleasurable, like the touch of her shoulder against his chest. His eyes darkened and he moved back abruptly. This wasn't the place, he told himself, even if he was crazy enough to make a move on her. He had to try to remember what was at stake right now. He had to keep his mind on business, not on Delia.

The casino looked different in daylight, she thought as they got out of the cab. While Marcus was paying the fare, Delia walked over to a bank of hibiscus and touched the red blossoms with a delicate hand. She loved flowers. She had a huge garden at home, full of every sort of blooming plant. But she didn't have hibiscus. They weren't comfortable in her part of Texas through the winter.

"Do you like them?" Marcus asked.

She nodded. "I can't grow them at home. The winters are too cold."

"I thought Texas was hot."

She chuckled. "It is, in the summer. But we actually have snow sometimes in Jacobsville in the winter, and it gets down to freezing. Tropical plants can only be grown in a greenhouse, and I can't afford one."

He reached down and picked one of the flowers, tucking it behind her ear. He smiled. "It suits you."

She laughed self-consciously. "I'm not pretty, but you make me feel like I am. That sounds silly, I guess."

He shook his head. He was searching her green eyes quietly, intently. She blushed, and he smiled. It amused him that she found him attractive, that she reacted to him so hungrily.

She was twenty-three. He was certain that she had some experience, at that age. He was curious to see how much. But he couldn't rush his fences. She was going to fit nicely into the scheme of things. He had to keep her around.

He took her hand in his again. "Let's go. I want to show you around my house."

"You don't live in the hotel?" she asked.

"The boss keeps a penthouse apartment there," he said evasively. "But I like my own space."

He led her around the grounds of the hotel to a wrought-iron gate in a white stucco fence. He unlocked it and ushered her in.

There was a huge expanse of grass and flowering shrubs and trees. Beyond it, just on the spotless beach, was a sprawling white adobe house with graceful arches and a red tiled roof.

"Wow," she said as they approached it. The porch had white wicker furniture, and there were pots of flowers everywhere, hanging from the eaves of the house, sitting on the ceramic tile of the wide, long porch.

"Do you like it?" he asked, smiling. "I thought you might. I love flowers, too. I planted most of these as seed. A couple of the shrubs were imported. The hibiscus and oleander were already here, but I planted a few more. There's a greenhouse, too, where I raise orchids. You can't see the driveway from here, but it's lined with royal palms."

"Those are the ones with the white trunks, aren't they?"

"Yes."

"Are those casuarina pines?" she added, nodding toward the trees lining the yard, near the beach. They looked like white pines, but with long fronds that waved gracefully in the breeze.

"They are," he said, surprised. "Don't tell me you have those in Texas," he teased.

She shook her head. "I bought a book on native plants and trees the day I got here," she told him. "Everything is so different down here!"

"I like the scenery, too," he said. "But there's something more. It's the sort of place that relaxes you, slows you down."

"In your line of work, I guess it's a relief to get away from brawls," she said.

"Huh?"

"Security work," she prompted.

He smiled ruefully. He'd actually forgotten the role he was playing. "That's right," he said. "I need a place that takes my mind off work."

He led her inside the beautiful house, through open rooms with stone floors that were cool and eye-catching. She thought about how wonderful that stone would feel under bare feet and had to resist taking off her shoes.

"I don't see a television," she remarked when they were in the living room.

"I've got one in the den," he said lazily, "along with all the electronic equipment I have to keep for the sake of security around here. Smith has some of it in his suite. I have the rest."

"Mr. Smith lives with you?" she asked, surprised.

"Well, not in the same room," he said at once.

She laughed at his indignation. "Sorry."

"Damn, woman," he cursed, and then laughed. "Smith takes care of the house for, uh, the boss," he added. "So do I, when I'm off duty."

She knew it was his house, but she didn't let on. She looked around with warm, approving eyes. "It must be great, living here, with the ocean so close."

"It gets a little hectic during hurricane season," he said.

"Which is when?"

He pursed his lips. "From May until late September or early October."

She gasped. "It's late August!"

He chuckled at her expression. "Don't worry. We don't get that many."

"Does the house flood?"

"It has, in the past," he said. "I...the boss, I mean...has rebuilt it once. Otherwise, we just drain it out and have a crew come in and clean out the water damage."

She nodded, as if she understood.

He knew she didn't. He turned and looked down at her. "Cleaning up water damage is a specialized job," he said. "The same people come in after a fire when the hoses have been used on furniture and drapes."

"Oh!"

He grinned at her. "Don't ever be ashamed to admit you don't know something, Delia," he said gently. "It's not a crime."

She smiled ruefully. "Sorry. I just don't want you to think I'm an utter idiot. I don't know a lot about the world."

"Stick with me, kid," he said in a teasing tone. "I'll clue you in."

She laughed with delight. "How exciting."

He pursed his lips and gave her slender body a mock leer. "You're the exciting one. Come on. We'll finish the tour and then we'll drive over to Blackbeard's Tower."

"I can hardly wait!"

He showed her the lavish master bedroom, with heavy Mediterranean furniture and carpet and drapes in earth-tones. There was a huge bathroom with a hot tub, and a vanity. The other two bedrooms were similar, if smaller. There was a laundry room, too.

"I don't use it," he told her with a grin. "We have a lady, Lucy, who comes in to cook every day, and two days a week she does laundry for me and Smith. And the boss, of course."

"I have a laundry room, too, but no Lucy."

He smiled. "And this is the garage," he added, opening a door.

She gasped. Inside were five cars. One was the stretch limousine that had taken her back to her hotel the night before. There were four others, none of which she recognized. Well, except for the silver Jaguar. The

Ballenger brothers mostly drove Jaguars, so she knew what they looked like. The others were unusual, and she hadn't seen anything like them.

"We'll take this one," he said, guiding her to a small red sports car.

"Wow," she said as he seated her. "This is cute."

He could tell that she didn't know what an Alfa Romeo was, so he didn't expound on how much it cost. "Yes," he agreed, starting the engine. "It's cute."

"Are we going to see Blackbeard's place now?" she asked.

He chuckled. "That's right. Hang on to your seat, honey. This is a car you *drive*."

He shifted gears, whipped it out of the garage, and sent it racing down the driveway. All she saw was a blur of green and white on the way to the road.

Once they were across the Paradise Island bridge again and on the paved road that led around the island, she began to relax. The wind in her hair was delightful. She didn't reach for a scarf or hairpins. She closed her eyes and enjoyed the feel of the wind.

"You're an elemental, aren't you?" he called above the roar of the engine.

"Excuse me?"

"You like wind and storms."

"Yes," she called back, smiling.

"Me, too," he murmured.

They passed small houses and public beaches, where local people were playing in the surf. There were houses recessed down past wrought-iron gates and roadside stands where tourists could buy drinks and food. Everything was colorful. A lot of the small houses were painted in pastel colors, pinks and blues and greens. They looked homey and welcoming, and the people seemed always to be smiling.

Marcus drew up at a deserted beach and pulled off into the small dirt track that led toward a grown-up, ruin of a building.

"This is it," he said, helping her out after he'd parked.

"The tower?" she parroted.

"The very same." He led her around the growth of vegetation to a stone ruin, a circular building that had relatively new wooden steps. "Most tourists don't know about this place," he told her. "They can't prove that Blackbeard watched out for treasure ships here, but they think he did. Local legends say so, anyway."

"A real pirate," she enthused. "That's exciting."

"Pirates were all over the Bahamas and the Carib-bean," he remarked, nudging her toward the staircase. "Woodes Rogers, who became governor of the Bahamas, was a pirate himself, like Henry Morgan, who later became governor of Jamaica."

"Renegades," she mused under her breath.

"Sometimes a reformed bad man makes a good man," he said quietly.

She laughed. "So they say."

She got to the top and looked out over the remaining gray stone blocks to the ocean. "It's beautiful," she said to herself, noting the incredible color of the ocean, the blistering sugar whiteness of the beach. Between the tower and the beach were sea grape bushes. One of the cabdrivers had pointed them out and told her that they were once used as plates in the early days of settlement.

"Do you like pirates?" she asked, glancing up at him with a wicked smile.

He shrugged. "They're my sort of people," he commented, looking down at her quietly. "I'm an outsider."

Her fingers itched to touch him, but she was nervous about it. He looked formidable.

"You'd be surprised at the number of tough guys who live in my town. We've got everything from ex-black ops to ex-mercenaries. I hear there's even a reformed gun runner in town somewhere. Our police chief, Cash Grier, was in black ops, we heard."

His eyebrows arched. "You don't say?" he mused. He didn't tell her that he knew Cash Grier quite well, or that he'd heard of Jacobsville. He'd helped Grier keep his wife, Tippy, from being victimized after her kidnapping back in the winter.

"I need to visit this town," he said, studying her.

"You'd be welcome," she replied, lowering her eyes shyly. "I could take you around our local points of interest. Not that we've got such exciting ones as this, but Jacobsville was once the center of Comanche country, and there was a famous gunfighter who had property there."

"You like outlaws, don't you?"

She grinned. "Well, they're interesting," she pointed out.

"And dangerous."

She stared at his chin. It had just a faint cleft and looked stubborn. "Life is boring without a little spice."

He moved a step closer and touched her hair. He'd been itching to, ever since he picked her up at her hotel. "Your hair fascinates me. I love long hair."

"I figured that out," she confessed breathlessly.

He chuckled. "Is that why you wore it down? For me?"

"Yes."

He lifted an eyebrow. "Don't you know how to lie?"

"It's a waste of time," she said simply. "And it complicates things."

He couldn't quite meet her eyes. "Yes. It complicates things." He dropped his hand.

She was going to ask him why he'd become so remote suddenly, but a tour bus drove up next to the Alfa Romeo and parked.

"It seems we've been discovered," he said, smiling at her, but not with the same sensuousness as before. "We'd better go."

She followed him down the staircase. They got to the bottom just as six tourists followed a heavyset, laughing, tour guide to the tower. One of the women was young, blond, sophisticated and dripping expensive jewelry. She gave Marcus a sultry look from her heavily shadowed blue eyes. He ignored her completely, locking Delia's fingers into his as he nodded politely at the tour guide and kept walking.

The blonde shrugged and turned away.

Delia was curious about his lack of interest.

He gave her a keen glance and laughed hollowly. "I

may not be Mr. America, but the car attracts women," he hedged. "Even though it's not mine," he added quickly. "I don't like women who find my possessions attractive."

"I guess it would be demeaning," she agreed, because she knew what he was saying. A lot of women over the years must have liked him for his money, his power, his position alone.

"Demeaning." He savored the word. "Yes. That's a good way to express it."

He opened the passenger door of the car and helped her in. "You're perceptive," he mused.

She leaned her head back against the seat. "Everybody says that, but I'm not, really. I just know how to listen."

He got in beside her and laid his arm over the back of her seat. He stared at her until her eyes opened and her head turned toward him.

"Listening is a rare gift," he said. "Most people only want to talk about themselves."

She smiled warmly. "I'm not that interesting, and I haven't done anything that would be worth talking about to people. I do alterations and make quilts. What's exciting about that?"

"As a fellow quilt-maker," he pointed out dryly, "I find it very exciting."

She leaned forward and whispered, "I know where to find some floral fabric that dates to 1948, and the lady's willing to sell it for the right price!"

"Darling!" he exclaimed.

She laughed with pure delight at the twinkle in his

dark eyes. "You're not anything like I used to picture security people," she told him. "The only bouncer I know is Tiny, who works at Shea's Roadhouse and Bar, and he's, well, he's not much to look at."

"Neither is Mr. Smith's pet iguana—who is also named Tiny," he chuckled ironically. "We should introduce them one day!"

"Funny coincidence." She lifted her hand daringly and traced his big nose, to the crook in the middle. "Has your nose been broken?" she asked.

He caught her hand and pressed the palm to his mouth. "Only once," he said. "But it's so big that I hardly felt it," he teased.

She smiled, looking hungrily at him.

He felt a sudden painful urge to bend and kiss the breath out of her. But it was a public place and this wasn't the time. He kissed her palm again and gave it back to her.

"We'd better go before the tourists get back," he said dryly. "Could you eat?"

"I could."

"Great. I had Lucy make us a seafood salad and slice some mangos last night. It'll be cold and sweet."

"I'll enjoy that," she murmured.

Marcus smiled at her radiant delight as the wind tore through her hair once more in the little convertible on the way back to his house. He noted that she didn't protest that it was messing up her hair, or complain about the wind. She seemed to love it.

It had been years since he'd driven a woman on a

date. He usually took the limo and had Smith drive him. When he wanted to impress a woman, which was rarely these days, the limo always did the job.

But he'd suspected that Delia wouldn't know an expensive sports car from a domestic model, and he was right. She was so honest, so natural, that she made him feel like a total fraud.

He pulled into a paved driveway that led up to white wrought-iron gates. He pressed a button in the car and the gates swung open.

Delia laughed with surprise. "How did you do that?"

"Magic," he teased. He drove through the gate and it closed automatically behind them.

"It looks different than it did when we left," she mused as she noted royal palm trees on both sides of the driveway, along with masses of hibiscus and bougainvillea and jasmine, all in glorious bloom. Farther along, tall casaurina pines swayed gracefully beyond the graceful white adobe house, its eaves dripping with flowers of every color and variety.

He laughed amusedly. "I get the message. I'll slow down so that you can see it this time."

"Your boss must think a lot of you, to give you such a spectacular place to live."

"You really like it?" he asked, pleased by her enthusiasm.

"Oh, I like it," she said in almost a whisper as he stopped and cut off the engine. Her eyes were everywhere, softening as they rested on the flowers. "It's so beautiful."

Other women he'd invited here had used different

adjectives: dull, boring, rustic. It was too small, or too primitive, or too remote from the city. The bottom line was that they hated it. He was crazy about the place. He spent hours working in the flowers, fertilizing and pruning and landscaping.

"You must be a terrific gardener," she murmured as they got out and walked across a stone patio to the wide steps and spacious front porch. "I've never seen so many flowers! And that tree looks like a...no, it couldn't be." She hesitated.

"It's exactly what it looks like, an umbrella plant," he confirmed. "And that one over there is a Norfolk Island Pine."

"But they're monstrous!"

"Compared to the potted plants back in the States, they certainly are. But here they're in their natural element, and they grow like crazy."

"They're beautiful," she said solemnly.

He smiled. "I think so, too."

He parked the car and led the way into the kitchen, sliding his car keys back into his pocket.

He opened the refrigerator and produced a huge covered bowl full of seafood salad and a covered plate with sliced mango. "There's a lemon meringue pie as well, if you like lemon."

"Oh, it's my favorite," she enthused.

He chuckled. "We'll have it for dessert. It's my favorite, too." He took down plates and glasses and she set the table, arranging the silver he gave her and the napkins as well.

"What do you want to drink?" he asked.

"I like iced tea, but milk is okay."

He gave her a curious glance. "I usually have coffee…"

"That would be even better, but I didn't want to impose," she added. "You went to a lot of trouble for this."

She was constantly surprising him. Nobody wanted to "rough it" by eating leftovers here, when there were five-star restaurants all over Nassau. Here she was worried about making more work for him. He was impressed by Delia's companionable spirit.

He had the light meal together in no time, and they lingered over a second cup of coffee on the veranda, overlooking the casuarinas and, beyond them, the blinding white sand and turquoise waters of the Atlantic Ocean.

Heavy, low clouds were building around them, blackened and towering into the heavens. The sun had been out earlier, but a storm was clearly on its way into the bay.

"Do you like storms?" she asked absently as she leaned back against a palm tree trunk, watching the churning of the waves on the beach.

"Yes. I'd already figured that you did," he replied.

She smiled. "I should be afraid of them, I expect, because lightning terrifies me. But I love a storm. I love the fury of the wind, and the sound of rain coming down. We have a tin roof on our house. When it rains, it's like a metallic lullaby, especially at night. I don't know why, but rain makes me feel safe."

He was studying her face with intent interest. His dark eyes slid down her trim figure in the gossamer-thin garments she was wearing, and he wondered hungrily what she looked like under her clothes.

As if in response to his mental images, the skies suddenly burst open and rain came down immediately, in torrents.

Delia gasped as the rain soaked her blouse and skirt and drenched her hair.

Laughing, Marcus caught her hand and ran with her to the protection of the roofed patio, where she stood dripping near a wall, trying to shake the water from her skirt.

Marcus's eyes were suddenly narrow and glittery, and he was looking at her with an expression she couldn't fathom.

When she looked down at herself, she understood. The fabric was transparent. He could see right through her clothes, right down to her flimsy bra and panties. It was like being naked.

She started to raise her hands. Seconds later, Marcus backed her against the wall and pinned her wrists to the smooth surface with his big hands, while his knee coaxed her legs apart and his eyes went to her breasts.

Instinctively she began to struggle, remembering Fred.

"I won't hurt you," he whispered softly, holding her gaze. "I won't force you. Trust me."

Her face flushed as he looked down at her again, slowly levering his hips into slow contact with hers while the wind blew wildly around them.

"Your breasts are incredible," he said huskily. "I ache just looking at them. And your mouth has the most seductive curve in your lower lip…"

As he spoke, he bent. He found her mouth and caressed it slowly, tenderly with his lips, while his tongue ran along the inside of her upper lip and drove her heartbeat over the edge. His mind was telling him it was too soon for this. His body wasn't listening.

Neither was Delia's. Throwing caution to the wind, she reached up around his neck, opened her mouth under his and held on for dear life.

Chapter Five

The reaction Delia got with her unexpected response was ardent and a little frightening for a woman who'd never indulged in heavy petting with a man she wanted. It was immediately obvious that Marcus was a man of experience, and that he knew exactly how to get past a woman's reserve.

His big body levered slowly down against hers in a sensuous, lazy movement that made her tremble with new sensations. His knee edged her legs apart so that he could fit himself between them.

She gasped and stiffened at the explosive pleasure.

He lifted his lips a scant inch from hers. His breathing was heavy, his eyes full of dark fire. "What's wrong?" he asked roughly.

She was out of her depth, but she didn't know how

to tell him. He seemed to think she was much more experienced than she was.

"Too fast?" he whispered, biting softly at her mouth. "I'll slow down. Is this better?"

Better? It was torture! His hand slid down her throat, around to her shoulder, and then with anguished slowness to the soft curve of her breast through the wet fabric.

Her legs were trembling. Her hands were gripping his broad shoulders for support. She was dizzy with sensation as his strong fingers worked magic on her soft skin. He teased up and down between her breasts with little brushes of pleasure that only built the hunger without satisfying it.

She arched her back gently and coaxed his fingers lower, but he lifted his head and looked at her curiously.

"You're shy," he mused, laughing tenderly. "I can't believe it."

"I've always been shy," she whispered, shivering as his fingers finally edged out toward the taut, sensitive tip of her breast.

"But there's nothing cold about you, is there?" he breathed at her lips. He nibbled the top one tenderly, tasting it with his tongue before his strong white teeth closed gently on the lower one.

At the same time, his hand shifted, and covered her breast under the dress. Her eyes rolled back in her head with the force of the pleasure. Her soft cry of pleasure was captured by the slow, hard assault of his mouth as it opened hers and his tongue began to penetrate it with long, deep thrusts.

Her body was no longer her own. She felt his hips

sink against hers, so that they were intimately pressed together between her long legs. The close contact was agonizing. His hands were under the blouse now, under the bra, against bare, eager skin. She lifted toward them, shivering rhythmically with the gentle thrust of his hips against hers.

"It's no good," he groaned. "I can't stop."

She couldn't even pretend to protest when he suddenly picked her up and strode into the house with her, his head pounding with a desire so sharp and profound that he couldn't even think.

She lay against his chest, feeling his heart beat, feeling his incredible warm strength, her breath catching in her throat with each step. She was trembling with wild little pulses of desire, so aroused that she couldn't bear even the thought that he might stop.

He carried her into the master bedroom, kicking the door shut behind him. He barely took time to lock it before he fell onto the patterned brown coverlet with her body under his.

He ripped at his shirt and hers until they were breast to breast while he kissed her with anguished, ardent passion.

His hands were relentless on her wet clothing, stripping it off expertly and tossing it onto the carpet. She lay nude under him, and her only thought was that his hands were heaven on her cool, bare skin. She moved helplessly as he touched her in ways and places that no man had ever touched her.

When his mouth drew down her throat and onto her breasts she actually gasped at the explosion of delight.

When it fixed on to her nipple and slid down over it, she shuddered. There was a wave of heat swelling in her lower body. She was blind, deaf, dumb to anything except raw sensation.

"Are you taking anything?" he rasped at her lips.

"You mean…like the pill or the shot?"

"Yes."

"No," she whispered miserably.

"It's all right," he said huskily. "You don't have to worry. I'm healthy as a horse. I've got something to use, and I'll be careful with you."

It would have taken more willpower than she had to question what was happening. She was twenty-three years old, and no man had really wanted her. Certainly she'd never wanted anyone so much. A little voice at the back of her head started screaming warnings, but she couldn't hear it.

He stood up and stripped, letting her watch. When he tore off the black silk boxer shorts and she saw him aroused, she gasped. She'd seen one or two pictures of men like that. None of them compared to him.

He liked her rapt stare, but it aroused him even more. He fumbled something out of his wallet and pulled her up into a sitting position.

"Put it on for me," he said gruffly.

She flushed rose red. "I'm sorry," she stammered. "I don't…well, I don't know how."

He grimaced, but the odd statement didn't register through the desire. His hands were unsteady. He couldn't remember being in such a state with a woman until now. Perhaps it was the long abstinence.

He managed to get the prophylactic into place in record time. He laid her back on the coverlet, his eyes intent, his body corded with desire.

"Don't...don't hurt me," she managed weakly.

He felt a hesitation in her that puzzled him, in addition to the quick little frightened plea. But he was much too far gone to ask questions.

"I'd cut off my arm before I'd hurt you, sweetheart," he whispered. "In fact, this is going to be the sweetest hour of your life. I promise."

As he spoke, he bent to her body and his mouth opened on soft, warm skin.

In all her reading—and there had been a lot— nothing prepared her for the minutes that followed. She was shocked, overwhelmed, delighted and drowning in sensations. She should have protested, at least once, but she couldn't manage a single word. Instead she opened her legs for him, lifted her hips for him, writhed in unholy torment as he kissed her slowly, expertly, and kindled such a flame of desire in her that she begged for relief.

He lifted his head and watched her face while his hand caressed her with deadly mastery, making her sob with building pleasure.

He bent to her mouth, brushing it with his lips. "You're ready for me," he whispered huskily. "Do you want to feel me inside you?"

She cried out in torment. "Yes!"

One long, powerful leg inserted itself between hers while his hand slid under her hips and lifted her into sudden, starkly intimate contact.

Her eyes snapped open as he began to move. He watched her wide-eyed shock with throbbing curiosity.

When she stiffened and her nails dug into his upper arms, and he felt the reason for her sudden stillness, he began to realize what was happening.

He paused for a second, his breath ragged as he searched her eyes. "If I'm your first man, you'd better tell me quick," he bit off.

Her eyes were tortured. The answer was in them, stark and vivid.

He drew in a quick, shaky breath. He swallowed, hard. "It's all right," he whispered reassuringly, taking deep breaths to slow down the anguish of need. "I'm not going to move again. You are," he said gently. "Come on. I'll let you control it."

"I don't know how," she whispered brokenly. "I'm so sorry…"

"For God's sake, there's nothing to be sorry about! Here. Push up against me," he said urgently. "Come on, honey, I can't hold it much longer. Push!"

She obeyed him, grimacing when the pain bit deeply into her.

"Easy," he whispered. His hand moved between them and found the tiny bud that controlled her pleasure. He touched her where his caresses had already made her sensitive, brushing her lightly until she gasped and began to lift toward him instead of away from him. "Do it again. And again. Just like that."

She felt the pain slowly lessen, the pleasure grow, with his expert touch.

"Good girl. That's it. I'll bring you to the edge of

pleasure and when you fall, I'll go into you," he breathed sensuously against her open mouth. "I'll go into you hard and fast and deep…"

She moaned hoarsely at the impact of the words and his sensuous caresses, and all at once, there was no more time. She cried out sharply as ecstasy rose up like a hot tide in her body and suddenly exploded into a symphony of pleasure.

She shuddered and shuddered, her eyes half-closed, her body moving rhythmically with his as he pushed down hungrily and she felt the power of him overwhelming her. Throbbing waves of hot sensation built to fever pitch as the sound of his harsh breathing echoed like her own. Waves of delight began to buffet her as the terrible tension finally began to shudder away in ecstasy.

She'd thought the pleasure had reached its peak, but with the sudden hard penetration of his body, her climax shot to an even higher level, one which she thought was certain to kill her. It was almost pain. She sobbed and sobbed as she felt him groan harshly and then shiver against her. His movements, like hers, were helpless, involuntary. It was so sweet that she wept.

When the world came back into focus, she was clinging to him with all her strength and still sobbing in the hot aftermath.

"Did you feel it?" she whispered brokenly into his hot, damp throat. "Did you feel it, too?"

"Of course I felt it!" He collapsed on her, giving her his weight as he tried to catch his breath. "I've never been so hot in my life! I'm still not spent. Can't you feel me? I'm dying for you!"

"You…are?"

He lifted his head and looked into her wide, curious eyes. Virginal eyes. She didn't have a clue what was happening. And now it was too late to go back. He moved his hips experimentally and she gasped and lifted toward him as what he'd said became starkly understandable.

"Can you go again?" he whispered tenderly.

"Yes," she replied, her body throbbing with every soft brush of his.

He ground his teeth together. "I can't stop," he groaned.

She reached up and touched his cheeks, slid her fingers into his thick black hair, lifting its crisp waves. "I don't mind," she whispered shyly, having never felt so close to another human being. He was part of her now. Completely part of her, in every way.

"Forgive me," he bit off as he kissed her passionately.

She wanted to tell him that there was nothing to forgive, but already the fever was rising in her body. She felt the first returning throbs of pleasure and closed her eyes.

Eons later, she opened her eyes and realized that they'd been asleep. As she looked at the wealth of bare skin on display under the light sheet, his and hers, she felt suddenly embarrassed and ashamed and guilty. She'd been saving her chastity for marriage. It had never occurred to her to give it away to a man she'd only known for one day! She was horrified at what she'd permitted to happen.

But she couldn't blame him. She hadn't made a single protest. It was her fault as much as his. She could still remember the hot urgency of the need, like an unquenchable thirst in both of them. There had been no way to stop it. It had happened too fast.

At least there wouldn't be any consequences, she consoled herself. He'd used protection.

He opened his eyes, stretched, and gave her a long, quiet look before he drew her into a sitting position beside him and cupped her face in his big, warm hands. "I didn't plan this," he said firmly, with dark, steady eyes. "It was never meant to happen. I just lost control completely when I started kissing you."

"I know," she said miserably. "I lost control, too."

He kissed her softly. "At least tell me you enjoyed it, so I won't feel like drowning myself."

He sounded genuinely upset. She lifted her shamed eyes to his. "It was the most incredible experience of my life," she confessed. "I...loved it."

"So did I," he replied roughly. "It was worth anything. Even my life."

She searched his eyes curiously. He didn't seem the kind of man who would think of sex as a solemn act. Quite the opposite. But he looked totally serious.

"Delia, I've never been with a virgin," he said in a deep, soft tone. His voice was husky, sincere. He touched her face tenderly. "I could barely believe it, even while it was happening."

She couldn't answer him. She was dumbfounded.

"I didn't hurt you too much, did I?" he persisted.

She shook her head. "Only a little. Honest."

He pulled her up off the bed with him and nudged her toward the bathroom. "Let's have a bath. Then we'll sit down and talk."

"A bath?"

"In the hot tub," he said.

He started the water and gathered up washcloths and towels. When the tub was full, he turned on the jets and coaxed her into the water. It was heavenly, although the water stung a little in her delicate feminine core.

"I was afraid of that," he murmured apologetically. "Is it bad?"

"Not at all," she said. "I'm fine. Really."

He leaned back against the edge of the bath and scowled.

"Something's wrong," she guessed. "What?"

"You do know that no sort of birth control is fool-proof?" he asked gently.

Her heart jumped. "Yes."

He sighed. "Delia, what I used is for one time. We went two."

"And...?"

"It tore."

She felt uncertain. Her eyes were troubled.

He grimaced. "Listen, I'd take care of you, if something happened," he told her.

"You mean...a clinic...?"

"No!" He looked horrified. He paused. "Would you...?"

She shook her head. "I couldn't."

He relaxed. He stretched, grimacing as muscles protested. He saw her watching him and he chuckled. "I feel my age sometimes. I'm older than you. A lot older." He looked at her worriedly. "Am I too old?"

"Don't be silly," she said, smiling.

He drew in a long breath. "Hell. I don't know where I am. It was going to be lunch and a tour of the pirate tower. Now look at us."

Her eyes dropped to his broad, hair-covered chest and his muscular arms. They were very strong. She remembered the power of his body above her, driving down against her with furious rhythm.

She blushed.

He lifted an eyebrow. "My, my," he murmured. "Pleasant memories?"

She threw her washcloth at him.

He liked that, and it showed. He caught the cloth and moved suddenly, making a huge wave, as he imprisoned her against the wall of the whirlpool bath. "Now, that was reckless," he whispered, crushing her mouth under his while his hands found her soft breasts and explored them hungrily. "You're sore and I'm wasted."

She linked her arms around his neck and kissed him back, hungrily. Her body was singing to her. She throbbed with remembered pleasure. "You're just dynamite," she whispered unsteadily.

"So are you. Explosive. Passionate. Delicious. I could eat you alive!"

"I thought that's what you were doing," she teased, kissing him sensuously, feeling, for the first time, her power as a woman.

"Delia, this is crazy. We're both out of our minds! We can't have this sort of complication," he groaned.

She lifted her breasts against his chest and moved them seductively. "We can't? Are you sure?"

He kissed her again, savoring the feel of her nude body against his. "You don't know what it's going to be like," he said worriedly. "We're going to want each other all the time. It will show. People will see it."

"Does it matter?" she murmured in a dazed cloud of pleasure.

"Yes, honey, it does," he replied solemnly, lifting his head. "You don't know who I am, what I am. You don't know how dangerous it could be."

That was when she remembered what Barney and Barb had said to her. It assaulted her mind with shattering reality. She looked up at him with wild, frightened eyes that betrayed her knowledge.

He frowned. "You know who I am, don't you?" he asked then. "You knew when I picked you up at your hotel."

She bit her lower lip worriedly.

He eased her away from him and got out of the tub, drying himself perfunctorily before wrapping his big body in a white terry-cloth robe that emphasized the soft olive of his complexion.

She scrambled out of the tub and grabbed one of the big bath towels on the warming rod, wrapping herself in it with growing embarrassment.

He turned with a long sigh and looked at the devastation in her face. "I didn't want you to know," he said gruffly. "At least, not yet. Not until you knew me better."

She laughed inanely. As if they could know each other any better physically!

"Did your sister tell you, or did Barney?" he persisted.

She drew in a long breath. "Both of them."

He didn't move any closer to her. He wanted to. He wanted to pick her up in his arms and cradle and comfort her. He actually winced as he realized what must have been said about him, about his past. He wasn't like that now. He was legitimate in every way, but he couldn't tell her that. He couldn't admit that he'd broken the old ties, given up the old life. So much depended on his actions. He couldn't afford to trust anyone, least of all a woman he barely knew—despite the unusual feelings she kindled in him. He'd already been sold out by one woman he trusted, and that incident had nearly cost him his life.

He was watching her, waiting, uneasy.

She felt sick to the soles of her feet. In the heat of the moment she'd forgotten everything she knew about him. Now, when it was too late, her reason came back.

"I'm not quite as bad as they made me out to be," he said after a minute. "I'm not wanted anywhere in the States. In fact, I was only arrested once, when I was about twenty, on conspiracy charges. But they were dropped. That's gospel."

That made a difference. She relaxed a little as she looked at him. "I don't know a lot about the real world," she said after a minute. "I've been sheltered all my life, by my mother and, especially, by Barb. I've only had one or two dates, and they ran for the border after Barb grilled them when we got home again."

He cocked an amused eyebrow. "Your sister intimidates men?"

She nodded. "She's formidable."

"Are you afraid of her?"

"Not afraid, exactly. But I've never disobeyed her much."

He frowned worriedly. "Did you tell her you were going out with me?"

She blushed scarlet.

"Uh-huh," he murmured.

"She'd have told me not to go," she explained.

That made him feel better. If she was willing to risk her sister's wrath for him, she must feel something.

"And you wanted to go," he said softly.

Her eyes searched his with pure anguish. "It was all I thought about," she confessed. "I wanted to see you, so much."

"I wanted to see you, too." He moved closer, his big hands reaching for her shoulders. He pulled her closer. "Take a chance on me," he coaxed. "I can't make any promises right now, but I can't bear the thought of losing you."

She smiled weakly. "Me, neither."

His warm hands reached up to her cheeks. He searched her eyes hungrily before he bent and kissed her with aching tenderness.

He wrapped her up tight and kissed her until her mouth felt bruised.

"Stay with me tonight," he ground out against her lips.

"All...night?"

"All night, Delia." He lifted his head. "Yeah, I know, we're both too sore to do much except hold each other, but I want that. I want it more than I can tell you."

So did she. "What can I tell the desk clerk at my hotel if Barb calls and asks where I am? She'll be frantic."

"I've got a friend named Karen." He smiled when she looked jealous. "She's sixty and she loves a conspiracy, especially a romantic one. She'll tell your sister that you met her here at the casino and accepted an offer to go sailing early in the morning. She's got a yacht."

"She does?" she exclaimed. "I've never been sailing!"

He chuckled at the excitement in her eyes. "Would you like to spend the day on the ocean? I'll call her right now."

He held Delia's hand as he went back into the bedroom and pulled his cell phone out of his slacks' pocket on the floor. He tossed the slacks into a chair and pushed a button on the phone.

He dropped down into an armchair and pulled Delia onto his lap. "Hi, Karen," he said with a smile in his voice. "How's it going?"

There was a pause. He tucked Delia against his shoulder and kissed her damp hair. "I've got a girl," he said. There was another pause, and he laughed. "No, this one doesn't gamble or drink. She's from Texas and she teaches quilting." Another pause. He laughed again. "That's exactly what I was thinking. How would you like to meet her? She's never been on a boat."

He turned his head and looked down at Delia with warm, sparkling eyes. "We'll meet you at the marina at 10:00 a.m. Bring a basket. You bet! See you."

He closed the flip phone. "What's wrong?" he asked when she frowned.

"I don't have a change of clothes," she said. "I'll have to go by the hotel…"

"Baloney. What size are you?"

"I'm…I'm a ten," she replied.

He picked up the phone again and spoke, but this time in fluent Spanish. He nodded and spoke again. He hung up. "They're sending over a selection of shorts, skirts, and sundresses. You've already got those cute little zip-up pink sneakers," he teased, indicating them on the floor.

"You can do that?" she stammered. "I mean, just have people send a shop to you?"

"Bibbi's my cousin," he said lazily. "She runs a boutique in the arcade down the street."

"But she doesn't know me."

"I told her to bring pastels, pinks and blues and yellows," he said. "I notice you like those colors."

"You're just…amazing," she managed to say.

He smiled and bent to kiss her softly. "Wait," he whispered. "You haven't seen anything yet. What do you want for supper?"

"It can't be that late," she began.

He pulled a clock around on the table beside the chair. Amazingly they'd been in the room for three hours.

She started to speak and couldn't.

He bent and kissed her eyelids shut. "I know it seemed quick, but it really wasn't," he whispered. "And we slept."

She looked at his face with wide, curious eyes. "I've never done anything like this," she said, trying to make him understand. "I take forever just ordering food at a restaurant. I'm very deliberate."

"But you rushed into this without being able to think and you're upset," he said perceptively. "If it's any consolation, it was just like that for me. I usually think things through myself. I'm not impulsive. But this was beyond my control."

"That's what I was just thinking."

He touched her mouth with his fingertips, noting its slight swell. "You were waiting until you married, weren't you?"

She nodded sadly.

"But you'd want kids, a home, a place you belonged."

"Yes."

His thumb rubbed at her lower lip and he scowled. "Would you want me, like that? Would you want me to belong to you?"

Her lips parted on a surge of feeling. "Oh, yes."

He was still scowling. "Nobody ever wanted me for long," he said absently. "For my money, sure, for a fling, an affair. But not with the works. A home and kids."

"Why not?" she wondered.

"Maybe I've liked the wrong sort of women."

"What sort?" she asked, because she was genuinely curious.

"Beautiful women with long legs and no scruples," he said simply. "Models, showgirls, even an actress.

They liked fancy cars and easy money and plenty of plunder."

"Girl pirates," she said, trying not to look jealous.

Her eyes were sizzling. "Why, you're jealous," he mused, surprised.

"Why would I be jealous of beauty and talent?" she asked wistfully. "I mean, I'm so drop-dead gorgeous and talented—"

"You're beautiful all over, especially your heart," he interrupted. "And I consider quilting an art."

"I've never been a man-killer."

"That's what you think," he said with a grin.

Delia's eyes twinkled. "But I'm nothing to look at," she protested.

He wrapped her up tight and smiled down at her. "I've already told you, beauty is in the eye of the beholder. To me, you're a knockout."

She was suspicious. "You aren't just saying that because you feel guilty?"

He shook his head. "I value honesty above everything. Just like you." He did feel guilty at saying that, because he was involved in the biggest lie of his life, and he couldn't tell her.

Chapter Six

The hotel sent their supper order over to his house in a van. They shared shrimp cocktail, steak and salad, and a bottle of champagne. But Marcus had her stay in the bedroom when it arrived, because he didn't want his staff to know that he had a woman in his house.

"It isn't that I'm ashamed of you," he told her when they sat at the table savoring the delicious food. "But I don't want it to get back to your people."

"Especially Barb," she agreed.

"Yeah."

She finished her meal and reached for a piece of lemon cake with a pudding center as Marcus refilled their cups with fresh coffee that he'd brewed.

"This is delicious," she said with real feeling, savoring it. "I can make a lemon cake, but not with this filling!"

"I'll have the chef share his recipe and you can make it for me."

"But you've got a chef," she argued.

He reached across the table for her hand. "Nothing wrong with home-cooked food. The way to a man's heart…?"

She smiled.

"Has Karen lived in the Bahamas a long time?" she asked.

He nodded. "She's British, but she came down here for a holiday and never went home. She used to be an anthropologist," he added. "She went on digs in Egypt in her younger days. Now, she's happy piddling around in her flower garden or knitting."

"Does she quilt?" she asked.

He nodded. "She taught me machine piecing, although I rarely use it. I much prefer hand-quilting."

"Me, too," she agreed.

The cell phone rang suddenly. He picked it up and listened. "No," he said curtly. "No, I can't. Not today." He looked over at Delia thoughtfully. "That was your fault, not mine. How long are you going to be in Miami? The end of the week. Yeah. You can call me when you get back. We'll see. I said, we'll see. Yeah."

He hung up, but immediately dialed again. "Smith? Listen, I don't want any more calls today. I'm forwarding everything over to you." He listened. "Tell them I'm unavailable until tomorrow night. Got that?" He pursed his lips. "None of your business. Do what I told you. If there's an emergency, you handle it. Yes, I'll back you up. Fine. Thanks."

He put the phone away and pulled his own slice of chocolate cake over to him. "Don't you like chocolate?" he asked.

"I get migraine headaches from it sometimes," she said. "I don't want to ruin tomorrow."

He grinned and dug into the dessert with gusto.

He liked the windows open at night, Delia noticed. She lay in his arms in the king-sized bed and thought how difficult it was going to be to explain this to Barb. Then she felt the warmth of his big body next to her, and the wonder of intimacy she'd had with him, and she didn't care. Whatever the cost, she was truly happy for the first time in memory. She'd take the consequences and deal with them, whatever they were. He felt her move and his arms brought her close, enfolded her in their warm strength.

"Don't leave me," he whispered, half-asleep. "Don't ever leave me."

"I never will," she whispered back. "I promise."

She curled into his body with a sigh and went back to sleep. If Barb called the hotel to make sure she was all right, they'd tell her that Delia was staying at Karen Bainbridge's house, and Karen would tell them the same thing. It was nice to have an alibi. She didn't consider that it would be the first time she'd lied to Barb. A lot of firsts were happening to her. She'd grown up and she was certainly old enough to make her own decisions, her own choices. Maybe this was terribly wrong, but she'd never wanted anything more than these days with Marcus.

A tiny voice in the back of her mind warned her that some things came at an exorbitant price. She refused to listen. All that mattered was this sweet feeling of belonging, of…love. She sighed softly and fell asleep.

The next morning, Delia was dressed and waiting in the living room when the boutique owner, a pert olive-skinned woman with dancing dark eyes, waltzed in behind two men carrying boxes.

"Hi, Bibbi," Marcus greeted.

"Hi, yourself. I brought a selection," she told Marcus, turning a cheek for his kiss. *"¿Esta ella?"* she added in Spanish, nodding at Delia. "Bonita," she added with a grin.

"She's pretty, all right," Marcus agreed with a smile. "Okay, honey, take a look and pick out what you want."

"Do you take credit cards?" she asked Bibbi.

"I'm paying," Marcus began.

"You are not," Delia said firmly, smiling at Bibbi. "I've got my credit card."

Bibbi gave Marcus a speaking glance. "A woman with principles," she said. "That's a novelty in your life, cousin," she added wickedly. "Yes, I take credit cards and you're in luck, because you hit a sale. All these are thirty percent off."

"Wow!" Delia exclaimed, and dug into the boxes.

An hour and six outfits later, Bibbi took down the information, shook hands, packed up her merchandise and followed the two men who carried it out. She waved at Marcus with a wide grin.

"You're going to be a pain in the butt, aren't you?" Marcus asked Delia as she tried to decide which outfit to wear sailing.

She glanced at him. "About letting you buy me things? Of course. Did you expect to have to pay me off for last night?" she added seriously.

He stuck his hands into his slacks' pockets. "I always expect to pay for whatever I get," he replied, his tone somber and disillusioned.

She could only imagine the sort of women he was used to. She put her new treasures down and went to him.

"I wanted what happened," she said in a gentle tone. "I didn't do it for personal gain. I don't play that sort of game."

He grimaced. "Sorry," he said tersely.

She searched his dark eyes quietly. "It's all right. We don't know a lot about each other. We're bound to make assumptions."

"A few, here and there, maybe," he agreed. He tugged her close. "We'll stop by a restaurant along the way to Karen's boat and get breakfast. I told her we'd be there about ten. That suit you?"

She smiled. "Yes. But I still haven't decided what to wear."

He went to the pile of clothing and tugged out pink Capri pants and a filmy white cotton top and a black and pink floral bathing suit. He handed them to her.

"You're going to be bossy," she surmised.

He grinned. "Count on it. I come from a macho culture. You'll have to be pretty tough to stand up to me."

"I think I'll manage," she replied, smiling back. "Okay, I'll go change."

She started toward the bedroom and suddenly stopped. She turned and found him watching her hungrily.

He cursed under his breath, hating his own weakness as he moved into the bedroom behind her.

He tossed her clothes on the bed and bent to her mouth, sweeping her up against him ardently.

"You're all I think about," he muttered against her mouth. "I'm sure it's unhealthy."

She linked her arms around his neck, tingling at the pleasure it gave her. "There's probably a pill for it."

"I don't want to be cured," he whispered, kissing her again.

His hands worked on her clothes, smoothing off everything except her bra and panties. He looked down at her with unbridled desire and his eyes asked a question as he brushed his thumb against her nipple through the lacy fabric.

She grimaced. "I want to," she assured him.

"But you're still sore," he guessed.

She nodded grimly.

He laughed shortly. "It's my own fault. I was greedy."

"So was I."

He kissed her lightly and reached for the Capri pants, holding them for her to step into. He fastened them around her small waist and then stuffed her into the blouse. He reached up and loosened the hair she'd tucked into a bun. "There," he murmured, studying her.

"Much better. I think I like having my own dress-up doll."

"We'll run out of clothes eventually," she said.

He shrugged. "I'll learn to make them."

She laughed. "I don't have to learn. I can already make clothes."

"Show off."

"I'll teach you," she promised.

His smile was wicked. "There are several more things I plan to teach you, too," he added, and he didn't mean sewing.

"Be still my heart," she whispered.

He kissed her slowly, fiercely. "We've barely touched the surface," he said. "Wait and see."

He put her away after a minute and tugged her by the hand. "Breakfast," he said again. "I'm starved, but food will have to do for now."

She laughed as she went with him.

He stopped at the little sports car and looked down at her for a long time.

"What are you looking for?"

"I was wondering what you looked like when you were a little girl," he said. "I was thinking that kids are nice."

Her heart jumped wildly. "We've only known each other for two days," she began.

"Hell. How long does it take to know how you feel?" he demanded. "Two days, two years, I'd feel the same. There's already a connection between us. Tell me you don't feel it. You want my kids. I can see it in your eyes."

She blushed. "I've always wanted children," she said in a husky, aching tone.

"I haven't really thought about having them until now," he told her. "Maybe I had some vague idea of the future, but nothing definite. You'd look right at home with kids around you."

She nibbled her lower lip. "Aren't you just making the best of a mistake, by saying that?"

"When you know me better, you'll see that I never make mistakes," he said blandly. "Being perfect, I'm above that sort of thing."

"Right."

He grinned. "Get in. We're wasting daylight, isn't that what you Texas girls say? I love Western movies."

"Listen, I can't even ride a horse," she protested.

"I'll bet you look smashing in a cowboy hat."

"We'll have to try one on me and see," she said.

"I'll take you up on that."

She wasn't sure if he was serious, but he certainly seemed to find her fascinating, because all the way to the restaurant he asked about her life back home.

The connection between them was staggering to Delia, who'd had very little to do with men all her life. She felt comfortable with Marcus in a way it should have taken years to accomplish. She loved just looking at him. He was big and dark and imposing, but he had a tender heart. She loved the way he spoke to little children they passed in the restaurant, the easy way he had with waitresses, making them feel at ease and not throwing his weight around. For a millionaire, and a gangster, he was remarkably polite.

The gangster part still nagged at her. So did her easy surrender to him. She'd lived by a code, one that didn't allow for such romantic escapades. She'd planned to get married and then sleep with her husband. She'd made no allowances for letting a man seduce her before then.

But she'd had no control whatsoever with Marcus. She still looked at him and ached to lie in his arms again and thrill to his kisses. It was scary.

She tried to hide it from him, though. It wouldn't do to let him see what a marshmallow she was.

There was also the problem of Barb, and that one wasn't going to go away. Barb was going to be disappointed in her, furious with her for cavorting with a known hoodlum.

There was one more complication that might arise—the consequence of a child. Even if Marcus was willing to do the right thing, how was she going to feel about having the child of a gangster?

She remembered reluctantly what Barney had said about Marcus and people who crossed him. He was a frightening figure to many people. If he had enemies, and surely he must, their child would be right on the firing line with Delia. It was a sudden and sobering thought. Marcus had asked her to trust him until she knew him better. She wanted to. For the moment, at least, she was going to make enough memories to last a lifetime. Just in case. And she wasn't going to think about tomorrow.

Karen Bainbridge was sixty, short, blond, and a live wire. She didn't look her age. She had beautiful skin and saucy blue eyes. And she liked Delia at once.

"She's just the way I pictured her," Karen told Marcus as they climbed aboard her yacht. She paused to talk to her captain and tell him where they were going, while Marcus handed the picnic basket Karen brought to the steward to be put down below in the galley.

"What's in this?" he asked Karen as he gave it to the man.

"Chicken and biscuits, salad, fruit and a lovely cherry pie," Karen told him. "We have champagne, as well. Tell me, dear, where did you meet Marcus?" she added, pinning Delia with those bright blue eyes.

"At the hotel," Delia began.

"She had an abusive date and I rescued her," Marcus said lazily. "What a shock I had when I took her up to my office and discovered that she knew how to quilt!"

"I'll bet." Karen turned to Delia. "You know, dear, he's never been around women who could sew, except me. And as sad as it is to admit it, I'm simply too old for him. You're much more his style," she added wickedly.

"Yes, she is," Marcus agreed, smiling warmly.

"Tell me about yourself," she encouraged.

Delia hadn't planned to talk much about herself, but Karen was easy to open up to; very much like Barb. She related the abbreviated story of her life, ending with her mother's recent death.

Karen was sympathetic without being artificial. She patted Delia's hand gently. "We all have to learn to let go of the people we love most," she said softly. "It's one of life's hardest lessons. But, just think, someday we have to let go of life, all of us."

"I suppose so," Delia replied.

"Not that you'd dwell on it, at your age," Karen said with an indulgent smile. "There's one little thought I'd like to share with you. I heard it from my mother when I was small. All the people we loved, who have died, are still alive in the past. The only thing that really separates us is time."

Delia eyed the older woman curiously. The thought really was comforting.

"See?" Karen added. "It's a matter of perspective. In other words, it isn't what happens to us, it's how we react to what happens to us. That's what separates optimism and pessimism."

"You're a deep thinker," Delia mused.

"I'm old, dear," came the laughing reply. "When you've lived as long as I have, you learn a lot, if you're the least bit observant." She glanced toward Marcus, who was talking to the captain in a relaxed, easy manner. "For instance, you're in love with my friend, there," Karen teased.

Delia drew in a long breath. "Hopelessly. I'm not an impulsive person, but I fell and fell." She met Karen's eyes. "It's only been two days," she said worriedly.

Karen didn't blink. "Love doesn't take a lot of time. It just happens."

Delia managed a watery smile. She stared at Marcus's broad back hungrily. "Do you…know about him?"

"That he runs around in, shall we say, shadowy company? Yes. But he's one of the best men I've ever known. He's a soft touch, and he never deserts a friend in trouble. Reputations are usually exaggerated, child," she added gently. "If I were your age, I wouldn't even hesitate. He's very special."

Delia wiped her eyes, smiling. "I thought so, myself. Sometimes, maybe taking a chance is the right thing."

"Count on it," the older woman advised. "And never judge a book by its cover," she added. "Or a quilt by its fabric alone."

"I won't forget."

They sailed out into the bay and then into the Atlantic Ocean. The high-tech fabric of the sails rippled in the wind and made whispery sounds. Seagulls darted to and fro. Delia sat beside Marcus and felt as if she belonged. Karen told her about the history of New Providence while they ate crisp salads and cold cuts.

Later, Karen drowsed while they sailed, and Marcus held Delia in front of him, idly kissing her neck and her ear and teasing her with the wind blowing noisily off the sea.

"This really is the Atlantic Ocean, isn't it?" she murmured, leaning contentedly back against his chest. "I used to think the Bahamas were in the Caribbean."

"A lot of people do. It's the Atlantic." He kissed her neck. "How do you like your vacation so far?"

"It's the best time I've ever had in my whole life," she said simply.

He hugged her closer. "Mine, too," he said huskily. "How much longer are you going to be here?"

"Three more weeks," she said, hating the thought.

"A lot can happen in just three weeks," he reminded her.

She turned into his arms. "A lot already has," she whispered, lifting her face.

He bent and kissed her warmly, hungrily, groaning deep in his throat as the kiss kindled fierce new fires in his big body.

"You're just incredible," she whispered when he lifted his head. Her eyes were misty with pleasure, her mouth swollen.

He enjoyed the way she looked. "So are you," he replied. "We need to make a quilt together," he mused.

She laughed. "I'd really like that."

"We'll talk about it."

"I like your friend Karen."

He glanced toward the elderly woman, still sleeping peacefully. "I like her, too," he said. "She's an odd bird. But then, so am I."

"Not so odd," she replied, touching his face with the tips of her fingers, exploring its broad strength, its nooks and crannies. "I like your face."

"It's a little banged up," he pointed out.

"It doesn't matter," she said. "It just gives you a sort of piratical look. I find it very attractive," she added shyly.

He chuckled, swinging her back and forth in his big arms. "I would have been a pirate in the old days, I guess." His face hardened. "Maybe I still am."

She put her fingers over his wide, sexy mouth. "You're just Marcus, and I'm crazy about you," she said simply. "Although maybe it's too soon to say that."

He shook his head. "I'm crazy about you, too, baby," he said huskily.

She laughed with pure joy, her eyes radiant with it as she looked up at him. "Is there really a future for us?"

He moved restively, thinking of all the complications in his life right now. He grimaced. "Look, we have to take this one day at a time," he said, searching her eyes. "It isn't what I want, but it's how it has to be. There's a lot going on that you don't know about."

"Not something…illegal?" she faltered.

He cocked an eyebrow. "Do you think I'd involve you in something illegal?" he asked openly.

She sighed. "No. Of course not. I'm sorry."

He touched her mouth with his fingertip, tracing its soft outline. "I will never hurt you deliberately. I promise."

She relaxed. "And I won't hurt you deliberately," she vowed.

"I now pronounce us dedicated to truth," he chuckled.

She reached up and kissed him. "Do we get to do what we did again?" she asked.

He drew in a long breath. "I want to get to know you," he replied. "Sex clouds the issues. Even if it is the best I ever had."

She brightened. "I like that idea, too. I'll bet you were a tough little boy."

"Very," he assured her. "I got in fights from kindergarten up. Broke my poor mother's heart."

"I never got in trouble at all," she replied wistfully.

"Unless you count pouring salt on another girl's mashed potatoes because she called me a fat frankfurter in second grade."

"Were you? Fat?"

"Roly poly," she admitted, smiling. "I lost weight."

"Don't ever get skinny," he said gently. "I like you just the way you are."

She beamed at him. It was, in many ways, the most perfect day so far.

They discussed movies and television shows and even politics, and found that they were amazingly compatible.

"Do you have a DVD player?" he asked her.

She grimaced. "I hate to admit it, but I can't figure out how to hook one up. I'm still using VCR tapes."

"Primitive," he remarked. "I'll have to come to Texas, if for no other reason than to show you how to move into the modern age electronically. Do you like music?"

"Yes. Latin music, especially," she confessed. "I have most of Julio Iglesias's albums, some Pedro Fernandez, some Luis Miguel, and half a dozen others. I even have some of Placido Domingo's opera performances."

"I'm impressed," he teased. "That's a fairly mixed bag."

"All terrific, too."

"Truly. How about reggae?"

Her eyebrows lifted. "What's reggae?"

He grinned. "We've got a Jamaican reggae band

playing at the casino. I'll take you there one night and let you see if you like it."

"Could we dance?" she asked hopefully.

He laughed. "I may not look it," he said gently, "but I won dance contests when I was younger."

She was delighted. "I'll bet you still could."

"We'll find out," he promised.

They were on the way to landing at a small, deserted island when Marcus's cell phone rang insistently.

He excused himself and Delia frowned at the expression on his face. He seemed first curious, then angry, then furious. He barked something into the phone and hung up, glowering at the ocean.

After a minute he came back. "Some businessmen from Miami have turned up unexpectedly. We'll have to go back. Now," he added when Karen joined them.

"There will be other days for sightseeing," Karen said in a conciliatory tone. "Marcus, go and tell the captain to make for port, will you?"

"Of course," he said, but he was distracted.

At the marina, Delia said her goodbyes to Karen and let Marcus call a cab for her instead of sending her back in the limo.

"There are plenty of reasons that you don't need to be seen with me right now," Marcus said gently. "And the least of them is your sister. I'm really sorry about today. But I'll make it up to you tomorrow. We'll go sightseeing all over the island. How about that?"

"I'd love it," she said radiantly.

He grinned. "Tomorrow it is, then." He opened the

door and put her into the cab without touching her. "See you in the morning."

"Yes. Take care," she said.

"You, too."

He closed the door. She looked back as the cab pulled out of the marina. He and Smith were still standing beside the limo, in deep conversation.

Chapter Seven

Delia was up at daylight waiting for Marcus to call. Her whole life was suddenly caught up in his. She could hardly bear being away from him at all.

Barb had phoned soon after Delia got in, and Delia was able to tell her about Karen's yacht and the ocean day trip.

Barb relaxed audibly as she listened. There was no mention at all of Marcus, of course.

"You're sure you're not seeing that gangster?" Barb insisted.

"I was out with a nice little old lady seeing the sights," Delia said in a forcibly relaxed voice. "I'd love for you to meet her when you get back. She's British, but she's lived in these islands for a long time. She knows all the best spots."

"I'll take you up on that," Barb said finally, laughing. "Okay, I'm convinced. But you do keep your door locked at night."

"I do. Honest."

"Have you seen Fred? I heard he might be back from Miami already."

"No, I haven't seen him. Why?" Delia asked, curious.

Barb hesitated. "It was something Barney let slip. I think Fred may be a lot more dangerous than we realized, baby. You steer clear of him, just in case, okay?"

"I will. But why is Fred dangerous?"

She hesitated again, lowered her voice. "Well, I heard Barney tell somebody that he was thick with the Miami mob and that he was laundering money for it."

"Fred?"

"Yes, that's what I thought," Barb chuckled. "But you can't ever tell about people, and mostly the bad guys don't wear signs. Just the same, it would explain why he was so eager to take you to that gangster's casino on Paradise Island. There's a connection there, you mark my words."

"I'm not going to the casino, honest."

"I know that. Are you having a bad time without us? I'm just so sorry…"

"I'm having a ball with Karen and the beach," Delia laughed. "Really."

"I'm not surprised that your idea of fun is hanging out with a woman in her sixties," Barb said softly. "Mama and I were too hard on you, weren't we, baby?"

"I turned out just fine, thanks," Delia laughed again.

There was a sigh. "All right, I'll let you go. But be careful sailing around on yachts. There might be pirates out there, for all you know."

"If I meet one, I'll introduce you."

"You do that. Good night, baby. We should be back late next week or the week after. You're sure you don't want to fly over here and stay with us until we go back?"

Delia was thinking about the extra time she'd have to see Marcus while her sister was away. "I'm very sure," she replied. "Take care."

"You, too. Love you."

"Love you, too." Delia hung up, relieved that Barb hadn't noticed anything suspicious. She was learning to lie very well, she thought sadly. Maybe, too well.

She didn't sleep worrying about what Barb had told her. If Fred was mixed up in money laundering for the mob, could that be why he'd gone to see Marcus?

She loved him with all her heart. But she had to admit that she didn't really know him very well. And what if he was mixed up in the mob? After the delight they'd shared, after she'd grown to care so much for him, could she really walk away even so?

It was barely six in the morning when she woke up and couldn't go back to sleep. She made coffee and sat out on the balcony of her room, watching the waves break on the sugar-white beach. Today Marcus was taking her sightseeing. Should she ask him if he and Fred were in business together? Did she dare? And what would she do if he said yes? The thought that he might end up in prison tormented her.

She tried to eat breakfast, but her stomach rebelled at the smell of eggs. That was so odd. She'd never had a lack of appetite in the morning. She touched her belly lightly and wondered. Could she tell, this soon? Or was she just becoming paranoid?

Paranoid, she decided firmly. All the warnings from Barb were making her second-guess her own judgment. She had to take it one day at a time and not borrow trouble.

So she was waiting when Marcus sent a cab for her the next morning. It was John, the same cabdriver who'd ferried her over to Paradise Island before. He was young and personable and seemed to love the conspiracy.

"You like the boss, huh?" he asked her cheekily, in a crisp, very clear British accent.

She laughed. "Yes. I like the boss a lot."

"He is a good man," he told her, the outrageous smile gone. "My brother drowned last year when his fishing boat capsized. He left a wife and six children. That Marcus Carrera, he set up a trust fund for them at a local British bank, so they never have to worry about money again. Some people say he is a bad man. But I do not think so."

She smiled warmly. "Neither do I. What's your name?"

"I am John Harrington."

"I am Delia Mason. And I'm very glad to meet you," she said sincerely.

"The same with me. I am sorry you have to hide your trips to Paradise Island."

"So am I. It isn't the way I'd prefer to do things," she added quietly. "But for some reason, Marcus thinks it's better if we aren't seen together at my hotel."

"He has enemies, ma'am," he replied. "He is protecting you."

Her heart warmed at the suggestion. She hadn't considered that. She began to smile and couldn't stop. Protecting her. She liked that.

Marcus was waiting for her at the door of his house where John dropped her off. He waited just until the cab was paid and waved away before he pulled Delia into his house, closed the door and kissed her half to death.

His hot face slid into her throat and he held her as if he feared she might be torn from his arms. "I can't bear this," he whispered roughly. "It's torture, being away from you even for a few hours."

Which was exactly how she felt. She kissed his warm neck drowsily. Her whole body throbbed. She wanted him. It was mutual, she could feel the instant response of his big body to her closeness.

His big hand slid around to the upper part of her thigh and tugged, pressing her hard against that part of him that was most male. He groaned.

She felt him shudder and her heart soared. He belonged to her. She'd never been more sure of anything.

"If you want to," she whispered, "I will."

He groaned again, sliding his mouth across her

cheek to find her hungry lips. He kissed her with aching need, both hands on her hips now, rubbing her body roughly against his until they both shuddered.

But abruptly, he pulled back, let her go, and turned away to the sliding glass doors overlooking the ocean. He opened them and let the eternal breeze off the ocean cool his fever.

Delia joined him, still unsteady from the unexpected burst of passion. She folded her arms across her chest with a long, heavy sigh.

He glanced down at her, his dark eyes stormy. "I want to," he said without preamble. "But we're not going to," he added firmly. "I'm not going to try to turn you into my mistress. I have too much respect for you."

She was surprised by his straightforwardness. "You aren't anything like your reputation, you know," she said softly.

He laughed harshly and turned his attention back to the white-capped waves breaking on the sugar-sand beach. "You don't know that part of my life at all," he said. "And I don't want you to."

"Everybody makes mistakes," she began.

He turned and took her by the shoulders. "My past is brutal. But I'm trying to start over, despite how it looks." His fingers contracted. "Listen, I want a family, children, a home—a real home—of my own." He looked tortured. "But there are things I have to do first. I have obligations that I can't share with you, people depending on me."

She was curious. "You're mixed up in something, aren't you?"

"Yes," he said bluntly. "Something bad and dangerous, and I can't share it."

"Are you…in danger?"

He drew in a sharp breath and looked out at the ocean over her blond head. "Yes." Her concern made him ache to tell her the truth. But he didn't dare. He looked down into her wide, trusting eyes and he grimaced. He touched her cheek with a tender hand. "You have to trust me, as hard as that may seem. I know it looks bad, but there is one great truth here—my feelings for you. Those are as real as that ocean out there." He bent and kissed her softly. "I adore you!"

She pushed close into his arms and kissed him back. She felt safe, treasured, comforted. She felt as if she were a part of him.

Marcus was feeling something similar. He should send her back to her hotel and have nothing else to do with her until this was all over. He was putting her life at risk. But he needed her, so desperately.

He stood in the wind, just holding her close, for a long time, his turbulent gaze on the ocean, which seemed as restless and tormented as he felt.

"When it's all over," he said huskily, "you and I will make plans for our future. Deal?"

"Deal," she whispered.

He bent and kissed her, one last time. "We'd better get going," he said gruffly. "Before I do what we both want."

She searched his eyes, uncomprehending. "Why don't you want to?"

He framed her oval face in his big, warm hands.

"I've already made one almighty mistake, taking you to bed on our first date. I'm not making it again. My mother raised me to respect innocence. It goes against everything I believe in to make a convenience of you."

"But I'm crazy about you," she whispered.

He actually flushed. "Yeah. I'm crazy about you, too. But we're building a relationship that will last a long time. We need to go about it slowly. Agreed?"

"Agreed," she said reluctantly.

"Besides that," he worried quietly, "I'm too careless with you. I want children someday, that's no lie. But I don't want them right now. It's impossible. My life is too complicated."

Her heart skipped. She could be pregnant, and he didn't want children right now. She gave him a pained look.

"Don't look like that," he said softly, smiling at her. "It was just one time. There's no real risk. Right?" he added, a little uneasily.

"Right," she lied, and forced a smile. "No real risk at all."

"So we won't take any more chances. I was careless. I won't be careless again, and neither will you."

"Got it," she agreed.

"Now," he said, releasing her. "I've got a great itinerary. In the next few days, Miss Mason," he added with a grin, "I'm going to educate you in the folklore and history of the most interesting group of islands on earth!"

And he did. They started out early in the morning and came back at sunset. He strolled her down Prince

George Wharf, through the gigantic straw market, where he bought her a beautiful purse and hat adorned with purple flowers. He took her on a carriage ride, where the horse pulling it wore a hat, too.

They saw the water tower, the artificial waterfall, Government House, and where a James Bond film was made. They went out into the ocean on a glass-bottomed boat, with a skipper who serenaded the crew in a reggae beat. They toured Fort Fincastle and Fort Charlotte. They walked along Bay Street and had lunch in quaint bistros. They toured the botanical gardens and Delia raved about the koi pond. They toured a hotel complex where an underwater aquarium was the key attraction. They saw a sponge warehouse and ate conch soup in a restaurant on the bay, where passenger ships were berthed at the wharf and tiny tugboats sailed to turn the big ships in the harbor.

Every night they had supper at Marcus's house, with Smith standing guard. And in the evenings, Delia lay in Marcus's arms on the patio near the big swimming pool, and listened to the waves crash on the beach as they talked about a future.

It was an idyllic time; two weeks of unbelievably sweet memories. During that time, Delia missed her period, and she felt nauseated not only in the morning, but at night, as well. She lost her appetite, and grew so tired that she started going back to her hotel no later than nine o'clock, pleading lack of sleep.

Marcus wasn't suspicious. He knew nothing about pregnant women, never having been around one—not even his sister-in-law when she was pregnant with his niece and nephew. He'd mentioned it once when they were talking. Delia was confident that she didn't have anything to worry about in that sense. But what was she going to do?

It was a problem she didn't want to have to face anytime soon, but the odds were against her being able to hide her condition. Especially when Barb came back. Her sister was a vacuum cleaner when it came to information.

Marcus made a lobster bisque while Delia made a fruit salad and poppyseed dressing, plus homemade rolls, to go with it. They'd shared food preparation only once before, but this particular night they didn't want to have someone bring food in.

Delia loved working in the kitchen with Marcus. They talked as they worked, and Delia teased Marcus about the size of his Shark Chef apron, which featured a cartoon shark grilling shrimp on a barbecue grill.

"We could try it on you, honey," he mused, "but I expect it would wrap around three times. You're tiny compared to me."

"I like that," she said with a warm smile.

He put the bisque off the burner to rest before it was served. Then he caught Delia close and kissed her hungrily. "I like it, too," he whispered at her lips. "You were almost too small for me in bed," he added with a dark affection in his eyes when she flushed. "That's why you got so sore." He bent and kissed her again. "But you'll fit me after the first few times," he added outrageously, teasing her lips with the point of his tongue.

She hid her face against his chest and laughed softly at the thrill of remembered pleasure the words provoked. "Are you…big?" she asked.

He roared.

She hit his chest, still without looking at him. "Well, how am I supposed to know about things like that?" she asked reasonably. "I've only ever seen men in magazines, and they sure didn't look like you did that night!"

He laughed deep in his throat. "You couldn't take your eyes off me," he recalled gently. "I loved it. I can't remember feeling like that in my whole life. It was like flying."

"I felt that way, too." She sighed and curled closer. "I love being with you."

"Yeah. Me, too," he said, but he sounded remote, distracted.

She lifted her head at the odd tone and gave him a long, curious appraisal. His face was taut and his eyes were troubled.

"Have I done something wrong?" she asked worriedly.

"As if you could," he chided. He bent and brushed his lips gently over hers. "I've got a problem or two that I can't share with you. Nothing major. Honest."

"It wouldn't be another woman?" she asked uncertainly.

He laughed softly. "No. It wouldn't be. I haven't had feelings for any woman in a long time." His big hand brushed her cheek. "None of them were ever like you," he added. "You're special."

"So are you," she replied.

"Besides," he added, "how far would I have to look to find another woman who knew quilts the way you do?" he teased.

She laughed. "Speaking of quilts," she added, tugging loose to go to her purse. "I found something in my pocketbook last night that I didn't even know I had. I want to give it to you. It's a pattern for a memory quilt that I'm working on."

She brought it to him. It was a small square with graceful curved lines and a tiny embroidered flower in the center.

"This is beautiful," he commented. "I don't embroider well, though."

"I do. It's one of my better skills. That's why I did the center square of the block like this. It's rather a variation on the Dresden Plate."

"Yes, I noticed, but you've pieced every wedge section individually. This is going to be a lot of work if you hand quilt it."

"I want to do it by hand," she replied. "It's a labor of love. The fabric in that block comes from dresses worn by my grandmother and my mother, Barb and me," she added, pointing out the different fabrics. "I want to make a quilt that I can pass down to my own children one day. If any of them quilt."

He was studying her face, the block held loosely in his big hand. "Maybe they'll like it as much as we do," he said quietly.

Which could only intimate that he was interested in fathering her children, and she brightened immediately.

"Thanks for letting me keep this," he told her. "I think I might do the same, with fabric from my niece and nephew's clothing and my sister-in-law Cecelia's. Maybe she's got something left from Carlo, as well."

"Carlo?"

"My brother. The one who died of a drug overdose." He didn't add that it was an injected overdose, that Carlo was killed for tipping off the feds about Fred Warner's Colombian money-laundering connection.

"How terrible for you. And for them," she added. "Your sister-in-law, does she come here to see you with the children?"

"From time to time, in the summer," he said. "The kids are five and six, respectively, and in school now. They're called Cosima and Julio." He smiled with re-membrance. "They're really cute. Smart, too. Carlo was brilliant with figures."

"What led him into drug use, can you tell me?"

He shrugged, moving away to put the quilt block on top of the counter. His fingers traced it lightly. "Why does anybody use them?" he asked coldly. "He was never strong enough for life, in the first place. Every time he and Cece had an argument, or he had pressure at work, or one of the kids got sick, he turned to nar-cotics for relief. I tried to stop him, Cece tried to stop him. We even had his parish priest talk to him. But he didn't want to quit. In the end, he took one hit too many and his heart stopped. He ended up in the hospital and we finally got him into rehab. It was a bad time," he added. "A real bad time. He was back on the right track and mad as hell at the people who got him hooked."

He stopped short of telling her that Carlo had gone after Fred Warner for revenge, since it was Fred who got him hooked. Fred wasn't aware that Marcus knew that. He thought Marcus considered him one of Carlo's friends. "Anyway, Carlo died of an overdose and Cece came apart at the seams. I ended up with the kids, down here in the Bahamas, with a nanny until she could cope again."

"Is she nice?" Delia asked, trying not to feel jealous.

"Yes. She's nice," he replied. "Pretty. Talented. She's a commercial artist. She lives in California now."

"Wow."

He gave her a long look. "Are you jealous?" he asked in a deep, husky tone.

She shifted restlessly. "Maybe. A little."

He laughed. "I've never even kissed her. She's definitely not my type."

"That's reassuring."

"How about you?" he wondered. "Do you secretly pine for Barney?"

She laughed, too. "Oh, sure, I hide under his bed at night hoping he'll notice."

"Barb would have you for breakfast," he commented.

"Probably. Barney's definitely her type, but I think of him as a big, cuddly brother. He's sort of like my hero, in a lot of ways. He's looked out for me since I was little, like Barb. Besides," she added with a flirting look, "I like big, dark men with deep voices."

He smiled broadly. "I like slight little Texas girls."

"That bisque is going to get cold," she said after a minute.

"So it is. We'd better eat it quick."

After they did the dishes, Marcus pulled her down onto a chaise lounge with him and they listened to classical music while the wind danced in the casuarinas pines and the ocean roared softly along the shoreline.

"It's so nice here," she murmured. "I love the Bahamas."

"Me, too. I feel as if I've come home, every time I come back here. The people are wonderful, and the climate is like paradise."

"It has so much history."

"Yes. And so much beauty." His hand contracted in her long hair. "But it can be a dangerous place, too. When Barb comes back, you and I are going to have to be distant acquaintances. You know that, don't you?"

She sighed. "Yes. I guess so."

"It's not what I want, either, Delia," he confessed. "But I can't afford to rock the boat."

"Can I do anything to help?" she asked him.

He moved restlessly. "This is something I have to do alone," he said, almost absently. His hand smoothed her hair. "Some people are coming here tomorrow," he added. "That means you can't phone me or come over here."

Her heart fell. "I can't talk to you?"

"The phones may be bugged," he replied. "I don't want you in any danger."

"Now you're scaring me," she told him.

His broad chest rose and fell heavily. He'd said too much. He had to backtrack to keep her from getting suspicious.

"They're just businessmen, but it's a big deal going down, and quickly. I can't have any distractions, is what I mean. Nothing dangerous. Okay?"

She let go of the fear. "Okay," she agreed.

His hand filtered through her soft hair. "Worried about me?" he probed.

Her fingers toyed with a button of his silk shirt. "Always," she confessed.

She made his blood sing. He felt her body in the red sundress warm and fluid against his on the chaise lounge. She smelled of flowers. He could feel the quickness of her breath. It was going to be a long dry spell after this.

His big hand moved under hers and flicked open shirt buttons. He guided her fingers under the silk and taught her the motion and pressure he liked.

He felt warm and strong and just faintly furry. She loved the feel of his chest against her. She bent and drew her mouth along his collarbone, noticing with pride the way his big body shivered at the caress.

"Turnabout is fair play," he said in a husky tone. He unbuttoned the sundress and discovered to his delight that there was no bra under it. He pulled her closer, so that her breasts were pressed into the thick hair that covered his chest. "That's nice," he groaned.

"Yes." Delia slid her arms around him under the shirt, reveling in the wonder of being close to him. She ached to merge into his own body, there in the starlight, with the waves crashing on the nearby beach.

He turned her so that she was under him. His long, powerful leg eased between both of hers and insisted on dominion.

She didn't fight him. She loved the warmth of his big hands on her breasts as he kissed her with ferocious hunger. She arched up to his hands, gasping as the pleasure began to grow all over again.

He moved, so that his hips were directly over hers, so that they were as close as possible without the clothes that separated them.

"Oh, baby," he groaned into her mouth. "This is the closest to heaven it gets in the world. Feel how much I want you, Delia."

What he felt was blatant. His skin was damp with the passion that grew in him by the second.

"What if I can't stop?" he ground out against her mouth.

She relaxed into the soft cushions. "I don't mind," she whispered with aching need. She meant it. She sensed that he was distancing himself from her. He did care, she knew he did, but something was terribly wrong. She didn't want to lose him.

"Delia," he groaned, "we can't do this."

"Why can't we?" she asked, opening her legs to admit the weight of his powerful body between them. She lifted into him.

"This isn't the place…God!"

Just as he protested, her hand went shyly between them and she touched him, shocked at his reaction as much as she was surprised at his potency. Her memory of his body in arousal was less intimidating.

He caught her hand and moved it against him with pure sensual fever. "That's it. Here. Here!" He undid fastenings and seconds later, her hand was against hard, velvety soft skin.

She tried to draw back, but it was too late. He had her firmly in his grip and he was insisting. She followed his whispered commands first with shyness, then with pride, then with abandon as he gave in to the aching need for satisfaction and shuddered violently in her hands.

"It's no good, I can't stop," he ground out, and he stripped her out of the sundress and her underwear with confident finesse.

His shirt hit the pavement along with his slacks and boxer shorts, in short order.

"Yes," he groaned as he went into her with feverish passion. He lifted his head and watched her body accept him, even if it protested just slightly at the power of his possession.

"Marcus," she cried out, shocked and delighted all at once.

He moved again, still watching her. "It's going to be magic," he gasped.

She watched him, watching her, as they moved together on the chaise, while the whispery, urgent sounds of skin on fabric grew loud, like their breathing, in the softly lit darkness.

"What if someone...walks in?" she asked in a last bit of sanity.

"Who the hell cares?" he moaned. "Let them watch…!"

His rough, deep motions sent her out of control, throbbing with hot tension that built and built until finally, abruptly, she stiffened and shuddered and cried out in a hoarse, almost inhuman tone that faded like the night around them as she climaxed over and over again.

He let her wring the last bit of silvery pleasure from him before he drove hard and fast for his own fulfillment. He found it so suddenly that his voice rang out in the darkness as he convulsed over her.

She held him afterward, cradling his weight, caressing his dark, damp hair while he shivered in the aftermath.

"It gets better all the time," she whispered brokenly, kissing his throat.

"It gets more dangerous all the time," he replied roughly. "Delia, I didn't use anything. I was too far gone. I don't want to make you pregnant, baby. I don't dare!"

"Would it really be so terrible?" she whispered daringly.

His teeth clenched. "It would be…the end of the world for me, right now," he said bluntly, shattering the last of her dreams. She didn't know the danger he was in, and he was thinking what a stick it would give his enemies to have a pregnant woman for them to threaten. "I've told you that already. I don't want kids, Delia. Not now!"

Chapter Eight

Delia clung to him tightly, her eyes closed as she hid her anguish at what he'd just said to her.

"I know you don't want to hear that," he said wearily. "I'm sorry. But there are things going on that you can't know about. We can't take any more chances. We can't be lucky forever."

"I understand."

"You don't, baby," he said heavily. "But that's all right." He eased onto his side, carrying her with him. "I'm crazy about you," he whispered. "That's the truth."

"I'm crazy about you, too, Marcus," she whispered back. "I'll never feel this way about anybody else as long as I live."

"You'd better not," he growled in mock anger. He

kissed her gently. "We'd better get dressed. I have to get you home early tonight. I've got company coming."

"Company?" She felt uneasy.

He smiled. "Male company," he whispered, and kissed her again.

Once they were dressed and he'd phoned for a cab, he held her gently in the hall. "Listen," he said quietly, "don't think I'm trying to back out. I have to keep away from you for a while. It's nothing to worry about, and you're not to feel rejected. Okay?"

She felt worried, and it showed. "I can't even talk to you on the phone?"

"Not until I call you, or get in touch with you through Smith. Got that?" He held her by the shoulders, his hands heavy and firm. "You can't be seen associating with me until I tell you it's safe. Promise me!"

"I promise, Marcus," she faltered.

"You look as if I've thrown you out in the street and it's not like that," he said gruffly. "You're the best thing that's ever happened to me. I'm not going to let you go. So when you're picturing me with other women and worrying about whether I've dumped you, remember what I said. I care about you, very much. As soon as I can, I'll be in touch."

She managed a wan smile. "Okay."

"You can't tell your sister or Barney anything about us. Got that?"

"I wouldn't dare," she confessed.

He looked at her with deep concern. "We've got a future together. I promise you, we have. I'll find a way."

She sighed. "All right. I'll live on dreams for a while."

He traced a line down her cheek. "So will I, and they'll be sweet ones." He bent and drew his lips softly over her swollen mouth. "My sweet innocent. There's nobody else like you on earth, and you're all mine."

She smiled under his mouth. "And you're all mine."

He kissed her hungrily until the sound of a horn outside the door distracted him.

"Can I send you a note?" she asked.

He glared at her. "No notes, no phone calls, don't wave if you see me on the street. You don't know me, except for that night I saved you from Fred."

"Fred," she sighed.

"And stay the hell away from him, no matter what else you do," he said firmly. "Fred is big trouble."

"I noticed," she said, not realizing that they were talking at cross purposes.

His dark eyes were troubled as he walked her to the front door. "Last month I was a happy, carefree bachelor," he murmured. "Now I'm not only losing my right arm, I'm seeing it off at the curb."

She laughed softly at the analogy. "I'm losing mine, too," she reminded him. "Or maybe I should say I'm going to be a needle without thread."

"Or a block without piecing," he countered, smiling.

She held his big hand in hers and looked up at him one last time. "Be safe," she whispered.

"I'll do my part. You do yours." He opened the cab's rear door for her. "John," he told the driver, slipping him a hundred-dollar bill, "you never saw me in your life and you just came from Karen Bainbridge's house with Miss Mason. Got that?"

"You bet, Mr. Carrera," John said with a grin.

Marcus stood and watched the cab pull away with a grim face. All too soon, he was going to be involved in a struggle he didn't anticipate with joy. But compared to losing Delia, even temporarily, it didn't concern him half as much.

Delia hid her misery until she was back at the hotel and in her room for the night. She took a long hot bath and cried all through it. She couldn't shake the feeling that Marcus might be trying to set her down gently, despite his affirmations that he cared for her. Hadn't she heard all her life that men would say anything to get a woman into bed with them?

Now that she didn't have him to reassure her, she lost her confidence. It was all she could do to make herself get up and dressed the next morning and go down to the restaurant for breakfast.

It wasn't much of a breakfast at that, she thought as she sat by the clear waters of the swimming pool under some palm trees. She sipped orange juice and nibbled bacon. She couldn't even look at a fried egg.

She was staring uncertainly at the bacon on her plate when a shadow fell over her.

"It's too late," a deep voice commented.

She lifted her head and looked into a pair of black eyes in a rough, tan face surrounded by dark blond hair. He was tall, slender, muscular, and pleasant. He didn't look the least bit threatening, but there was something about him that made Delia tense inside.

"I'm sorry?" she stammered.

"The bacon. You can't set it free."

She got it. Her face brightened as she laughed. "Smart mouth," she commented.

He grinned. "My middle name," he replied.

She frowned. "I've seen you around here."

"Really?" he asked with a straight face. "When?"

She chuckled. At least he'd taken her mind off the bacon. "I'm Delia Mason," she introduced herself.

"Dunagan," he said, extended a hand.

"Just Dunagan?" she queried, wondering why his name sounded familiar. Hadn't Barney mentioned a man named Dunagan? She couldn't remember.

He grinned. "Mind if I join you?"

She hesitated.

"Let me guess. You're involved," he surmised.

She sighed. "Yes."

"No problem. So am I." He had a thoughtful look. "Of course, she doesn't know it, but why should that worry me?"

She blinked. "You're involved with a woman and she doesn't know?"

He shrugged. "I keep secrets. Are you here alone?" he added.

"With my sister and her husband," she said.

"Thought I recognized you. Your brother's Barney Cortero, right?"

"He's my brother-in-law," she corrected

"He's a good egg," he replied, studying her closely. "Why aren't they with you?"

"They had to go to Miami. But they're due back tonight," she volunteered.

He smiled. "I like Miami," he said. "I spend a lot of time there."

"I've never been to Florida," she said, smiling. "In fact, I've never been anywhere until now."

"Where are you from?" he wanted to know.

"Texas," she said. "You?"

His eyebrows arched. "You aren't going to believe this. I'm from Texas, too. Near El Paso."

"I'm from near San Antonio."

"We've got sagebrush and cactus," he bragged.

"We've got pecan trees and palms."

He shrugged. "To each his own. Maybe I'll see you around, again," he added with a congenial smile.

"Yes. Maybe so."

He winked and sauntered off toward the bar.

She smiled to herself. There was nobody who could compete with Marcus, of course, but her new acquaintance was definitely attractive. Back home, she'd had one date in two years. Now in the space of weeks, she was suddenly irresistible. But it didn't help to know that she was separated from Marcus indefinitely, and that she was almost certainly pregnant to boot. Marcus didn't want children now. What was she going to do?

The first thing was to make sure she really was pregnant. So she went to a drugstore and bought a home pregnancy kit. She used it. The result was positive.

She sat on the edge of the bathtub and stared down at the blue tile floor with her mind in limbo. She was going to have a child. She was twenty-three, unmarried and the child was fathered by a man who'd already said he didn't want children until much further down the road.

Now Delia was faced with a dilemma. Barb couldn't know about it; that was the first priority. She'd be inconsolable and furious, and so disappointed in her sister that it was agony to even contemplate her reaction.

The second priority was to make sure that she didn't slip up and show any symptoms that Barb would recognize. She had to make sure she slept late and didn't get exposed to scrambled eggs. She had to say that she exercised so much during the day that she was exhausted at night. Barb would buy that, because she'd never been pregnant. She couldn't have children at all. Delia wondered why. It was a subject that had never been discussed.

But as to what she was going to do about her child there was no question. She was keeping her baby, no matter what she had to do. If it meant moving overseas for nine months and pretended that she'd adopted a child, she'd do that. She'd do anything. She placed her hand protectively over her flat stomach and smiled dreamily. She was going to be a mother!

She tucked the pregnancy test kit into a plastic bag, shoved it in her purse, and disposed of it in a trash bin in a nearby arcade. There was now no chance that Barb would find it.

She contrived to look rested, alert and happy when the hotel door opened and a weary Barney walked in with Barb.

"We're back, baby!" Barb exclaimed, and rushed forward to hug Delia warmly. "I'm so sorry we had to be away so long! Are you okay? There wasn't any trouble, or anything…?"

"Barb!" Barney inserted abruptly, and gave his wife a threatening look.

"I meant Fred hasn't been around?" Barb backtracked quickly.

"No, I haven't seen him," Delia assured her sister. "Did you have a nice trip?"

"It was business," Barb said evasively. "Have you been hanging out with the yacht lady?"

Delia chuckled. "Quite a lot. You have to meet her, too," she added with perfect composure. "She's a hoot. You'd never guess she was in her sixties. She's so full of life—and she quilts!"

"Aha," Barb said with a grin. "That's the draw, is it?"

"We've been trading patterns," Delia lied. Of course, she and Marcus certainly had traded patterns.

"And you haven't been seeing that gangster?" Barb added suspiciously.

"Barb, she already told you she hasn't," Barney groaned. "Stop grilling the girl."

Barb grimaced. "I'm sorry. It's just that I worry, especially now…"

"Barb, for God's sake!" Barney interrupted.

Barb flushed, holding up both hands, palms out. "Okay, okay!"

"Have you eaten supper?" Barney asked Delia.

"No, and I'm hungry," she said. She wasn't really, but she couldn't admit that.

"Let's all go get something to eat."

"Have you connected with any of the guests here?" Barb asked as they all went out the door together.

"Actually, I have, with one. His name's Dunagan."

Barney turned to her, frowning. "Dunagan?"

"He's from Texas, too," Delia chuckled.

"Yes, we know," Barb said absently.

"He's dishy," Delia said, playing it to the hilt. "Wavy blond hair, black eyes, nice body, weird sense of humor—just my type."

Barb pursed her lips and her eyes twinkled. "Well, well, progress!"

"Will you stop trying to marry her off?" Barney muttered. "She's just a baby."

"I was eighteen when you married me," Barb pointed out.

Barney gave her a grin. "So I robbed the cradle. That doesn't make it all right."

Barb made a face at him. "Spoilsport. I want to see my…sister happy like I am. What's wrong with that?"

Not for the first time, Delia found it curious that Barb always hesitated before she said 'sister,' as if she had a hard time with it. There was a tremendous age difference, of course, and she'd spent much of her life taking care of Delia. Probably she felt more like a mother than a sister, and who could blame her.

"I'll bet I ruined your love life," Delia mused. "Mama said you took me on your first date with Barney."

Barb didn't look at her. "That was Mama's idea. She thought you'd keep us straight."

"Didn't she trust you?" Delia asked innocently.

"Leave it alone, there's a good girl," Barb replied. "Quick, catch the elevator or we'll be stuck here for ten minutes!" She ran for it, with Barney and Delia trailing behind.

Dunagan was at the restaurant when they walked in, sitting all by himself, waiting for his order. He was wearing white slacks with a patterned silk shirt and a stylish jacket. He looked very masculine and expensive.

He spotted Delia and grinned as she and her party came even with him, behind the waiter.

"Great minds do think alike," he told her. "Care to join me? I need protection! I'm sure that at least two women in this restaurant have evil designs on me." He glanced around covertly.

She smiled. "Sorry. I'm with my sister…"

"Barb, you mean?" he persisted. "Hey, Barney, how's it going?" he added, greeting Delia's brother-in-law.

"Slow and tricky," Barney said. "You're still here, then?"

Dunagan shrugged. "Some jobs take a lot of patient work."

Barney and the younger man exchanged a puzzling look. There was something strange about the way they looked at each other. It was almost as if they were putting on an act.

"What do you do, Mr. Dunagan?" Delia asked as Barney seated Barb and then himself.

"I'm in real estate," he replied, smiling. He produced

a card and handed it to Barney. "Right now, I'm trying to peddle some acreage on Paradise Island."

Barney lifted both eyebrows. "That's still on?"

"Definitely," Dunagan said easily. "I've got a buyer on the hook."

"Well, well," Barney replied.

The waiter arrived, and the small talk vanished as the menus were produced.

It was the strangest meal Delia could remember, and she was quietly suspicious of the easy rapport between Barney and Dunagan. Barb didn't seem to be aware of it.

Afterward, Dunagan went into the lobby with them and asked Barney if he knew anything about a statue just outside the hotel door.

The men walked away, talking animatedly.

"What's going on?" Delia asked her sister.

Barb looked innocent. "What do you mean, baby?"

"Barney and Mr. Dunagan are talking on two levels," she said. "I don't understand much, but they know each other. I'm sure of it."

Barb laughed. "You've got a very suspicious mind."

"It runs in my family," Delia said mischievously. "Now, give. What's going on?"

Barb was serious all at once. "I wish I could tell you," she replied. "But I can't. It's a very secret sort of project Barney's working on."

"With Dunagan?"

Barb turned and looked down at her sister. "I can't tell you anything."

Delia grimaced. "I get the feeling that nobody trusts me."

"That's silly. Of course I do. But this isn't my project, and I can't discuss it. Not even with my very favorite sister."

"I'm your only sister," Delia pointed out.

Barb hugged her. "My very special only sister."

Delia relaxed. She was very tired. It was her condition, she supposed. At least she hadn't been sick.

"Sleepy?" Barb asked curiously. "You're usually a night owl."

"I don't know what it is about the Bahamas," she said with a straight face, "but I've been sleepy like this for two weeks. Maybe I'm coming down with something."

Barb chuckled. "The paradise syndrome," she teased. "It's making you lazy."

"That'll be the day," she laughed.

"Yes. It truly will. Why don't you go on up to bed?" Barb asked, nodding toward the two men who were talking outside the hotel, with grim faces. "They may be out there all night."

"That looks like a distinct possibility," Delia said. "I think I will go on up. You sleep good, Barb."

"You, too, baby. Tomorrow we might go out in a glass-bottom boat, would you like that?"

"Yes!" Delia said with forced enthusiasm. "I'd really enjoy it."

"Then we'll do some sightseeing," Barb said. "You're not sick, are you?" she added worriedly.

Delia laughed. "Not me. Good night."

"Lock the door behind you. We've got our key," Barb called after her.

* * *

Delia did go up, but she didn't sleep. She laid awake worrying if the driver of the glass-bottom boat she and Marcus had gone out on would recognize her and say anything. They'd been careful most of the time, but on occasion, they'd been careless.

She realized that it would be ridiculous to assume that a boatman would recognize one couple out of the thousands that came through the Bahamas during the summer. But she couldn't help herself.

As it happened, she didn't need to worry. She had a phone call early the next morning.

"It's for you," Barb announced, poking her head into Delia's room. "Some lady with a British accent."

"Karen!" Delia exclaimed, grinning as she dug for the phone. "Hello?"

"Good morning, dear," Karen's accented voice replied. "Would you and your sister and her husband like to come sailing today?"

"I would," Delia said at once. "I'll ask my sister. Barb!" she called, with her hand over the mouthpiece.

Barb opened the door again. "What?"

"Would you and Barney like to go sailing?" she asked. "Karen's invited us out on the yacht."

Barb's eyes widened. "Would we!" she exclaimed. "Sure!"

"Barb said yes," Delia told her friend. "And thanks."

"Come over to my slip at the marina about ten, dear, and I'll pack a nice picnic lunch for us. See you then!"

"We'll be there," Delia promised, and hung up.

"A yacht. Wow!" Barb murmured. "Even Barney's friends don't have yachts. Nobody sails!"

"Karen doesn't, not often." Delia smiled. "You'll love her. She's sweet and British and very eccentric."

"My sort of lady," Barb agreed. "When do we leave?"

"About nine-thirty, to get to her slip at the marina by ten. We'll have to take a taxi."

"I'll tell Barney."

The door closed and Delia's heart raced. She couldn't see Marcus, but being with Karen was almost as good. Perhaps Karen had seen him and had a message for her. If not, perhaps she could take one for Delia. She felt as if she'd had her lifeline cut.

They took a cab to the marina, and Karen was waiting on the pier, all smiles, wearing a huge straw hat with roses all over the brim.

Delia introduced them, and Barney and Barb were immediately charmed by the elderly lady.

"I'm so glad you could all come," Karen said, leading the way down the pier to the slip where her yacht was moored. "It's old, but I love it," she added, leading them aboard the grand white floating mansion. My husband bought it new in the eighties."

"It's glorious," Delia said with a sigh.

"Very nice," Barney agreed, smiling at Karen. "Barb and I went on a cruise once, but we've never been nautical. A ship like this could change my mind."

"I love the ocean," Barb agreed. "Thank you so much for inviting us," she added. "Delia's been singing your praises ever since we got back from Miami."

"She's a dear girl," Karen replied, smiling at Delia.

"And so kind, to keep an old lady company. Guests are thin on the ground for me these days," she added with a meaningful look at Delia, who was immediately alert and concerned. Had something happened to Marcus?

Karen read the expression and shook her head quickly as Barb and Barney wandered off to explore the yacht.

Delia nodded and followed after them, with Karen in the rear.

They sailed for the Out Islands, chatting and listening to Karen's outlandish tales of her first days on New Providence.

There was a swimming pool onboard, although Marcus and Delia hadn't used it. But Barb and Barney were like fish in water. Karen offered them suits and as much time in the pool as they liked before lunch. They took her up on it.

Delia didn't because she wanted to talk to Karen, and she couldn't risk having her sister overhear them.

When they heard splashing in the pool, Delia turned quickly to Karen. "How is Marcus?" she asked at once. "Have you heard from him?"

"No, dear," Karen said worriedly. "I was hoping that you might have."

"Not a word," Delia replied. "In fact, he told me not to contact him. Not even to wave at him on the street. Something's going on. Something bad, I'm afraid."

Karen took Delia's cold hands in hers. "My dear, I feel the same apprehension, but I don't know what we can do about it. I tried to phone him, twice, and that nice Mr. Smith said that he wasn't able to take any calls. Something about an ongoing business deal that he had to concentrate on. But I usually see him going in or out near my house, and he hasn't been."

Delia gnawed her lower lip. "You think he's in some sort of trouble?"

"I can't think of any other explanation. But I'm sure he's all right," she added when she saw Delia's expression. "I'm sure he is."

"I wish I could be," Delia replied, worrying about something else that she couldn't share with Karen, about the child she might be carrying.

"You might talk to Mr. Smith," she said.

"If Marcus doesn't want me to call him, I'm sure he doesn't want me talking to Mr. Smith, either. But if you hear anything, anything at all, will you call me at the hotel?"

"Of course," Karen said quietly. "And you must make me the same promise. I've known Marcus for many years. I'd stake my life on his honesty. And I'll never believe some of the outlandish things I've heard about him."

"Neither will I," Delia agreed. "Not ever."

It was an idyllic day, but disappointing, because Delia had hoped against hope that her friend knew something about Marcus. Now she had no way to find out what was happening in his life.

Barb was suspicious. She kept watching Delia as if she knew Delia and Karen were talking about something they didn't want overheard. Once they were back at the hotel, and getting ready to go downstairs to the restaurant for supper, Barb let Barney go on ahead to get a table. She urged Delia out into the room and closed the door.

"You and that sweet little old lady were trading more than quilt patterns, or I'm a drunken sailor," Barb said gently. "Now what's going on?"

Delia forced herself to look innocent. "Of all the suspicious people," she exclaimed, laughing. "Karen and I were talking about potted plants!"

Barb studied her worriedly. "No. I'm sure it's more than that. It has something to do with Marcus Carrera or I'm a turkey."

"Gobble, gobble?" Delia teased.

"This is serious," came the quiet reply. "Listen, Marcus Carrera is mixed up in a really bad plot, baby. He's working with a gang in Miami to take over gambling on Paradise Island. I overheard Barney talking about it on the phone with someone. But he's been sold out by one of the mob. Federal agents are on his tail. They're going to arrest him."

Delia's face went pale. She couldn't even manage a reply.

Barb grimaced. "So you do know him, don't you? And it's more than just having him rescue you at the casino. I thought so. Baby, you can't go near him again. He's going to go to prison. You don't want to throw your life away on a man like that!"

Delia swallowed hard. "He's not like that."

Barb's eyes widened. "In only three weeks, you know him better than the federal government does. I see."

"No. It's…hard to explain." Delia took a calming breath. "He won't let me near him. He said it was dangerous, that I could get hurt. He said he wouldn't risk me, in any way, and that I wasn't to speak to him on the street."

Barb groaned. "Oh, baby," she said miserably, and hugged her sister hard. "I'd have cut off my arm to spare you this."

"He's not a criminal."

"They don't arrest people for being nice."

"He hasn't done anything illegal, I know it. And he couldn't have killed people," Delia said fervently. "He's kind, he has a wonderful heart! He makes the most beautiful quilts...!"

"There's a mass murderer who was kind to animals," Barb replied.

"Marcus is not a mass murderer!"

"But he is a criminal, baby," Barb said heavily. "And nothing you can say about him, nothing you can do, is going to keep him out of prison."

Delia swallowed. "I have to warn him," she whispered. "I can't let him be killed!"

"Baby..."

"I love him," Delia choked.

Barb ground her teeth together. "There's something else. I was afraid that you were involved with him, and I wanted to try and spare your feelings. But there's no need now. Listen, he's involved with a woman," she added. "She's been seen at the casino and the hotel with him, at all hours of the day and night. She's young and beautiful and the daughter of one of the gangsters in Miami that he's connected with."

Chapter Nine

Delia felt her world crumbling. Marcus had told her to stay away from him, for her own protection. But he was going around with a beautiful woman and connected with the mob in Miami. What if he'd just wanted her out of the way so that he wouldn't make his girlfriend jealous? What if he'd been involved with the other woman all along?

But if he was, why had he slept with Delia?

"He said he was crazy about me," she mumbled miserably.

Barb was looking at her as if she'd lost her mind entirely. "And you believed him?" she exclaimed. "Do you think a man like that cares about the truth?"

"He's not a mobster, he's a good man," Delia protested. "I can't let him go to prison, Barb. I have to go and see him. I have to warn him!"

"You can't go near that casino!" Barb said firmly. "I'm not going to let you get killed! Besides, if you go, Barney will know that I told you about Carrera."

"It will be our secret," she promised. "Barb, I have to know!"

Barb was hesitant. Her face was contorted with worry. "Baby, I don't want you to take the chance. Maybe I can get Barney to go," she added with uncharacteristic flexibility.

"Get me to do what?" Barney asked from behind them.

Barb jumped. "Don't sneak up on me!" she exclaimed huskily.

Barney was looking from one to the other with quiet curiosity. "What have you been talking about?" he asked.

"Marcus Carrera," Delia said bluntly. "I know he's in some sort of trouble with the government. I want to go to Paradise Island and…talk to him."

Barney didn't seem at all surprised by this statement. He cocked an eyebrow. "That might be possible, if you go with a friend of mine. And if you carry a note to Carrera for me."

Barb's jaw dropped. Delia sat down.

"You two must think I'm an idiot," he said easily, perching himself on the arm of the sofa. "I know more about what's going on than I'll ever tell you. But all you need to know is that there's a deep project going on, and I'm involved. Sort of. Anyway, I need to send a note to Carrera and Delia's the only hope I've got of getting it to him. I can't phone him or send a courier over without arousing suspicion."

"You're involved?" Delia asked.

He nodded. "And that's all I'm going to say."

"Is Marcus in danger?" she persisted.

His face was somber. "More than he even realizes right now. I can't afford to let him die. He's essential to what's going on. Are you game? It will be dangerous."

"She's not going!" Barb came out of her trance to protest. "I won't let her get in the line of fire."

"I won't let Marcus die," Delia replied. "I care too much about him."

"He's running around with another woman, and you want to save him?" Barb asked bitterly.

"Even if that's true, I don't want him dead," Delia said with quiet pride, oblivious to Barney's intent stare.

"I'll call my friend. You be ready to go in an hour," Barney told her.

"Barney!" Barb exclaimed, and she took off after him. "I am not letting you get involved with gangsters!"

All Barb's arguments didn't sway either Delia or Barney. She threw her hands up with a harsh groan.

"Don't I have the right to say anything at all?!" she exclaimed.

"Sure. Say 'good luck.'" Barney told her.

"We're talking about my…my sister!" she persisted, almost in tears. "She could be killed!"

"Carrera most certainly will be, if I don't get this note to him," Barney replied, handing it to Delia. "Don't open that," he added firmly. "It could cost you your life, and I'm not joking."

"I won't," Delia replied. "Thanks, Barney," she added, grateful to her brother-in-law for almost the first time in their long acquaintance.

"You do know that most of the things they say about him are true?" he asked, but in a kind tone.

She nodded. "It doesn't matter."

He grimaced. "That's what I thought you'd say. Good luck, kid."

There was a quick knock at the door. Barney went to answer it.

"You be careful," Barb said in a choked tone. "If anything happened to you…"

"I'm going to be all right," Delia said confidently.

Before Barb could say anything else, Dunagan walked in, wearing dress slacks with an expensive white shirt and a dinner jacket and black tie. He wasn't smiling. He gave Delia a cursory glance and nodded.

"You look good," he said.

"So do you, but why are you here?" Delia prompted.

"He's your date," Barney said. He held up a hand. "The less you know, the better this is going to go down. Just pretend you're out for a night on the town. Nothing more. And try not to be too obvious when you talk to Carrera. Talk about him rescuing you, and nothing else. Got that?"

"Got it," she agreed. Her knees were beginning to feel like jelly. She was a quilting teacher. How in the world had she gotten herself involved in mob warfare? And what involvement did the mysterious Dunagan have in all this? Was he working with Barney, and were they for the mob or against it?

"Pity people don't wear placards," she murmured, getting her purse and velvet wrap. She was wearing a black velvet dress, strapless, with red roses embroidered on the skirt. The wrap also had embroidered roses. Her blond hair was up in a complicated hairdo. She looked elegant and dignified.

"You can tell the players if you know what to look for," Dunagan said. He took her arm. "I'll take care of her," he told Barb, who was fighting tears. "I give you my word."

Barb managed to nod. "I love you, baby," she whispered to Delia.

"I love you, too, Barb."

She went out the door with Dunagan.

Just as they got to the hall, she heard Barb's furious voice yelling, "You never told me you were collaborating with gangsters! And just how much trouble are you in?!"

A cab was waiting at the curb. To Delia's surprise, it was John.

"How are you this evening, Miss Mason? To the Bow Tie, Mr. Dunagan?" he added.

"Yes," he said. "And hurry, John."

"Yes, sir!"

Delia kept glancing at Dunagan. She couldn't help it. The smiling, carefree tourist she'd become accustomed to was suddenly someone else. He was somber, watchful, and there was a noticeable bulge under his jacket.

He noted her concern and forced a smile. "Don't look so worried," he teased. "Everything will work out."

"Think so?" she asked. She sighed and looked out the window as they approached the high arch of the bridge that led past the marina and over to Paradise Island. "I really hope it will."

She was thinking of all sorts of terrible possible futures. She was pregnant, and nobody knew, not even Marcus. Life was very complicated.

The Bow Tie was crowded. Tourists milled around between the hotel and the casino with its gaming tables, slot machines, and entertainment complexes with live shows.

Delia kept looking around for Marcus. She'd felt overdressed when she walked in, but she saw everything from people in torn jeans to women in evening gowns and men in tuxedos. Apparently the dress code was very flexible.

Dunagan took her arm and guided her through the carpeted expanse toward the floor of the casino near the cash booths. It was like a scene from a James Bond movie, she thought, fascinated by the roulette wheels and blackjack tables.

"It's like a movie," she murmured.

He chuckled. "More than you realize," he replied.

They approached the entrance to the elevators when Delia spotted Marcus. He was wearing a tuxedo. He looked elegant and wealthy. Next to him was an olive-skinned woman, very beautiful, with long black hair. She was wearing a white silk dress, and she looked as expensive as Marcus. She had him by the arm, and he was smiling down at her.

Delia felt more insecure by the minute. It had seemed so easy when she was planning it. She even had Barney's note in her evening bag as an excuse to speak to Marcus. But when it came right down to it, she got cold feet. She remembered unpleasantly that he'd told her not to contact him. He'd been explicit. Certainly he had a reason, if he was really mixed up with the Miami mob. But where did that gorgeous brunette come in? And was she part of the deal Barney talked about, the secret project that nobody wanted her to know about?

Dunagan urged her forward. She hesitated.

Just as her feet froze, Marcus turned his head, laughing at something the brunette had said. He spotted Delia and the smile wiped clean off his face in an instant. He scowled furiously.

Delia felt unwell. Her stomach was queasy. She wanted to turn around and run. But it was already too late. Marcus and the brunette were moving right toward her.

"Hello, Miss Mason," Marcus said in a deliberately casual tone.

"Mr. Carrera," she replied, nodding at him. It was hard to pretend not to care, when the very sight of him was like water in the desert.

"You know each other?" the brunette asked, her dark eyes snapping.

"Mr. Carrera saved me from a drunken guest here at the casino last month," Delia volunteered.

"A real rat," Marcus drawled. "Doing okay, Miss Mason?" he added.

She forced a careless smile. "Doing fine, thanks."

"Nice place," Dunagan murmured, smiling. "Is there a bar?"

"There are three," the brunette said, running her eyes over him like seeking hands.

"You don't say? I'm Dunagan," he said, moving closer. "Do you mind pointing the way to me?"

"No problem," the young woman replied. "I'll just be a minute, Marcus."

"Delia, wait here, okay?" Dunagan told her. "When she shows me the bar, I'll get some chips on the way back."

"Okay," Delia replied, smiling sweetly.

They were no sooner out of earshot when Marcus exploded. "What the hell is your problem?" he demanded with blazing dark eyes. "I told you…!"

She slid her hand into his, pressing the note into it. "Don't fuss," she said under her breath.

He felt the note and scowled.

"Barney," she said without moving her lips, looking around as if she were searching for Dunagan.

"What has he told you?" he demanded.

"Nothing."

He didn't believe her. The situation was dangerous. Terribly dangerous. He turned and unobtrusively tore open the small envelope, running his eyes over the block printing. His whole face tautened. He slid the note into his pocket and looked down at Delia with an expression that would have stopped a bank robber cold.

"Get out of here," he said coldly. "Don't come back. Ever."

The heartless words made her heart stop. What had

been in that note? "Is it that woman?" Delia asked, feeling her heart turning to ice.

"It always was," he said without meeting her eyes. "We had a fight. She was in Miami and I got lonely."

She was pregnant. He'd said he adored her. And all of it, everything, was because he'd been missing his girlfriend?

He looked down at her, and his expression was cruel. "You heard me. Running after me isn't going to win you any points. Don't you have any pride at all? She's wearing my ring!"

Delia knew she was going to die later. He couldn't have made his feelings plainer.

"I'm here with another man, didn't you notice?" she said, gathering the tattered remains of her pride. Her heart was shaking her with its racing beat, and she felt sick all over. "I should think that speaks for itself. I'm a messenger. Nothing more."

"Good," he returned. He jammed his hand into his pocket. "Get out and go back to Texas. You're out of your league here."

"I noticed."

She turned her head and saw Dunagan returning with the brunette, who was glaring daggers at Delia.

"Do you love her?" she asked Marcus in the last second they were alone.

"With all my heart," he said flatly.

She looked up into his hard eyes. "And you cheated on her?" she asked on a hollow laugh.

"We had a fight," he said simply. He smiled cynically. "Did you think you had a chance? You're sweet, honey, but you're plain as old shoes and about as so-phisticated as a sand crab. You believe everything a man tells you."

"Not ever again," she replied with a tight smile. She searched his eyes. "They were right about you all the time," she said unsteadily. "You're just a gangster."

"Count on it," he agreed with cold eyes.

She turned away on shaky legs and smiled warmly at Dunagan. "Did you get the chips?"

"Sure did," he told her with a grin. "She showed me where to go. Thanks," he added to the gorgeous brunette.

"No problem," she said carelessly, moving right up next to Marcus with a possessive glance and a speaking glare toward Delia. "Have a good time."

"Oh, we will," Dunagan assured them, steering Delia toward the tables. "Good evening."

Dunagan stopped to speak to a man he knew. While he was distracted, Delia took a minute to catch her breath and try to pull herself together. She'd never dreamed that Marcus would treat her so cruelly. And the way he'd looked at her, as if she were an insect, beneath his notice. Her heart felt as if it had been shattered.

She put a tissue unobtrusively to her wet eyes, but as she put it away in her purse, she noticed a small, dark man with big ears that had curly lobes. His earlobes were so odd looking that she almost missed seeing the pistol that he was pulling out of his jacket. He was looking straight at Marcus.

Without even thinking of the danger, she turned and walked into him, knocking him off balance.

The small man cursed, gave her a seething glare, quickly stuck the pistol back into his belt and blended immediately into the crowd. He was out of sight seconds later. Marcus hadn't seen anything. Neither had Dunagan.

Delia's heart raced madly as she rejoined Dunagan. "Did you see that?" she asked quickly, without raising her voice.

"See what?"

"There was a small man with a gun. He pulled it out of his belt and was about to shoot Marcus with it. I knocked him off balance and he took off," she said, her eyes worried. "What is going on here?"

Dunagan ground his teeth together. "Where is he?"

"I don't know. He's very ordinary looking except for his earlobes. He just blended into the crowd. I don't know where he went."

"Did he realize that you saw the gun?"

"I don't think so," she replied curtly. "Why is someone trying to kill Marcus?"

He hesitated, just as Mr. Smith came striding into the room, alerted, no doubt, by his closed circuit camera. People moved out of his way as he joined Dunagan and Delia. Marcus, curious and solemn, glanced toward Smith, with his arm tightly around the brunette as if he wondered why Smith had approached Delia.

"Did you see him?" Smith asked Dunagan.

"I didn't," he replied tersely, "but Delia did. Were you watching?"

"Yes, on my monitors, for all the good it did me. I

don't think Marcus noticed anything." He turned to Delia with an urgent expression. "What did you see?" he asked her gently.

"Surely you saw him, too?" she asked softly, careful not to let anyone overhear. "Wasn't he on your monitor?"

He grimaced. "I got a nice shot of his back and the back of his head on tape, along with just a flash of the gun when he pulled it out and put it back up. The other monitors had a sudden, very convenient glitch, which means that he either has an accomplice or he knows his way around surveillance equipment."

"Suspicious," Dunagan murmured.

"Step outside with me, would you?" Smith asked quietly.

They went with him to the entrance. Delia managed not to look back at Marcus, who was still staring toward them, even though her heart was breaking at what he'd said to her.

"Was he aiming at Marcus?" Smith asked Delia the minute they were alone.

"I'm sure of it," she replied. "I walked into him deliberately, but I'm sure he didn't connect me with Marcus."

"What did he look like?"

"He was dark, small, ordinary, but he had unusual earlobes."

"Would you recognize him if you saw him again?" Smith persisted.

"Yes," she said with confidence.

Smith sighed roughly and ran a hand over his smooth head. "I didn't see it coming. That's a first."

Delia's blood was running cold. Someone wanted Marcus dead. Was it the government? Surely they'd go after him with a subpoena, not a hit man?

"Will he try again?" she wondered.

"Of course," Smith replied angrily. "And we won't see him coming next time."

"Maybe we could get a sketch artist," Dunagan ventured.

"No time," Smith replied. "He'll try again tonight. He can't afford to wait now." He looked at Delia. "I need you to stick around. Will you wear a wire, so that you can alert me the instant you see him, if you do?"

"Y…yes, of course," she said, although she wanted desperately to run to Marcus and protect him with her very life.

Smith looked at Dunagan.

"I won't leave her for a minute," he promised Smith.

"Are you packing?" Smith asked surprisingly.

To Delia's surprise, Dunagan nodded, opening his dinner jacket to expose a shoulder holster with an automatic pistol.

"Okay. We'll go to my office and do what's necessary."

"Why is Marcus in danger?" Delia wanted to know.

"I can't say," Smith said tersely. "Let's go."

Delia had a small battery-pack appliance attached to her dress under the belt at her waist, and the wire ran up just under the shoulder strap of her dress where it was clipped in place by Smith's efficient hands. It was black, and it didn't show. He inserted an earpiece in her ear, as well. She felt the danger like a living thing, more for Marcus than for herself. If he were killed, despite her misery tonight, she didn't know how she'd go on living.

"All you have to do is sing out," Smith assured her, indicating the receiver in his ear. "I'll hear you. I'm going to have the casino ringed around with volunteer staff. He won't get through us."

Delia managed a weak smile. "Gosh, I hope not."

"Keep your eyes open. And be careful," he added. "If this guy is a contract killer, he won't hesitate to shoot anybody who gets in his way, including you."

"They didn't waste any time, did they?" Dunagan said bitterly.

"Not a second," Smith agreed.

Delia glanced from one to the other, totally in the dark. Everyone seemed to know what was going on, except for her. But the thought that some stranger was trying to kill Marcus made her sick at heart. She was carrying his child, and he didn't know. How could she bear it if something happened to him?

"I'll be right beside her," Dunagan added.

It was only then that Delia realized he was wired already. He had an earpiece in his ear, too.

"Gosh, this is cloak-and-daggerish," she murmured.

Smith cocked an eyebrow. "You have no idea," he mused, green eyes sparkling. "All right. Are we ready? Showtime."

"What about Marcus?" Delia asked. "Does he know that somebody's trying to kill him?"

"If you gave him Barney's note, he does," Dunagan replied.

Her breath caught. That explained his expression, his determination to get her out of the casino. He didn't want her out of his life at all. He was protecting her! She felt her heart lift like a balloon.

"But he didn't see the assassin, did he?" Smith persisted.

"I can't be sure, but he didn't even look our way until the man blended into the crowd."

"Come on," Dunagan coaxed. "Let's get back downstairs. I'll be right with you every step of the way."

She gave him a curious smile. "You're not a tourist, are you?" she asked.

He chuckled. "Sort of."

"Don't ask him any questions," Smith told her firmly. "What you don't know keeps you safer. And you watch yourself," he added. "We don't want to lose you."

"I'm going to be fine," she assured him. "The thing is to save Marcus."

"Amen," Smith said.

"Let's go," Dunagan said.

"I'm right behind you," she replied, glancing one last time at Mr. Smith.

Her spirits dwindled a little when they were back on the casino floor and she saw the brunette curled into Marcus's big body while they stood on the staircase overlooking a bank of slot machines, talking to a customer. He was holding her with one arm, still smiling down at her with possession. It broke Delia's heart to see it. Had he really been trying to protect her, or was he genuinely involved with that dynamite brunette? From where she stood, it didn't really look as if he were pretending to be interested. Especially when his big hand strayed down to the brunette's hip and caressed it. She thought of the child she was carrying and fear rippled across her body. She was taking a chance not only for herself, but for the baby, as well, and nobody knew. But she couldn't back out. Nobody else would recognize the man who was trying to kill Marcus. Only her.

She didn't look directly at Marcus, but her eyes were everywhere else, darting to and fro while she tried to locate any sign of the odd man who'd aimed the gun at Marcus earlier. What a lucky break for her that he hadn't realized the bump she gave him was deliberate. It had saved Marcus's life.

Dunagan steered her to a slot machine just below Marcus and gave her a handful of quarters. "Go for it," he coaxed. "Just keep your eyes open at the same time."

She noted that he'd placed her so that she had a clear view of Marcus, who was standing just above her on the staircase between the first and second floors of the casino. He didn't move from the spot. Obviously, Smith hadn't yet spoken to him. Out in the open like that he made a good target, but it was also easy to see anyone approaching him. That had to be deliberate, to keep the hit man from thinking Marcus was aware of his presence, but it was dangerous. Smith was taking a terrible chance on Delia's ability to recognize the assassin.

The only bad spot came when Delia had to make a quick trip to the rest room, but she'd given Dunagan the best description she could and she hoped he could recognize the man if he reappeared.

As she walked out of the cubicle to wash her hands, the gorgeous brunette was waiting for her at the elegant, gilded bank of sinks.

She was primping, pushing at her perfectly coiffed long black hair. She gave Delia a cold going-over.

"I saw you talking to Marcus, while your boyfriend lured me away," she said icily. "Just don't get your hopes up. He belongs to me."

"Does he?" Delia asked.

"And nobody poaches on my territory," she said in a thick northern accent. She even smiled. "Not if they want to stay healthy."

Delia wanted to hit the woman. She was elegant, beautiful, rich, everything Delia wasn't. And Marcus had said he loved her.

"Have you known him long?" she asked.

"Long enough to know that I love him," the woman said smugly. "And I can afford him. You can't. A woman like you would be useless to a man like Marcus. You don't even know how to dress!" she said rudely. "A country rube at a place like this. What a joke! He'd have to hide you in a closet to keep his friends from laughing if they got a good look at you!"

Delia's eyes sparked, but she pretended surprise. "You're kidding, of course," she retorted. "As if I'd want to be seen going around with a gangster!"

The woman's eyes opened wide. She hadn't expected that response.

"I come from respectable, decent people," she

added haughtily, "who wouldn't be seen dead in company like this! I have too much pride to lower myself to that level!"

"How dare you!" the woman snapped. "Do you have any idea who I am? My father is filthy rich and so am I!"

Delia washed her hands and dried them nonchalantly. "Filthy is a good word for the sort of rich you are," she said. "Do have a nice evening." She smiled coolly and walked out.

"You…!"

The vulgar word floated on the air so loudly that a couple of heads turned when Delia walked out into the casino, but she paid no attention to her sudden notoriety. Her blood was boiling. She'd have liked nothing better than to knock the woman down. But she had other concerns.

"Wow," came a soft, deep chuckle in her ear. "Remind me never to make you mad."

It was Smith. He'd heard every word. Delia grimaced. She glanced behind her, watching the brunette storm up the staircase toward Marcus. "I'm a bad girl," she whispered.

"She's worse," Smith replied, and walked off toward the roulette wheel, his eyes still on the crowd.

Delia moved back to her slot machine, aware that Dunagan was trying to get her attention from halfway across the room. Her earpiece wasn't working! Dunagan indicated a solitary figure heading for the staircase.

"Oh, my God! That's him!" Delia exclaimed.

Smith and Dunagan came from different directions, trying to converge in time. Delia was closer, and faster.

She went up the staircase like a whirlwind just as the little man aimed the gun a second time at an oblivious Marcus.

Delia ran at him, pushing him just as he fired. He backhanded her with the strength of his whole body and she felt herself go backward, over the railing, down onto the casino floor. She landed with a horrible crash, and she felt as if her body were broken in two. The pain was so terrible that she blacked out.

Meanwhile, Marcus had struggled with the little man when they both wrestled over the railing and they, too, fell onto the carpeted casino floor.

The little man rolled and got to his feet, but by then, Smith had him in an inescapable hold and had handcuffed him seconds later.

Marcus, like Delia, was unconscious from the fall.

"Call an ambulance!" Dunagan growled into his microphone.

There were screams and muffled speculation as people gathered around Delia and Marcus with fascinated horror. The brunette was lying over Marcus's chest, crying hysterically when the ambulance sirens began to sound.

Chapter Ten

Delia came slowly back to consciousness. She moaned. Her stomach felt as if it had been ripped open. Her head was splitting.

"Baby?"

She opened her eyes and looked up at Barb with blank, curious eyes. "Barb?"

Barb was crying. "Oh, baby, thank God you're alive," she whispered hoarsely. "We were scared to death when Dunagan called us! I thought you were dead when we first got here!"

"I fell." Delia's mind was swimming. "There was a man with a gun...Marcus?!"

"He was still unconscious when we got here," Barb said coldly. "And good enough for him!"

"Is he going to live?" Delia asked worriedly. "Please!"

Barb hated Carrera. She didn't want to answer the question, but Delia did look so miserable. She couldn't refuse her. "I haven't seen him, but Barney said they think he'll live," she said reluctantly. "It was a concussion, just a little worse than yours. That brunette is all over him like measles," she added disgustedly.

Delia closed her eyes. She was sick with grief, anguish, bitterness. At least Marcus was alive, even if the venomous brunette was in possession. Then like lightning striking, she thought about the baby she was carrying and the terrible pain in her stomach. She gasped.

Her hands went to her stomach. She looked up at Barb with icy fear, wanting to ask but afraid, too.

Barb's face was eloquent. "You lost the baby, Delia. I'm sorry."

Delia's eyes clouded. Tears rolled helplessly down her cheeks. It had been Marcus's child. He wouldn't know. He was still unconscious. If he had concussion that severe, he could die, too, despite what the doctors were telling people.

Barb moved as close as she dared and held the younger woman gently. "Damn him!" she choked. "Damn him!"

"I loved him," Delia whispered brokenly. "I wanted our baby."

Barb ground her teeth together. "Why didn't you tell me?"

"Because I knew what you'd think," Delia said miserably. "You're so upright, Barb. You'd never have made a mistake like that."

Barb's face was contorted with pain, although Delia

couldn't see it. "I would have done anything I could for you," she replied. "Anything, baby!"

Delia held her closer, her face awash with tears. "I'm so sorry I didn't trust you!" she said, knowing how much it had hurt her sister to be kept in the dark.

"There, there," Barb whispered, stroking her hair. "It's going to be all right, you'll see. You're safe now."

"Dunagan?" Delia asked.

"He and Barney have gone off with some men in suits," Barb muttered. "Good grief, I feel like a mushroom lately! Nobody tells me anything!" She lifted her head. "Just what were you doing when you fell, Delia? How did you fall?"

Delia didn't want to involve Barb. If Dunagan and Barney had kept quiet, she had to do the same.

"The railing at the casino gave way," she lied.

Barb sat up and stared down at her curiously, and not with an expression of trust. "Barney said you got knocked off the staircase by a man who stole from the casino and was trying to get away from security."

"Did I say the railing gave way?" Delia touched her temple. "I must still be in shock."

"I must be wearing a sign that says, Lie To Me," Barb corrected darkly.

"It's for your own good," Delia replied. Her hands went back to her flat stomach. She was in shock right now, but it was going to be bad when it wore off. She didn't even want to have to face it yet.

Barb got up from the bed and sat down in a chair, grateful that the nurses hadn't seen her. Sitting on beds was strictly forbidden.

"Did they arrest a man in the casino, or did Barney say?" Delia asked hesitantly.

"The Bahamian police arrested a man for attempted murder, in fact," Barb told her. "Dunagan had put handcuffs on him and Carrera's head security man was sitting on him when the police arrived, according to Dunagan."

"Ouch," Delia murmured. "Mr. Smith is huge and the would-be killer was only a little guy—" She stopped abruptly.

"I am *so* ready to thump you when you're better!" Barb said through her teeth. "You saved that gangster's life, didn't you? And risked your own to do it!"

Delia closed her eyes. "I'm really tired, Barb," she whispered, becoming conveniently drowsy. "I just want to sleep for a while."

Barb relented, but her eyes were worried. "Okay, baby. We'll talk when you feel better. I'm just happy that you're going to be all right. Delia," she added slowly. "I'm sorry about the baby. But you don't have a clue what it would have been like to have it and keep it and be unmarried. You just don't."

"Like *you* know!" Delia said with loving sarcasm, her eyes still closed.

Barb's eyes were haunted. "I'm going to go and see where Barney got to. I'll be back soon, I promise."

Delia was getting drowsy for real. "Okay," she sighed.

Barb went out of the room and down the hall to intensive care. She paused at the desk.

"Marcus Carrera," she said slowly. "Can you tell me how he is?"

"Are you a member of the family?" the nurse asked.

"No," Barb replied, glancing through the window where the slinky brunette was leaning over Marcus in his bed. "But my sister saved his life."

"Then she must have been the young woman who knocked down the man with the gun," the nurse said at once, smiling. "My brother is a policeman, he told me. What a brave young lady!" She didn't notice that Barb paled and gasped. The nurse was looking through the glass into the intensive care room where the brunette and Marcus were. "He's just recovered consciousness. He's going to be fine. Well, in time," she added, leaning closer. "He doesn't know who he is, though," she whispered. "He's lost his memory completely."

Barb was secretly relieved. That might spare Delia a lot of pain down the road. At least it would make the last week of Delia's vacation a peaceful one, once she knew how things stood. Barb was going to make sure that she had a good time.

"Thanks," Barb told the nurse. "I won't say anything about it, except to my sister."

The nurse just smiled.

Barney was coming down the hall when Barb approached Delia's room. He was alone, and he looked worried.

"How is she?" he asked.

"Sleeping, when I left," Barb replied. She folded her arms tight across her chest. "Am I ever going to find out what's going on?" she asked him. "According to a nurse, my sister foiled an assassination attempt on the gangster down the hall!"

He pulled her down the hall to the waiting room and sat down with her in a corner, away from other visitors.

"I'm sorry I couldn't tell you sooner, but it was impossible. They've got a contract killer in stir over in Nassau," he told her. "He was sent here from Miami with explicit instructions to take out Carrera."

"Who sent him, the government?" she asked, still shocked from what the nurse had told her.

"No," he replied tersely. "It was a renegade gangster who's trying to set up a money laundering operation down here with the first of many casinos he hopes to buy. He's living in Miami and bucking the northern mob, and they don't like it. But so far he hasn't ticked any of them off. This will change things. Carrera has friends. Lots of them." He took a breath. "That hood in Miami made a big mistake using a killer with a rap sheet the size of this guy's. He's still wanted for two murders in New Jersey, and federal marshals are already on the way to pick him up after his extradition hearing."

"We're going to be in the middle of a turf war," Barb groaned.

"No," her husband replied. "You don't understand. Carrera's little brother was knocked off by a money launderer right here in the Bahamas, a banker with mob connections and ties to the Colombian drug cartel. Carrera's been after him for weeks. He's working with the feds."

Barb's jaw fell.

"I thought you'd take it like that," Barney murmured. "You can't tell Delia," he added firmly. "She's already done more than I'm comfortable with. She saved Carrera's life last night, twice. The first time she bumped into the assassin and put him on the run, before he knew who she was. The second time, she stopped him just as he fired. She and Carrera went over the banister in the struggle." He shook his head. "Smith and Dunagan were just a few feet away, but they'd never have been in time. They had a communications breakdown. When Carrera's back on his feet, Smith's going to be in serious trouble, I'm afraid."

"Barney, Carrera won't know him," she said slowly. "He won't know anybody, including Delia. I just came from intensive care. Carrera's regained consciousness, but he's got amnesia. He doesn't remember a thing."

"Amnesia? Oh, that's just great!" Barney growled. "Just great! We're in the middle of a sting, and he's the pivot. Without his cooperation, the little Miami rat we're trying to trap may just get his foot in the door down here!"

"That's not our problem," Barb told him. "I just want to get my sister out of the hospital and back home."

"I know that. But we can't leave just yet," he said apologetically. "I'm working with Dunagan because I'm thick with the money laundering banker," he added. "I have to finish what I started."

"Why are you mixed up in this?" Barb demanded. "And who is Dunagan?"

He grimaced. "I did a little artful doctoring of my

taxes last year. If I do the feds this little favor, I get to pay the penalty and not lose half my livelihood."

"Barney!" she exclaimed. "How could you!"

He patted her hand. "No need to sound so selfrighteous, doll, we both know you're not."

"Delia doesn't know, and she's never going to!" Barb shot back.

He was hesitant. "There's something I have to tell you. You aren't going to like it," he added. "The money laundering banker's name is Fred Warner."

She stiffened. "Fred, who tried to assault Delia?!"

"It gets worse. Fred got mad at Carrera for punching him over Delia that night, and he reneged on the deal he'd made with Carrera. He ratted him out to the Miami guy. That's why the assassin came after him. They know Carrera's working with the feds, and they're planning to take him out. Right now, he's the only one who knows what they're up to—except for me and Dunagan—and with his memory gone, we're in the hot seat together."

Barb felt sick. "There's more, right?"

"Fred's not through getting back at people," he told her. "He's been talking to a private detective. I don't know what he's after, but he's looking for revenge on me, too. It's just as well they detected my little income tax artwork, because Fred would have turned me over to the government in a heartbeat."

"He couldn't find out about my past, could he?" she asked worriedly. "Mama's dead. Nobody else alive knows…"

"We know, though, don't we?" Barney said quietly.

"There may be records somewhere that he can get into. I don't know. I just thought you should be prepared."

"I should have told her years ago, after we got married," Barb said miserably. "She'll never forgive me."

Barney pulled her close and held her. "Cross bridges as you get to them, honey. Don't anticipate them. We've been through more than this together. We'll manage."

"If we could just rewrite the past," she said sadly, resting her cheek on Barney's shoulder.

"Nobody gets to do that." He kissed her forehead. "Did you tell her about the baby?" he added sadly.

"Yes, but I'm sure she guessed," Barb said. Tears stung her eyes. "My poor Delia. She loved the fourteen-karat heel. She wanted that baby so much."

"We know how that feels," he replied, smoothing her hair. "A baby in the family would have been nice. I don't guess she told Carrera?"

"Of course not," she replied. "And he's practically sewn to that hard-wired brunette who's staying with him at the hospital, so it's just as well."

"I suppose. Amnesia. Imagine that." He sighed. "Dunagan and I are going to have our work cut out for us now."

"Well, you just keep my baby out of any future plans, you hear me, Barney?" she added firmly. "We're not going to risk losing her, too. No matter what."

"You know I'd never let Delia get hurt," he said with a sad smile. "Has it occurred to you that we've made a tragic error of judgment? Your mother helped it along, but we could have overridden her."

"It was too late by then."

He grimaced. "Most of it was my fault."

"I helped," she reminded him gently. She reached up and kissed him. "I do love you, so much," she whispered. "It was worth everything!"

"For me, too, honey," he replied, and kissed her back.

"We can't let Delia be hurt anymore," she said.

"I'll do my best to prevent it. You don't think it might be wiser to just tell her the truth about her past now?"

She shook her head. "Not until I have to."

"Then we'll try to head off Fred. Come on. Let's get a bite to eat while Delia's sleeping. I'm starved and they must serve breakfast around her somewhere!"

She went along with him, only later remembering that he never had told her who, or what, Dunagan was.

Marcus had a hell of a headache, and it didn't help that Roxanne Deluca wouldn't stop fussing over him. He hadn't recognized her, but she'd introduced herself and told him they were engaged. He noted the ring on her left hand and took it for gospel.

"What do I do for a living?" he asked her, sounding dazed.

"You own hotels and casinos all over the world," she told him easily. "And you and my father are in business together."

"We are? What sort?"

She gave him a calculating look. "I'll tell you all about it later."

He put a hand to his head. He felt sick and his temples were throbbing. "How did I end up in here?"

"You accidentally fell in the casino and hit your head," she lied glibly.

"Am I clumsy?" he mused.

"Not usually."

He closed his eyes. "I'm sleepy."

"Go to sleep, then, darling," she told him sweetly. "I'll be right here when you wake up."

"Okay," he mumbled.

She stayed until she was certain he was asleep, then she went out into the hall next door to the restroom and used her cell phone. "Daddy?" she said after a minute. "He's in the hospital. He doesn't remember anything. No, he's not faking, I'm positive, I asked a doctor. You can say anything you want to and he won't be able to contradict it. Pity, he's quite attractive. I know, Daddy, I'm not going soft. We can take him down at our leisure. Let me know where and when, and I'll get him there when you've got somebody to do the job. And please get somebody efficient! I'll be in touch. *Ciao.*"

She closed up the cell phone and walked back to Marcus's room. Barb opened the rest room door cautiously and made sure the brunette was out of sight before she walked back down the hall toward Delia's room. She had something very interesting to tell her husband.

The second day that Delia was in the hospital, she had an unexpected visitor—Karen Bainbridge, who walked in the door with an enormous bouquet of tropical flowers tied with a ribbon.

"I'm so glad that you're both going to be all right," Karen said. "But for Marcus to have lost his memory— I'm so sorry."

Delia forced a smile. "I'm sorry, too, but at least he's still alive. Do sit down! I'm so glad you came."

"Your sister isn't here with you?" Karen asked curiously.

"She and Barney went back to the hotel to get me some more nightwear," Delia said. "We thought I'd be released today, but they want to keep me until tomorrow."

"You're all right?" Karen asked, concerned.

"Yes. I...just had some minor complications," she replied, not wanting to tell the sweet elderly lady about the miscarriage.

Karen gave her a slow, penetrating look. "I told Marcus what you did, you know," she said gently. "That you saved his life. He doesn't remember who you are at the moment, but he was surprised and very grateful that you took such a risk on his behalf. I wanted to stay longer, but that woman with him seems very possessive. It wasn't until Mr. Smith walked in that she backed off and stopped interfering."

"Mr. Smith?"

She nodded. "He's been running the enterprise while Marcus is here. He's quite intelligent."

"Yes," Delia agreed.

"That woman almost didn't let me into Marcus's room. Mr. Smith moved her aside and invited me in. Marcus had no idea what was going on, but I imagine Mr. Smith will tell him sometime."

Delia was miserable at how possessive that other young woman was, and she couldn't hide it.

"There, there, dear," Karen said softly, reaching out to touch Delia's hand. "You mustn't give up. I'll never forget the way Marcus looked at you, the day we went out on the yacht together."

"She's wearing an engagement ring, and she says he gave it to her," Delia replied solemnly. "At the casino, before we fell, Marcus told me they'd had a fight and that was the only reason he had anything to do with me. He said I had no place in his life."

Karen was shocked. "He can't have meant it."

"He won't remember it now," Delia continued. "He won't remember me, either. But he made it very obvious that he didn't want anything more to do with me. At first," she added hesitantly, "I thought he was in danger and he was protecting me by telling me not to come near him. That was before she told me about the engagement. He told me, too, at the casino."

Karen's face fell. "I'm sorry. You seemed like such a perfect couple—and so much in love with each other."

"It did feel like that, for a while." She leaned back against her pillows with a deep breath. "You know, I felt as if I'd known him forever. Now I feel like a fool." She looked at Karen. "Life teaches painful lessons."

"Indeed it does, my dear. My fiancé was killed in Vietnam. I was never able to love anyone else," the older woman replied gently.

"Karen, I'm so sorry."

She smiled wistfully. "We might have been divorced

a week after the wedding, who knows? But the memories are very sweet. He was an American, from Oklahoma. His parents had a ranch that had been in his family for a hundred years." She stared down into her lap. "He was riding in a helicopter, airlifting wounded men, when the helicopter was shot down."

"It must have been devastating," Delia ventured.

"It took years to get over it," Karen agreed. She looked at the younger woman sympathetically. "Death or rejection, it's all loss, and it hurts. But you can get over this, too, my dear. I'll help. Any time you want to go sailing, all you have to do is call me."

"I'm very grateful," she replied. "Thank you."

"And now, let's talk about something cheerful! What do you think of my new crop of orchids?" she asked, indicating the bouquet she'd brought with her. She refrained from mentioning that Marcus had given them to her over the years and that her orchids were descended from his. Poor Delia. Her heart ached for the girl. She'd heard about the baby Delia lost, and she knew without asking that it was Marcus's. She'd told Smith that Delia had lost the child she was carrying. Smith had been shocked. She'd asked him not to share that with Marcus, because of the brunette. Smith had been utterly furious, and hurt. Karen sensed that he felt a responsibility for that loss. But he'd promised he wouldn't tell Marcus that in addition to losing his memory, he'd lost a child, as well.

Roxanne was raising so much havoc in Marcus's room that the nursing staff finally ordered her out. She vowed to return with an attorney, but she left.

Smith stood beside Marcus's bed like a stone statue. "Have you remembered anything, Mr. Carrera?" he asked his boss.

Marcus still felt as if his head was coming off. The nausea was easing a little, thanks to his medication. He stared up at the big, bald man with wide, blank dark eyes. "I don't know you," he said. "I don't know that woman who keeps coming in here, either, but I'll never believe I was stupid enough to get engaged to her. She's a lunatic!"

Smith grimaced. He didn't dare tell Marcus the truth. It would put the boss in more danger than he was already in.

Marcus was glaring at him. "You know all about me, don't you?"

"I've worked for you for a year, now," Smith said.

Marcus grimaced. "There was an old woman who came to see me. She said a young woman down the hall threw herself at a man who was trying to shoot me. She saved my life. I don't remember her. And why was someone trying to kill me?"

Smith ground his teeth. "Your doctor says we can't tell you anything yet. He says your memory will come back all on its own, but you have to give it time."

"I could be dead before then."

"I'm not letting anybody kill you," Smith promised him. "You may have lost your memory, but I've still got mine. I know all I need to know, in order to protect you. I'm afraid you'll just have to trust me."

"Why is that young woman in the hospital?" Marcus persisted.

Smith drew in a calming breath. If he didn't say, Marcus would ask a nurse, and that might provoke gossip. "She was pregnant," Smith said flatly. "The father of the child didn't know, if that was your next question. She's not married."

Marcus thought about that for a minute. His face was taut with strain, as if he were trying to remember anything about his past. He sat up in the bed and swayed a little. "Will they let you walk me down the hall?"

Smith hesitated. "I'll go ask."

He knew where Marcus wanted to go. It was possible that seeing Delia would trigger his memory. But if he meant to do it, it needed to be before Roxanne came back and took over again.

He asked the nurse, who agreed that Marcus could go down the hall if Smith was careful to support him.

"Your nurse says you can go walking," Smith said, helping Marcus into a burgundy bathrobe.

"Good. I want to see that young woman before my so-called fiancée gets back here. Let's go."

Delia saw her door open with a feeling of apprehension, especially when she realized that Marcus had come to see her.

He looked dazed, and he was moving very slowly. Smith gave her a quick warning glance, which she interpreted to mean that she wasn't to tell Marcus anything. She nodded back.

Marcus stopped at the foot of her bed and stared at her. He saw a plain, green-eyed young woman with tangled blond hair and a slender body. She wasn't pretty or exciting. She didn't seem his sort of woman at all.

He frowned. "Smith said you saved my life," he said without preamble.

"So they tell me," she replied in a heavily Texas-accented voice.

His eyebrows arched. "My God, what an accent!" he laughed. "Where are you from?"

She glowered at him. "A little town in south Texas that nobody from Chicago probably ever heard of."

He glanced at Smith curiously. "Am I from Chicago?"

Smith nodded.

Marcus looked back at the young woman in the bed. "How do you know where I'm from? Are we acquainted?"

She looked at Smith worriedly.

"Don't look at him, look at me," Marcus grumbled. "Do I know you?"

Delia took a breath. "You saved me from an assault at your casino," she said, compromising with the truth. "I saved you from an assault. We're even."

"Not quite." Marcus stared at her while odd flashes of sensation wound through his big body. "You were pregnant, they said. You lost your child."

Delia fought to keep her feelings from showing. "God's will," she said in a tight tone.

His eyebrows arched. "You're religious?"

She avoided his eyes. "Yes."

He was scowling again. "I think I was, too... Did you want your baby?" he asked bluntly.

She ground her teeth together. It hurt to answer that question. It hurt to look at him and have him know about their baby, and not be able to tell him that it was his, as well.

"Yes," she bit off. "I wanted it."

"The father, did he want it, too?"

She glared at him, fighting tears. "He didn't know. But if he had, it wouldn't have made any difference. He didn't want me. He certainly wouldn't have wanted a child of mine."

He couldn't let it go. He felt something when he looked at her. He didn't understand why he should feel sad. "Did you love him?"

She couldn't force herself to meet his searching gaze. "Yes. I loved him."

He didn't say anything. He just looked at her. "I'm sorry," he said finally, "about your child."

She didn't look up. "Thank you."

"Thank you for what you did," he replied.

"As I said," she choked, "I was repaying a favor."

He winced. He didn't know why it hurt him to hear her say that. His mind was spinning. He moved and almost lost his balance. Smith caught him, but he noted an instinctive surge forward from that young woman in the bed. She was concerned for him, even in the midst of her grief. Why should that make him feel guilty?

"We should go," Smith said deliberately, "before your fiancée comes back and misses you. There'll be a scene."

"God knows, we've had enough of those," Marcus

muttered. He was still watching Delia. "They say I'm rich. If you need anything, all you have to do is ask."

"I don't need a thing, but thanks," she replied, forcing a smile. Her eyes wouldn't go up far enough to meet his.

"Get better," Marcus said as he turned away.

"You, too."

"I'll be fine. My condition's not a patch on yours," she said without thinking.

A patch. A patch. A four-patch, a nine-patch, those were quilting terms. He turned so quickly that he almost fell again. "You make quilts!" he said abruptly.

Chapter Eleven

Delia felt her heart rise into her throat. He'd remembered! Would that trigger other memories?

But his lack of recognition was evident as he looked at her. "I don't know where that came from," he said, looking blank. He smiled politely. "*Do* you quilt?"

"I teach quilting back home," she replied. "We... spoke about it after you saved me from the man I was with."

He put a hand over his eyes as if he wanted to wipe away the fog that concealed his past. "Someone mentioned that I quilt, too, as a hobby."

"You've won competitions with your designs," she agreed.

He nodded, but he wasn't thinking so much about quilts as he was wondering why he'd had such an extensive conversation with a woman who didn't appeal to his senses at all. She seemed like a kind woman, but she didn't stimulate him or make him wish for a closer acquaintance. There couldn't have been anything between them, he decided.

He smiled politely. "Thanks again. I'd better be going."

"I hope you regain your memory," Delia said, with equal politeness.

He shrugged. "If I don't, it's probably no great loss," he said, chuckling. "It might be nice to start fresh."

"It might, indeed," Delia agreed, although he was twisting a knife through her heart.

He nodded to Smith, who got under his arm and steadied him down the hall to his own room. Smith felt sick to his soul about Delia. He gave her a last look, grimacing at the moisture growing in her eyes. Poor little thing, he thought miserably.

The next day, they released Delia and let her go back to the hotel, with instructions to rest for a day or two before doing anything strenuous. Since her plans had to do with sunbathing and sightseeing, she didn't think of that as a problem.

Marcus was also released. Roxanne followed behind the limousine as Smith drove him to his beach house. She carried in her suitcase and looked as if she had plans to take over.

"You'd better stay at the hotel," Marcus told her.

"We're engaged," she retorted.

He stared at her for a long time. "I want my memory

back. That's more likely to happen if I'm here on my own with no distractions."

"He's here," Roxanne fumed, glancing at Smith ruefully.

"He cooks," came the reply. "Besides, he'll be running the casino and the hotel in my absence, so he's unlikely to be around much anyway."

Roxanne paid close attention to that statement. She looked thoughtful.

Smith noticed and decided to make a couple of phone calls. He was going to add some extra gardeners to the house as well—men he'd worked with before who were handy with sidearms. He didn't trust Roxanne or her father one bit, and he was suspicious of her concern for Marcus, as well as the mysterious engagement that nobody knew anything about. It could be real, he decided, but only Marcus would know. And Marcus had no memory.

"Smith, take her over to the hotel and book her into a suite," Marcus said.

"Yes, sir."

Roxanne glared at him but she backed down. "All right, darling, if that's the way you want it. But all you have to do is phone me if you get lonely."

"Thanks," he replied.

She pulled her suitcase on wheels back out the door as Smith led the way. Marcus watched her go with mixed feelings, the most prominent of which was suspicion.

Later, when Smith returned, Marcus was dressed in lightweight white slacks with a red and white patterned shirt. He was standing out on his balcony with the wind ruffling his hair. He'd been drawn to the balcony, as if something important had happened to him there. He wished he knew what it was. The harder he tried to remember, the worse his head throbbed.

He turned at Smith's approach. "Who is that woman?" he asked.

"She's Deluca's daughter. He's a Miami hood who wants to own crooked casinos down here and launder money through a local banker," Smith said honestly. "Her father doesn't like you, so don't believe it when she tells you he's your biggest fan. You didn't have any plans to marry her, either."

Marcus put a big hand to his forehead and groaned.

"Sorry, boss," Smith said at once. "I shouldn't have said that."

"I wanted to know." The pain was terrible. He lifted his head, trying to focus. He looked right at Smith. "Who tried to kill me?"

"An insignificant little contract killer with a four-page rap sheet," Smith said. "Listen, boss, I'm not sure I should be telling you this stuff."

"There's nobody else who can." Marcus moved to the balcony overlooking the ocean. "Who sent him after me?"

Smith hesitated.

Marcus pinned him with threatening dark eyes. "Spill it!"

"Deluca," he said.

Marcus raised both eyebrows. "Why?"

Smith ground his teeth together. Well, it might save

the boss's life if he knew. He had to tell him. "You're trying to shut Deluca down," he said tautly.

"That doesn't make sense!"

"Yes, it does." Smith moved closer. "You had a brother, Carlo. He married Cecelia Hayes, his childhood sweetheart. They had two beautiful little kids, Cosima and Julio. Carlo finally got off drugs and straightened out, but before he could get his life back together, he was killed by the banker Deluca's working with, because he informed about some Colombian cocaine shipments to the feds. He died and you swore to get even. You've been working with the feds to shut down the banker and keep Deluca from coming in here and starting up crooked gaming." Smith cleared his throat. "The banker doesn't know you found out about him being involved in Carlo's death, but he did find out you were working for the government, and he was angry that you hit him to save Delia Mason from him that night at the casino. So he sold you out to Deluca and Deluca sent a cleaner after you. That's it in a nutshell."

Marcus felt ill. He leaned hard against the balcony. He had a brother, a niece and nephew, and he didn't remember any of it. A man was trying to kill him.

"Where does Roxanne come in?" he asked.

"She was hanging around you with a peace offer from her father that you were considering. She was supposed to keep you unsuspecting while the killer did his work. But Delia Mason got in the way. When you got amnesia Roxanne moved in and pretended you were engaged. She was overheard talking to her father on a cell phone to tell him you were vulnerable and they could take you on at their leisure."

"In other words, he'll send someone else to tie up the loose ends," Marcus guessed.

"Exactly. But you have amnesia and you trust Roxanne, so they won't play such a close hand this time. They'll feel safe."

Marcus smiled. "Good. Can you get me in touch with the feds I'm working with, unobtrusively?"

"That's going to be tricky. One of them cuffed the perp in plain view of Roxanne. He was playing the part of a tourist, but he's blown his cover. He was seen in the company of Delia's brother-in-law, who's also helping the government with this sting operation. That means I can't get you close to the feds. And if I'm seen with them, the jig's up, too."

"What about the woman, Delia?" he asked.

Smith grimaced. "Good God, boss, she's been through enough!"

Marcus glared at him. "Do you think she's safe? She foiled the hit, didn't she? Do you think Deluca will let that slide?"

"I hear from my sources that he's got something on her sister that he's planning to use, by way of revenge. He can't kill her, everybody would know who did it."

"Everybody will know who did it if he hits me, too," Marcus reminded him.

"Maybe. But Deluca's daughter is supposedly engaged to you, which means he's not got a visible motive for killing you."

Marcus sighed angrily, and glared out over the ocean. "I can't remember a damned thing. I still don't understand why the Mason woman risked her life and her child's life to save mine. She isn't my type. I don't even find her interesting. Surely I didn't encourage her?"

Smith didn't dare answer that question. "You saved her from the money-laundering banker," Smith said, trying to sound nonchalant. "It's hero worship."

Could it be that simple? He turned back to Smith and saw nothing in that calm countenance. He shrugged. "I guess that could explain it."

Great, Smith thought, relieved.

"Who was the old woman who came to see me?" Marcus persisted.

"Karen Bainbridge. You're friends. You got her interested in orchids. She grows them for nurseries now."

"Orchids. Karen." He frowned. "I grow orchids?"

"Yes. You've got a greenhouse full of them."

"And I make quilts." He shook his head. "I can't believe I do that."

"Why not? I knit."

Marcus's eyes were shocked. Smith was over six feet, solid muscle, with a military special ops background. He was a dead shot as well. "You knit?"

Smith shrugged. "I quit smoking because it bothered Tiny." He saw the blank look he was getting. "Tiny is my iguana. She lives in my room, in a giant cage."

"A giant iguana." Marcus frowned. "Do I like her?"

"Yes. But the point is, since I quit smoking, I've got to have something to do with my hands. You used to smoke cigars. You said that's why you started quilting."

"Orchids. Cigars. An old woman for a friend and a plain, uninteresting girl from Texas saved me from a hit man. It wouldn't pass as fiction, much less fact!"

Smith pursed his lips. "It would make a great novel."

Marcus glared at him. "I pay your salary, right?"

"Right."

"Get out there and find the feds. Tell them I'm game to help them nab this Deluca guy, but I'll need direction. I don't remember anything, and I won't know the players. They'll have to work out the logistics."

"I'll get right on it."

"That girl," Marcus said hesitantly. "Maybe I should send her some flowers or something."

Smith hesitated. It would give Delia false hope, and make her recovery even more difficult. "Not a good idea," he replied finally. "Roxanne might get upset and do something unexpected."

He sighed. "Good point. Okay. I'm going to stick around here. Get busy."

"Yes, sir."

Delia laid on the beach, soaking up the sun and trying not to go crazy thinking about the child she'd lost. It was every bit as bad to remember the look on Marcus's face when he'd stared at her in the hospital. She could tell that he found nothing remotely attractive about her, that he was supremely disinterested in her. It broke her heart because it made her question if he'd really felt anything more than desire for her when they were together. Perhaps it was exactly as he'd said; the brunette and he had argued, and he'd gone out with Delia for revenge. It made sense. A man like that wouldn't be attracted to a plain woman. It went against the grain.

She watched the water lap up on the shore with sad eyes, one hand lying quietly on the flat stomach that no longer contained her child. It was going to be hard to get over that. She probably never would.

A shadow fell over her. She looked up and Barney was standing there, wearing a neat suit. Amazing how familiar he looked sometimes, she thought. She'd always been fond of Barney, and he'd spoiled her rotten as a child. It was one of her greatest blessings that her sister's husband was honestly fond of her.

"Hi, Barney," she said, and smiled.

He pulled up a chair and sat down, facing her. "Hi, baby," he said, addressing her exactly as Barb always had. "I need to talk to you."

"It's about that Miami guy that Marcus is mixed up with, isn't it?" she asked. "Marcus is still in the line of fire. Is the government after him? "

He nodded. "No. Marcus is working for the government," he told her bluntly, "but you can't say that to anybody, you hear me?"

"I do." She looked at him, wounded now that her faith in Marcus had paid off just as he'd pushed her out of his life. He'd been a good guy all along. "Then who's after him?" she asked.

"Deluca is, and he isn't going to quit. Marcus

doesn't remember anything, but he wants to go ahead with the sting."

"But Deluca's hit man missed!"

"Deluca won't mess up if he sends another one. We have to get him off the street as soon as possible. We found a way to communicate with him through a cab-driver, but we're going to bait a trap for Deluca and it's dangerous. All of us think it would be a good idea if you went back to Jacobsville before it goes down."

Delia looked at him with pained eyes. "Why do I have to go? Nobody knows I was going out with Marcus, we kept it very low-key. Besides, he's engaged. That brunette stingray's living with him, isn't she?" she added coldly. "I'm no threat to anybody."

"She isn't living with him. She's staying in the hotel." He studied his clasped hands, trying to find a way around what he knew he should be telling her. "Delia, it's best if you go home. I can't tell you why."

"Is it because Marcus's enemies might target me?"

He hesitated. "You're not in any physical danger," he said.

"Barney, you're hiding something from me," she said with certainty. "This isn't like you."

He grimaced. "There are things you don't know," he began. "Like who your father is."

"Who my father is?" she ventured, shocked. "But my father died before I was born. I was premature...!"

He cleared his throat and there was a dull flush across his cheeks. "Well, that isn't exactly how it was. But what you have to know is that Fred's mad at us. He told Deluca that Marcus was going to sell him out, and that's why a hit man got sent in Marcus's direction."

That explained a lot. "But Marcus doesn't remember that!"

"If he does, he's dead. The Deluca woman told her father that Marcus doesn't remember anything about him, so he thinks he's safe. Deluca will be working on a replacement for the hit man. We're watching Marcus like a hawk. They won't catch us off guard again. But you're another matter. Fred's got some… well, some information he shouldn't have, about you."

She sat up, concerned. "What could he do with it?"

Fred looked pained. "Damn it, I told Barb she should have talked to you about this. She won't. She's scared to death to tell you."

"Barney, you're scaring me."

He took a deep breath and looked into her eyes. "I don't mean to. It's just, you need to know what's going on. I guess I'll have to tell you…"

"Barney!"

Barb's taut voice carried down the beach as she walked toward them in platform sandals, sinking to her ankle in the deep sand with each step. She grumbled all the way.

"What are you two talking about?" she asked suspiciously.

Barney sighed. "I was about to tell Delia…"

"…About our plans for dinner?" she finished for him. "We're taking you to this exclusive seafood place. There's a movie star in town and he eats there every night." She mentioned the name of a Texas movie star who'd been in a recent Western. He was Delia's favorite.

"That would be nice, Barb," Delia said, but she knew Barb had interrupted them deliberately. Whatever Barney knew, Barb didn't want Delia to know.

"I was telling her that we want her to go back to Texas, as soon as possible," Barney added coolly.

Barb didn't say anything for a minute. "At the end of the week," she said then. "Let her have a little vacation first."

"The longer she stays, the worse the risk," Barney reminded his wife.

"What risk?" Delia asked. "You just said I wasn't in any danger."

"Not that kind of danger," Barney said.

Barb and her husband exchanged an odd look.

"The end of the week, then," Barney said, rising. He kissed Barb's cheek. "You should tell her," he added softly.

"Tell me what?" Delia exclaimed, exasperated.

"Barney was only teasing," Barb said when he left. "Now, suppose we wander down Bay Street to the straw market? I feel like a new hat!"

Delia was still weak, but she knew the exercise was good for her. She bought a small wooden elephant and a new straw bag to take home with her. Barb was unusually animated, but not very forthcoming. Something was definitely going on.

That evening at the restaurant, Marcus came in with

Roxanne on his arm. Delia tried not to look at him. It hurt so much to see him with the other woman.

He paused at their table to speak to them. He looked at Delia carelessly, summing her up as part of the furniture. He smiled at Barb and invited them over to see his orchid collection the next day.

"We'd love to, thanks," Barney said at once, taking advantage of the public invitation to do some private business with Marcus.

Roxanne grumbled, "But we were going out tomorrow!"

"You may be. I'm not," Marcus told her. "I'll see you about eleven, then?" he asked Barney and Barb. He didn't look at Delia at all as he and Roxanne passed on to their table. Delia felt like sinking under the carpet.

Marcus had orchids everywhere, but especially in the enormous, expensive greenhouse with its own climate control.

He acquainted them with the various species of orchid, and showed them how the beautiful flower grew only in bark, not in soil. The colors ranged from pink and white, to spotted yellow and deep orange. There were huge bracts of flowers, and tiny ones. The containers that held them were as unique as the orchids themselves.

While Barney and Barb were enthusing over one particular species, Delia found herself briefly alone with Marcus. He was wearing light Bermuda shorts and a patterned green and white shirt that made his eyes look even darker. She had on a blue and white sundress with white sandals, her long hair hanging around her shoulders. She was still pale from her ordeal.

"You seem to be doing well," he remarked, feeling uncomfortable with her.

"So do you, Mr. Carrera," she replied politely. "Your orchids are…"

"Who are you?" he asked huskily, his gaze as intent as his tone. "I don't know you, but it upsets me just to look at you. Why?"

She sketched him with her eyes, her heart breaking as she realized that he might never remember anything that had happened between them. Amnesia was unpredictable. "We were only acquaintances," she lied. "Nothing more."

"I know that," he said irritably. "You're not my type of woman at all. You're not glamorous or particularly pretty, you obviously buy your clothes off the rack, your body is too thin, you don't even wear clothes well. I could never have been involved with you," he agreed angrily. "But it was more than a nodding acquaintance. Were you connected with the casino somehow?"

Her heart felt as if he'd stepped on it. He couldn't make it plainer that he had no romantic interest in her. He was certain he couldn't have cared for her.

She lowered her eyes to the orchids nearby. "No," she said. "I don't gamble."

He sighed angrily. "Why do you do that?"

"Do what?" she exclaimed, looking up.

"You look at me as if I'm killing you," he bit off.

She forced a laugh. "How silly. I'm having a nice

time looking at the orchids. What sort is this?" she added, pointing to an ordinary purple and white phalaenopsis.

He hesitated, as if he wanted to press it, but he gave in and answered her question. Then he stepped close to show her the way the bracket of flowers grew and the tension exploded between them. He turned to her, a breath away, and saw every quick beat of her heart moving the fabric at her breasts. He felt an electricity that grew quickly explosive as he felt the heat from her body.

His jaw tautened almost to pain as his dark eyes met her green ones at point-blank range. His lips parted on a rush of breath. His big hand went to her cheek and his fingers drew down it involuntarily. Heat exploded in him.

Delia felt it, too, but she'd had enough. She moved away from him and back to the safety of Barney and Barb without a word.

Marcus stared after her, scowling, feeling as if he were on the brink of some incredible revelation. But it hung there, just out of reach, taunting him, tormenting him. She meant something to him in the past, he could taste it. What had she been, a minor amusement? Why was he attracted to such an ordinary, dull woman? It must be the concussion, he decided finally, still knocking him off balance.

For the rest of the visit, he ignored Delia, hating the sensations he'd felt with her. He showed his guests the new koi pond he was building of sandstone, a mammoth undertaking with plumbing for all the necessary filters and an expensive liner to boot. He

wondered if he'd liked the colorful Japanese fish
before? Until he lost his memory he'd apparently not
had a yen for koi. The pond had a waterfall, also of
sandstone. It was going to be beautiful, when it was
finished.

He found time to get Barney alone, and they spoke
about Deluca. Then, all too soon, they were ready to
leave.

While Barney was getting Barb into the back of the
cab, Marcus hesitated beside Delia. "You lost your
child saving my life," he said sadly. "I'm sorry."

Tears stung her eyes. "Tragedies happen to most
people at one time or another," she said, trying not to
let it show that it was killing her to stand beside him like
this and pretend they weren't involved. She loved him!

He felt empty somehow, especially when he saw the
tears she was trying valiantly to stem. "You really loved
that baby, didn't you?"

She nodded jerkily. She couldn't speak.

"Why?" he ground out. "Why did you take the risk,
to save me, a man you didn't even know except as a
chance acquaintance?"

She couldn't look at him. "It was an impulse. I saw
the gun in the man's hand and I just reacted."

"At what cost!" he said heavily.

She forced her eyes to lift. He looked tormented.
She adored him. It was so strong a feeling that she
couldn't hide it, and he saw it in her face.

It was like peering into a dark room and seeing just
a sliver of light. He wanted to force the memory, but
he couldn't. "Tell me," he said under his breath.

She managed a sad smile. "Dragging up the past benefits no one. I'm glad you're still alive, Mr. Carrera. The other…" She took a deep breath. "I believe in acts of God. It wasn't meant to be, for whatever reason. I have to accept that and live with it."

He searched her soft eyes and felt again that jolt of sensation. He frowned. "I don't understand why it hurts me to look at you," he said under his breath.

She averted her eyes and moved away. She couldn't bear to talk about the past any more. He'd made it clear that she didn't appeal to him in the least. He didn't want her except physically; he probably never had. He was engaged, after all, to the sort of woman he'd told her he liked—beautiful, sophisticated and rich. "You've already made your feelings clear. After all, what would a rich, powerful man like you want with a dull, plain nobody of a woman like me? Goodbye, Mr. Carrera," she said, and felt as if her heart was breaking right into. "I hope life treats you better than it's treated me."

As she went to get into the cab, Delia met Marcus's eyes across the car and she winced at his closed, angry expression. She didn't look at him again.

He stood and watched the car drive away. Her sarcasm had made him angry. But he felt as if he'd just cut off an arm, and he didn't know why.

That night, while Barney and Barb went to a show downstairs in the lounge, Delia answered the phone and found herself talking to Fred Warner.

"Think you scored real good against me, didn't you,

honey, but the joke's going to be on you. Why do you think a millionaire like Barney married a little school-girl from Texas when he could have had a debutante, ever think about that?"

"What?" she exclaimed, too shocked to fight.

"You idiot, he looks just like you, and you never noticed? Barney married Barb because she had his baby! He was married when she got pregnant, so your grandmother went away with Barb and told everybody it was her kid. Barb's not your sister, you dope. She's your mother!"

He hung up.

Delia was sitting on the sofa with her head spinning. She couldn't move. She couldn't breathe. Barb was her mother. It had to be a lie. Surely it did!

But things kept going through her mind. Barney did look like her. They favored more than Delia and her late mother had. Barney had been affectionate toward her all her life. He loved her. Barb loved her. It was more than sibling love.

Why hadn't Barb told her? Why had she let her grow into a woman believing that her grandmother was her mother? Why?

She sat and worried and seethed for the next hour and a half until Barney and Barb came back.

They came in the door laughing, having been dancing most of the time after the floor show ended. They were happy, upbeat, cheerful. Until they saw Delia's rigid features.

"I had a phone call from Fred Warner," Delia said coldly, staring at them.

Barb let out an unsteady breath. She put down her evening bag with careful deliberation.

"And…?" she said, trying to sound casual.

"He said that Barney was my father and you were my mother." Her eyes pleaded with them to deny it.

Barney seemed to slump. He sat down on the sofa, leaning forward. "It was only a matter of time, I told you," he said to Barb in a subdued tone. "I told you to tell her the truth!"

"Then…it's true," Delia choked.

Barb burst into tears and ran for the bedroom. She closed the door behind her.

Barney was left, staring at Delia, who looked as if the whole world had fallen on her.

"Why?" she asked harshly.

He spread his hands expressively. "I was married, baby," he said heavily, "to a woman who would have done anything to hold on to all that nice money I had. She never loved me. She only wanted what I could give her. I met Barb while I was in San Antonio on a business deal." He smiled reminiscently. "She was staying overnight with a girlfriend and she went to the same bar where I was. She was dressed real sexy and she was wearing some sophisticated makeup. I thought she was in her twenties." He sighed. "One thing led to another. When I realized what a kid she was, and how innocent, it was already too late. She went home and never mentioned me to your mother, not even when she got pregnant. It was two years before I found out. By then I was divorced, and your grandmother had told everyone that you were her baby, to save Barb's reputation. You were born seven months after your grand-father died, so they said you were premature."

"All these years," Delia said on a sob.

"I wanted to tell you a million times," Barney said, in anguish. "But Barb couldn't bear to have you know. You were brought up so carefully, sheltered so much, so that you wouldn't make the same mistake Barb did."

"But I did anyway," she said flatly.

"Yeah." He grimaced. "If we'd made you go home, maybe you'd never have had to find out. Damn Fred!"

She looked up at him. "It would have come out one day, Barney," she said, feeling oddly sorry for him. He did look so devastated. Not unlike Barb…

"What will you say to Barb?" he asked gently.

Her face closed up. "I don't want to see Barb again right now. I want to go home, Barney. In the past week, my whole life has fallen apart. I'm leaving tomorrow. First thing."

"Okay," he said after a minute. "If that's what you want."

"That's what I want," she said flatly. Then she hesitated. "What about Marcus?" she asked reluctantly. "Will they try again to kill him?"

Barney sighed. "I don't know, baby, but I imagine they will. He's got friends," he reassured her. "Good friends. We'll do everything we can to keep him safe. I promise."

She swallowed hard. "Thanks."

"Barb and I ruined your life," he said. "You don't owe me a thing."

She looked up, her eyes wet with tears. He was her

father, and she'd never known. She wished she'd never had to find it out like this. Life, she thought miserably as she went back to her own room, could be cruel.

Chapter Twelve

The next morning, Delia was up just after daylight and packed when Barb knocked and immediately came into the room.

Delia stared at her as if she were seeing a stranger. Barb's eyes were red and swollen and she looked as devastated as Delia felt.

"I know you don't want to talk to me," she said quickly. "But just give me one minute, please!"

Delia didn't speak. She was still devastated by what she'd learned.

"I was sixteen. Mama was very strict and I thought she was an old fogy," Barb said huskily. "So I snuck off one weekend and went to San Antonio with a friend of mine. We bought some cheap dresses and smeared on lots of makeup and went to a bar. Barney was there

alone. We started talking and when he left, I went with
him. I didn't know he was married," she added miserably, wiping at her eyes with a tissue. "But I knew I
loved him, and he loved me. I had to go home, and I
was afraid to tell him how old I really was, so I just left
without a word."

Delia sat down and folded her hands, waiting for the
rest.

Barb sat down, too. At least Delia was listening, she
thought. "When I knew I was pregnant, it was devastating, not only because I didn't know what to do, but
because I was going to have to tell mama what I'd
done. I knew she'd be ashamed of me, but I couldn't
hide it. Daddy had just died and she was miserable. But
the thought of a new baby sort of snapped her out of
the depression," she added with a faint smile. "I dis-
guised my condition with big clothes and tent dresses
until I was almost due, and then we went away for a
couple of months and stayed with a cousin of Mama's.
We said the baby was Mama's when we came back
home."

"Why?" Delia demanded.

"Because even today in small towns it's hard for a
child to grow up illegitimate," Barb said, her tone sad
and resigned. "I didn't want your childhood to be any
harder than it had to be. I figured Barney would hate
me if he ever found out how young I'd been, and that
I'd probably never see him again. So we let you think
that my mother was your mother, too. But when you
were two years old, Barney finally tracked me down.
By then he was divorced, and he was still crazy about

me. When he saw you, he just fell in love. So he married me. We wanted to take you with us," she added, "but Mama went crazy. She said she'd do anything to keep you, right up to running away with you to another country and hiding out like a fugitive." She grimaced. "Barney and I were afraid she might do it, so we got a house in San Antonio and I was at the house almost every day until you graduated from high school and got a job. We didn't move to New York until you were self-supporting."

"I remember," Delia said heavily.

"We loved you so much, both of us," Barb said, studying her closely. "We still do. We've been bad parents, and we've made a lot of mistakes. I know you need time to come to grips with it all. I won't push and neither will Barney." She stood up. "But I hope someday you can forgive us."

Delia was too confused and still too grief-stricken over Marcus and her baby to manage forgiveness for that big a deception. She didn't look at Barb. After a minute, the other woman's hopeful expression drifted into one of despair and she turned away.

Barb lowered her head and moved to the door. She hesitated, but she didn't look back. "We'll always be there if you need us, baby," she said gently. "And we'll always love you. Even if you...can't love us back, because of what we did."

Her voice broke with tears. She went out the door and closed it firmly behind her. Delia stared at it with dead eyes. It was just too much at one time. She had to go home, she had to get away from here! Maybe when she was back in a normal place, she could get her life back together again. Maybe she could accept that Barb had done the only thing she could have done, in the circumstances.

The plane ride home seemed terribly long, because Delia dreaded arriving back in Jacobsville. So much pain overwhelmed her. She'd lost Marcus, her baby and now her own identity, all in less than a week.

Her heart was broken. She cried until her eyes were swollen. She didn't know how she was going to cope with it all. She loved Marcus. That was never going to change. But he didn't remember her, and he might never. She couldn't get their last meeting out of her mind. He knew there was something between them, but he had no memory of it. The sight of his tormented face, his sad eyes, would haunt her always. But what they'd had for those few weeks would last her all her life.

She needed time to mourn her child, get over Marcus, and come to grips with what she'd just learned about Barney and Barb. They were her parents. She'd always believed that her father had died before she was born, and that Barb's mother was also her mother.

Now she began to see the past for what it was. Barb had always been more protective of her than her grandmother had, and she'd been sheltered by both of them. But her grandmother had always blamed her for Barb's lapse of judgment. Her grandmother had taken out all her resentments and anger on Delia, without Barb knowing. Looking into Barney's face was like looking in a mirror, not to mention that she shared Barb's coloring, but Delia hadn't wanted to see those things. She'd accepted a lie. Now she knew everything.

She had to find a way to cope. It would take time to get used to the idea of her changed identity. She knew that, in the end, she couldn't hate Barb. She'd done what she thought was best for Delia, without realizing that Barb's mother was going to make Delia pay for Barb's mistake by persecuting her child. She was only disappointed that Barb and Barney had lied to her for so many years. Maybe they did have a legitimate reason. And they certainly didn't know how hard her grandmother had been on her all those years.

Marcus had been brooding ever since Delia's visit with her sister and brother-in-law. The feelings he had were unexpected and inexplicable. She wasn't his type of woman, so why did he feel such turmoil when he was with her? Why did she look at him as if he meant something to her? Why did she look as if he was hurting her every time they were together?

He couldn't find any answers, and nobody would talk to him about Delia, not even Karen Bainbridge. His memory wasn't any closer than it had been, either. All of it combined to make him irritable and frustrated.

Roxanne Deluca was still around, and she was behaving very suspiciously. She was trying to coax him into taking her to one of the deserted islands in the Bahamas chain. She'd even chartered a boat without telling him.

"You need to get completely away from here for a day,

and I'm taking you to a deserted island with me, tomorrow morning." she said, cuddling close to him. "We'll be like Adam and Eve, darling," she teased breathily.

He knew she was up to something, and it probably had to do with a new contract on his life. He was grateful that Smith had been so forthcoming about the situation, or he might have been killed without ever knowing the reason.

"Okay, then," he said. "Come on over about nine in the morning, and we'll go from here. That suit you?"

She smiled broadly. "Yes, it will. I'm so glad you're better, darling."

"When were we getting married?" he asked her.

She hesitated. "Oh, in December," she said, thinking fast.

"December." He nodded, pretending to go along with it.

"We're going to be so happy," she exclaimed.

Later, when she'd gone back to the hotel, he called the cab company and asked for John to come to his house. He paid the cabbie, John, for a double trip that he wasn't going to take, to allay suspicion, and gave him a note for Dunagan.

"Give it to Barney Cortero," he told John quietly. "He'll get it to Dunagan. Don't do it yourself. Got that? And make sure he gets it today. Or you can come to my funeral."

John grimaced. "Yes, sir, Mr. Carrera. You can count on me."

Unfortunately John went across the bridge too fast and T-boned a passing jitney. The wreck gave him a light concussion and a broken rib and sent him directly to the hospital for treatment. It wasn't until the next morning that he was conscious enough to remember the note. He asked the nurse for the shirt he'd been wearing. She handed it to him. He extracted the note and grimaced as he read it. Carrera and Roxanne were going to the marina at nine for a trip to one of the Out Islands. It was now ten o'clock.

"I must have a telephone, at once," John croaked to the nurse. "It's a matter of life or death!"

Barney was just about to leave the room to join Barb downstairs for brunch. They'd overslept and he was still a little groggy. But as he reached the door the phone rang. He ignored it and went out into the hall.

But something nagged at him. He hadn't heard from Carrera, and he'd expected to. What if it was Marcus?

He unlocked the door and went back inside, lifting the phone just as it stopped ringing.

"Hello? Hello?" he repeated.

A thin, weak voice came on the line. "Mr. Cortero?" a husky voice queried. "This is John. I drive a cab. Mr. Carrera sent me with you last evening with a note, but I was in an automobile crash. I'm in the hospital."

"I'm sorry. What's in the note?" Barney asked.

John read the note to him. "You know which island this is?" he added and gave directions.

"Thanks, John. There isn't a minute to lose!" Barney

hung up and dialed Dunagan on his cell phone. "It's me," he said when Dunagan picked up. "We've got an emergency."

Marcus had packed a gun, just in case, and he wore it in an ankle holster under the flaring denim of his jeans. If they took him out, he was going to go down fighting.

Roxanne was dressed in a flirty white sundress, her long dark hair sleek and expertly cut. She smelled of expensive perfume, and she was beautiful, but she had the eyes of a cobra.

"You love to go exploring undeveloped islands," she said in a chatty tone as they sailed out of port. "We've done this several times, but not lately."

He didn't believe her. She didn't look like the sort of woman who liked exploring primitive places. He was betting that she planned to lead him right into a trap. He was going along with it. By now, Barney and Dunagan would be waiting for the gangsters when they made their play. He smiled to himself, thinking how surprised Roxanne was going to be when her father found himself in federal custody.

The crew of the sailboat seemed oddly familiar, but Marcus couldn't place them. He was getting bits and pieces of his life back, in odd dreams that woke him in the middle of the night. A shadowy woman had been the main attraction in them, a woman with a loving, sweet personality who made him whole. It hadn't been Roxanne, he was certain. He'd thought that perhaps he'd run into the unknown woman at the casino. It was a magnet for beautiful, rich women. He was sure that she was extraordinary. He sensed that he hadn't been involved with anyone for a long time, until just recently. But so far, he hadn't run across the mystery woman. Sometimes he could almost feel her in his arms, the sensations were so real. Then he woke up, and he had no memory of what she looked like. It was, he thought absently, like the powerful, odd sensations he felt with Barney's sister-in-law Delia. His attraction to her was as inexplicable as it was shocking. But, then, Delia was a plain, sweet down-home sort of girl, not the type to appeal to his sophisticated tastes. It couldn't have been her.

Well, he had plenty of time, once he got rid of Deluca, to search for his mystery woman. He'd have the leisure, then, to wait for his memory to come back.

"You're very quiet," Roxanne commented as they approached the deserted island she'd described to him.

"I was just trying to remember my recent past," he said easily. "I remember my childhood, my parents, the place I went to school." He shrugged and slid his hands into the pockets of his beige slacks. "But I can't remember what I did a week ago."

Roxanne seemed to relax. "Don't force it," she said. "It will come back."

He glanced toward her. "Think so? I wonder."

"We're here," she said, pausing to give the crew the order to drop anchor so that she and Marcus could go ashore in the small rowboat.

"You can still row, can't you?" she teased.

"I suppose I'll remember how when I start," he

agreed. He gave the crew a searching look, because they still looked familiar to him.

One of them, a tall Berber with the traditional mustache and beard, raised an eyebrow and gave an imperceptible jerk of his head to indicate that Marcus shouldn't look at him too hard.

That was when he knew that the crew of the sailboat wasn't working for Roxanne. He actually grinned before he climbed down the ladder into the dingy.

"You're very cheerful all of a sudden," Roxanne remarked.

He chuckled. "I have a feeling that I'm going to get my memory back very soon. I don't know why, but I do."

"You may be right," she said, without looking at him.

He rowed the boat into the shallows and they jumped out. He tugged it up on the beach so that it wouldn't wash out to sea.

"Now what?" he asked Roxanne.

"Now, let's go exploring!" she said enthusiastically, catching his big hand in hers. "If I remember right, there's a little shack just through there…"

All his instincts for self-preservation were standing up and shouting at him. He moved along with her, but vigilantly, his eyes ever searching for the glint of the sun on a gun barrel, or a shadowy figure nearby.

"I'll bet we'll find a nice cozy little nook in here," she told Marcus, and went up onto the porch of the rundown shack. "Why don't you go on in, and I'll look around for some driftwood so that we can build a fire in the fireplace, like we did before," she added deliberately, smiling. "I'm sorry you can't remember it. We had a really good time here!"

She turned to go down the beach.

He stepped up onto the porch. But instead of going inside, he bent, as if to retie the rawhide lace on his deck shoes. As he squatted down, he palmed the ankle gun.

His heart raced madly. He wondered what the sailboat crew had in mind. If a contract killer was hiding here waiting for him, he'd have to manage alone.

Roxanne, sensing something, turned around and frowned. "What's wrong?" she asked, trying to sound nonchalant.

"Nothing, I just had to tie my shoelace," he called, rising.

"Go on in and wait for me, darling," she cooed.

Wait, the devil, he thought, gritting his teeth. He opened the door and threw himself to one side just as a shot rang out.

He fired without even thinking, reacting to the shot as he had in the old days. The old days…

Everything became crystal clear in seconds. The man in front of him clutched his chest with an expression of disbelief and slumped to the floor, a red stain spreading over the back of his shirt as he landed facedown on the wooden floor of the shack.

"Did you get him?" Roxanne yelled.

"No such luck, baby," Marcus returned. He kicked the killer's gun aside and stepped onto the porch, his dark eyes blazing as he looked over the rail at her.

"And that's the second time you and your father have struck out."

Roxanne's mouth fell open. Before she could do anything, say anything, three men came out from the back of the shack with leveled guns.

"Put your hands up, Miss Deluca," the Berber said pleasantly, "unless you want to join your father's hired man in hell."

Roxanne put her hands up at once. She could hardly believe what she was hearing. "He's…dead?"

"Looks that way," Marcus said, his voice even and cold. He came down the steps with the pistol still in his hand. "Was he the only one?" he asked the Berber.

"Yes. We searched thoroughly. Are you all right?"

Marcus laughed hollowly. "Apparently." He gave the taller man a curious appraisal. "Who the hell are you guys?"

"Friends of Mr. Smith," the Berber told him with a grin. "And that's all you need to know. We were barely in time to bluff the crew Miss Deluca had hired and tell her they had a prior engagement and sent us to replace them. Luckily she swallowed it. Dunagan said to tell you that he's found an 'associate' of Mr. Deluca's who's willing to spill his guts in exchange for immunity. His name's Fred Warner."

"Fred!" Roxanne exclaimed. "The weasley little coward…!"

"Sticks and stones, Miss Deluca," the Berber said. "Let's go."

"What about him?" Marcus asked, nodding toward the shack.

"Bahamian police are already on the way. They were looking for the guy in Nassau, but we figured Miss Deluca here had him waiting for you in a secluded place. So we came along for the ride."

"Thanks for the backup," Marcus told them.

"Our pleasure. Now, we'd better get going."

Barney, Barb and Dunagan had supper together that night, after statements had been given to the police and the body of the contract killer had been tucked away in the local morgue. The man, like Deluca's other hired gun, had a rap sheet as long as a towel. Deluca had been picked up in Miami on federal racketeering charges stemming from statements made by his banker, Fred Warner. Roxanne Deluca was arrested for conspiracy to commit murder. Once jurisdiction was established, the two of them could expect a lengthy stay in jail.

They'd invited Marcus to eat with them, so they could fill him in on everything that had happened about Deluca. Even Barb hadn't protested. She was so lonely for Delia that she'd given up her vendetta against the man who'd wronged her. Marcus hadn't completely regained his memory, but he felt more optimistic that he would, despite all the unsettling business of the day. Bits and pieces of the past were fitting themselves into place with each passing hour. He noticed that Barney and Barb were positively morose. Dunagan was manfully trying to keep the conversation going all by himself.

"You two look like the world just ended," Marcus commented.

"Personal problems," Barney replied.

"We all have them," Marcus said heavily.

"It's a good thing you're a dead shot," Dunagan said. "Because John was in a wreck and we didn't even know what was going down until you were halfway to the island with Roxanne."

Marcus smiled, having heard that from the Berber. "Your guys showed up, at least, but they couldn't go ashore with us without arousing Roxanne's suspicions. But I always carry a hide gun. Old habits die hard." He scowled. "How did I know that?"

"Looks like your memory's trying to reboot," Dunagan said, grinning.

"I wouldn't mind. It's like living in the dark." He stared at Barney curiously. "It's odd how much your sister-in-law looks like you," he said out of the blue.

"That's because she's actually my daughter," Barney said miserably.

Barb took a big swallow of her drink. "And my daughter, too," she added. She gave Marcus a wry glance. "It's almost funny. I was so determined to keep her away from you, because I thought you'd wreck her life. And Barney and I did it all by ourselves."

Marcus frowned. "What do you mean, keep her away from me?"

Barney was trying to give Barb hand signals but she was already three sheets to the wind and she wasn't looking at him.

"She was going around with you while Barney and I were in Miami," she said heavily. "She thought the sun rose and set on you. I didn't know how far things had gone until...ouch!"

She rubbed her shin, where Barney had kicked it. He gave her a hard look, which she finally interpreted. Marcus had lost his memory and they'd said not to tell him a lot about the past. It could be dangerous.

"Don't mind me," Barb said, trying to backtrack. She laughed inanely. "I'm drunk. I think we'd better go, Barney. I need some sleep."

"Me, too," Barney agreed. "Good to see you all in one piece, Marcus," he said.

"And thanks for the help," Dunagan added, rising. "We won't forget."

Marcus shrugged. "It's been my year to play Good Samaritan. Back in the spring, I helped bag a guy who kidnapped Tippy Moore. Remember her, the super-model who became a movie star?" he recalled with a smile. "She married an old friend of mine, Cash Grier. He's a police chief in a small town in Texas." He paused, shocked. Those memories had come back without any work at all.

"Jacobsville," Barb informed him. "That's where Delia and I are from."

Marcus was very still. Jacobsville. Small town. Texas. Cash Grier. Tippy's kidnapping. He remembered! He'd visited Tippy in the hospital in New York. He'd been in the hospital in Nassau with a concussion. Delia had been down the hall. He'd gone in to see her without knowing why. She'd looked so familiar to him. She'd been pregnant...

"Good night," Barney called as he and Dunagan shepherded a weaving Barb out the door.

Marcus waved, but he barely heard them. His mind

was going full tilt. Delia had been pregnant. She'd
saved his life. She'd lost her baby. Her baby.

He signed the tab—no big deal, because he owned
the hotel—and went up to his office. Smith glanced at
him with subdued concern.

"I heard what happened," he said. "I'm sorry I
wasn't there. It was all I could do to get the guys
together and send them after you. They were working
on a job for a friend of mine, in the area. It was a lucky
break for me, because I couldn't find Dunagan or
Barney and I had no idea what was going on."

Marcus waved away the apology. "Tell me about
Delia," he said curtly.

Smith hesitated.

"Barney's wife said I was going around with her."

Smith grimaced. "Well, yes."

Marcus stilled. "Smith—she was pregnant. Was
it…mine?"

Smith's eyes closed and opened. "Yes," he said
huskily.

Marcus sat down behind his desk. The baby was the
key that opened the lock. He had sudden, sharp flashes
of memory. Delia, laughing up at him with the wind
blowing through her blond hair as he drove her in the
convertible. Delia, in his arms, loving him with unbridled passion despite her utter innocence. Delia,
looking at him as if he were some sort of hero when
he saved her from Fred. Delia, with tears in her eyes,
understanding that he didn't remember her or know
about the baby. Delia, walking away from him with her
heart breaking…

"Dear God, I let her go!" he burst out. "She was pregnant. She lost the baby, lost me, lost everything. I told her she wasn't my kind of woman, that she could never appeal to me. I actually said that to her. And then, I just let her walk away, without a word! She must have been devastated!"

"Boss, you didn't know who she was," Smith said gently. "She understood."

He put his face in his hands and groaned in utter anguish. "She lost our baby, saving my life," he whispered. "She fell!"

Smith didn't know what to say. He said nothing.

Marcus continued, "She ran right into that little weasel and knocked the gun out of his hand. He was going to kill me. She saved my life and what did I do? I acted as if I couldn't have cared less about her! I was convinced that I'd never have gotten mixed up with some plain little small-town woman from Texas. I was looking for the mystery woman in my past, for someone beautiful and rich and sophisticated. Delia was standing right in front of me, and I treated her like a stranger. What an idiot I was!" He moved to the balcony and opened the sliding glass doors to let the wind in. He stood there, shattered, vulnerable, hating himself.

"She went home, didn't she?" he asked belatedly.

"Yes," Smith replied.

"And why not? I suppose she thought I'd never get my memory back. I know I looked at her as if she couldn't have interested me any less. She'd been hurt, she'd lost the baby, she'd lost me…" Marcus's eyes were tormented. "No wonder she looked at me as if I were killing her, when I walked into her hospital room." His eyes closed and he fought tears. "After all she'd been through, I turned my back on her, too."

"You didn't know," Smith said again.

"I should have known," Marcus said heavily. He pushed back his unruly hair with a big hand. "I lit up like a rocket whenever she came near me. I ached to hold her when she was close to me. Even that didn't register."

"You were hurt, too."

"Not enough," he said icily. "Everything I got, I damned well deserved. There was going to be a baby," he added, and the pain almost doubled him over. "A baby, Smith. My baby. She...lost it."

Smith closed his eyes. He couldn't bear to see the torment in that dark face. Marcus Carrera was one tough customer, but he was melting in front of Smith's eyes.

"I'm sorry about that," Smith said.

"She just found out that her sister was really her mother, and her brother-in-law was really her father," Marcus added dully. "That, the baby, me...I guess she figured she didn't have any reason to stay here. She probably felt as if we all sold her out."

"She needs time," Smith said wisely. "It's a lot to have to adjust to."

"Yeah." Marcus moved back into the office, his manner distracted. "I'd like to just rush down to Texas and scoop her up and bring her right back here. But you're right. She's going to need time. So I'm going to give her a few months, to get over the worst of it. Meanwhile, I've just thought of a project that may help my case when I go after her."

"Go…after her?"

Marcus smiled faintly. "Half a man can't live, Smith," he said simply. "Not for long, anyway. I'm going to marry her."

Smith's green eyes sparkled at the idea of his boss, a loner by nature, being so smitten with a woman.

Marcus gave his bodyguard a speaking glance. "You've never married, I guess?"

Smith shook his head, smiling. "I'm too picky."

"There were rumors that you were crazy for Kip Tennison," Marcus added.

"I was responsible for Kip and her son for several years, you know," Smith told him. "I'm terribly fond of them both, but her heart always belonged to Cy Harden and I always knew it."

"You didn't stay with them."

Smith chuckled. "Harden and I didn't quite come to blows, but we're too much alike to get along. Besides, since they had their second child, Kip's given up most of her work for the Tennison corporation and she's working as a vice president for Harden's companies. It's her former brother-in-law who's in the line of fire now. I wasn't needed." He cleared his throat. "Harden never did take to Tiny. I think he had a secret lizard phobia."

"Maybe it was an excuse to get rid of the competition," Marcus chuckled.

Smith shrugged. "A man as good-looking and

talented as I am would inspire jealousy in most men," he said with a straight face.

Marcus grinned. "Just as well I got landed with you. When Delia comes back, you're going to be needed more than ever. I expect to found a small dynasty down here," he added, the smile fading to sadness as he thought of the child he'd lost before he even knew it existed. "Babies are nice. In fact," he mused, breaking out of his somber mood as he turned, "I've got some nice blue and pink batik prints and a few fat quarters of whimsical fabric that would make the sweetest little quilt…"

He was gone before Smith had to hide his amused smile.

Chapter Thirteen

Delia had always loved Christmas. It was her favorite season. Jacobsville pulled out all the stops for the holiday season, beginning just at Thanksgiving, decorating everything in sight. There were garlands of pine and colored lights strung across the street that went around the town square, and every door had a wreath and a red bow. There were Christmas trees in almost every window, including one right next to the statue of Big John Jacobs. There were lighted reindeer, Santa Clauses and snowmen, and wreaths on the lawns of businesses and homes. In holiday dress, Jacobsville was absolutely without peer.

It was getting easier to look back, Delia thought, although she still grieved for Marcus and her baby. But she felt the pain grow dimmer as time passed. She missed Barb and Barney, as well. She hadn't spoken to them, but she had sent Barb a card just a few days ago for Thanksgiving, and had one sent right back in return. By Christmas, she hoped, they might be speaking again and visiting. She'd never spent a Christmas without Barb and Barney that she could remember.

She was sorry she'd been so hard on them. It must have been difficult for them to have to give her up to Barb's mother, and more difficult to keep the secret all the long years in between. They loved her. Of course they did, and she loved them. But they should have told her the truth years ago.

She wondered if Marcus had gotten his memory back. She supposed not, because he hadn't been in touch with her all these months. But, then, would he contact her? He'd looked at her without any spark of interest most of the time. He'd even told her that she could never appeal to him as that Deluca woman did. Anyway, it was probably just revenge and desire and nothing more on his part. It even made sense. He'd gotten mad at his fiancé, picked up Delia, seduced her and then felt guilty. It would explain why he hadn't wanted her to contact him after their night together. Whatever had gone before, or whatever might have been, he was engaged. He might even be married by now. Certainly he might even welcome his loss of memory, because it would keep him from having to explain his lapse of fidelity with Delia to Roxanne Deluca.

She did write to Mr. Smith, however, in care of the Bow Tie, without putting her name or return address on the envelope. To her surprise, he wrote back immediately. She learned that there had been another attempt on Marcus's life, but that some mercenaries who were friends of Smith had saved him. The perpetrators were now in custody, including a Miami mobster who'd planned it all—and Fred Warner was right in custody along with him. He cautioned her not to mention it to anyone. As if she knew anyone who'd even be interested, she mused. She was so grateful that Marcus was still alive and out of danger, even if he did marry that Deluca woman. Amazing, she thought, that he'd been targeted by the Miami mobster yet he was engaged to the same mobster's daughter. It didn't make sense.

Nevertheless, it had been a joy to know that Marcus wasn't doing anything illegal, that he'd worked with the government to shut down the illegal operations. Sadly, it wouldn't have mattered if he hadn't been. She'd loved him so.

She hadn't heard from Mr. Smith after that. It was as if there was a conspiracy to keep her in the dark. Perhaps he'd mentioned that he'd written her to Marcus, and Marcus hadn't approved.

All her rationalizing didn't keep Marcus out of her thoughts. She dreamed about him every night. When she put a quilt block together, she thought about him. When she taught a quilting class, she thought about him. Her life was empty in a way it never had been before. She felt as if she'd been cut in two. Even worse was the loss of her child. She'd loved babies all her life. She'd dreamed of having one of her own. Now she could hardly bear to look at baby clothing, or furniture, or even photos of her customers' children and grand-children. It was like a knife through her heart.

But she was adjusting. She felt far more mature than she had been. She was less unsure of herself, less nervous around people. She'd grown emotionally. She was certainly stronger than she'd ever been. But she missed Marcus. Oh, how she missed Marcus!

She was putting the final touches on the second shortened sleeve of a garment she was altering when she heard the bell go out front, where she had her small office open to the public. Leaving the shirt on her sewing machine table, she walked to answer the door, smiling automatically as she opened it. It didn't occur to her to wonder why the customer didn't just walk in. Everybody else did.

But when she saw who her caller was, she was dumbfounded. She couldn't even manage a single word of greeting.

Marcus was doing some hard looking of his own. She'd grown thin in the three months they'd been apart, he thought. She was finer-drawn, from the grief. But her green eyes were wide and surprised and brimming over with delight that she couldn't hide. He relaxed, just a little.

"Mr. Carrera," she greeted hesitantly.

"I know who you are, Delia," he said quietly. "I know what happened. My memory came back. Fortunately it came back before Deluca's second hit man took his best shot at me."

She stared at him hungrily. "I'm so glad he missed," she said softly.

He shrugged. "I guess you didn't know exactly what

was going on, did you?" He grimaced. "Can I come in?" he asked, glancing behind him uneasily. "I've never had so many people stare at me before. I feel like a lobster at a seafood restaurant."

"Certainly," she said belatedly, stepping aside to let him in. She paid great attention to closing the door behind him while she tried to get her wits back about her.

"I was just at the police department to see Cash Grier," he explained.

"You know our police chief?" she asked, surprised.

"Yeah. One of the guys who kidnapped his wife Tippy, back in the winter worked for me at one time. I helped the feds put him away," he added.

She didn't know what to say. She didn't know why he was here. "Are you married now?" she asked, trying to sound nonchalant.

"Married?" he asked blankly.

"Roxanne Deluca said you were engaged to her."

"She told me that when I lost my memory. Roxanne's dad was setting me up for another hit," he replied blandly. "I knew Roxanne, but we were never engaged. She wanted me to believe we were, so that she could lead me into a trap."

"But...why?" she asked. "I don't understand."

He perched himself on the edge of her desk and studied her intently. She'd cut her beautiful long hair. He grimaced, because he'd loved the length. She was wearing a dress that was obviously homemade, and not sexy at all. She dressed, and looked, like a woman who didn't care how she appeared to men ever again. He was responsible for that. It hurt him.

"The trap?" she prompted, because it made her uncomfortable to have him look at her that way.

"I've been working with the feds to shut down
Fred Warner."

"Yes, I know."

"Do you?" he asked quizzically. "Well, Fred was
laundering money for Deluca, who wanted to move in
on Paradise Island and set up his own casino. You can
probably imagine what sort. Crooked. Anyway, Fred
was already doing dirty banking for one of the bigger
drug cartels in Colombia."

"Your brother was killed by them," she recalled.

He looked at her, surprised. "I guess I did tell you
that." He smiled apologetically. "Some things are still
a little blurry. Yes, Carlo was killed by the cartel when
he tipped off the feds about a shipment. They injected
him with an overdose of cocaine to make it look like
an overdose, but the medical examiner wasn't fooled."

"Was he working for the government, too?" she
wondered.

His face was taut. "No. He wanted to get back at
the guy who got him hooked. Your old pal Fred
Warner," he added.

Her lips parted on a soft rush of breath. So that was
the connection.

"But the Colombian cartel Fred was laundering
money for wanted revenge for that lost shipment, so
they went after my brother and killed him," he said
sadly, his face hardening. "I swore I'd get Fred for
doing that, so I cultivated him with a phony offer of
working with me and Deluca. Deluca had contacted

me, that's true, and I drew the feds in before I approached Fred."

"But it didn't bring back your brother," she murmured sympathetically.

"No," he agreed, his tone sad. "If he'd just left that damned Fred Warner alone, and not tipped off the law about the cocaine shipment, he might still be alive," he added coldly.

She felt his sadness. "He did the right thing, though. You know he did."

"Yes. The right thing. But he died for it." He grimaced. "I never could understand why he couldn't stop using. I smoke cigars occasionally, but I can quit any time. I don't like addictions, so I don't have any. Carlo was different."

"I've known people who drank and couldn't stop," she replied gently. "I've always connected alcoholism and drug addiction with chemical imbalance. It seems to me that addictive personalities are basically depressed people who are trying desperately to find substances that will lift their moods. In fact, it does the opposite, and just makes it worse."

He searched her face quietly. "That's one of the first things I liked about you," he said. "You're not judgmental. You always look for reasons why people do the things they do. Me, I just shoot from the hip."

She lowered her eyes. "I thought you didn't like anything about me."

He ground his teeth together. He hated the memory of that last conversation they'd had before she left the Bahamas.

She turned. "I'm glad you came by," she said. "But I really have to go back to work now."

"Delia."

She didn't want to look at him again. It hurt too much. But she forced herself to face him.

He was holding something in a bag. She hadn't noticed until now. He held it out to her, almost hesitantly.

She took the carrier, set it on the desk and opened it. Tears blinded her to its beauty for a few seconds. She lifted it out, blinking away moisture, and spread it slowly on the surface of the desk.

It was a baby quilt. It had a block with a Texas landscape and one with Navy Pier in Chicago. Another one was of Blackbeard's Tower in Nassau, and a house with casuarina trees on the ocean. It had a block of a man and a woman at a table on the beach. It had one of a yacht, another of a woman making a quilt, and a man cutting a pattern. In one, there was a couple holding hands silhouetted against the ocean and the moon. In the center, there was a baby dressed in a lacy white gown and a white cap, with a halo over its head.

"It's our baby," she whispered brokenly, without choosing her words.

"Yes," he bit off.

She looked up. His face was tragic, as she imagined her own might be. There was a suspicious moisture in his own eyes.

It was too much. She ran to him, one arm holding the quilt, the other open to embrace him.

He swept her up without a word and stood just

holding her, rocking her, while she cried and cried. Tears ran down her cheeks and into the corners of her mouth. She cried until the pain became almost bearable, and still he held her close.

"The past three months have been pure hell," he whispered roughly at her ear. "A hundred times I've picked up the phone to call you and put it down, or started to write a card, or thought about buying an airplane ticket. But I didn't think you'd even speak to me, and I didn't want to upset you any more. Barb and Barney said you weren't having anything to do with them. Well, until three days ago, they got a card from you." He chuckled, although his voice sounded oddly hoarse. "Then I figured, hey, if she can forgive them, maybe she can forgive me. So I got on a plane and flew to San Antonio. It's taken me two days just to get up the nerve to come down here."

She rubbed her wet eyes against his throat. "Did you rent a car?"

"Hell, I rented a limo. I'm not driving you around in some budget sedan and having your friends say I was too cheap to do the thing right."

She pulled back and looked up at him with her whole heart in her eyes, smiling through the tears. He looked older, too, and almost as worn as she did. She reached up, hesitantly, to touch the dark circles under his eyes. There was moisture there.

He caught her hand and pulled it to his mouth, as if he didn't want her to know how it had affected him, when she saw the quilt.

"I was so glad that Dunagan and Mr. Smith's friends

kept you safe," she confessed, smiling through her tears.

His eyebrows lifted. "How did you find that out? You haven't been talking to Barb or Barney. They'd have told me."

She looked sheepish. "Mr. Smith wrote to me," she admitted, "and I wrote back, to a post office box he's got in Nassau."

He caught his breath. "So that's how you knew what was going on! If I'd known that, I wouldn't have been so miserable. I'll shoot Smith for not telling me!"

"No, you can't do that," she said with a smile. "I made him promise not to tell you. I was worried, and since I wasn't speaking to my...parents," she said the word for the first time, "there was no other way I could know how you were."

"You cared how I was, after the way I treated you?" he asked with humility.

She touched his wide mouth with her fingertips. "You didn't remember me," she said softly. "You couldn't help it."

"You gave up on me," he accused. "You went away and left me with that poisonous brunette."

"I thought you might really be engaged to her," she pointed out. "She said you were, and you'd already told me not to contact you, after we went out with Karen on the yacht. I knew about her father, but it wouldn't be the first time a woman got involved with a man against her father's wishes. For all I knew, I could have been a fling."

"Some fling," he murmured, his eyes eating her. "I

breathed you from the minute we met. I've been half a man for months."

She managed a weak smile. "Me, too."

He lifted an eyebrow.

"Figuratively speaking," she corrected.

He bent and touched his mouth to her soft lips, tenderly. "I want to take you out to supper tonight. I've got something for you. There's a hotel in San Antonio, the Bartholomew," he added. "I booked a table for seven o'clock. Okay?"

"Why do you have to go to San Antonio to give it to me?" she wondered. "It will be expensive, to have the limousine go there and back again..."

"I'm rich. Didn't you notice?"

She sighed. "I was too busy noticing how sexy you were," she confessed.

He grinned.

She lifted the quilt in her hands and looked at it again, this time with pleasure as well as pain. "This is beautiful."

"We'll keep it in a special place. But I'm working on another one," he added. "One with blocks with numbers and letters in them, and little animals in separate blocks. I'm going to do a blue and pink and yellow one, so it will work for a boy or a girl."

She was confused. "Why?"

He looked down at her with poignant feeling. "I thought, if I asked nicely, you might give me another baby."

Her heart felt near to bursting. That didn't sound like he wanted an affair.

"We'll talk more about it tonight."

"It isn't very fancy, is it?" she worried. "I don't have a lot of nice clothes, Marcus."

"Anything you wear will be fine," he promised, but in the back of his mind, a plot was already forming. "What time do you close up?"

"At five."

"I'll be here about five-thirty. That okay?"

She nodded.

He reached down to kiss her, softly. "Don't forget."

"How could I?" she wondered in a breathless tone.

He turned to go, pausing with his hand on the door handle. "I'm glad you're better," he said. "I had hell living with the things I said to you. It was worse, knowing you lost the baby saving me."

"You think I could have stood by and let him shoot you?" she asked sadly.

"No more than I could have let him shoot you, honey," he replied huskily.

She fed her eyes on him. He was beautiful to her. She never got tired of looking at him. And a man like that had come all this way to take her out to eat. She was amazed.

"I'll see you later," he promised, and winked as he left the shop.

He walked right into an elderly lady who'd been standing outside the door. He apologized and backed into a young couple. As he turned to apologize again, three people he hadn't seen excused themselves for being in the way. A few yards away, a woman was taking pictures of the black super stretch limousine sitting outside Delia Mason's combination house and shop.

"Nice day, isn't it?" the elderly woman asked, grinning from ear to ear.

"Yeah. Real nice."

Marcus dived into the limousine with a total lack of grace and slammed the door. "Get me the hell out of here!" he told the driver.

At precisely five o'clock, Marcus knocked on Delia's front door, peering warily around him while the limousine sat at the curb with its motor running.

Delia opened the door, still in the dress she'd been wearing earlier, shocked. "You said five-thirty!" she exclaimed. "I haven't even started to dress…!"

"I know." He took a long box from under his arm and handed it to her. He put another box on top of that one. He pulled a jewelry case out of his pocket and added that to the stack. "Five-thirty," he said.

She knew the labels on the boxes. One was that of a couture fashion house, the other a leading shoe manufacturer. He hadn't got these things off any rack. "But you don't know my size!"

"I called Barb," he replied.

He climbed back into the limousine and it took off. Delia closed the door. It felt like Christmas.

Inside the big box was a black silk dress, just her size, and cut to emphasize her slender figure. It fell to her ankles in soft ruffled folds. In the shoe box was a pair of high heels to match. In the jewelry case lay a thick gold necklace encrusted with emeralds and diamonds, and two matching earrings lay in the center of it. She knew before she looked that the gold was 18 karat and the stones were genuine and of the highest quality. Barb had taught her about fine jewelry.

She got out her best underwear, which was still a poor match for the finery Marcus had brought, and started dressing. Fortunately her blond hair had some natural wave, and it didn't look bad at all to her. She used more makeup than normal and pulled out a fancy black velvet coat that Barb had given her to wear with the dress.

When Marcus knocked at the door, she was ready.

"I forgot about the coat," he remarked. "We can get you a fur if you want one. I'll phone and have one sent down right now—"

"I can't wear fur, Marcus," she interrupted softly. "I'm allergic. Sorry."

"Are you allergic to cats and dogs?"

"No. I've got a dog, remember? Sam has a fenced yard out back and a doghouse. My pet chicken Henrietta has her own little fenced corner and a henhouse. I'll introduce you to them another time. I'm only allergic to fur coats."

"Thank God." He noted her curious stare. "While I had amnesia, I adopted two big Persian cats."

"Why?" she asked.

He shrugged. "Search me. That was just after I put in a koi pond."

"I remember you showing it off before I left the Bahamas. I still can't believe you have a pond full of those beautiful, colorful Japanese fish like the ones we saw in that botanical garden we visited."

He was surprised she knew about koi. He hadn't remembered. Or had he?

She was fascinated. "When we walked around the garden, I told you that I loved them. You said you weren't that interested in fish!"

He laughed. He had remembered. "I've thought about doing some koi quilts."

Her eyes brightened. "Oh, I'd love to do some of those, too."

"Then we'll have to talk about having you come live on Paradise Island," he murmured dryly. "Because I don't think my nerves will let me live here."

"Why?" she asked blankly.

He turned and pointed to the limousine. On the sidewalk near it, the same woman was taking photographs of it again. A new couple was standing near a tree, apparently talking, but they were both staring at Marcus and Delia. An elderly woman down one end of the street was pruning roses. Two girls in the upstairs window of the house next door were giving Marcus thumbs-up signals. And a police car was going slowly down the street while the officer driving it looked at the floor show. Out back, the dog was raising the devil. He was going to upset her hen, Henrietta, in her nice little caged lot, and there would be no eggs for days.

"I forgot that Callie Kirby and her stepfather lived here before she married Micah Steele," Delia said on a sigh. "They still tell stories about their courting days."

"The crowds, you mean?" he asked, glowering at the crowd nearby.

"It's a very small town," she pointed out. "The only real crime we've had in years was when our local mercenaries shut down a notorious drug dealer. Oh, and Tippy Moore batting a would-be assassin on the head with an iron skillet. They say when Cash Grier got there, the man ran out to the police cars pleading for the officers to save him from Tippy."

He chuckled. "I've met the lady, and I don't doubt the story."

She smiled up at him. She touched the emeralds gingerly. "You shouldn't have done this," she said.

"You needed a dress and some accessories," he said simply, catching her by the hand. "Lock the door and we'll take a bow before we leave."

She fiddled with the lock, only half hearing him. "A bow?"

He pulled her into his arms, bent her back against one of them, bent and kissed the breath out of her.

When he let her go, the elderly woman had her hand on her heart and looked as if she might faint. The couple nearby was watching, openmouthed. The girls at the window were cheering. The woman taking the photo of the limousine was now snapping pictures of Marcus and Delia. And the police car was stopped in the road, blocking traffic, while the man inside leaned out the window to shout at them.

"I'd give that a Nine-Plus on a scale of Ten!" Police chief Cash Grier called to Marcus.

"You're blocking traffic, Grier!" Marcus called back.

Grier just chuckled and waved as he drove off.

Marcus escorted Delia to the car with continental flair, waited while the uniformed driver opened the door, put her inside and dived in after her.

"So much for satisfying our public," he teased, laughing at her still-dazed expression.

The restaurant was crowded, and Delia was still reeling from Marcus's stage kiss. She gave her coat to the clerk at the coat room and took Marcus's hand as they followed the waiter to their table.

Sitting at it were Barney and Barb, dressed to the nines and looking nervous and even a little frightened.

That softened Delia's heart even more. She went straight to Barb with her arms wide open.

Barb ran into them and hugged her close, crying. "Oh, baby, we've missed you so much!"

"Hello, stranger," Barney added, opening his own arms to be hugged.

"I'm sorry," Barb began.

"No, I'm sorry," Delia said at the same time, and laughed because they sounded like echoes. "I just had to get used to it," she added. "But now I'm glad. I'm so glad! I love you both very much."

"We love you, too, baby," Barney said, and turned away before he lost his composure.

"I told you it was going to be a surprise," Marcus told Delia with a grin.

"It really was," Delia said, laughing through her tears. "Oh, I'm so glad to see all of you!" she exclaimed, including Marcus as she swept her eyes over the three most important people in her life. "I'm sorry I've been such a pain," she added softly, to her parents. "I'll try to make up for it, honest."

"You had so many hard knocks, baby," Barb told her. "It's no wonder it hit you so hard. We understood." She glanced at Marcus with a wry smile. "And Marcus has kept our spirits up, too."

"We were all sort of in the same boat," Marcus explained. "None of us wanted to rush you, but it was a lonely game."

He seated Delia while Barney seated Barb, and the waiter bought menus for them.

After they ordered, Delia looked around the table. "I don't understand why we're here tonight, though. Is it some sort of special occasion?"

"You might say that," Marcus mused.

Barb and Barney smiled mysteriously.

"What, then?" Delia persisted.

"You'll just have to wait until after dessert," Marcus teased. "But I promise, it will be worth waiting for."

Dinner was exquisite. Delia had never eaten food so wonderful. And the desserts were rolled from table to table on a trolley, so that the guests could choose their own. Marcus liked a deep chocolate cake. Delia picked a crème brûlée and savored every single bite.

With the dinner came wines, a delicious white with the fish and a dry red with the beef, and champagne with dessert.

The bubbles tickled Delia's nose. She laughed. "I don't think I've had champagne more than once in my life. Mother didn't approve of spirits," she added. Then she stopped, and looked at Barb. "I mean, Grandmother didn't approve of spirits," she corrected, and her eyes were full of love.

Barb bit her lower lip. "Thank you, baby," she said softly. "But I know it's going to be hard for you to get used to calling me Mother. You just go right on calling me Barb. It doesn't matter, honest."

But it did, and Delia knew it. She reached over and touched Barb's hand gently. "You've been like a mama wolf all my life, protecting me and sheltering me and taking care of me. I've always thought of you as more mother than sister, and especially now. I'm glad you're my mother. And I'm glad Barney's my dad," she added, smiling at him, too. "It was a surprise, but it's not a bad one. It was just that so much was going on at the time. I think I went a little crazy."

"No wonder," Marcus replied. "You lost everything, didn't you?"

"Yes. But what doesn't kill you makes you stronger, don't they say?" she replied. "I've matured."

"You have," Barb said.

"But you're still my baby," Barney told her with a loving smile.

"Thanks."

He shrugged. "What are dads for?"

"That's something I can't wait to find out for myself," Marcus murmured, giving Delia's shocked face a speaking glance. "And that reminds me…"

He reached into his jacket pocket and pulled out a small, square jeweler's box, one that matched the box

Delia's necklace and earrings had been in. He opened it and sat it just in front of Delia's dessert plate. Then he waited, watched, his breathing all but suspended.

She stared at the rings openmouthed. There was an emerald solitaire in an exquisite heavy gold setting, surrounded by small diamonds, next to what was obviously a matching wedding band.

"It looks like…" she began.

"It is," Marcus said quietly. "I'm asking you to marry me, Delia."

Chapter Fourteen

Delia stared at the rings with her heart in her throat. He was telling her that he wanted to marry her. She shouldn't have been surprised, not after he brought her the baby's memory quilt. But she was.

She looked up at him with tears in her eyes.

He grimaced. "I know. You're remembering what I said to you, that you weren't my type, that I didn't believe I could ever have been interested in you. But the doctors explained it to me. Even when I had amnesia, I was still trying to protect you. Deluca was after me and you were in danger if you were near me." He smiled gently. "You see, it wasn't that I didn't care. I cared so much that even amnesia didn't affect it."

She curled her small hand into his big one and

looked at him with her heart in her eyes. "Yes, I'll marry you, Marcus."

"They weren't kidding, you know, when they said I had a reputation," he added, his expression solemn. "I have got a past, and I was a bad man."

"No bad man could make a quilt like the one you brought me today," she said simply, and swallowed hard to keep the lump in her throat from choking her.

His fingers tightened on hers.

Barb and Barney exchanged puzzled looks, but Marcus and Delia weren't sharing that memory. It was too personal.

"Yes, Marcus," Delia repeated. "I'll marry you."

He grinned from ear to ear.

"We're going to need a lot more champagne," Barney said on a chuckle, and signaled to a waiter while Barb mopped up her tears.

"Would you like to be married in Jacobsville?" Marcus asked when they were briefly alone in his hotel room while he planned to phone for the limo driver to pick them up.

"I would," she agreed.

"We can get a license and a blood test and a minister in three days," he said. "Or would you like to wait until Christmas?"

She searched his eyes hungrily. "I'd rather starve to death than wait."

His eyes flashed. "So would I."

In a matter of seconds, the phone call to the limo driver was forgotten, her dress was on the floor, followed by his jacket, and a trail of hastily-removed clothing made a trail all the way to the king-sized bed.

They barely made it under the covers before his big body was crushing her down into the crisp, cold sheets.

"I'm sorry, I really am starving," he groaned as he nudged her long legs apart and lowered himself between them. He looked into her wide, misty eyes. "Is it all right?"

"What do you mean, is it all right?" she gasped.

"Are you taking anything?" he emphasized.

She shook her head.

He hesitated.

She looked straight into his eyes and deliberately lifted her hips and brushed them against his in a long, slow, sensuous plea.

He shivered.

He bent and brushed his mouth softly over hers. The urgent ferocity was suddenly gone. He hesitated, shifted, took a deep, long breath and kissed her with aching tenderness. The sudden shift from raging passion to exquisite tender patience caught Delia by surprise. She met his eyes with patent curiosity.

"I'll explain. Here," he whispered, tugging her legs up beside his so that they were lying curled together like an intimate puzzle. "If we're going to make a baby, we have to do it with love, not lust," he added, and his voice actually trembled.

She caught her breath and tears misted her eyes. "A baby?" she whispered brokenly. "Do you mean it? It's not too soon for that?"

"No. It's definitely not too soon," he whispered,

closing her wet eyes with kisses. "A baby will only make everything more perfect than it already is."

"Yes," she sobbed at his ear, clinging closer as she felt him pressing intimately into her body.

He shifted against her, smiling as his hands began to caress her slowly, with aching tenderness. He kissed her face, brief little teasing kisses that matched the infinitely slow, sweet movements of his big body. The only sound in the room was the soft whisper of flesh against flesh, the tiny sounds that pulsed out of her throat as the pleasure began to build.

His big hands cradled the back of her head. "I'm sorry you cut your hair," he said. "I loved it long."

"I was grieving," she replied. "I'll let it grow…" She cried out as his hands found her more intimately than they ever had before.

"Do you like that?" he murmured. "Let's try this."

"Marcus…!"

His mouth explored her as if she were a flower, touching and tasting, and arousing sensations that lifted her completely off the bed.

By the time he reached her breasts, she was shivering. One big hand was between them, coaxing her body to accept him.

Her short nails bit into his big arms as he began to possess her with slow, deep, intimate strokes.

"It wasn't…like this," she tried to tell him.

"No, it wasn't," he whispered. His eyes were somber as they held hers while his body moved into stark, total possession. "We've never made love like this, before, not even when it was the very best pleasure we shared.

But this is different, my darling. This is…creation itself."

She throbbed. Her body pulsed with every brush of his powerful body. She made a sound she'd never heard, deep in her throat, as the pleasure began to climb like a fever.

"Hold on, tight," he whispered. "We're going to fall right…over…the edge…of the world…!"

He pushed down, hard, and she lifted up to meet him. The motion was frantic, potent, fierce. All that tenderness that had led up to it made the culmination even more shattering. They clung to each other, shuddering, pulsating, as the pleasure burst into a thousand fiery explosions and lifted them into near unconsciousness.

She heard his harsh voice throbbing in her ear as he convulsed over her shivering body. She wept, because it was unbearable. She didn't think she could live through it.

"I'm…dying," she sobbed.

"So am I," he ground out unsteadily, his body moving helplessly against hers in the pinnacle of ecstasy.

She couldn't let go, not even when their hearts stopped racing out of control. She clung to his damp back, holding on as he rolled sideways, with her still pressed to him.

He shivered one last time. "I never had it like that in my life with anyone, not even with you," he whispered, awed.

"Me, neither."

He laughed wickedly, deep in his throat. "Yeah, but I wasn't a virgin," he whispered outrageously.

She laughed, too, amazed that intimacy could be so sweet and so much fun at the same time.

He curled her against him and rolled onto his back with a rough sigh. "Now we have to get married quick, so that we don't have to let out the wedding gown I packed for you."

"Wedding…gown?" she stammered.

"It's gorgeous," he said wearily, tugging her into a more comfortable position. "Acres of lace, a keyhole neckline, an embroidered hem of white roses to match the embroidered veil, and a white rose garter."

"You bought me a wedding gown?" she exclaimed. "When?"

"A few days after my memory came back," he murmured drowsily. "I was going crazy, I missed you so much. I knew you had to have a little time, but I had to do something to keep myself sane. So I flew to Paris and went through all the couture houses looking for just the right gown. It's in a hanging bag in my closet. Want to see?"

"Do I!" she replied, touched.

He dragged himself out of bed, opened the closet, and drew out a couture bag. He hooked it over the closet door and unzipped it. Lace flowed out onto the floor. Delia jumped out of bed and went to look at it, fascinated by the almost ethereal beauty of it.

"Marcus, this must have cost a fortune," she exclaimed.

"It did," he mused. "But I'd have mortgaged the

hotel to get it. I think you'll be the most beautiful bride this town ever saw."

She looked up at him with eyes that adored him. "You'll certainly be the most handsome groom," she told him.

She moved against him and reached up to lock her arms around his neck and coax his mouth down to hers. Neither of them was wearing clothing, and it had been a long time that they'd been apart. He felt her bare breasts and long legs against his and his body hardened at once.

She lifted her eyes to his and pursed her lips. "Well?" she asked. "Are you up to it?"

He bent and swung her up into his arms with a bearish grin. "Honey, suppose you tell me if I am?"

He tossed her into the middle of the bed and followed her down.

It was morning before they woke. He rolled over and looked at the clock and sighed. "I guess the limo driver gave up on us and went to bed, too," he told her with a wry grin. "I booked him into the hotel, just in case."

"You wicked man," she teased.

"Hey, it's been a long dry spell," he defended himself. "I haven't touched another woman in all this time, you know."

She beamed. "I hoped you hadn't, but it's nice to know for sure."

"Trust me, do you?" he asked.

She nodded. She nuzzled her face against his. "I love you, Marcus," she whispered. "I love you so much, it hurts."

He buried his face in her throat. "I love you just as much," he groaned. "I never knew it could hurt so much to be separated from someone!"

"Hurt…?"

"You lost our baby, and you were gone before I even knew it. I couldn't even comfort you. Worse, I had to live with the knowledge that I'd caused it."

"But, you didn't," she said at once. "Marcus, you didn't! I couldn't have let that man kill you! What sort of life would I have had, without you?"

"Maybe a better one than you will have," he said worriedly. "I've still got enemies. We might have some bad times yet."

"I don't care. I'll stand with you with our backs to the wall and fight right alongside you, if I have to!" She lifted her head and stared at him with a ferocious, loving expression. "Texas women have always been fierce when their families were threatened. You're my family, now, too," she whispered. "And I'll love you all my life."

He bent and put his mouth softly over her parted lips. "I would die for you, baby," he whispered in a choked tone. "I'll give you anything you want!"

She snuggled close, feeling safe and loved and cherished. "I only want a baby, Marcus," she said softly.

His arms tightened. "So do I!"

She closed her eyes. "I have a feeling that we won't have a long time to wait," she murmured with a smile.

When they got back to town, Marcus checked into the Jacobsville hotel to allay any gossip about him and his Delia, and he invited his friends Cash and Tippy Grier to have dinner with them, along with Barb and Barney.

But what started out as a simple social evening mushroomed.

Cash had arranged for his friends Judd Dunn and Marc Brannon, as well as Jacobsville police officers Palmer and Barrett, and Sheriff Hayes Carson, to meet him in the lobby of Marcus's hotel just after supper. And he didn't mention it to Delia.

He left her talking with Barb, Barney and Tippy while he tugged Marcus out to the lobby on the pretext of discussing something personal with him.

"Oh, no," Marcus said when he saw the lawmen, most of whom were wearing their uniforms. "No, you're not to arrest me on some old, forgotten charge like jaywalking and lock me up before my own wedding…?"

"Nothing of the sort," Cash replied immediately, grinning. "No, we have another objective in mind."

Marcus shook hands all around, but he was puzzled at why these guys were gathered around him.

"We asked the Hart brothers how to go about this," Cash said merrily. "They arranged each others' marriages even when their brothers didn't want them to. And they gave us a rundown of the entire process. So here's how it goes. I'll take you over to get the license first thing in the morning. Judd's arranged for Dr. Lou Coltrain to do the blood tests tomorrow at eleven. Marc's arranged for the county ordinary to perform the ceremony two weeks from Friday in her office." He grimaced. "I forgot to ask, did you want a minister, as well…?"

Marcus was reeling. In shock, he nodded and mentioned that he and Delia had barely had time to discuss that, but they were agreed on the denomination and said they'd take care of that, also.

"We'll rent you a tux," Cash added, pursing his lips when Marcus gave him the size.

"I'll phone Neiman-Marcus and have them ship one down for me, with the accessories," Marcus waved that detail away.

"That leaves the invitations," Cash continued.

"All in hand," tall, blond Officer Palmer said with a grin. "My wife works for a big engraving company. They print invitations and business cards and such."

"I've lined up caterers for the reception," Officer Barrett added, smiling. "And I've arranged for the local bank's community room to hold it in."

"I've taken care of the flowers," Marc Brannon chuckled. "Josette's friends with our best local florist."

"Who put the announcement in the local weekly and daily papers and alerted the news media?" Cash asked.

There were shocked gasps.

Cash held up a hand. "Tippy and I will take care of that."

"News media?" Marcus asked darkly.

"Not to worry," Cash said, grinning. "I know exactly the people to call. We won't have any tabloid reporters here. I've already asked Matt Caldwell to run down that local ordinance that he used to keep reporters away from his wife Leslie when they were after her a few years back. It works great!"

"I think that's about everything," Hayes Carson mentioned, "except for the escort to the airport, and I'll do that personally. Can't have our newlyweds hassled by traffic on their way out of the country, right?" he chuckled.

Marcus shook his head. "And I was just wondering how to go about getting the details wrapped up." He smiled sheepishly. "Thanks, guys. Thanks a million."

"Don't worry about the dog and the chicken, either," Hayes added with a wicked grin. "I've already got places ready for them out at my ranch until you decide when you want them shipped to the Bahamas."

Delia just beamed. "Thanks, Hayes. You, too, guys!" she added to the others.

They all managed to look humble. They hadn't mentioned the tin cans, the confetti, the soap and ribbons they planned to affix to the rented limousine while the reception was going on. Or that they'd already phoned Mr. Smith in the Bahamas and given him explicit instructions about Marcus's house for when the newlyweds went home after their week on St. Martin in the Caribbean.

Every detail of the service had been worked out, perfected and carried out without a hitch by Marcus's willing accomplices, to Delia's surprise and secret amusement. It didn't even bother her that preparations for it had been taken out of her hands. She helped address the invitations and they were hand-carried by

cowboys that worked for the surrounding ranches—
most specifically the Harts, the Ballengers, the Tre-
maynes and Cy Parks.

The wedding was incredible. News media from two
continents showed up with satellite trucks and reporters. Print media sent reporters with cameras and tape
recorders. Limousines came to town bearing men in
dark suits, two groups of which seemed to line up to
glare across the pews at each other. Another pew was
populated by rough-looking men who kept watching
the men in the dark suits. Lawmen covered one, including police chief Cash Grier and his wife, Tippy, along
with assistant chief Judd Dunn and his wife Christabel, former Texas Ranger Marc Brannon with his wife
Josette Brannon, Jacobsville police officers Palmer
and Barrett and their wives, and Sheriff Hayes Carson.
Another group of local mercenaries and their wives
covered a separate pew—Dr. Micah Steele and his
wife Callie, Eb and Sally Scott, Cy and Lisa Parks—
with Harley Fowler who wasn't married. All five Hart
brothers, Justin and Calhoun Ballenger, the Tremayne
brothers attended, with all their wives, and so did the
doctors Coltrain and Dr. Morris and his wife. Tom
Walker and his wife showed up with Ted Regan and
his wife, the Donavans, the Langleys and even the
attorney, Blake Kemp with his secretary Violet. Any of
the local gentry who didn't attend simply weren't in
town at the time. It was an event, with a capital "E."

There were some unexpected guests, too, including
a man named Tate Winthrop from Washington, D.C.,
with his wife, Cecily. He worked in personal security,

or so Marcus told Delia, and Marcus had done him a
favor to help keep Cecily of danger.

Delia also noticed some well-known national politicians, two movie stars, three or four singers and a
whole rock band of the notorious type. She couldn't
say that Marcus wasn't gregarious, in his way. He certainly had a duke's mixture of friends and acquaintances.

But the one person Delia noticed most was Barb,
standing at her side at the altar, having served as her
matron of honor. Mr. Smith had flown up just for the
day and he was serving as best man for Marcus.

The church leader, an elderly man with a contagious
smile, performed the service with dignity and affection,
and at the end, where they exchanged rings and kissed
each other tenderly, there wasn't a dry eye in the house.

Later, at the reception, Delia's gown was the center
of attention.

"You can tell it's from Paris," Barb remarked,
hugging Delia warmly. She'd been ecstatic ever since
the announcement in the newspapers when she and
Barney were listed for the first time as Delia's parents.
It had stirred quite a lot of local gossip, but the nicest
possible kind.

"It's just beautiful," Violet Hardy sighed, smiling at
Delia. "I don't suppose I'll ever get to wear anything
like that," she added. Violet was just a little overweight,
although she had a beautiful face. She worked for local
attorney Blake Kemp, who'd brought her to the
wedding, to everyone's surprise. Kemp's aversion to
women was well known.

"You never know, Violet," Delia whispered with a speaking glance at Blake Kemp, who was speaking to Cy Parks. Violet actually giggled.

The local people who didn't go to the wedding were waiting outside at the end of the reception, as the couple left in a shower of rice and good wishes.

The limo driver, long-suffering but a good sport, stood dignified and silent beside his elegant vehicle, which was now covered with soaped well wishes, ribbons and bows, with a string of cans, shoes and ribbons dangling from the rear bumper.

"Congratulations, Mr. and Mrs. Carrera," he said with a smile, and opened the door for them with a flourish.

"Thanks," they echoed, diving inside under another barrage of rice.

They waved at the crowd one last time before the door closed.

The next morning, they were cuddled together like spoons, in a king-sized bed in a luxurious beach house in St. Martin. It had been a long, passionate wedding night and they'd slept late. Marcus had woken first and called room service to send up breakfast. Then he'd curled Delia into his body and dozed until it arrived.

There was a knock on the door.

Marcus kissed his wife awake warmly and threw on a terry cloth robe so that he could answer the door, while she stayed in bed behind a closed door.

It was room service, with breakfast. Marcus let the waiter in, with his cart, and directed him where to leave it. He gave the smiling waiter a big tip and saw him out.

Before he went to get Delia, he lifted the lids from the dishes and took a deep breath of the delicious scrambled eggs, bacon, sausage, and toast.

He went back into the bedroom, tugged the cover from Delia's pretty nude body, bent and kissed her breasts with breathless tenderness.

"I don't want to stop, but we need to eat something," he whispered, pulling her gently to her feet. "For my part, I'd keep you like this," he added, smiling.

"We'd never be able to go out and see the sights," she laughed.

He kissed her. "Spoilsport. Who wants to see other sights when these are so perfect?" he asked. "Come on. We've got food. I don't know about you, but I'm starving!"

"Where's my gown?"

He slid it over her head. "Waste of time to put it on, baby," he told her with a grin. "It's coming right back off after breakfast."

She tucked her hand into his and let him lead her to the table. But an unexpected thing happened when she smelled the scrambled eggs.

She barely made it to the bathroom in time. He was right behind her, wetting a cloth to bathe her face when she could get up. He helped her wash out her mouth so tenderly that she could have bawled, then he picked her up, cuddling her like a small, frightened child, and carried her right back to bed.

He put her against the pillows with breathless care. "Oh, baby," he said softly, "I never dreamed we'd do it this quick!"

She met his eyes and managed a watery laugh. "Me, neither," she replied. "Marcus, I think I'm pregnant!"

"Yeah," he agreed, smiling from ear to ear. "Doesn't it look like it, though?"

She drew him down to her and kissed him until her mouth hurt.

"Now we've got a real dilemma," he whispered.

"Hmm?"

He grinned against her lips. "Who do we call first?"

"My parents!"

"Mr. Smith will be ticked," he said. "And he's the best babysitter we'll ever find. He was with Kip Tennison's little boy from birth."

She beamed. "What a lovely thought!"

"I've got it," he said. "You call Barb and Barney on the room phone." He went to the dresser and picked up his cell phone. "I'll phone Smith with my cell phone!" He stuck it in his robe. "But, first, we have breakfast. I'll bring you a nice glass of milk and some toast. You can have breakfast in bed!"

She sighed and smiled up at him with love glowing from her eyes. "You are going to be the nicest husband and best daddy in the whole world," she said with heartfelt conviction.

And he was.

* * * * *

She came to take his company... but would she lose her heart instead?

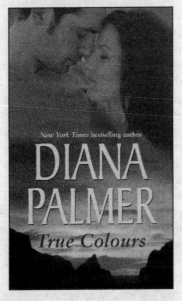

New York Times bestselling author

DIANA PALMER

True Colours

As a pregnant teenager, Cy Harden's family had driven her out of town. Now Meredith Ashe runs a multi-national corporation – and she's back to take over Harden Properties.

Meredith plans to let Cy think she's the same naive girl he abandoned years ago. But when Meredith falls for Cy again, even her carefully made plans can't protect her.

His passions were as tempestuous as his temper...

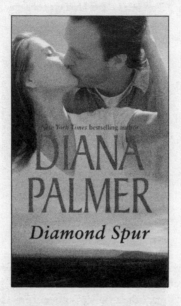

Even though Kate Whittman was young and inexperienced, she wanted moody Texas rancher Jason Donovan more than anything. But he offered her only brotherly protection.

So Kate pursued another fantasy – becoming a successful New York fashion designer. But just when it seemed that her fairy tale was coming true, fate brought her back to Texas. And to Jason.

Secrets always find a place to hide...

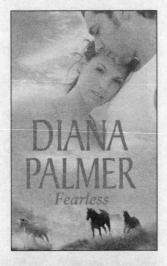

When DEA agent Rodrigo Ramirez finds
undercover work at Gloryanne Barnes's nearby
farm, Gloryanne's sweet innocence is too much
temptation for him. Confused and bitter about
love, Rodrigo's not sure if his reckless offer of
marriage is just a means to completing his
mission – or something more.

But as Gloryanne's bittersweet miracle and
Rodrigo's double life collide, two people must
decide if there's a chance for the future they
both secretly desire.

Two men have vowed to protect the women they love...

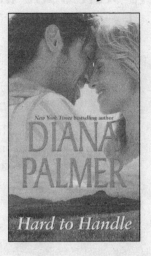

New York Times bestselling author

DIANA PALMER

Hard to Handle

Hunter

On a top secret operation in the desert, chief of security Hunter knew Jennifer Marist needed his protection. Soon he discovered the lure of Jenny's wild, sweet passion – and a love he'd never dreamed possible.

Man in Control

Eight years after DEA agent Alexander Cobb had turned Jodie Clayburn down, Alexander could hardly believe the beauty that Jodie had become... or that she'd helped him crack a dangerous drug-smuggling case. Would the man in control finally surrender to his desires?